SHE WA[S] SOMETHING WHITE, LACY, AND FEMININE . . .

Angie was stretched out before him, wearing that damn piece of enticement, and asking him to put his hands on her. Whatever sins he had committed in the past, the Lord sure had figured out the way to make him pay for them now.

Scooping some salve on his hands, Giff slicked it on her shoulders. It was a mistake. The moment his hands made contact with her warm flesh, they seemed to have a will of their own. His fingers spread, caressing the satiny skin more than kneading it.

"Oh, Giff, that feels so good."

The sigh was as provocative as the feel of her under his fingertips. Driven by passion, he slid his hands under the camisole, stroking her back, not wanting to stop. He wanted to run his hands over her breasts, to hold them . . . they were so near; it would be so easy.

A burst of laughter from beyond the campfire jolted him from his thoughts. Good God, he'd forgotten about them! And he was so hard, he couldn't move.

"Thanks, Giff, I feel better already," Angie said softly.

At least one of us does, he thought frustratedly.

Other **AVON ROMANCES**

THE MACKENZIES
PETER

ANA LEIGH

AVON BOOKS  NEW YORK

AVON BOOKS, INC.
1350 Avenue of the Americas
New York, New York 10019

Copyright © 1998 by Ana Leigh
Inside cover author photo by Fantasies Photography Studio
Published by arrangement with the author
Visit our website at **http://www.AvonBooks.com**
Library of Congress Catalog Card Number: 98-93176
ISBN: 0-380-79338-5

First Avon Books Printing: December 1998

AVON TRADEMARK REG. U.S. PAT. OFF. AND IN OTHER COUNTRIES, MARCA REGIS-TRADA, HECHO EN U.S.A.

Printed in the U.S.A.

WCD 10 9 8 7 6 5 4 3 2 1

*I dedicate this book to Patti and Rick,
my daughter and son-in-law.
May their love be as eternal
as Angie and Giff's.*

Prologue

St. Louis
February 1880

Oh, no! Angie blushed profusely when he dropped the sheet and stood there stark, staring naked!

Get a hold on yourself, Angeleen MacKenzie. After all, you're twenty-one years old—too sophisticated to be upset by the sight of a naked man.

Her gaze moved over him slowly. His muscular upper torso looked powerful and beautifully proportioned. She hesitated, unable to follow the symmetrical lines of his body any lower until curiosity overcame modesty—then she lowered her gaze.

"Oh, my goodness!" she gasped.

"What did you say?" Jeanette asked.

Nervously Angie shoved back the mahogany curls that had fallen over her forehead and glanced at Jeanette Bordeau, sitting beside her. "He's quite ... muscular, isn't he?"

"Built like a bull, you mean," Jeanette said, her eyes gleaming with pleasure.

Having been raised on a cattle ranch in Colorado, Angie understood the bawdy innuendo. She

1

threw Jeanette a forced smile, then picked up a charcoal pencil and began to sketch the male model.

When the class ended, Angie closed her drawing book with relief. Then she saw that the model, who had covered himself, was headed in her direction.

"Oh, Good Lord! He's coming over here, Jeanette," she whispered.

"Of course," Jeanette replied calmly.

With mouth agape, Angie stared in astonishment when the young man took Jeanette in his arms. "Hello, *chérie*," he said, kissing her cheek.

Jeanette sighed. "Armand."

Angie gathered up her supplies for a hasty exit, but Jeanette stopped her.

"Wait, Angeleen, let me introduce you to my husband, Armand."

"Your husband! I thought you said your husband was a waiter."

Nodding, Jeanette said, "He is, but Armand does modeling occasionally to pick up extra money. Armand, this is my classmate Angeleen MacKenzie."

"Bonjour, mademoiselle," Armand said, with a pleasant smile and a heavy French accent.

Angie was amazed how the handsome young man could remain so poised when only minutes before he had stood naked before her and the whole class. "How do you do, Mr. Bordeau."

"If you will excuse me, I must dress," he said.

"Of course," Angie replied. Fearful he intended to do so on the spot, Angie again prepared to leave. "It was a pleasure to meet you, Armand."

"Armand and I are going to the waterfront carnival," Jeanette said. "Why don't you join us, Angeleen?"

Angie had nothing to do for the rest of the weekend, and it would be fun to go down to LeClede's Landing and join the festivities. "I would enjoy that. Are you sure I won't be intruding?"

"Of course not," Jeanette said. "Hurry, Armand. As soon as you dress we will leave."

When he went elsewhere to do so, Angie sighed with relief.

After a brief stop at Angie's room to dispose of her drawing supplies, they took a landau to Le-Clede's Landing. Located on a hill overlooking the Mississippi River, the area abounded with sights, smells, and sounds. Bright balloons fluttered in the crisp breeze; storefronts were draped with red, white, and blue bunting; the whiff of baking croissants and roasting pigs floated from restaurants; and dozens of vendor stands and tents had been erected for the occasion. Strings of colorful banners and guidons flew from the masts of several steamboats docked along the wharf, and in an exhilarating cacophony of sound, the loud blasts of their whistles blended with the sound of a hurdy-gurdy and the three-piece band playing in a beer garden.

After an hour of strolling among the crowd, they sat down at a table in the walled courtyard of a small restaurant.

"You speak our language excellently, Armand, but it's obvious from your accent you were not born in this country," Angie said as they savored steaming mugs of chocolate and delicious hot apple-filled crepes.

"That is right, Angeleen," he said. "I came to America last year." He picked up Jeanette's hand and kissed her palm. "I met my lovely Jeanette and fell in love. I could never leave her and go back to France."

"Oh, Armand, how romantic! My sister Thia— Cynthia—spent some time in Paris and often spoke of the magnificent cathedrals and galleries. She told me that's where I should be studying art."

Armand nodded his dark head. "Your sister is correct, Angeleen."

Angie sipped her coffee for several seconds, wondering if going to France would give her a renewed enthusiasm to continue studying art. "I imagine St. Louis has little to offer compared to a famous city like Paris."

"Not at all, Angeleen. Paris does not have Jeanette." Armand smiled with adoration at his wife.

A shiver raced down Angie's spine. Would she find such a love someday? The couple reminded her of Thia and Dave, just recently married. A special message seemed to pass between them every time they looked at each other.

When they finished eating, Armand suggested they walk down the hill and look at the array of steamboats docked along the riverfront.

"I can't believe I let myself be talked into entering a singing contest on a riverboat," Angie whispered a few hours later, as they waited for the woman onstage to finish her song.

"You have such a lovely voice, you can't lose, Angeleen," Jeanette assured her.

"The contest has ended," Armand said, "and our lovely Angeleen was most easily the best. Which prize will you choose, *chérie*? The ten dollars or a chance to perform for a week?"

"I haven't won, Armand!" Despite an attempt to remain indifferent, Angie was trembling with excitement.

"You will," Jeanette said confidently.

"Shhh," Angeleen whispered, "Mr. Perkins is about to speak."

"Attention, ladies and gentlemen," the stage manager called out. "The competition is over, and if all the contestants will return to the stage, the judging can begin. And, ladies, hold on to your bonnets, because Edward Emory, our leading actor, has agreed to assist me in the judging.''

Gasps of pleasure went up from the women in the audience when the actor stepped out from behind the curtain.

The handsome man was tall and slenderly built, elegantly clad in a black coat and trousers, gray satin cravat, and a silk brocade vest of gold and silver. Doffing a black silk top hat, he made a sweeping, theatrical bow.

"Oh, I feel as if a hundred butterflies are fluttering around inside my stomach," Angie said.

"Good luck, *chérie*," Armand and Jeanette called out in unison as she hurried away.

Standing on the stage with the other four contestants, Angie realized that a year ago she never would have had the courage to do anything so bold. Her singing had always been confined to family gatherings and the church choir. Leaving home and coming to school in St. Louis had given her much greater self-confidence. And even if she didn't win, she had enjoyed the competition. Performing in front of an audience had been very exciting.

"Miss Angeleen MacKenzie, who sang Stephen Foster's 'Beautiful Dreamer.' " Perkins's voice jolted Angie out of her musings.

The audience broke out with loud whistles and clapping, and much to Angie's amazement, she was the undisputed winner.

Edward Emory took her hand, leading her forward on the stage. Glancing up at him, she saw that the actor was older than he had appeared from below, but still very handsome. His gray eyes, ringed with long, dark lashes, were topped with neatly curved brows. His nose was narrow and well formed, and his face was clean-shaven except for a tidy mustache that rested above thin lips now drawn into a charming smile as he lifted her hand up for a kiss.

"My congratulations, Miss MacKenzie," he said in a resonant voice.

"Thank you, Mr. Emory."

"And have you made a choice for your prize?" Perkins asked.

"I will take the ten dollars."

Edward Emory was clearly disappointed. "I am sorry to hear that, Miss MacKenzie," he whispered in a voice made mesmerizing by intimacy. "I was hoping for the opportunity to see you again."

Perkins handed her the prize. "You're very talented, Miss MacKenzie. If you ever decide to go on the stage, look me up."

"Thank you, Mr. Perkins, but that's very unlikely," she said.

Later, after leaving Jeanette and Armand, Angie hurried home to her boardinghouse. She dared not miss the curfew Miss Danvers insisted upon; the old battle-ax locked the front door at nine sharp.

Once in her room, she lay in bed thinking about the handsome Edward Emory and how exciting it would be to perform on the stage every night—free of dull art classes and nine-o'clock curfews.

Angie suddenly sat up in bed. Why not? What was stopping her from shucking her boring existence for an exciting life on the stage? As Thia would say, she should test her wings. In the morning she would go back to the riverboat and see if Perkins had meant the offer he had made to her.

Chapter 1

April

As she waited to go on, Angie stood backstage and listened to Edward Emory and Stella Crawford sing their romantic duet. Despite her love for Edward, Angie had to admit neither of the stars had the greatest singing voice—but they were more than adequate for the riverboat *extravaganza*, she thought derisively.

She looked down at her own costume. How she hated it. She felt vulgar every time she put it on. The skimpy, bangle-studded red dress hugged her breasts and hips like a second skin. White stockings and thigh-high laced red boots covered, but failed to conceal, her legs. Reflexively her hold tightened on the ends of the white feathered boa that she clutched across her breast.

This certainly wasn't what she had anticipated when she took the job months earlier. She had expected to be able to come out and sing a lovely ballad as she had done the night of the contest; instead, Perkins had put her in the chorus with five other girls.

There was nothing exciting about appearing in front of strange men who whistled and hooted every time she appeared. The cruder ones even tried to paw her, and only the presence of Big Ike, one of the riverboat's bouncers, prevented them from succeeding. She would have quit the job long ago were it not for Edward. Her loving glance swung to him again. Edward made it all tolerable for her, and he had promised her that once the ship returned from New Orleans, they would leave and find employment elsewhere.

Now they were back. Tonight when he came to her after the evening's performance, she would tell him her wonderful news. She had not had her menses from the time he first made love to her, two months ago. She just knew she was carrying his child! They would leave the ship and get married. Perhaps he would be willing to go to the ranch while she awaited the birth of their child.

Thinking of the life ahead of her with Edward, Angie sighed with pleasure, then cringed when Stella hit a sour note. Edward tried to cover it up. Angie couldn't understand what he had ever found appealing about the brash redheaded woman. She was coarse and assertive, too brassy for a man with Edward's refined sensitivities.

Although he had convinced Angie that for the peace and harmony of the show, Stella must not know that he loved someone else, she was disturbed that even now, rather than tell Stella the truth, Edward would sneak away to Angie's cabin for a tryst with her. Well, tonight that would all end, because the boat had docked and Edward had promised her they would leave the *Mississippi Belle*.

Edward and Stella finished their song to polite applause, and the chorus girls lined up, awaiting their cue. As he left the stage, Edward winked at Angie in passing, the band struck up a new song, the six women moved out on the stage, and the audience exploded with a burst of whistles and applause.

Her trunk long packed, Angie paced the floor of her tiny cabin as she anxiously waited for Edward's arrival. The small room seemed more confining than ever. She could stand with outstretched arms in the center of the floor and touch the opposite walls with her fingertips. Her trunk and the narrow bunk reduced the walking space to about a four-foot-square area.

At the sound of a light tap, she eagerly pulled the door open. Edward slipped into the cabin and closed the door.

"I thought Stella would never go to bed, my love," he said, pulling her into his arms.

Angie closed her eyes as his lips claimed hers. She sensed by the fervency of the kiss that he intended to make love to her.

"My lovely, lovely Angeleen," he murmured, and began to release the buttons on her bodice. He slipped the blouse off her shoulders, and his mouth traced a moist trail to her breasts as he untied her skirt and it dropped to the floor.

"Edward, I'm packed. Ready to go," she said breathlessly. "You said we were leaving tonight."

"Yes, I know, my love, but there's been a slight complication." Pulling the chemise over her head, he reclaimed her lips, cutting off her protest.

She drew a quick breath when his hand closed around her breast, his thumb stroking the nub to tautness. A mild wave of passion flooded her senses, but she managed to hold on to her thoughts. "What complication, Edward?"

"Later, my love. Later." Taking her by the hand, he led her to the bunk. After he quickly removed the rest of her clothing, they sat down on the edge of the bunk. There was a possessive, almost greedy glint in his eyes. For an instant, she felt self-conscious under his intense stare.

The thought was quickly obliterated when he reached out and slowly ran his fingertips along the base of her neck. "Your skin is like silken alabaster, my lovely," he said in a whispered murmur as provocative as a caress. She sucked in her breath as he continued his tactile exploration, tracing the slope of her breasts and then down the plane of her stomach until a tremor rippled her spine.

He smiled. "Your body is like a finely tuned instrument, my love. A few mere touches and it is ready to be played."

She lay back when he stepped away, and his gaze held hers as he stripped off his clothing. "What complication, Edward?" she repeated. "You said we would leave as soon as we reached St. Louis."

"Stella took to her bed early with a headache, so I haven't had a chance to tell her I am leaving."

"But you said Stella delayed you."

Then his body pressed to hers: his lips and hands—his whispered words—became an erotic stimulant, blotting out any further requests for explanations. Within seconds he had aroused her passion, sensation obliterating any need for reasoning, excitement removing any need for restraint.

"Oh, Edward, I love you. I love you," she murmured again and again.

Later, with her head resting on Edward's chest and his arm around her, Angie snuggled up against his side. "Edward, I have something wonderful to tell you."

"What is it, my lovely?" His hand stroked her spine and she sighed with pleasure.

Raising her head, she smiled at him. "Edward, we're going to have a baby."

"What?" he exclaimed, looking stunned.

"Isn't it wonderful—the utmost testimony of our love?" She snuggled back down beside him. "As soon as we wed, I would like to go back to the ranch and await the birth there."

Edward's handsome face drew into grave lines. He slipped out of the bunk and began to dress.

Angie's joy dissolved. "What is it, Edward? Aren't you happy about the baby?"

"Of course. It's just that this is all so sudden. I need time to think it all out."

After he finished dressing, he leaned down and kissed her lightly on the cheek. "You get some sleep, my dear. You need your rest. Let me decide what we'll do."

"Why don't we just leave? We can get married and go to my family's ranch."

"Haste makes waste, my dear. It's best we think everything out thoroughly. We'll talk again in the morning."

Disappointed, Angie lay thinking about Edward's hasty departure. She had believed it would be such a special moment between them, but he hadn't seemed the least bit happy about the baby.

But of course he was happy, she told herself. The news just came as a shock to him. In the morning everything would be different. She closed her eyes and began to plan their future. Come morning they would marry. Or should they wait to marry in Denver? It would be so lovely if Beth and Thia could attend the wedding, and Dave and Giff. Giff must be present; he was her best friend. And Middy, String, and Red. Yes, it would be so much nicer to have her whole family present at her wedding.

She and Edward would get married at the Roundhouse, she decided blissfully just before succumbing to slumber.

*   *   *

As soon as Angie opened her eyes the next morning, her first thought was of Edward—they would be leaving the *Mississippi Belle* that day! She practically skipped with happiness as she joined the cast for breakfast. Much to her disappointment, Edward was not among them.

"Good morning," Angie said, sitting down at the table with the other girls in the chorus.

"Morning, hon," Ruby Adams said. The redhead was the oldest of the group. The rough existence had given her a jaded viewpoint on life, but underneath all the rouge and powder, she had a good heart. "Did you hear the good news? Edward and his prima donna are gone."

Angie paled. "What do you mean?"

"They snuck away during the night. Didn't even tell Perkins they were going."

Angie's heart seemed to drop to her stomach. "Maybe they just stepped out for a short while."

Ruby shook her head. "No. Perkins said both cabins are empty. They moved out bag and baggage."

"And good riddance!" one of the other girls exclaimed. "It's a blessing to see that bastard go, and Stella was a real bitch. They deserve one another."

Angie couldn't believe it. She was *sure* Edward hadn't deserted her. He most likely had moved his things out knowing he was leaving. That was it! Even now, he probably had found them a room where they could stay—and any moment he'd be back for her.

"You mustn't say those unkind things about Edward. He doesn't deserve them."

"Don't tell me that good-for-nothing snake didn't try to get you in bed, hon," Ruby said. "If he didn't, you're the only one in skirts he's missed." The other women laughed and nodded. "With Sir Edward's roving eye—"

"And hands," interjected Rita Moralez, a Mexican girl who was a member of the troupe.

"That's for sure," Ruby agreed. "Stella won't know a day's peace of mind."

Smiling, Rita said, "Poor woman." The remark brought forth another burst of laughter.

"Ruby, did Perkins say he was going to replace them?" Sheila Dazzle asked. The brunette usually attracted the most attention on the stage because of her generously endowed breasts.

"He didn't say," Ruby replied. "He told me he was going to add another number for us to do."

"Damn!" Sheila declared. "That weasel told me that when he had the chance, he'd let me do a solo. What better chance than now?"

"Guess sleeping with him didn't pay off after all, huh, Sheila?" Rita intoned drolly.

"Ain't seen where it did you much good either, honey," Sheila snapped back.

Angie only half listened to the conversation flowing around her. They had to be mistaken. Edward would *never* have done the things they suggested. He wasn't a womanizer. He was a sensitive, honorable man who loved her . . . who'd fathered the baby she now carried. He'd *never* desert her and the baby. They were wrong! All wrong! Edward would come back for her. Numbly she rose and walked away.

The women stopped their chatter. "That low-down bastard!" Ruby declared bitterly as Angie walked out of the room.

She returned to her cabin to await Edward's arrival. After packing her nightgown, she sat down on the edge of the bunk, prepared to leave the moment he returned. How they'd all have to eat their words when he showed up!

At noon Ruby tapped on the door and asked her if she wanted lunch. Angie declined and continued to wait. She wanted to be certain she'd be there when Edward came for her.

Dusk came and the cabin grew dark. She missed the evening meal. Perkins rapped on the door. "Fifteen minutes until showtime," he shouted.

Angie stood up, lit a lamp, and unpacked her trunk. Desolately she put on the red dress for the evening's first performance.

Edward wasn't coming back.

Chapter 2

"Thanks, Katie," Pete Gifford said, tossing some money on the dresser.

The saloon girl lay back and tucked the sheet up to her neck. "Giff, you're my only regular who ever thanks me," Katie said.

"You're a good woman, Katie. Time you got out of this business, found yourself a husband, settled down to raise a family."

"You're one to be givin' advice, Pete Gifford. A tall, good-lookin' fella like you's got no reason for needin' a whore. Any woman in the territory would be glad to marry you."

Any woman but the one I love, he thought wistfully. He had loved Angie from the time she was eighteen, but two things stood in the way of his telling her: not only was he ten years older than she was, but she also considered him a brother.

"Reckon we're two of a kind, Katie. I'll see you around."

"Sure, Giff."

He went downstairs and sat down at one of the tables. After ordering a steak, he settled back with a beer and thought about his conversation with Katie.

15

Maybe she was right: maybe he should just find himself a nice gal and settle down. What difference would it make if he didn't love her? They could still have a good marriage, and children. Maybe he'd do just that, as soon as he finished the house he was building on the spread the Chief had willed him. In time, he might even grow to love her. Tipping back his chair, Giff reaffirmed that maybe he'd do just that.

Yeah, like hell he would! He'd never get Angie out of his blood.

"Here's your steak, Giff," Slim Collins said. The bartender put down a plate containing a huge steak and a heaping pile of fried potatoes. "You want another beer?" Giff nodded and Slim grabbed the empty glass. Returning shortly with the refill, he sat down. "How's things goin', Giff?"

"Can't complain. How's business?" he asked the ex-cowboy who had once ridden for the Roundhouse.

"Mighty fine. I'm sure glad the Chief talked me into openin' this place. Otherwise, I'd of long spent my savin's and been a bum by now." Slim shook his head. "I still look up when the door opens, expectin' the Chief to come in," he said sadly, remembering Matthew MacKenzie, the man who had owned the Roundhouse ranch and the Rocky Mountain Central Railroad. "Don't seem possible he's been dead goin' on a year."

"Yeah, it'll be a year in October." Giff noticed the old range rider had begun rubbing his leg. "Does that still bother you much, Slim?"

"Acts up when it's cold or damp. Middy tells me the gals are all doin' fine."

"Yeah. Beth stays busy running the railroad, Thia's happily married to Dave Kincaid, and Angie's away at art school."

"Figure yuh must be almost done with the roundup or you wouldn't be here."

"Yeah, just have the north range to go. Probably finish up next week."

"How's the steak?"

"Damn good, Slim," Giff replied, popping another bite into his mouth.

Slim grinned. "Oughta be; it's Roundhouse beef."

When two men came in and bellied up to the bar, Slim rose and limped away on the injured leg that had sidelined him from punching cattle.

Giff finished his meal, then tipped back in his chair again to finish the beer. He felt good: Katie had taken care of one need, Slim the other. He tried to decide whether to stay in Denver and laze around in town the next day, or ride back to the ranch that night and spend Sunday working on the house he was building.

A loud burst of laughter broke his train of thought. Then he jerked to attention at the mention of Angie's name. Giff grimaced in disgust when he saw that Jamie Skinner was the speaker. The loudmouth had tried to woo Angie for years, but she had always rejected him.

"I know now I was too nice," Skinner declared. Anyone in the place would have to be stone-deaf not to hear him. "I treated Angie MacKenzie like a lady, instead of the cheap little tart that she is."

Giff's chair screeched across the wooden floor as he shoved it back and slammed down the glass he'd been holding. In seconds he reached the bar, spun Skinner around, and with a well-placed punch to the jaw, sent him crashing into a table. Before Skinner could shake off the effects of the blow, Giff was on him again, this time punching Skinner's nose.

With clenched fists, Giff stood over the man. "Come on, get up, Skinner."

"What in hell did I do to you?" Skinner asked.

"I've never liked hearing any lady's name bandied about in a saloon—and I especially can't tolerate it when the lady is someone I'm especially fond of. You care to take back those lies, or do I have to wipe up this floor with you?"

"I saw her with my own eyes, Giff," Skinner said, getting to his feet. "She was wearing red tights and singing on a riverboat in New Orleans."

"You're a goddamn liar, Skinner. Angie's in art school in St. Louis." Another blow knocked the man to the floor. Reaching down, Giff clutched a handful of Skinner's shirtfront and yanked him to his feet.

Swiping at the blood dripping from his nose, Skinner said, "It's the truth, Giff, I swear it! I know Angie MacKenzie when I see her. You can beat me bloody, but it still don't change what I saw."

"I'm warning you, Skinner, if I hear of you spreading any more of those kinds of lies, I'll do more than bloody your nose." Giff grabbed his Stetson from the table and stalked out of the bar.

Elizabeth MacKenzie glanced up in surprise when he entered the study. "Giff! I thought you were going to spend the weekend in Denver."

"I was, but I had a change of mind," he said.

"You just can't stay away from the Roundhouse, can you?" Putting aside the pen, Elizabeth sat back and tucked an errant strand of long auburn hair behind her ear.

"Beth, when was the last time you heard from Angie?"

"Funny you ask. I'm just writing her a letter. She hasn't written since February."

She leaned forward anxiously, her sapphire eyes

clouded with concern. "Giff, you look like you're ready to explode. What's bothering you? It's something to do with Angie, isn't it? What is it? Is she okay?"

"I can't say. I ran into Jamie Skinner tonight. He claimed he saw Angie performing on a riverboat in New Orleans." Giff intentionally neglected to tell her Skinner's description of how Angie was dressed.

Beth scoffed. "Angie performing on a riverboat; that's ridiculous! Why, poor Daddy would be turning over in his grave. Thia might have had the nerve to try something that reckless before she met Dave, but not Angie."

"Well, Skinner seemed pretty sure of it. He stuck to his story even after I hit him a couple times. You gonna be around here for a while?"

"To my knowledge," she said. "Why do you ask?"

"I'd figured on going to St. Louis to set up a buyer for the fall herd as soon as we finished this roundup. I think I'll go now and look up Angie while I'm there. It'll kill two birds with one stone and put both of our minds at rest."

"That's a good idea, Giff. Jamie Skinner may be sincere, but I think he was mistaken. I'm sure she's okay. You know Angie as well as I do; she's not the type to run off impetuously. In the last letter I got from her, she mentioned she was thinking of leaving art school and coming back to Denver." She sat back and relaxed again. Her voice softened with compassion. "When are you going to tell Angie how you feel about her, Giff?"

"We've been through all this before, Beth. It's not gonna happen. You know my reasons—and they haven't changed. She thinks of me as an older brother. It's best we leave it at that." Giff headed for the door. "I'll take the morning train."

* * *

Accustomed to riding a wide-open range, after two days of riding trains, Giff felt like a caged animal. As soon as he arrived in St. Louis, he hailed a carriage and went directly to Angie's boarding-house. Two young girls were sitting on a porch swing, so he smiled and tipped his hat. "Howdy, ladies." Putting down his carpetbag, he rang the bell.

"Isn't he gorgeous?"

Giff grinned when the whispered comment from one of the girls carried to his ears.

As Giff waited, he read the sign beside the bell: MISS DANVERS' BOARDING HOME. SINGLE WOMEN ONLY.

The door opened and an elderly woman, her gray hair drawn back severely into a knot at her nape, eyed him suspiciously. Removing his Stetson, Giff asked, "Miss Danvers?"

"Yes." The woman glanced at the bag he had set beside him, then turned her cold gaze to him in a scrutiny that didn't miss anything from the top of his wheat-blond hair to the toes of his boots. "I don't rent to men, young man."

"I'm not looking for a room, ma'am. My name is Peter Gifford and I'd like to speak to Miss Angeleen MacKenzie."

"She doesn't live here anymore." When she started to close the door, Giff managed to step in enough to wedge his shoulder into the opening.

"How long ago did she leave?"

"It's been a few months. Now, if you don't get out of my house, I'm going to whistle for the police." She groped for a metal whistle hanging from a cord around her neck.

"Please, Miss Danvers, that's not necessary. I'm just trying to locate Miss MacKenzie. I'm the foreman of her family's ranch. Do you have any idea where she went?"

"No. She packed her trunk one morning and up and left. I haven't seen or heard a word from her."

"And she didn't give you any hint where she was going?"

"No. I've told you all I know. I'm not responsible for what these young girls do on their own. They're supposed to be going to school, and as long as they keep their rooms clean, don't bring in any boys, and are in by the nine-o'clock curfew, I don't give them a here or there, Mr. Gifford."

"Well, if Miss MacKenzie should return, will you tell her to wire her sister Elizabeth?"

The woman folded her arms across her chest. "Oh, so she didn't tell her family she was leaving school."

"No, she didn't, ma'am, and we're quite concerned about her."

"It's not likely she'll return here since she's been gone all this while. Besides, I've rented her room."

"Thank you for your time," Giff said, and stepped away. The door slammed firmly behind him.

Giff picked up the carpetbag. He felt foolish carrying Beth's brocade bag. Anything he ever needed always fit into saddlebags, but Beth and Middy had convinced him that carrying around saddlebags in a big city would look even sillier.

"I bet I know where you can find Angie," one of the girls on the swing said. She elbowed the girl next to her, and they both giggled.

"Is she in St. Louis, Miss, ah . . ."

"Brenner—Christine Brenner."

"Is she here in St. Louis, Miz Brenner?" he asked.

"She is now, I suspect." When the girl next to her bumped her with a hip, Christine said, "Oh, this is my friend Pokie Purcell."

"Prudence Purcell," her friend corrected.

"My pleasure, Miz Purcell," Giff acknowledged. He drew a deep breath, trying not to lose his patience. "So you ladies think you know where I can find Angie?"

"Well," Christine said, raising a curved brow, "when Angie left school, she took a job on the *Mississippi Belle* sailing south."

So Skinner hadn't been mistaken. That probably meant the rest of his story was true, too. He'd go to the shipping line and try to discover where the boat was now.

"You gals have been most helpful. Thank you."

After receiving another elbow in her side, Christine spoke up. "The boat just returned this afternoon. It's docked at LeClede's Landing. Pokie and I saw it."

Giff couldn't believe his good fortune. "The *Mississippi Belle*. Appreciate your help." He tipped his hat. "You ladies have a good day."

As he walked away, he heard Pokie repeat, "He's so gorgeous."

This time he felt nowhere like grinning.

After checking into the hotel, he learned that LeClede's Landing was just a short walk away. As Giff changed his shirt and Levi's, his thoughts were on Angie. He still didn't want to believe she was actually performing on a riverboat. But the alternative might be even worse. What if he couldn't find her?

When he reached the wharf, he saw the vessel tied to the dock. A majordomo, dressed in a red and white uniform with gold fringed epaulets on the shoulders, directed him to a huge, smoke-filled salon located on the second deck. The room, once ornate with dozens of crystal chandeliers hanging from a painted ceiling, now looked run-down and neglected.

A large stage was set at one end of the long room, and the chairs were filled with spectators awaiting the night's performance. Giff stopped at the long bar at the other end of the room and ordered a beer. Mug in hand, he turned and gulped the drink, then moved closer to the stage. Leaning against a wall, he anxiously waited for the show to begin.

The band finally struck up the introductory strains to a lively tune, and to the hoots and whistles of the men in the audience, six girls traipsed out onto the stage. One of them was Angie.

Relief surged to his head in a gush of hot blood— she was well and unharmed. He felt the lift of spirits he'd always experienced at the first sight of her. He wanted to rush to the stage and hug her, to feel her in his arms, to offer that same reassurance to his body.

But it was clear what had provoked Skinner's bawdy remark: a red sequined dress stretched across her breasts and hips, and a pair of skintight hose hugged her long legs. What the hell was she doing in a rig like that! Disgusted, he worked his way to the front, much to the disgruntlement of many in the audience. As he neared the stage, the song ended and the curtain closed. The crowd began stamping and whistling, shouting for more.

Giff hurried over to the piano player. "How do I get backstage?"

"You don't, brother. It's off-limits to stage-door Johnnies."

"I know one of the girls."

The musician scoffed. "Sure you do—or would like to."

"Look, friend, just tell me how to get backstage," Giff said, beginning to become irritated.

The piano player nodded toward a nearby door. "Good luck, cowboy."

As soon as Giff opened the door a big black man, who dwarfed Giff's own six feet two inches, stopped him.

"Sorry, suh, ah can't let nobody in here."

Pointing to Angeleen in a far corner, Giff said, "I'm with Miss MacKenzie. She's . . . my sister."

Stepping aside, the black man smiled broadly. "My apologies, suh. Dat woman sure has a mighty fine voice iffen they let her sing like she should. And she's a real lady, too. Not like some of dem on this here boat. You tell her Big Ike said so, suh."

Giff reached out for a handshake. "Thanks, Ike, I will."

For an instant the black man looked surprised, then he shook Giff's hand.

Angie had her back to him, staring into space. He walked up behind her. "Hello, Angel."

She turned, her eyes rounded in surprise. "Giff! Is it really you?" She threw herself into his arms. It took him several seconds to realize she was crying.

Giff hugged her tighter. She felt so good in his arms—she belonged in his arms. He never wanted to let her go. As her sobbing continued, he sensed she was not crying from joy. He stepped back, his gaze devouring her face: the rosy flush to her cheeks, the delicate curve of her jaw, the full red lips he yearned to taste. Then he saw that her wide sapphire eyes, usually glowing with warmth, had black circles under them.

"Oh, Giff, it's so good to see you," she managed to murmur between sobs. He was there before her—he had come in her time of need. She finally composed herself, wiping her eyes and smiling weakly. "You must tell me how everything's going at the Roundhouse. How is Beth? And Middy? Oh, and how is Calico? I miss him so much. Are you working him out every day?"

"They're all fine and missing you, Angel. We can talk about that later. Right now, let's get out of here."

"I can't go yet. I've another number to do."

"No you haven't," he declared. "You've done your last *number*. You're leaving right now. Where are your clothes?"

Confused, Angie said, "In a trunk . . . in my cabin."

"Then you go change your clothes while I get us a carriage."

"But, Giff—"

"No buts, Angie. I'm taking you out of here whether you like it or not."

"Giff, you don't understand. I need this job."

"Like hell you do."

Her heart leapt with hope, and for a brief moment she closed her eyes. He'd take her out of the hell she had slipped into, wipe away her tears, and make everything right again—the way he had done her whole life. "All right, Giff. I'll go and change my clothes."

He waited until she disappeared down a hallway, then left to go out and hail a carriage. He had just reached the entrance to the salon when a loud explosion rocked the boat. He spun around and saw that a man had stepped out on the stage, reassuring the audience there was nothing to be alarmed about.

Seeing one of the crew running from the stage area, Giff grabbed the man's arm when he passed. "What happened?"

"One of the boilers down below exploded. Blew a hole right through the floor above it."

"What's above it?"

"The dressing rooms. Good thing they're empty now."

Angie! His stomach jumped to his throat. "Are you sure they were empty?"

"Should be. Almost time for the gals to line up for their next number. Better hope so; that area took the worst of the blast."

Giff raced toward the stage. *Please, God. Please?*

"Look! The boat's on fire," a woman in the audience screamed, pointing toward the black smoke creeping out from under the curtain.

Pandemonium broke out as people began screaming and scrambling out of their seats. Giff pushed his way through the terrified crowd shoving him back in their panic to get to the door. Reaching the stage, he leaped up on it and ducked under the curtain. Chaos reigned backstage. Amidst black smoke and hot steam, crew members rushed about, putting out burning props with buckets of water.

"Have you seen Angie MacKenzie?" he shouted to a group of chorus girls huddled in a corner.

"She's not with us," one yelled back.

"Where's the dressing rooms?"

"What's left of them is down that hallway where all the smoke's coming from," the woman said. "Everything I own is in one of those damn rooms. Hey, mister, are you crazy? You can't go back there," she yelled after him.

Vapor of hot steam hung in the air like a suffocating fog. He saw Big Ike among the crew who had succeeded in putting out the fire.

"Have you seen Angie?"

"No, suh. Ain't she with dem other gals?"

"Which cabin is hers?"

"The one at the end of the hall. You can't see it with all dat smoke, though, so I'll show you."

The two men slip-sloshed their way through the water, and often the wall of the narrow passage was the only thing that kept them from falling.

They reached the gap in the floor that had been made by the explosion and peered across the twisted and shattered metal of the huge steam boiler below.

"Angie!" Giff shouted. Heavy smoke still shrouded the end of the hallway like a black curtain. When there was no reply, he shouted again. "Angie, it's Giff. Where are you?"

"Giff." The reply came back weakly.

He wanted to cry with relief. "Thank God she's alive," he said to Ike, "but if we don't get her out of there, this smoke will suffocate her."

The gap was too wide to leap. Giff looked around frantically for something to span the opening. Spying a cabin door hanging partly off its frame, he rushed over and began to yank at it. Ike joined him and the two succeeded in pulling the door off the hinges. They quickly angled it across the gaping hole, precariously anchoring the other end on a narrow ledge that had not collapsed.

"Ike, you better stay behind. In case that ledge doesn't hold, get yourself some help down here."

"Yes, suh. You be careful now," Ike said.

Giff stepped cautiously onto the makeshift bridge. It didn't budge. Several more steps took him to the ledge, then he was on solid footing and rushed to the door of the end cabin. The door was sprung and wouldn't open.

"Angie? Angie, can you hear me?"

"Giff, help me," she called back weakly.

Giff threw the full force of his weight against the door. It gave slightly, but held. Once again he threw himself against it, and this time the wood splintered away from the jamb. After several hard kicks, the door sprung open.

Through a haze of smoke he saw Angie on the floor, still wearing the red dress. Coughs wracking her body, she reached up weakly to him. Swooping her up in his arms, he hurried down the passage until he reached the hole.

As Giff cautiously worked his way across the makeshift bridge, Ike watched nervously. "Should I take her, suh?"

Giff held his precious burden closer. "I'm not letting her go."

The backstage appeared to have resumed some normalcy, with the exception of several piles of charred debris. The orchestra had struck a tune and the master of ceremonies was onstage making jokes and reassuring the audience, who had begun returning to their seats.

"Five minutes, folks, and our dancing and singing beauties will be back onstage."

Angie's coughing had finally subsided, and after several deep breaths, she felt recovered. "You can put me down now, Giff."

"Not until I'm sure you're all right. Do you hurt anywhere?"

"No, I don't hurt anywhere. I feel one hundred percent better now that I'm out of that smoke. Now, put me down, I feel foolish."

"I'm not letting go of you until we're out of here."

As he headed for the door, the stage manager came up and grabbed his arm. "Where the hell are yuh going, Angie? Yuh've got another number to do. And who the hell is this guy?"

"She's out of here, mister," Giff declared, shoving ahead.

"I'm sorry, Mr. Perkins," Angie said pitifully.

"If yuh leave now, Angie, don't bother to come back," he shouted after them. "I've got no use for gals who run out on the show. And what about them clothes yer wearin'? They belong to us."

"I'll bring them back when I pick up her trunk in the morning," Giff said, without halting. "She'll have no further use for this trashy rag she's wearing."

"You takin' that gal outta here, mistah?" Big Ike asked, when they reached the stage door.

"That's right, Ike. I hope you're not gonna try to stop me."

His face split in a wide grin. "She ain't no more your sis than I'm yer brot'r, is she, suh?" Giff grinned back at him. "You wants to go with him, Miz Angie?" the big man asked. Angie nodded and buried her head against Giff's chest. "Dat's good. She's too fine a lady for this place," he said to Giff. "You take her home where she belongs, suh."

"I will. Thanks for your help, Ike. Say, would you consider doing us one more favor and bring her trunk over to the hotel?"

"It'd be my pleasure, suh."

Giff shifted Angie enough to dig in his pocket and pull out a gold eagle. "My name's Pete Gifford and I'm in room twenty-one on the second floor." He handed the bouncer a coin. "I appreciate it, Ike."

Once outside, Giff told the majordomo to hail them a carriage. Goggle-eyed, the man complied.

On the ride back to the hotel, Angie sat huddled in the seat of the carriage, burrowed against him, not saying a word.

Chapter 3

When Giff registered Angie, the desk clerk's disdainful glance swept her bedraggled form and flashy attire.

"Does the lady have luggage?" the man asked.

"Miz MacKenzie's trunk will arrive in the morning." Giff yearned to smash the contemptuous look off the man's face. "She was attending a costume ball and suddenly took ill."

Though he looked skeptical, the clerk was too well trained to challenge the explanation. "Miss MacKenzie's room is number twenty-three ... directly opposite yours." He shoved the key across the desk. "And how long will Miss MacKenzie be a guest here?"

"Well, sir, I reckon as long as I will."

"I see," he said haughtily.

"I was sure you would," Giff replied with a tolerant smile.

"Do you wish the services of a bellboy, sir?"

Grinning broadly at the pretentious man, Giff said, "No. I reckon I can tote her myself." Sweeping Angie into his arms, he carried her up the stairs.

After depositing her on the bed in her room, he crossed the hall and returned with one of his clean shirts. "Here, Angie, change into this." She did not reply, but continued to sit on the bed and stare into space.

Giff went over and knelt down before her. He quickly unlaced her boots and removed them. Then he picked up the shirt he had laid beside her. "Angie, if you're not gonna remove that damn costume, I'll do it for you."

She rose woodenly and began to undress. He quickly turned his back. "You'll feel much better once you get a good night's sleep. You know what Middy always says: 'A good night's sleep will cure anything that ails yuh.'"

When her silence continued, he ventured a peek and saw that now, dressed in only his shirt, she had sat on the edge of the bed and once again was staring into space.

His heart ached for her. She looked so forlorn. A ridiculous-looking red plume was still in her hair, so he went over, squatted down before her, and removed it. Tossing the plume aside, he said, "Everything will be fine, Angel. Tomorrow we'll take the train back to Denver."

She looked at him sorrowfully. "I can't..." Bursting into tears, she reached for him. "Oh, Giff, I can't go back. I've made such a horrible mess of everything."

Her body trembled as her crying increased. Shifting to the edge of the bed, he sat down and embraced her. "Nothing's that bad, Angel."

"Yes, it is. I've been such a fool. I'm so ashamed of myself." He could barely understand her because she was crying so hard.

"Now, stop the crying. Look, honey, we've all done things at one time or another that we aren't proud of. And some of them are a lot worse than running off and getting a job on a riverboat."

She looked up at him with tears sliding down her cheeks. "I'm going to have a baby, Giff."

He felt as if a knife had been thrust into him. He knew she was waiting for him to say something, but he couldn't breathe, much less speak. Her words were choking him—cutting off his breath like a cord tightening around his neck. For the past three years he had tried to fortify himself against the day when she told him she was in love, against the day she carried another's man child. Now he discovered how useless the effort had been. His hands slid to his sides and he got to his feet. Wordlessly he walked to the window and stared out into the darkness.

"Now you understand why I can't go back."

Still unable to look at her and expose his true feelings, Giff said woodenly, "Why should that keep you from going home?"

"Because two weeks ago, when I told him I was expecting, my baby's father ran off with another woman."

A wave of hot anger rushed to his brain. "How could you marry a son of a bitch like that?"

"I'm not married to Edward Emory." Her voice had become steady, free of the self-pity and incrimination that had suffused it previously.

His sudden sense of relief made Giff feel he was as rotten as the bastard who had run out on her. He turned to look at her. Angie had risen to her feet, and now, despite the overlarge shirt that hung past her knees and dangled off the ends of her wrists, she stood with her shoulders squared and her head unbowed.

"So you'll have to live down some scandal. Thia did, didn't she?" he said, reminding her of the scandalous affair her sister had had with an Italian count before she married Dave Kincaid.

"Thia didn't come home as an unwed mother, Giff."

"You think that would have stopped her if she'd had to? She has spunk, Angie, and was always willing to face the consequences of her actions. And you've no call not to do the same. You're a MacKenzie, aren't you?"

"That's more reason to stay away. I won't disgrace my father's memory."

"You trying to say the Chief would have been ashamed of you? He loved you, for God's sake. And he'd be proud to see you tough it out."

"And what about my child, Giff? Must that innocent tough it out too, because of its mother's sin? Denver society can be very cruel. I'm not going back. I'm sure if I ask, Mr. Perkins will reconsider and give me my job back."

"And how long before that red dress becomes too small for you to get into, Angie? What then? Like it or not, you're coming home with me, even if I have to tie you up and pack you on my back."

"Oh, Giff." She walked over and stood before him. Grasping his hand, she brought it to her cheek. "Please, let's not quarrel. You've always been like a big brother to me—and to Beth and Thia. Someone we could take our troubles to when we needed a shoulder to cry on. And you always listened, picked us up when we fell, and fought our battles for us. But you can't fight this one for me, Giff. Don't you think I *want* to go home? I've thought about nothing else for the past two weeks—and I thought about Joey Burke, too. Remember poor Joey, Giff? Remember the gossip because his mother never married? How people never let Joey forget he was born a bastard? How the cruel taunted him to his face and the less cruel behind his back? Do you remember how many times he was bloodied defending his mother's name?" Tears glistened in her eyes. "And do you remember the day they cut Joey down from the rafter he hung himself from?"

Angie wiped away her tears. "And what if my child's a girl? It will be even worse. Think of the names she'd be called, and what she'd have to endure from boys and then from men who would brand her because of her mother's folly." She shook her head emphatically. "I could tough it out if I were the only one hurt by it, but I'll never subject my child to what Joey Burke had to endure, until he couldn't endure it any longer."

As Giff looked into her stricken face, images from the past swirled through his mind: the curly-headed moppet reaching up her little arms to him, the leggy adolescent with skinned knees and sun-burned nose, the self-denying teen who, shadowed by the vibrancy of two extraordinary sisters, had been unaware of her own blossoming beauty. Three years ago, he had recognized the depth of his feelings for her: he was in love with Angie. He would love her the rest of his life. And in that bittersweet moment he'd also realized she would never reciprocate that love. In her eyes he was her best friend, the one she turned to in time of need— not passion; the arms she sought for comfort—not in desire.

The Lord knew he was far from being any psalm-spouting saint, but he'd always held a deep reverence for God's mastery. Now suddenly Giff recognized that through the grace of heaven-sent intervention, he was being given the opportunity not only to solve Angie's predicament but also to fulfill his forbidden dream. He wanted to shout with joy.

"No one's gonna hurt or slander you and your child, Angie." He grasped her shoulders. "Because I'm going to marry you. Then when the baby's born everyone will believe I'm the father. We'll get married tomorrow."

Stunned, she looked up at him. "I won't let you do that, Giff. You've got your life to live."

"I want to do this. I swear to you, Angie, I'll love that child as my own."

"I know you would. That's not the issue."

"Then what is? Are you still in love with this Emory fellow?"

"I don't know what I feel for Edward. Knowing how he lied and took advantage of me doesn't change the memory of how I felt when he made love to me—of how much I loved him at the time. Now love . . . guilt . . . shame, and anger are all running together in my mind. I'm all mixed up, Giff. I can't think straight."

"All the more reason why you should listen to me."

Angie shook her head. "Giff, I love you—you know that—but I couldn't live with you as a wife." She blushed and turned away.

"You mean share my bed."

Her head bobbed in reply.

His joy plummeted as fast as it had risen. Wanting her the way he did, he knew it would be impossible to share a day-in-day-out existence with her and promise not to take her to his bed. Even now, despite her despair, he could barely keep his hands off her. Everything he had dreamed and hoped for was within his grasp. He couldn't let it slide through his fingers—but he couldn't lie to her either.

Giff put his hands on her shoulders and turned her around to face him. "I don't expect you to now, Angel. It would be a marriage in name only that we'd be doing for the baby's sake." He smiled tenderly, yet pleadingly, for her understanding. "But I would hope that someday your feelings would change and it would become a real marriage between us."

He watched her internal struggle intently. "I can't promise that, Giff, so you'd be jeopardizing your own chance for happiness. What if you meet a woman who you could love, who could bear *your* children—not another man's? Why would you do this, Giff? Take such a risk?"

"You MacKenzies are the only family I have—and that baby has MacKenzie blood. I don't know of a better reason than that. As long as I can draw a breath, no one's ever gonna call it a bastard." He grinned and brushed aside a tear sliding down her cheek. "Besides, I turned thirty-one last week. There ain't a woman alive who wants to marry an old, broken-down cowpoke like me."

"Oh, sure!" Angie said, smiling through her tears. "That's why every girl in Denver is hoping you'll ask. Why *haven't* you married before, Giff?"

He couldn't look her in the eye and keep up the pretense that he wasn't in love with her, so he quickly fended off the question. "Hey, are we gonna try to solve my problems or the baby's?"

Angie sighed deeply. "Oh, Giff, your offer is so tempting, but it would be so selfish of me to take advantage of your loyalty. Everyone in Colorado knows you'd be willing to die for a MacKenzie."

"Who said anything about dying? I might not be that lucky. Marriage to one of you headstrong MacKenzie gals could turn out to be a fate worse than death," he teased. "Reckon I should have gotten Dave Kincaid's advice before I made the offer." He tucked a finger under her chin and tipped it up. Smiling down into her upturned face, he said gently, "I'd be mighty grateful if you'd do me the honor of marrying me, Angeleen MacKenzie."

"I'll always love you, Giff. And it's shameful of me to take advantage of your love and kindness.

But it seems like I've done it my whole life." Her lips quivered and tears streaked her cheeks as she smiled gamely up at him. "So, yes, I'll marry you." Sobbing, she buried her head against her chest. "God bless you, Giff."

He felt the moisture in his own eyes and hugged her closer, aching to kiss her, but he knew it would be a mistake. It would only frighten and confuse her more. She wasn't ready for another man's kiss—and it was better to be thought of as a brother than to lose her entirely.

Awaking from the first good night's sleep she'd had in two weeks, Angie thought about her conversation with Giff. Now, in the bright light of morning, she wondered if she should go through with the outrageous scheme. It would be so unfair to Giff. Then she thought of the baby. Her baby's interests had to come before anyone else.

She got up and saw that her trunk had been set in the corner and every piece of the costume she wore on the riverboat was gone. For a long moment she felt a flash of resentment at Giff's high-handedness. Why hadn't he awakened her? The thought of him moving freely around her room while she slept disturbed her. Then she shrugged aside the foolish thought. It was just Giff—trying to make things easier for her, the way he had done all her life.

Angie opened her trunk and chose a simple blue cotton gown. Gripped with nostalgia, she felt the rise of tears. How she had dreamed of and planned this day! Now there'd be no wedding gown of white satin. There would be no lacy veil on her head—not even a sprig of orange blossoms. And just as heartbreaking, Beth and Thia would not be there with her—or her father, beaming with pride.

Determined not to shed any more tears of self-pity, she went down the hallway to the bathroom, bathed, and returned to her room to dress. She was sitting on the edge of the bed waiting when Giff rapped on the door.

"Angie?"

"Come in, Giff."

"Good morning." He looked uncomfortable. Funny, she hadn't realized how big he was; his tall frame filled the entrance. "Are you ready?"

She nodded and walked over to him. "Giff, are you sure you want to go through with this? I'd understand if you've had second thoughts."

He ignored her question. "There's a dining room right here in the hotel. I thought we would have breakfast and then go to city hall and get married by a judge or justice of the peace."

"That's fine with me," she said. At least they wouldn't go through the blasphemy of having the marriage performed and blessed by a man of the cloth.

Giff handed her a small bouquet he'd been concealing behind his back. "You make a lovely bride, Angel."

"Thank you, Giff." Recalling her pallor and the dark circles under her eyes when she looked in the mirror, Angie shook her head. "Pete Gifford, have you forgotten how Middy used to wash our mouths out with soap for telling such lies?"

"I'm not lying, Angie," he said solemnly, and took her by the arm.

As soon as they were seated in the dining room, Giff ordered them both a breakfast of ham, eggs, and potatoes.

"Giff, I can't eat a breakfast that size," Angie protested immediately. "Toast and tea will be fine."

The waiter looked inquisitively at Giff. "Bring her what I ordered," Giff said.

Angie gave Giff an angry glare, then sat in silence until the waiter returned and put down two large platters before them.

Appalled, she stared at the plate of food as the waiter departed. "There's enough here to feed an army. I told you I can't eat all this food."

"Just try."

"Giff, you know I've never been a big breakfast eater."

"Time you start. You're eating for two now."

Ignoring the potatoes entirely, she ate one of the eggs and half of the ham slice, then shoved the plate at him. He finished the rest for her as she drank a cup of tea.

After taking a long look at the two empty platters, she teased, "Are you sure you've had enough? Just because I do doesn't mean you have to."

He looked confused. "Have to what?"

"Eat for two." She couldn't hold back her laugh. "You're going to regret passing up the ham and eggs when you taste the food they give you on the train."

"Then thank goodness I'll be traveling with someone who's eating for two. I can always snatch a spare bite." She burst out laughing again, but stopped when he grinned at her. "What is it?"

"You're laughing, Angel. I was afraid you'd forgotten how."

Angie smiled self-consciously and shifted her gaze away. The warmth in his clear blue eyes only added to the guilt she felt at his sacrifice. He was trying so hard to put her at ease, and she was acting pernickety and treating him as if he were a stranger, not someone she'd known her whole life.

Two hours later, they were married by a justice of the peace in a civil ceremony at the city hall. Once outside the building, Angie studied the gold band that Giff had slipped on her finger. She had recognized it at once: Buck Gifford, the ranch fore-man, had worn the ring as a fob on his pocket watch after his wife's death. Upon Buck's death five years before, the watch had been passed on to his son. Moved by the sentimental gesture, Angie said solemnly, "Giff, this is your mother's ring."

"I hope you don't mind. I know Dad would be pleased to know my wife is now wearing it."

"I'll treasure it always." She smiled mistily at him.

"Ready to go home now, Angel?" He slipped his arm around her shoulders as they walked down the stairs of the city hall.

Sighing, she said, "Oh, Giff, it will be so won-derful to be home again."

"Our train doesn't leave until noon, and I have a quick stop to make at the cattle broker's office before that. Do you want to wait at the hotel or come with me?"

"I'll come with you."

"Good. I don't like the idea of leaving you alone." He grinned. "That round-eyed look you're wearing reminds me of a scared filly that's gonna bolt the minute someone tries to put a rein on her."

She glanced at him askance. Giff always had an uncanny knack for reading her mind. For the first time since she'd known him, the thought made her feel uncomfortable.

That afternoon, after wiring Beth to let her know they were headed home, they boarded a train that would take them to Denver.

Chapter 4

Despite Angie's determination to shake off her self-pity, she spent most of the trip home desolate and ill, throwing up in the train's water closet.

"We'll be reaching Laramie by morning and then it's just a short ride home, Angel," Giff said gently as he tucked her into the bunk.

"I feel bad that you have to sit up to sleep, Giff."

"I don't have any trouble sleeping, Angel." Grinning, he added, "I can even sleep in the saddle when I'm tired enough. If you need anything, just call out."

"Thank you, Giff," she said, grateful for his understanding. In truth, the thought of the two of them squeezing into the narrow bunk was not an inviting thought. In addition to which, once the curtains were closed, there was no circulating air.

Angie thought of her big, airy room at home. How good it would feel to get back again and sleep in her own bed. She nervously twisted the ring on her finger. Would Giff move into the house or remain in the small house he occupied on the ranch? And what would she tell Beth? Angie knew Giff

41

had wired her sister to tell her that they had married. Should she tell Beth about the baby? She knew Giff would never betray her secret if she asked him not to say anything to Beth or Thia. Of course, once the baby came early, her sisters would know that Giff wasn't the father. She'd have to decide by tomorrow—that was for sure.

She awoke the following morning without being ill. Just knowing she'd be home by nightfall was enough to make her feel better. In the bright light of a new day, her thinking was clearer than it had been the previous night. Once she and Giff had settled in, she'd sit down with Beth and tell her everything—*but not until she and Giff had settled in.*

In Laramie, as they transferred to the Rocky Mountain Central, the railroad line owned by her family, Angie was greeted by Jacob, the black man who had been a porter on the line from the time of its inception.

"Ah sure do miss the Chief, Miz Angie," Jacob told her. "Hard to believe he's been gone near to a year now."

"I miss him, too, Jacob," she said fondly.

She felt pride in knowing how much her father had been revered by all his employees: the cowboys who rode his range as well as the men who worked his trains. After striking it rich in the California gold fields, he had moved to Colorado and built the Roundhouse, a thriving cattle ranch. Then in '69, he had ventured into building railroads in Colorado and linked his line to the recently completed Union Pacific transcontinental railroad farther north in Wyoming and Nebraska. His dream had been to one day build a railroad between Denver and Dallas. Despite the illness that ultimately consumed his body, her father had lived to see the construction of that line begun under the supervision of Dave Kincaid, the brilliant and conscien-

tious engineer he had chosen for the task. Any
hope for the Rocky Mountain Central to remain in
the family now lay in the capable hands of Cynthia's husband—and in Elizabeth's ability to raise
enough capital to complete the ambitious project.

Throughout the day, sentimental memories of
her father flickered through her mind as her anxiety continued to build. Finally, five miles north of
Denver, the train pulled into MacKenzie Junction.
Located on the fringe of the MacKenzie ranch, the
small station was her family's private depot. As the
train ground to a halt, her gaze swept the tiny log
station house and small roundhouse where her father had kept his private railroad car. She thought
fondly of the many times he had taken her for a
ride in the luxurious car, and the dozens of times
she had stood on the wooden platform and waved
good-bye to him as he waved back from the deck
of that car. Now he was gone. Even the car no
longer remained there, because Thia and Dave
were living in it at end of track somewhere in New
Mexico or Texas.

Peering out the window, Angie saw that Elizabeth was waiting at the station. Her heart leaped
with love at the sight of her auburn-haired sister.
Four years her senior and the eldest of her sisters,
Beth had always been the businesswoman in the
family, as dedicated as Dave Kincaid to seeing the
railroad completed.

Angie hopped off the train before Giff or Jacob
could even assist her. The two sisters reached out
to one another, their love, excitement, and joy flowing through each hug and kiss they exchanged.

"Oh, Angie, it's so good to see you," Beth exclaimed, giving her another quick hug before opening her arms to Giff. "And I'm so happy about the
marriage. Now you truly are a brother to me, Giff.
But couldn't you two have held off getting married

until you were home? You cheated us out of a big wedding."

Giff hugged Beth and kissed her cheek. "We saved you a lot of money by doing it."

Beth's eyes were glistening with tears. "I'm just so happy for both of you. I can't believe you finally asked Angie to marry you. I want to hear every word of how it came about."

Glancing uncomfortably at Angie, Giff said, "Let's get to the house first. Angie had a hard trip home and she'd probably like to rest."

"Oh, I'm sorry, honey." Tucking her arm through Angie's, she said contritely, "You should have said something sooner. Let's get going."

The two women climbed on the buckboard while Giff loaded the luggage, and in a short time he pulled up in front of the big house. Angie felt overwhelmed with emotion. All the tension eased from her body, and all the doubts and reservations from her mind—she was home again.

As her gaze drew in the huge house and its surroundings, she glimpsed a dun horse in the distant corral. Recognizing her beloved stallion, she cried out, "Calico!" Tossing aside her hat, she sprang from the buckboard and rushed to the corral.

Laughing and shaking her head, Beth climbed down and entered the house. Giff tethered the team, then followed Angie down to the corral.

Mindless of her gown or safety, Angie climbed up on the fence as the horse trotted over to her. Flinging her arms around the horse's neck, she cooed, "I missed you, boy." The horse's head bobbed up and down as if responding to the greeting.

Impulsively grabbing a rein, Angie climbed over the fence and began to halter the animal.

"What do you think you're doing?" Giff asked, arriving just as she finished.

"I'm going for a ride."

"It's too dangerous for you to ride in your condition."

"Nonsense. Daddy told me my mother never stopped riding when she was carrying me and my sisters." Pulling her skirt up to her knees, she swung herself up on Calico's bare back.

Giff grabbed the halter. "You've been sick for days. The horse isn't saddled. You could fall."

"Pete Gifford, I won't fall, you know that."

"I'll make sure you don't." He swung up behind her, and she found herself encircled in his arms when he took the reins.

"I guess we're just going to have to tolerate his overprotectiveness for a while, Calico," Angie said, patting the horse's neck. Then she turned her head and cast a reproachful glance at Giff. "For a short time, anyway."

"I take it I've been warned," Giff said, amused. He goaded Calico lightly with his knees and the well-trained animal broke into a slow, loping gait. Angie settled back against Giff and he tightened his embrace. Her hair smelled of lavender and he wanted to bury his nose in its thickness.

"This reminds me of how you used to give me a ride when I was too young to ride alone," she said. "Do you remember, Giff?"

"Yeah, you were as pesty then as you are now," he said gruffly, hoping he sounded displeased. In truth, as she pressed against him in the shelter of his arms, Giff wished the ride could go on forever. "I'm surprised you even remember that, Angel. You weren't much more than five or six years old."

"Oh, I'd never forget that. It meant too much to me."

"Yeah, I can see you now, waiting at the corral when I'd ride in with Dad and the other hands.

One look at your little face and I knew what you were hoping for."

"And without my asking, you'd reach down and pull me up in the saddle in front of you."

"I never could resist those big blue eyes of yours." He turned the horse toward home, and they settled into the silent companionship they had shared through the years.

As soon as they reached the corral, Giff slid off the horse and swung Angie to the ground. "I'll take care of Calico. You best go and say hello to Middy or there'll be no living with her tonight."

Giff watched her walk up the path to the house, his gaze following her graceful stride and the sight of the dark curls bobbing on her shoulders. He'd lost count of the number of times he'd done the same thing in the past few years. Chastising himself for being a lovesick fool, he led Calico into the barn to rub him down.

With outstretched arms, Middy greeted Angie at the entrance of the huge foyer. "Saints alive! My baby's home again!" The white-haired housekeeper could barely contain her pleasure, and her eyes glowed with love and affection as she hugged and kissed her.

Matilda McNamara had been the housekeeper at the Roundhouse for over twenty years. The widow had even assisted in the delivery the night Angie was born. Upon their mother's death, when Angie was ten years old, Middy had taken over the task of mothering the three sisters.

Snatching up the hem of her apron, Middy wiped away her tears. "And Giff's wife now, too. I can't believe it! Where is that boy?"

"He's in the barn, Middy, taking care of Calico," Angie said.

"I might have knowed you'd see your horse before comin' inside and givin' old Middy a kiss."

Angie slipped her arm around the housekeeper's waist and they entered the house. "That was only because I saw Calico when we drove up, you old darling."

"Well, I best get to the kitchen and see what that worthless cook is up to. I had her make your and Giff's favorite meal."

"Chicken and dumplings!" Angie exclaimed.

"What do you think? Trouble is, she ain't got the touch for it."

"Middy, are you ever going to stop fighting with the cooks?" Angie teased.

"Soon as I find a halfway decent one. It's good to have you home again, darlin'," Middy added as she hurried away.

"I agree," Beth said. "It's good to have you home, Angie. You have no idea how lonely it is in this big house with everyone gone. You and Giff are planning on living here, aren't you?"

"I don't know, Beth. We haven't discussed it."

"I hope you will. You should take Daddy's bedroom. It's larger."

Uncomfortable with the question, Angie lowered her gaze to the marble tiles of the foyer. The thought that she and Giff would be expected to share a bedroom hadn't occurred to her. "Oh, I'm sure Giff wouldn't want to do that."

"Do what?" he asked, coming through the door with her trunk.

"I was just suggesting to Angie that the two of you move into Daddy's room," Beth said.

"I don't think so."

"Why not, Giff? The room is so much larger than Angie's, and the attached sitting room will give you two a private place to get away from me when you want to."

That was so like Beth, Angie thought fondly. Her

eldest sister always considered other people's interests.

"Now, why would we ever want to get away from you?" Giff said, tactfully avoiding giving her an outright answer.

"I thought newlyweds preferred privacy." Spontaneously Beth slid an arm around Angie's shoulders. "I just can't believe you two are married! I'm so happy."

"We kind of like the idea, too," Giff said. "I'll get this trunk out of here."

"Why don't we go into the drawing room, and you can tell me all about the wedding over a hot cup of tea," Beth said.

In the glow of Beth's happiness, Angie knew she couldn't tell her sister the truth about the wedding yet.

"I'd like to get out of these clothes first." Angie started to climb the wide circular stairway. "Then we can talk afterwards."

She intercepted Giff, who was on his way down, and pulled him back into her room. "What should we do, Giff?"

"Why not tell her the truth?" he said. "I don't like lying to Beth."

Angie slumped down on the edge of the bed. "You saw how happy she is. I hate to spoil it for her. If I tell her the truth, I'll have to tell Thia and Dave . . . and Middy, too."

Angie felt as if the walls had begun closing in on her. She jumped to her feet and walked to the window. "I feel so guilty. I've made such a mess of everything. I never should have come back."

Giff went over to her and looked her in the eyes. "Angie, that is a ridiculous thing to say; you couldn't stay away forever. Furthermore, there's nothing so bad that the truth won't cure. What you did was for the baby's sake, so it's time you start looking at the future, instead of the past."

With all the wallowing in self-pity she'd been doing in the past few days, she had allowed that
thought to slip away. Giff's words buoyed her spirits, and Angie turned to face him. "That's right.
The baby's future is all that matters, isn't it, Giff?"

He hugged her, holding her in his arms to give
her the reassurance she was seeking. "I don't believe you can keep the truth from Beth. But I'll go
along with whatever you decide to do."

"I have to think about it some more. I'm just so
tired." She snuggled deeper in the sanctuary of his
arms.

Giff picked her up effortlessly and carried her
over to the bed. Laying her down gently, he smiled.
"Go to sleep, Angel."

"I shouldn't. I told Beth I'd join her for tea."

He sat down on the edge of the bed. "I'll explain
you're napping. She'll understand."

Overcome with drowsiness, Angie slipped her
hand into his, then closed her eyes. "I don't know
what I'd do without you, Giff." Her voice drifted
off as she fell asleep.

His gaze rested on her sleeping countenance.
How he cherished her. If only it *were* his child she
carried. If only their marriage weren't a sham. He
lowered his gaze to their entwined fingers and
smiled. Someday it wouldn't be. The day would
come when Angie looked upon him as more than
a friend—the day would come when she looked
upon him as her lover. He raised her hand to his
cheek. It felt cool and satiny against his heated
flesh. Sliding it to his lips, he kissed her palm, then
lowered her arm and tenderly placed it on the
counterpane.

He stood to pull a folded afghan off the cedar
chest at the foot of the bed, and covered her. For a
moment he stayed looking down at his sleeping

wife, yearning for what might be, instead of what was. Finally he lowered his head and pressed a light kiss to her lips before he slipped quietly from the room and closed the door.

Angie didn't know whether it was exhaustion or just being back in her own bed that made her sleep so well, but she woke up to the sound of Beth tapping on the door and calling out that dinner was ready.

Getting up quickly, Angie straightened her clothing, touched up her hair, and hurried downstairs. Expecting to see Giff at the table, she was surprised to find Beth alone.

"Giff's eating in the bunkhouse with the boys," Beth said. "They'll be heading out to finish the roundup tomorrow and he said he's got a lot to go over with them."

The lucky guy, Angie thought. *Now he doesn't have to face Beth's questions.*

To avoid discussing her marriage, Angie steered the conversation to Cynthia and Dave. Beth brought her up to date on the married couple and the progress of the railroad.

"We're in Texas now—the homestretch. Barring any unforeseen problems, the line should be completed in less than a year."

"I thought for sure the Rocky Mountain Central would go under after the disaster at the end of last year. How do you do it, Beth? Wherever did you raise the money to replace the engine and flatcars we lost?"

"It wasn't easy, that's for sure. You name it, I tried it. I'm running out of sources—short of stealing, that is," Beth said, laughing. "And at times that's even a temptation."

"You think you'll make it?"

The gaiety left her eyes. "God willing."

Having managed successfully to get through the meal without having to answer one question about her marriage, Angie used the excuse of having to unpack to return to her room. She knew she had probably hurt Beth by rushing off the first night they were reunited, and knowing her sister as well as she did, there was no doubt in Angie's mind that Beth wanted to know more than the cursory things they had told her. If she and Giff continued to skirt the questions, Beth would surely become suspicious.

Angie wasn't mistaken. The tap on her door came sooner than she expected, and Beth poked her head in the room. "May I come in?"

"Of course."

Beth sat down on the bed. "How much longer before you tell me what's going on?"

"What do you mean?" Angie asked.

"Angeleen MacKenzie, I'm Beth—your older sister—remember? You've never been able to fool me. What's wrong, honey?"

"There's nothing wrong, Beth." The denial sounded weak even to Angie.

"Nothing wrong, huh? Most new brides are glowing with love and happiness—you look like you've just been sentenced to hang. If there is any glow in your eyes, it's dimmed from those black circles under them. And Giff is so tense, he looks like he's ready to snap. Granted I'm no authority on the subject of marriage, but the two of you sure don't act like newlyweds; you both try to avoid looking at each other, much less make any physical contact. If you weren't wearing his mother's ring, I'd question if the two of you were even married."

"I can assure you we're married, Beth. The situation's just a little awkward, that's all. And I think Giff isn't comfortable with the idea of living here in the house."

"Oh, that's nonsense. As long as I can remember, Giff's had free run of this house as much as the one he's living in." Patting the bed beside her, Beth said, "Come over here, honey."

As soon as Angie sat down, Beth clasped her hand. "I should have kept my mouth shut, because I have no right to interfere in where you live. It's a decision that you and Giff must decide for yourselves."

"You know how much Giff and I love you, Beth. I'd never accuse you of interfering in our marriage. I just need a couple days to get settled in. I feel that you—and Giff—are still treating me like the baby of the family. I've outgrown that role; I'm a married woman and I'm going to have . . ." Angie stopped before she could say more. She still wasn't ready to talk about the baby—and Edward.

"Going to what?" Beth asked. "What were you about to say?"

"Going to have to ask you to have patience until we all get used to that."

"Of course, dear." Beth hugged her and stood up. "But married lady or not, honey, you're not a visitor here. This is your home—and Thia's—as much as it is mine. The same is true of Giff. Good night, Angie. I'll see you in the morning."

Beth stopped at the door and turned to her with a broad grin. "Gosh, it seems so long since the last time I said that. I sure like the sound of it."

Knowing she must talk to Giff, Angie sat up in bed reading until he came into the room. "I've stalled as long as I could, but Beth outlasted me," he greeted her. "Dammit, Angie, I've had about all I can take of this pussyfooting around."

"Please don't raise your voice or Beth will hear you."

"She won't hear me. She's downstairs in the library. Just where do you suggest I sleep? Tomorrow I'm riding out to the roundup and I'd like to get one decent night's sleep."

"I guess the only thing to do is for you to sleep in here until we figure out what to do."

"You mean share a bed?"

"Under the circumstances, what choice do we have? This is an emergency."

"How can you be so naive, Angie?"

"What do you mean?"

"If we're lying in the same bed, the outcome's inevitable."

"What outcome?" she asked, confused.

"We'd become intimate, of course."

Her eyes rounded in astonishment. "Just because we share the same bed? That's ridiculous. It's inconceivable to me how it can even cross a man's mind to become intimate with a woman he doesn't love."

"Well, there's enough whorehouses around to prove how *conceivable* it is."

"Are you implying that all men are so driven by their passion—by lust—that they can't lie beside a woman and control..." She was so upset, she couldn't get the words out.

"Maybe not *all* men, but the thought sure as hell would occur to most."

"I don't believe that. And I can't believe it of you."

"Don't try reading that fairy tale, Goldilocks, or you might be disappointed with the ending."

Frustrated, she threw her hands up in the air. "I'll never understand men."

He went over and raised the window.

"What are you doing?"

"Getting the hell out of here," he said grumpily. "I'll sleep in my own bed, tonight, but this is the last time I'm climbing out of windows. Tomorrow, either you tell Beth the whole story or I will."

"You told me you'd agree to whatever I wanted to do," she protested as he started to climb out.

He turned his head and looked back at her. "I know I did, and I know it's necessary to lie to people to protect the baby. But lying to the family we both love sticks in my craw."

He swung over and grabbed the limb of the tree outside the window. She watched as he worked his way down until he reached the lower branch. Before he could jump the short distance to the ground, he lost his hold and fell, landing on his rear end. A string of expletives followed the fall.

"Giff, are you okay?" she cried worriedly.

"Yeah," he said gruffly, standing up and brushing himself off.

Despite the situation, Angie couldn't help smiling as he strode away, kicking at the loose pebbles in his path.

That night Angie lay in bed thinking about Giff's words. He was right. She couldn't lie to Beth any longer. Nothing but anxiety would be gained by putting off the truth. In the morning she would tell Beth the whole miserable story.

Chapter 5

Angie had the shock of her life when she woke up the following morning to discover her menses had started. Stunned, she struggled with a mixture of emotions: relief that she wasn't carrying Edward's baby, yet sadness that she wasn't carrying one, too. How could she have been so stupid? Her menses had always been irregular, although *never* as late as she had been this time. Still, she'd been wrong to just assume she was pregnant. She should have consulted a physician.

Then she had compounded it by marrying Giff! What was she to say to him now? Sorry I've ruined your life, but I miscalculated!

Dumb! Dumb! Dumb! It's a good thing you weren't pregnant, Angeleen Caroline MacKenzie . . . Gifford. You're too dumb to raise a child.

But at least she wouldn't have to go to her sister and confess she was carrying Edward's child. She'd tell Beth that she and Giff had made a mistake and the marriage wouldn't work out.

"Oh, God! Another lie," she moaned. "I can't believe I'm standing here formulating another lie!" Tossing down her brush, she leaned forward and

55

studied her image in the mirror. "No. I'll tell her the whole story. No more lies and deceit."

Prepared to confess all, Angie went down for breakfast only to encounter Beth on the verge of departing.

"Oh, good, you're awake," Beth said. "I was just going to write you a note. I'm about to leave for end of track. Dave wired and said there's a problem he wants to go over with me, but he can't leave the site. I'm grabbing a ride on the freight train this morning."

"When will you be back?"

"I imagine in a couple of days. I really feel bad about running off this way the day after you've gotten home. Maybe it's for the best, though. You and Giff can get settled in comfortably without me around."

"Oh, don't worry about that, Beth. I just hope the problem's not too serious. I wish there was something I could do to help. You've had to bear this burden so long."

"Well, I asked for it, honey."

"Do you want me to drive you to the station?"

"That won't be necessary. String's waiting in the buckboard for me right now. 'Bye now; I've gotta go." She rushed off with a wave.

Angie stood at the door and watched the dust raised by the departing wagon settle back to the ground. Then she went upstairs and dressed.

After eating breakfast, Angie offered to help in the kitchen, but the cook shooed her away with an emphatic no. Upon offering her services to assist with the housecleaning, Middy informed her it wasn't necessary; the hired girl was due in that day.

With nothing but time on her hands, Angie wandered from room to room, reacquainting herself with familiar objects: the paintings on the walls, and the delicate pieces of porcelain and crystal that her mother so loved. In the drawing room, she sat down and played a polonaise.

"Well, that should set poor Mr. Chopin shuddering in his grave," she murmured, moving on to the study. Pausing beneath her father's picture hanging over the fireplace, she said to it, "Daddy, you sure raised one worthless daughter. Everyone seems to have a function in life except me. I failed miserably at art, I failed at music, I failed on the stage, and I most certainly will fail Giff as a wife." *Giff!* She buried her head in her hands. She now had to face him and tell him the truth about the baby! Angie glanced up again at her father's portrait. "You know, Daddy, I think I just figured out that I do have a function in life—failing." Despondent, she turned away.

As she passed through the dining room, she grabbed an apple from a bowl on the table and went outside to the barn.

Calico's ears perked up at the sight of her. When she held out her hand, the horse plucked the piece of fruit from her palm.

Patting his neck, she said affectionately, "Good morning, my love. Looks like Giff's been neglecting to give you your favorite treat. Well, I'm home now, so I'll make sure it won't happen again."

She walked out of the barn when String returned with the buckboard. "Good to see you, String. How have you been?"

"Mighty fine, Miz Angie," he said, doffing his hat.

"And how's Red doing? Still talking about moving to a warmer climate?"

He grinned broadly. "Red ain't never gonna change, Miz Angie. That's for dang sure."

Now in their forties, the cowboy and his younger brother had ridden for the Roundhouse for over twenty years. Although the brothers had been christened Wallace and Ethan at birth, their parents were the only ones who had ever called them by their proper names. With a last name of Bean and the fact that he was as skinny as a rail, standing six and a half feet in his stocking feet, Wallace had been dubbed String. A full head of red hair had earned Ethan the nickname of Red Bean.

"We sure wuz pleased to hear about you and Giff hitchin' up."

"Thank you, String. Where are Giff and Red?"

"North range. They rode out early this mornin' to finish roundin' up the herd. We told Giff it weren't proper fer a new bride to be left alone."

"Oh, I know what spring roundup is like, String," Angie said. "Say hello to Red for me," she added, and strolled back to the house.

Later that evening, sitting alone at the dining room table, Angie had a sense of exactly how lonely Beth must have felt this last year. Memories of her father and sisters seated at the table flickered through her mind, and the sound of their voices and laughter seemed to echo in the room.

After finishing the lonely meal, Angie got a favorite novel from the library and retired to her room. For the next few hours, she lost herself in the chivalry and treachery of jousting knights, Normans and Saxons, the Lady Rowena and Rebecca.

Finally putting *Ivanhoe* aside, she turned off the light and snuggled down into her bed. The past few months had soured her belief in romance. It was a pity that handsome knights who rode to a damsel's distress no longer existed, she reflected with the embittered wisdom of all her twenty-one years. Just before falling asleep, in what she told herself was a totally unrelated thought, Angie wondered why Giff hadn't ridden back that evening.

Angie tossed and turned in a dream where she

was held prisoner in the tower of a huge round castle, guarded by a mammoth black dragon snorting fire. Her gaoler, who looked suspiciously like Edward, forced her to paint nude pictures of him, until the day Wilfred of Ivanhoe rode up to the castle in a flourish of clarions, the sun gleaming on his steel armor inlaid with gold. As the valiant knight raised his lance to slay the dragon, the beast suddenly changed into a long train and chugged away, puffing smoke.

Jolted awake, Angie sat up in bed and shook her head to try and clear it. In the bizarre dream, the armored knight hadn't been mounted on his gallant steed, but on Giff's chestnut gelding.

Boredom set in about the same time Angie opened her eyes the next day. After receiving the same refusals of her offers to help, she spent another restless morning. It was Middy's day off, and after she'd left for Denver for the night, Angie tried to sketch, but gave it up. By midday, when it was obvious Beth would not be returning, she made a decision. In the past, she had always participated in the spring and fall roundups. She was tired of trying to keep herself occupied, and since she wasn't pregnant, there was no reason why she shouldn't be taking part in this one, too.

Racing up the stairs, she pulled off her dress. Freed of the restraints of her corset, cumbersome bustle, and train, Angie donned a split riding skirt and plain white blouse. Boots replaced fancy pumps, and her well-worn, small-crowned Stetson felt better than any fancy chapeau.

After saddling Calico, she shoved several strips of white linen into the saddlebags to provide for the feminine needs of her condition, and added apples as a snack for Calico.

It felt good to be back in the saddle again. Putting all her heartaches and misgivings behind her, Angie galloped across the countryside, feeling really alive for the first time in months. She shoved the hat off her head and lifted her face to the warmth of the sun and the rush of exhilarating wind through her hair.

She chose a shortcut to the north pasture across a rocky terrain they called Devil's Peaks. Bare of grass and vegetation, other than a few scrub draws and an occasional ash tree that appeared to be growing out of the rocks, the area was treacherous, full of fissures and narrow gullies furrowed by centuries of rain and wind. Knowing that Calico was as surefooted as a mule, and having ridden the tract so often it was as familiar to her as a keyboard, Angie never skirted the area.

She goaded Calico to leap over one of the wider cracks, then reined up when she heard a noise. Listening intently, she waited until the noise was repeated. It sounded like a bawling calf. Dismounting, she explored a nearby draw and soon spied a calf, its legs tangled in the twisted scrub.

"Poor baby," she cooed as she freed the frightened animal. "How'd you get down here, little one?" She wondered what had happened to its mother, because heifers were very protective of their young. "Did those mean old cowboys drive off your mama and leave you behind? Well, we'll just have to take you to her. I've hefted enough calves in my day, but you're a bit larger than I'm used to handling. If I knew I'd have to come to your rescue, little one, I sure would have brought a rope."

The calf continued to bawl.

"I'll send one of the men back to get you," she said. Looking into its limpid eyes, though, Angie felt as if the calf was pleading with her. She

couldn't bear to leave the frightened animal behind.

Exerting all her strength, she managed to lift it
onto Calico's back and swung up behind the bawling calf. "What are you crying about? I'm the one
who did all the work," she panted. "I haven't done
anything that strenuous in a year."

Despite the physical exertion, she felt good as
she resumed the ride. "At least I'm good for something, aren't I, little one?"

Giff was bending over a fire when she rode into
camp. He looked up and grinned at the sight of
her. "Looks like somebody hitched a ride."

"Yeah, this little guy was left behind."

He walked over and relieved her of the squirming calf. "The poor little thing is probably hungry,"
she said. "I'll cut out one of the heifers."

Angie rode over to the herd and skillfully separated one of the cows from the herd. In the meantime, Giff got a rope and towel from the supply
wagon. After Giff tied the heifer to the tree, Angie
covered its eyes with the towel, and Giff carried
the calf over to the tethered heifer. The hungry little
calf immediately began to suckle.

Clutching his arm, Angie exclaimed, "Look, Giff,
it's eating."

After the calf ate its fill, Angie removed the towel
from the cow's eyes. She held her breath waiting
to see if the heifer would reject the mewling calf.
The cow stood docilely and allowed the calf to nuz-
zle her.

Giff released the heifer and it trotted back to the
herd, with the calf at its side.

Angie clutched his arm. "Oh, Giff, wasn't that
precious?" Her eyes glowed with warmth as she
looked up at him.

She looked so beautiful his stomach tied in a
knot. "Reckon that little maverick has found a

mother," he said. "I noticed it wasn't wearing a brand. Where'd you find the calf?"

"In Devil's Peaks."

The grin left his face, replaced by displeasure. "Dammit, Angie, that place is dangerous."

"Giff." Exasperation was thick in her tone.

"Don't give me that look. I don't gave a damn that you know it like the back of your hand. That doesn't mean Calico can't step in a chuckhole or crack. You've got to start thinking about the baby." He spun on his heel and strode away.

Angie followed on Giff's heels, trying to keep up with his long strides. "If you're going to get mad at me every time we're together, I'd have been better off remaining in St. Louis."

He stopped and turned around so abruptly that she bumped into him, almost knocking her off her feet. Giff grabbed her shoulders to keep her from falling. "I'm only thinking of our baby."

"Our baby!" she exclaimed. "You mean *my* baby—you had nothing to do with it. Furthermore, there is no baby." The words had slipped out so quickly that Angie couldn't believe she had blurted it out so insensitively.

"*What* did you say?"

"There is no baby." The fight had gone out of her and she turned away from him.

"I don't understand, Angie."

"I thought I was pregnant, Giff, and I was wrong."

"You were wrong! You mean you weren't . . . How could you make a mistake like that?"

She pivoted, and more out of guilt than anger, she lashed out at him. "I *said* I am sorry. It was a logical mistake at the time. I hope you don't think I said it to trap you into marrying me or something stupid like that."

"Come on, Angie, you know better than that."

"Anyway, you ought to be happy."

"Well, I'm not. I was kind of looking forward to raising a baby."

"Don't you think I was too?" she murmured, on the verge of tears.

"Yeah, I reckon you were." He put his arms around her. "I'm sorry, Angel. I know you're disappointed. Let's get out of this sun and sit down." He led her over to a clump of pine and aspen and tethered her horse next to his gelding.

Angie slumped down on the ground and he handed her a canteen. "Here, take a drink."

She took a quick swallow and handed it back to him, then looked up with a weak smile. "I shouldn't keep you, Giff. How's the roundup going?"

"Fine. We've been rounding up strays. We should be moving the herd in the morning." He gave her a long, worried look. "You okay, Angel?"

One of the beautiful qualities of their relationship was that they never could stay angry with one another for any length of time.

She nodded. "I'm fine, Giff. You know, human nature is sure odd. When I thought I was having a baby, it seemed to be the source of all my problems. Now that I'm not pregnant, I feel such a loss." She looked at him quizzically. "Isn't that crazy? How can you lose something you never had to begin with?"

"Do you feel the same way about Emory?"

"It's not the same, Giff. Edward was real—he was flesh and blood. The baby never existed."

"Yeah, but it's the same principle, honey; you can't lose something that you never really had to begin with." Giff stood up. "I better get back to work." He pulled her to her feet.

"Any chance that you could use another wrangler?" she asked.

"You looking for a job, cowboy?"

"Sure am. And I work real cheap. My only problem is that I forgot to bring a lariat or bedroll with me."

"Lariat's no problem. We've plenty of rope in the wagon. No blanket, though. How do you feel about sleeping with the boss?"

"That's my intention."

"Then the job's yours." Chuckling, he added, "Welcome home, Angel."

For a long moment he gazed pensively down at her. He knew Angie was covering up her disappointment over the baby, and he wanted to tell her how bad he felt for her. Yet he figured this was the best way she could put Edward Emory behind her forever. The baby would have been a constant reminder of the man who fathered it. Keeping his thoughts to himself, he walked over to the supply wagon. Angie followed him.

"You hungry?" he asked, without looking at her. "I was about to rustle us up a pot of coffee and something to eat."

"Let me do it, Giff. I'll call you when it's ready."

"Seems like old times." For a moment they stood grinning at each other like two kids. "String and Red should be riding in soon," Guff said. "If you're sure you don't want any help, I'll ride out and give the boys a hand."

"I'll be fine."

Watching him swing up on the back of his chestnut gelding, Angie recalled her bizarre dream. She turned away quickly.

Seeing that one of the men had shot three rabbits, Angie immediately set to skinning them. After cleaning and dressing the rabbits, she sat down in the shade to peel and cut up potatoes for frying. For a moment she sat back and relaxed, enjoying the sweet fragrance of pine permeating the air, and comforted by the low mewling from the grazing herd.

By the time all the men returned to camp, she had the rabbits roasting on a spit.

"Somethin' sure smells good," Red said, taking a deep sniff.

"Something smelling like roasting rabbits?" she teased.

"I'm more inclined to think it smells like a purty lady. Sure glad to see yuh've come home, Miz Angie."

"It feels good to be back," Angie said. She did enjoy being out in the fresh air—she had missed that in St. Louis. "Nothing smells as good as this mountain air, Red."

"Yeah, but trouble is, once that wind starts a-howlin' through these peaks, it gets mighty dang cold. Gotta find me a warmer climate."

"Oh you've been saying that as long as I can remember. Go wash up, Red." She plopped the sliced potatoes into a large skillet sizzling with melted bear grease. "Dinner'll be ready in ten minutes."

Darkness had descended by the time they finished picking the rabbit bones clean.

"Mighty fine-tastin' vittles, Miz Angie," String said. "Sure better than anythin' Red cooks up."

"Iffen yuh don't like my cookin', Mr. String Bean, do it yerself," Red grumbled. "Time yuh take a hankerin' to the taste of yer own cookin' anyway, 'cause come next winter I'm ridin' out of these hills. Think I'll head west to that Californee. Been told it's warm there all the time."

Giff winked at her. Then, tossing a rabbit bone into the fire, he stretched out with his hands under his head.

"What are you grinning about?" she asked.

"Just feels good, Angel—you here on the

roundup with us . . . the guys chewing around the fire."

She'd been thinking the same thought. It seemed like an eternity since she last ate out under the stars with the guys. She hadn't realized how much she had missed it. But the sleeping arrangements were very different this time. She asked nervously, "Are you sure you don't mind sharing your bedroll, Giff?"

"Just so you promise not to hog the blanket." He made no attempt to conceal his wicked grin. "Besides, why should I mind our sharing a blanket—you're my wife, aren't you?" He stood up, then pulled her to her feet. "Come on, Angel. Let's clean up. We want to get an early start in the morning."

By the time Angie closed up the supply wagon, String and Red were already bedded down for the night and snoring away. Giff put several logs on the fire and then rolled out his bedroll.

"Days are warm, but it still gets pretty chilly at night out here," he warned.

"As if I don't know, Pete Gifford," she said, lying down beside him.

"Just remember my warning about hogging the blanket, lady."

They both were making a concerted effort to try and not touch, but it was impossible to avoid under the narrow confines of the blanket. Occasionally an arm would inadvertently touch, or a leg would make contact.

Angie finally gave up trying and just relaxed. After all, they were man and wife, even if it was in name only. There certainly wasn't anything unusual or scandalous about sharing a bedroll with her husband. Matter of fact, it was downright comforting, considering the chill that settled on the mountains after dark.

"It's still possible to wake to frost these mornings," she said.

"I figure we're pretty safe, unless we have a late snow. You never can tell in these mountains. *The Old Farmer's Almanac* did say we were in for a mild spring, though."

Sighing, she glanced up at the stars. "Isn't the sky beautiful tonight, Giff? It looks so serene and . . . infinite."

"Yeah, real peaceful."

"I think everyone should sleep out under the stars."

"I bet you'd have sung a different tune a couple months ago. Damn cold then."

"I mean, just think of how long they've been up there and how large those stars must be if we're able to see them. It gives you a real perspective of how infinitesimal we are compared to the heavens."

"You gonna sleep, Angel, or ponder the universe all night?"

"But it's so fascinating. Don't you ever stop and think how miraculous it is that everything up there is somehow balanced and related?"

"Angel, my main concern is that God up there will see that it rains before the grass dries out. It's been a dry spring so far. If we don't have rain soon, we're gonna run out of graze for the cattle."

She closed her eyes. "Starlight, starbright, first star I see tonight. Wish I may, wish I might, have the wish I wish tonight." She opened her eyes and giggled. "I haven't done that for so long. Beth, Thia, and I used to do it so often when we were younger. I wished for rain. Did you make a wish, Giff?"

"Yeah, I wished that you'd go to sleep. You always did talk through half the night." He turned over, his back to her. "Dawn'll come sooner than you think, and we're moving the herd at sunrise. The boys want to be through with the roundup by the weekend.''

Long after he fell asleep, she lay glowing in the contentment of his nearness and the warmth of his body.

Chapter 6

The warmth of her woke him. Sometime during the night he had turned over and she was now cuddled against him, her body curved to his, one arm flung across his chest, and her head resting on his shoulder. Her closeness set his loins to aching. Hot blood pulsed through him with every beat of his heart hammering against his ribs. He was hard and throbbing. Cursing himself for being a fool, he wondered how much longer he could honor his promise to her. Every conscious thought warned him to get out of the bedroll, but his body was so heavy with lust, he couldn't move.

In the dim glow, her profile looked ethereal. He couldn't help thinking how much she looked like one of those stars shining in the dark sky that she so admired—the luminous flush of her exquisite face set against her dark silken hair.

Reaching out, he pushed a stray curl off her cheek. Then, unable to resist touching her again, he pressed his lips to hers.

He felt her stir under the pressure and forced himself to pull away. She opened her eyes and he couldn't tear his gaze away from the sight of her slumberous sapphire eyes. Clenching his hands to keep from pulling her into his arms, he sat up, shifting her off him.

She covered her mouth and yawned. "Is it time to get up already?"

He nodded, not trusting himself to speak. Getting to his feet, he hurried to the fire before she could notice the telltale evidence of his arousal. The cold, crisp air helped to quash his passion and he busied himself at the fire—stoking the flame with fresh wood as determinedly as he quelled the flame within himself.

"You might as well stay tucked in until I get this fire built up," he said when he felt he was under control. "I'll get the coffee on."

Despite the temptation to remain in the bedroll, Angie got up, and after removing several granny rags from her saddlebags, she sought the privacy of some nearby trees to change her padding. Giff was prodding String and Red awake with a nudge of his boot when she returned.

Angie rinsed off her face and hands, the shock of the cold water dousing any lingering drowsiness. Then, borrowing Giff's tooth powder and hairbrush, she rinsed out her mouth and brushed her disheveled hair.

With her morning toilette completed, she felt refreshed and ready for a new day.

"I'll take over," she said, brushing Giff aside at the fire. Angie fried strips of smoked bacon, and she had eggs bubbling in the bacon grease by the time the men joined her at the fire.

"Eat it while it's hot," she said.

They didn't have to be asked twice, and by the time the men finished wolfing down the food and hot coffee, the gray sky had begun to streak with carmine.

When the wagon was hitched up and ready to roll, Giff laid out their jobs.

"Angie and I will drive the herd; you fellas ride ahead with the wagon to the big hill near the Willow. I want you to build a temporary corral with those posts and slats we brought out last week."

"Dad-blame it, Giff! Why'd you pick a hill to run fence on?" Red grumbled.

"Because that's the best grazing closest to the tracks. The corral's just to contain the steers we're keeping until we drive the rest of the herd to the depot."

"That still don't make it no easier to run a line of fencing on a hill."

"Red, it's just temporary. You don't have to make the fence perfect. We'll be breaking it down once we ship out the rest of the herd. Let's roll, fellas," Giff said.

After tying their horses to the back of the wagon, the ranch hands moved out. Side by side, Giff and Angie worked in companionable silence as he saddled Brick and she saddled Calico.

"Let's get that herd on their feet, Angel," he said, once they were mounted.

As soon as they got the bellowing cows moving, Giff and Angie split up, each taking a flank. The herd was strung out for about a quarter of a mile, and the site where they were headed was a little more than five miles away, with the Willow River between. Giff didn't want any pounds worked off the cattle this close to selling them, so they moved them slowly.

With just the two of them, though, it was an arduous task. Angie had to repeatedly ride up and down the flank, whistling and hazing the steers. Time and time again she drove a straying calf back into the herd before it could wander too far away from its mother.

When they reached the banks of the Willow, the real work began. The steers had a mind to stop and drink; Angie's job was to make certain they continued to the other side so the herd didn't get bunched up in the middle of the river. She shouted and yelled at them, delivering stinging slaps to their rumps with her lariat.

When the last steer finally stepped out on the opposite bank, Angie finished driving them to where Giff and the Beans had started to cut the younger bulls and heifers out of the herd into the hastily erected corral. Then she rode back across the river and checked the route they had followed for any possible strays. It was dusk when Angie finally rode back into camp, driving four steers ahead of her, and she turned them over to String.

Sipping from a coffee mug, Giff leaned against a tree and watched Angie ride in. She had done a hell of a job all day, never shrinking from the task at hand, and stopping only to take an occasional drink from a canteen. He was so damn proud of her, he wanted to go over and hug her. Her time away from the Roundhouse hadn't dulled her skills at all; she was still as proficient as any hand they ever had.

But she looked exhausted. He started to go to her, then changed his mind. In the past, she had always resented it when he didn't treat her like any other hand.

He watched her unsaddle Calico and swing the heavy saddle to the ground. After she removed the blanket and halter, she spoke to the horse, gave Calico a pat on the rump, then watched it trot away to graze.

Giff straightened up when he saw her limp over to the fire. Concerned, he hurried over to her. "You're limping. Did you hurt yourself?"

She tried to stretch, then winced. "Ouch!" Then

she laughed nervously. "Guess I'm just out of condition. I'm kind of sore."

"There's a tin of unguent in the wagon. That should help."

She never uttered one word of complaint as she ate the meal Red prepared, but when she finished, she headed over to where Giff had laid out the bedroll a distance away to give her privacy. He purposely lingered at the fire, talking to String and Red, in order to give her time to tend to her needs. When he finally went over to her, she was stretched out on her stomach.

"Feel any better?"

"Yes, much. I can't reach my back, though. Will you put some of this unguent between my shoulders?" She sat up to remove her blouse, and handed him the tin. Then she lay back down, her cheek against her folded hands.

She was wearing something white, lacy, and feminine. God, how he lusted after this woman! And here she was, stretched out before him, wearing that damn piece of enticement, and asking him to put his hands on her! Whatever sins he had committed in the past, the Lord sure had figured out the way to make him pay for them!

Quick and fast. He'd get it over with before his loins even got the message!

Scooping some of the salve on his hand, he slicked it on her shoulders. It was a mistake. The moment his hands made contact with her warm flesh, they seemed to have a will of their own. His fingers spread, curling around the soft slope of her shoulders, caressing the satiny flesh more than kneading it.

"Oh, Giff, that feels so good."

The sigh was as provocative as the feel of her under his fingertips. Driven by passion, he increased the pressure, sliding his hands under the camisole. Her body felt even warmer there. He didn't want to stop. He wanted to turn her over, to trace his hands over her breasts—hold them—fondle them—taste them. They were within his reach. It would be so easy. He grasped her sides to turn her over.

A sudden outburst of loud laughter from String jolted him out of his thoughts. He jerked his hands away and glanced across the camp, where String and Red were preparing to bed down for the night.

Good God! He had forgotten about them! He was obsessed—and he was so hard, he couldn't move.

"That should do it," he mumbled.

Angie sat up and put on her blouse, then lay back, her hands tucked under her head again.

"Thanks, Giff, I feel better already," she said softly.

It's good one of us does, he thought churlishly.

"It's been a while since I've spent a whole day on a horse, and I haven't worked so hard in a long time."

"You'll feel better by morning."

Her grateful smile ripped at his guts. He felt like a lecher.

"Thanks to you." She closed her eyes and took a deep breath. "But you know, Giff, despite the aches and pains, it felt good out there today. There's such a sense of peace out here."

"Yeah, I know what you mean."

She opened her eyes and her tender gaze warmed him. "I can't imagine you doing anything else, Giff. You were born for this life."

"I've always thought the same thing about you, Angel."

"I do love it. I could never see myself behind a desk like Beth, or in a schoolroom like Thia." Her eyes deepened with intensity. "Will you keep a secret, Giff?"

"I always have, haven't I?"

"I really don't like crowds and big cities. When I used to listen to Beth talk about New York and Washington, D.C., or Thia talk about London and Paris, they always sounded so exciting. But big cities are crowded and smoky. And noisy! I couldn't believe how noisy St. Louis was, even at night. Have you ever thought about what a wonderful life you have, Giff? Nothing compares to the fresh air here and the beauty around us. And it's so peaceful and quiet."

He chuckled warmly. "There's a couple hundred mewling steers out there, Angel. Many people wouldn't call that quiet."

She giggled, a delightful sound which threatened the passion he had just brought under control. "Why, that's a symphony, Mr. Gifford. Music to my ears! If I rode out there right now, I could sing them to sleep like babies." Her mouth settled into the loving and trusting smile he remembered so well from her childhood. "Have you ever thought of doing anything else, Giff?"

"Like what?"

"Maybe build a railroad like Dave?"

"Hell, no! Getting through a winter in these mountains is enough challenge for me."

"What about seeing Paris? Or the ancient pyramids?"

"Most of what they've got to offer is man-made. Reckon I lean toward God's handiwork. I don't have to go around the world to figure out that there can't be anything much more beautiful than these Rockies."

"But aren't you the least bit curious about the people who live in those distant places?"

"No. I reckon people are pretty much alike, no

matter where they live or what language they speak. Different habits maybe, or different clothes and customs. But human beings are the same: some are good, some are bad—no matter where you live."

For a long moment she lay in silence. Figuring she was going to sleep, Giff started to get up, but her words stopped him.

"You know, Giff, I've been thinking all day about what you said yesterday regarding Edward. You're right. A person can't lose anything they never had to begin with. For weeks I anguished over losing Edward, when in truth, he was the loser. I offered him the greatest gift I had to give: my love. And he rejected it. Why should I feel any guilt—or misery? He's the fool, not me."

"He sure is, Angel."

"But I'd be the fool if I ever lost you, Giff. You're my best friend."

"You're not going to lose me, Angel," he said gently.

She grasped his hand. "No matter what happens, you'll always be my best friend, won't you, Giff?" Her voice began to drift off.

"Yeah, Angel. No matter what—I'll always be your best friend."

Long after she fell asleep, he continued to hold her hand. He couldn't go on deceiving her much longer. Even though she might not be ready for it yet, now that the baby scare was behind them, they were going to start sleeping together—in all ways.

The next morning, he knew he could not spend another frustrating night lying beside her with the camp's lack of privacy, so he told her to go back to the house.

"Giff, I feel fine; you don't have to send me back."

"That's not why I'm doing it, Angie. We've just got a few more steers to cut out here, then a short drive to the depot. The boys and I can handle that without any problem." He gave her a foot up when she mounted Calico, then checked her stirrups. "We'll be riding in tomorrow. How about you telling Middy to make the boys a special meal? They're about due for one."

"You know Middy," she said, laughing. "I can ask her, but I sure can't *tell* her. 'Bye, Giff."

" 'Bye, Angel."

He watched her gallop away until she disappeared over the crest of the hill. Then he mounted Brick and went back to work.

Chapter 7

Frowning, Middy met her at the door. "About time you showed up here, gal." She dug into her pocket. "This here wire came for you. Your sisters are comin' home today."

"Thia, too!" Angie exclaimed joyously. "Oh, I must get out of these clothes. They smell of woodsmoke."

"Where's that handsome husband of yours?"

"He and the boys won't be riding in until tomorrow. That handsome husband of mine also has a message for you. He told me to tell you that he wants you to make the boys a special meal."

Her face pinched into a frown. "He said that, did he?"

"Yes, he did," Angie replied, amused.

"You tell that young buck for me that he might be runnin' the ranch, but I'm runnin' the house."

"Knowing your obliging disposition, Middy dear, I already called that to his attention."

"Besides, he knows I always see to it them boys get fed proper when they get back."

Angie headed for the stairs but came to an abrupt halt when Middy said, "Sure hope Thia's got some good news to tell us."

"Good news about what?"

"Time we had some little ones runnin' around this house. It's been a long drought." She eyed Angie slyly. "And from the way you and Giff are actin', I figure the dry spell will continue."

Embarrassed by the woman's perceptiveness, Angie stamped her foot in indignation. "Middy McNamara, that's none of your business."

"You're dang tootin' it's my business. Everything that happens in this house is my business."

"Because you're a meddling old woman."

"Watch your words, missy. You ain't so big that old Middy still can't wash your mouth out with soap." She stomped off, mumbling under her breath about young gals who were too big for their britches.

After reading the wire from Beth, Angie thought of how good it would be to see Thia again. There was never a dull moment when she was around. Three years her senior, Cynthia had never been content to play the role of the "forgotten middle child." Vibrant and adventuresome, at twenty she had quit Wellesley College and gone off to Europe, become engaged to an Italian count, and for two years traveled to all the exciting capitals of Europe with him, until the previous year when she'd broken her engagement and returned to Denver prior to their father's death. The clash between her free-spirited sister and the serious, hotheaded Dave Kincaid had been the spark for a great romance. They were so in love that one could feel the energy when around them.

Shaking her head in amusement, Angie raced up the stairway to bathe before they arrived.

Angie could barely contain her excitement when the freight train arrived at MacKenzie Junction. The locomotive had barely squealed to a halt when, looking as lovely and vibrant as ever, Cynthia stepped down from the platform of the Mac-Kenzies' elaborate private car.

The two sisters embraced and kissed, then with her sapphire eyes glowing with excitement, Cynthia stepped back. "Let me look at you, Pumpkin. I just can't believe my little sister's a married lady now! And where's Giff? I've got to congratulate him for finally getting up the courage to ask you."

Before Angie could pursue the odd remark, they were joined by Beth and David Kincaid. Dave gave her a bear hug and kissed her cheek. "I'm happy for you, Angie. You couldn't have made a better choice for a husband."

It was no secret to anyone how well Pete Gifford and Dave Kincaid got along. The two men had a deep respect for one another. The differences in their vocations prevented them from being rivals, and both men had been devotedly loyal to Matthew MacKenzie, who had loved and regarded them both as sons.

"I don't think I made such a bad choice, either," Thia said proudly, slipping her arm through her husband's.

"You won't get any argument from me," Dave said. "Where's the lucky groom, Angie?"

"Giff and the crew are on roundup, but he'll be back tomorrow."

Cynthia sighed theatrically. "Oh, my, a man's work is never done. Even on his honeymoon. Or should I say *especially* on his honeymoon?"

"No, you shouldn't," Beth declared. "I swear, Thia, you're never going to get over trying to shock people with your scandalous remarks."

"And on that happy note, I'm going to duck away to help uncouple the car," Dave said.

While he was gone the women loaded the luggage onto the buckboard, then sat down to await Dave's return.

Angie smiled with pleasure. "Thia, you look lovelier than ever. And I swear Dave's gotten handsomer, too."

"Marriage agrees with us, Pumpkin. Just wait; you'll find out for yourself."

Having made certain the car was securely stored in the roundhouse and that the freight train had resumed the trip to Denver, Dave rejoined them and took the buckboard's reins.

"How's the new track coming along, Dave?" Angie asked.

"Oh, please, you're as bad as Beth," Cynthia groaned. "Let's try not to mention the Rocky Mountain Central for twenty-four hours."

"Don't be so flippant, Cynthia MacKenzie Kincaid," Beth scolded, "just because you don't care a hoot or holler about the future of the Rocky Mountain Central."

"You tell her, Beth," Dave said, goading her on.

"Must I remind you that same Rocky Mountain Central is your husband's livelihood?" Beth continued.

"And what a superb job he does, too," Thia said, her eyes flashing with pride. "At *everything* he does. That's why I love him so much."

Dave glanced back at his wife and the two exchanged one of those special glances they often shared.

"Look, my darlings," Thia protested, "I *do* care about the future of the line. I care about it deeply. It's just that I live with the railroad every day, and now that I'm home, I want to hear about Angie's wedding." She slipped an arm around Angie's shoulders. "And how dare you and Giff get married without the rest of us present!"

*   *   *

Later, alone in her bedroom, Angie pondered the conversation they'd had on the way back from the station. Fortunately, the talk had moved on to their father, so she hadn't had to discuss her marriage. But how long would that last? She was just postponing the inevitable.

She walked over to the dresser and lovingly touched a small moroccan leather music box, the special gift from her father given to her after his death.

Why a music box, Daddy?

Cynthia had finally guessed the message behind the silver thimble she had received at the same time; Elizabeth was convinced that her gift of a miniature replica of their father's first locomotive was his way of telling her to continue to preserve his dream. But why a music box to her? And one that played his favorite tune? What was he trying to tell her?

She wound up the box and a tutu-clad equestrienne standing on the back of a black stallion pranced around in a circle to the poignant strains of "Londonderry Aire."

She was tempted to open the letter that accompanied the gift, but her father's instructions had been clear: each of them was not to open her individual letter until the time when she missed him or needed him the most.

Oh, Daddy, I miss you every day, and I need your advice now more than ever.

Opening the top drawer of the dresser, she removed the lid of a small ceramic curio box and extracted the envelope she had tucked among lavender-scented sachets. Her gaze fondly traced the word *Angeleen* written in her father's familiar script.

Had the time come to open it or should she wait

for a more critical crisis in her life—or, God willing, a happier time to share with him?

Let's face it, Angie, you haven't exactly been making the wisest decisions these days!

A tap on the bedroom door solved the issue for her. "Angie, may I come in?"

She hastily returned the letter to the box and closed the drawer. "Come in, Thia," she called out.

Cynthia came in and sat down in the center of the bed, her legs crossed under her.

"This room doesn't look like a man's moved in. Where are some of those divine masculine reminders—like discarded holey socks in the corner or scruffy old boots smelling of horse manure?"

"Giff's been on roundup since we've been home. And we haven't decided just what we'll do yet."

"Beth mentioned she thought you and Giff should take Daddy's room."

"I might have guessed the two of you have already discussed it."

"Your marriage caught us all by surprise, Pumpkin. Just when did you and Giff decide to get married?"

"It was kind of sudden for Giff and me, too," Angie said uneasily.

"Had you discussed it in letters, or what? You both sure were close-mouthed about it all. Beth said Giff had gone to St. Louis because they hadn't heard from you for a while."

"That's right. I had quit school and was working on a riverboat."

"My little sister was working on a riverboat! I can't believe it!"

"Thia, will you stop referring to me as if I were a child! I'm twenty-one years old. Do I have to remind you what you were doing when you were twenty-one?"

Cynthia's startled look made Angie regret her

unkind outburst. It was only natural Thia would be curious—as was Beth. As sisters they had always been close and were accustomed to sharing their secrets with each other. The added fact that the man they had known all their lives was also involved made the situation even more mysterious.

"All right," Angie said, theatrically flinging an arm across her brow to soften her earlier remark. Plopping down, she joined Cynthia on the bed. "I can see there'll be no peace in this household until you and Beth get the whole story. Get her in here."

"Beth, get in here right away," Cynthia called out at the top of her voice.

A worried Beth rushed into the room. "What is it? What's wrong?" Seeing the familiar sight of her sisters sitting on the center of Angie's bed, heads together, legs tucked under them, Beth didn't have to be told. She recognized the ritual they had practiced since childhood—they were about to have one of their sisterly chats. Relaxing, she joined them and assumed the same position. "What's going on?"

"Angie's about to tell us why she and Giff decided not to invite us to their wedding."

"You ninny!" Angie said affectionately. She reached out and grasped a hand of each of them. "You know how much Giff and I love both of you. We would never intentionally do anything to hurt either one of you."

"We know that, Pumpkin. And we feel the same about both of you," Cynthia said.

"When Giff arrived in St. Louis, he discovered I had quit school and taken a job on a riverboat."

"Oh, no!" Beth exclaimed. "That loudmouth Jamie Skinner was right after all."

"Why? What did that toad say?"

"Apparently he shot his mouth off that he saw you on a riverboat in New Orleans. Slim Collins told me later that Giff beat the Sam Hill out of Jamie and threatened to do worse if he didn't keep his mouth shut."

"What would we have done through the years without Giff to champion us!" Cynthia said.

"Well, the night Giff found me," Angie continued, "a fire broke out on the boat, and if it weren't for Giff, I might have been seriously hurt."

"Giff to the rescue again!" Cynthia exclaimed.

Angie hesitated. Up to that moment she had intended to confess all: to tell them the whole truth about Edward and her mistaken belief that she was pregnant. She suddenly realized that as much as her sisters loved her, they also adored Giff. Both of them were so caught up in a romantic aura that she hated to tell them that she and Giff weren't in love, that it had been a marriage of convenience. She doubted that either of them would appreciate that she had taken advantage of his good heart to serve her own purposes.

Angie was sure that Beth, who had a more practical and businesslike approach to life, would come to terms with her sister's arrangement with Giff. But Thia was another matter. Even though she had lived a scandalous life herself, she had always stood accountable for her own mistakes and believed wholeheartedly that one married only for love.

What if it led to them quarreling among themselves? Factions lining up against one another as to the right and wrong of it? She could never forgive herself if that happened. At first the baby had been her only consideration—now she had to think about the effect on the whole family. In a resolution not made out of a sense of shame or embarrassment, but rather a heartfelt hope to avoid any friction, Angie decided the best thing she could do for family harmony was not to tell them the truth.

Somehow she would have to convince Giff to agree to do the same. She felt as if a burden had been lifted off her shoulders.

"Giff picked me up, told my boss that I was leaving, and carried me off the boat."

"Oh, my goodness!" Cynthia gasped. "He literally swept you off your feet! Don't you just love it, Beth?"

"Go on, Angie; then what happened?" Beth asked, leaning forward. The heads of the three girls were practically touching.

"Well, Giff took me to his hotel—"

"This is getting better by the minute," Cynthia said.

"Thia, stop interrupting her."

Beth and Thia waited expectantly. "And that's when he asked me to marry him. The next day we went to the city hall and were married by a justice of the peace. That's it."

At least everything she told them had been the truth.

Cynthia drew back. "That's it! Is that all you're going to tell us? We want to hear how he asked you—what did he say?"

"Thia! Have I ever asked you how Dave proposed to you?"

"Good thing, too. She probably did the proposing," Beth said, giggling.

"Oh, is that right, Miss Smarty Britches!" Picking up a pillow, Cynthia tossed it at Beth.

"On bended knee, no doubt," Angie added, swatting Cynthia with one of the fluffy cushions.

Within seconds the three of them were off the bed, laughing and chasing each other through the upstairs hallway in an all-out pillow fight.

Attracted by the commotion, Middy and Dave hurried to the foot of the stairway. Shaking her head, Middy stood with hands on hips. "Appears like we'll be cleanin' up goose feathers again for another week. I've lost count of the pillows them gals have ruined. I swear, don't matter none how old they get, them three gals ain't never gonna change."

"I hope not," Dave said, grinning with pleasure.

Chapter 8

When Angie came down for breakfast the next morning, the first thing she saw was Beth and Thia with their heads together. "Uh-oh! What are the two of you up to?"

"We're planning a wedding celebration," Cynthia said.

"Thia's even going to stay over to help with the arrangements," Beth added.

Dave glanced up from the week-old newspaper he was reading. "Cyn, planning that kind of affair takes time. I can't stay that long. I have to get back to end of track."

"I thought of that," Cynthia said. "You'll have to go back without me. I'll remain here and help with the arrangements, and you can come back for the actual party."

"We'll need two weeks to get out the invitations and make all the arrangements," Beth said.

Cynthia gave her husband an apologetic glance. "I hadn't planned to be separated from Dave that long. I'd think we could do it in less time, Beth."

Beth shook her head. "Melissa Cranshaw's wedding is a week from this Saturday. So we can't plan this for any sooner than two weeks."

Cynthia jumped up from the table and circled it excitedly. "I've just had a fantastic idea. As long as we have to wait two weeks, why don't we have an actual wedding—bridal gown and all! It's fine and legal to get married by a justice of the peace, but after all, the marriage should be blessed by a clergyman."

Angie had sat dumbstruck throughout the whole discussion. The idea of repeating their vows to a clergyman horrified her.

There was no way she could stand before a clergyman and have him bless the marriage, making a mockery of every young couple in love who had ever entered into that union. The hypocrisy of a big wedding and celebration would be an abomination—not to mention blasphemous—in the sight of God.

"No! No! No!"

Cynthia spun around, startled; Beth put down her coffee cup; and Dave lowered the newspaper. All stared at her with shock.

Angie cleared her throat. "I'm sorry. I know you mean well, but I don't want any big celebration. Giff and I are legally married. It's not . . ." She faltered. "It's not necessary to get remarried."

"Well, at least let's have a reception, Angie," Beth said. "That would be perfectly natural, as well as proper."

"Yeah, Pumpkin," Cynthia added. "We just can't ignore anything as important as your and Giff's marriage."

Dave stood up and came around the table to stand behind her chair. He put his hands on her shoulders, and Angie felt the strength and comfort he was offering. "Ladies, it's Angie's decision to make, and I think she's made her wishes very clear. So drop the subject."

Cynthia and Beth stared at Angie's distressed expression.

In an effort to ease the tension, Dave walked over to Cynthia. "Besides, Miz Sin, I don't think we'd last two weeks apart." He gave her a light kiss and hug.

"I think you're right, Kincaid," she said with a smile, and leaned her head on his shoulder.

Groaning, Beth buried her head in her hands. "Lordy, everyone! You know what we've all forgotten? This coming weekend is our annual roundup barbecue! My goodness, everyone in this area will be expecting it. We can make an official announcement of the marriage at the barbecue. How do you feel about that idea, Angie?"

Angie smiled in relief. "I think that would be just fine."

"I've always looked forward to the barn dance," Cynthia said. "This year more than ever, because I'll have my husband to dance with instead of Willard Hepplewhyte."

"I hope the weather cooperates," Beth added. "We've been hoping for rain, and with our luck, we'll get some Saturday."

As they all chatted at once about the forthcoming dance, Dave Kincaid stood observing them. He knew no words to describe the depth of his feelings for these remarkable MacKenzie women. Each one was entirely different from the others, and yet their essence came from a shared unity.

He shifted his gaze to his wife. As if she felt his stare, Cynthia glanced up and smiled at him. Pulled by the need to be near her, Dave walked back to the table, sat down, and resumed reading the newspaper.

Angie had hoped to talk to Giff in time to warn him, but he and the boys rode in late. By the time he cleaned up, they were ready to sit down to dinner.

The conversation during the meal centered around the plans and preparations for the forthcoming barbecue, and much to Angie's relief, nothing was mentioned about their marriage.

"How'd the roundup go, Giff?" Beth asked as they enjoyed the peach cobbler that Middy had baked especially for Cynthia's visit.

"It went fine. We've got a couple hundred steers to sell."

"Hear that, Kincaid?" Cynthia said, playfully putting a hand up to her ear. "Can't you hear the ring of those coins dropping in the coffer right now? I bet you and Beth can't wait to get to the library and figure out how many rails you can buy with it."

"Cynthia, you know darn well we do not take Roundhouse money to finance the railroad expansion," Beth declared.

"Uh-oh! Sister Elizabeth called me Cynthia. I'd better change the subject. It's good you were home to take part in the roundup, Angie. I'm glad that stuffy art school didn't change you. It would break Daddy's heart."

"Why do you think that?"

"He was always so proud of your ranching skills, Pumpkin," Cynthia said.

"Actually, I only rode out for a couple days. Giff seemed to want to get rid of me early."

They all turned to Giff with perplexed expressions. Seemingly caught off guard, he stammered for an excuse. "It was no place for her . . . We were rounding up cattle."

"So-o-o?" Cynthia asked, forcing a further explanation.

Giff was clearly at a loss. "Ah, cattle wander into draws and ravines. It's very dangerous."

"Giff, Angie knows every inch of this spread as well as you do," Cynthia said. "Furthermore," she added, winking at Angie, "she can sit a saddle better than most men."

"I wish I understood the railroad business as well as she does cattle," Beth interjected. "I remember the day Giff told me and Daddy that Angie was the best wrangler on the ranch. If I recall, the exact words were, 'Angie can rope cattle, haze cattle, knows what ails cattle and how to cure cattle, and can estimate the size of a herd with a single glance.'"

"Really? Giff said that?" Angie asked, surprised but pleased.

"When you three women draw on a fella, he's down and buried before his gun clears leather," Giff groaned.

"That's another point in her favor," Cynthia declared. "Daddy always claimed Angie was a sure shot with a Colt revolver and lethal with a rifle."

"Help me out here, Dave, will you?" Giff pleaded.

"They've got you against the ropes, pal," Dave said, laughing. "I think it's time to throw in the towel."

"Oh, that reminds me," Cynthia exclaimed. "Did I ever tell you all about the time Dave boxed John L. Sullivan?"

"Sullivan? You mean that up-and-coming prize-fighter?" Giff asked.

Cynthia nodded. "The very same."

"I remember reading in the paper that he's one of the best," Giff said. "They're predicting that one of these days he'll be the world champion."

"A quote, no doubt, from the mouth of Mr. Sullivan himself," Cynthia remarked drolly.

Beth cringed with disdain. "He doesn't sound

like too pleasant a chap. Why would you ever box him, Dave?"

"Ask your sister. It was her idea." He tousled Cynthia's hair affectionately.

Giff chuckled. "I figured you had more sense, so Thia had to have been behind it."

"It's a long story," Cynthia said. "But since I'm dying to tell it, you'll just have to sit back and listen. It happened one day last year in a small town in New Mexico."

As Cynthia related the incident, Angie only half listened. Her mind was on her blundering statement about Giff wanting to get rid of her. She'd meant it merely as a joke, but she'd put Giff in the awkward position of defending his actions. She should have immediately jumped to his defense. Good Lord! If anyone should have to defend her actions, it was she!

Angie ventured a guilty glance at him and felt a fluttering pull in the pit of her stomach. Lately, his nearness evoked this confusing reaction. He laughed at a comment of Cynthia's. Funny how she'd never before been aware of the appealing warmth of his chuckle. His ruggedly handsome face suddenly shifted into somberness, and she wondered what he was thinking at the moment—probably what a disappointment she was to him.

Giff was relieved that the conversation was no longer focused on him and Angie. What should he have said to them? *I sent Angie back early because I wanted to make love to her and that's not part of our marriage arrangement?*

He glanced at Angie to discover her looking at him. Their gazes held momentarily and her mouth curved in a tender smile. He winked and smiled back.

Lord, how he loved her! Everything the girls said was true. Angie was a born rancher; it was in her blood. She never complained about hard work or rough trails. Rain or shine, hot or cold, she worked the herd—and always with an energy that rejuvenated even his tired old bones. And while it was all hard work, it still was a labor of love to her. Why couldn't she recognize this? Why did she think to look elsewhere for happiness? She belonged right here on the Roundhouse.

But she still had to learn that lesson for herself, he reflected sadly. However, there was plenty of sky over the Roundhouse to test her wings, and even though he'd never clip them, he'd make damn certain this time that she didn't fly too far from the nest.

As soon as dinner ended, Angie excused herself and went upstairs to her room, expecting that Giff would follow. She had to tell him of the decision she'd reached that afternoon. Eventually she heard the others come upstairs and go to their respective rooms, but there was still no Giff. Finally she gave up waiting, undressed, and went to bed. She'd talk to him in the morning before they sat down to breakfast.

Angie was just preparing to turn off the light when Cynthia knocked on the bedroom door. "Everybody decent in there?"

"What do you want, Thia? I'm just getting ready to go to sleep."

"Here I come—ready or not," Cynthia said, opening the door. "Listen, you two, Beth and I just had this great idea . . ." Her voice trailed off when she saw Angie was alone. "Where's Giff? I thought he was with you."

"He prefers to sleep in his own bed."

"Oh," Cynthia said in obvious bewilderment. "And you prefer to sleep in your own bed."

"That's right."

"Rather an unusual arrangement for newlyweds, isn't it?"

"We had an argument," Angie said, hoping it would be enough to satisfy her sister's curiosity. "Good night, Cynthia dear." She extinguished the light and turned over with her back to her. "Please close the door on your way out." When she heard the door click shut, Angie heaved a sigh of relief and closed her eyes.

She had just settled into that lethargic stage in which the woes of the day had become blanketed by the shroud of drowsiness, when she heard Cynthia's frantic call from below.

"Angie, come quickly. I need help!"

Instantly jarred to wakefulness, Angie bolted out of bed and rushed to the stairway. "What's wrong? What is it, Thia?" Angie asked as she hurried down the stairs.

"Beth and I went out to the privy, and on the way back to the house she fell down. She can't get up. I think her leg's broken. I need help to get her back inside."

Robeless and barefoot, Angie rushed outside ahead of Cynthia. In her anxiety over Beth, it didn't occur to Angie to ask why Cynthia hadn't called for David. When the door slammed behind her, she looked back and saw that her sister had not followed. Angie stopped in her tracks.

"Oh, no!" Realizing her sister's trick too late, she tried to open the door, but knew it was locked. She also knew it would be useless to check the other doors.

The thin cambric gown she was wearing was little protection against the sting of the cool night. Shivering, she pounded on the door and shouted, "Come on, girls, open the door. I'm freezing."

Stepping back, she glanced up at the window of Beth's room just as it was raised. As she anticipated, her two sisters appeared and leaned out on their elbows to look down at her.

"Beth, can you believe she still falls for that same trick she always did as a child?" Cynthia said.

Beth shook her head with mock gravity. "I guess some people just never learn from their mistakes. Looks like going off to college hasn't smartened her up one bit."

Angie gritted her teeth. "And I can't believe the two of you haven't outgrown your need for childish pranks. Sorry to spoil your fun, but I'm not afraid of the dark anymore, so open the door. It's cold out here."

"Thia, look at all the sparks and smoke coming from Giff's chimney," Beth said innocently. "Bet it's real nice and warm in his house."

"Yep," Cynthia agreed. "I bet that bed of his—which he prefers to sleep in—is real cozy, too. Especially with him in it."

"Is that all you think about, Thia MacKenzie?" Angie yelled indignantly.

"Thia MacKenzie Kincaid, darling," Cynthia corrected. "The Kincaid part is *why* that's all I think about."

The remark set Beth and Cynthia to giggling, which only added to Angie's irritation. Her teeth had begun to chatter. "All right, you've had your fun. Open the door now; my feet are turning blue."

"Speaking as a married woman, I can tell you that husbands are great feet warmers."

"And speaking as an unmarried woman, Angie," Beth advised, "do what you always did whenever we locked you out: run to Giff for help."

"We're just doing what we think is best for you, Pumpkin," Cynthia said. "A woman belongs in her husband's bed."

"You're meddling, that's what you're doing.

And if I catch pneumonia out here, it'll be on your conscience."

"It *is* getting chilly in here. Time to close the window." Beth started to lower the sash. "Good night, Angie."

"Good night, Pumpkin," Cynthia called out before the window closed entirely.

"I'll get even with both of you," Angie shouted. She would have liked to shake her fist at them, but she had her arms wrapped across her chest trying to stay warm. Too cold to consider any alternative, she raced barefoot across the clearing to Giff's house.

Giff was bent over on one knee adding a log to the fire when Angie burst through the door. She slammed the door quickly and leaned back against it, shivering. His slow perusal trailed down her slim outline, faintly visible through the thin gown she wore.

"My sisters locked me out of the house."

He laughed with rancor. "So that explains this visit. For a minute there, I thought you had something else in mind."

Angie didn't miss the innuendo. "Is fornicating the only thing that occupies people's minds?" She came over to the fireplace and rubbed her hands to warm them.

"Why did they lock you out? And it's not fornicating if you're married." His throat had gone dry at the sight of her body silhouetted against the fire, and he rose to his feet, brushing off his hands on his pants legs.

A blush colored her cheeks. "I can't tell you."

"Okay, so it's none of my business." He turned away and grabbed the poker, then knelt again to firmly anchor the log on the grate.

"You're angry with me, aren't you?"

He didn't look at her. "What right have I to be angry?"

"I guess you have more right than anyone. They locked me out because they said I belong in my husband's bed."

Giff drew a deep breath. "Well, I reckon I wouldn't argue that." He stood up and put the poker aside. "I'll get you something warmer to put on." Returning quickly from the bedroom, he handed her a maroon robe.

"I remember this robe," she said, slipping into its warmth and belting it around her waist. "I gave you this for Christmas five or six years ago. It still looks new." Rolling up the sleeves, she added, "As if it's never been worn."

"That's right. I don't wear belted robes."

"Why didn't you say so when I gave it to you?"

"Angie, you were fifteen years old. I wasn't about to hurt your feelings. Besides, it's the thought that counts."

"Damnation!" she muttered. "They were right about that, too."

"Who was right about what?"

Her chin quivered as she tried to suppress a smile, but failed at the attempt. Looking up at him with a sheepish grin, she said, "Beth and Thia. They warned me you'd never wear it. Cynthia said you wouldn't be caught dead in a belted robe."

Giff couldn't help chuckling.

"You don't know how fortunate you were not to have two older sisters who always knew more than you did."

"I don't know about that. You don't look any worse for the wear," he said.

It was a pity Angie didn't understand him as well as her sisters did, he thought. She'd have guessed his true feelings years ago.

"I gather from the conversation at the dinner table that you didn't tell them, did you?"

"I tried, Giff. Truly I did."

"I warned you, Angie, that if you didn't, I would." He grabbed his shirt and started to put it on. "Come on. I'll take you back to the house and we'll straighten out this mess once and for all."

"Wait, Giff, you must listen to me. Believe me, I intended to tell them; then I was afraid of how they'd react to my . . ."

"Your what?" he asked, irritated.

"To my taking advantage of you."

"What the hell are you talking about?"

"My sisters are as opposite as day and night, you know that, Giff. They could easily take different viewpoints on this, and no matter what my motives were for marrying you, it might lead to arguments not only between me and them, but between Beth and Thia. Perhaps even drive a wedge between all of us. Look at Cynthia: when our father died she was against continuing building the railroad, but she agreed to it, rather than cause friction between us."

"Angel, nothing could drive a wedge between you and your sisters. Love will always win out in the end. In your position they both would have considered what was best for the baby, the same as we did at the time."

"Yes, that's true. But now because there is no baby, I don't think they'd really understand my desperation at the time we decided to get married. Everyone can always point out mistakes and offer better solutions after the damage is done." She hung her head. "So I . . . didn't tell them about the baby . . . or Edward. I let them go on believing we married for love." Moisture glistened in her eyes when she raised her head and looked at him. "Please don't embarrass me in front of them, Giff."

"All right, Angel. If it's that important to you."

"They wanted to plan a big wedding celebration, but I refused."

"Thank God for that, at least."

"They do plan to announce our marriage on Saturday at the barbecue."

"I see." He went over to the small area that served as a kitchen. "Coffee?"

"None for me, thank you. Giff, I know you're not comfortable continuing to pretend we're happily married."

"No, I'm not." He turned around, leaned his hips against the counter, and took a few sips from his cup. "One lie always leads to another."

"That's for sure. I remember Shakespeare once said, if you lie to cover up a sin, it becomes two sins."

"Actually, it was the English theologian Issac Watts. He said, 'If you lie to hide a fault, the fault then becomes two.'"

"Then I guess my faults will soon stretch as long as my arm."

She walked over to one of the many shelves stacked with worn books that lined the fireplace. "All these books. You never could get enough to read."

"When you live alone, there's not much else to do on long winter nights."

Angie moved away and began to roam the room, studying the framed photographs and old daguerreotypes on the wall. She paused before a picture of a young man and woman in their late teens. "Your parents were such a handsome couple, Giff. I wonder why your father never remarried. He was so young when your mother died."

"I reckon for the same reason your father never did. With some men there can only be one true love in their lives."

"But your father wasn't much older than a boy

himself when your mother died giving birth to you. I can't imagine how he ever raised you alone. And I want to cry just thinking about you growing up without any mothering."

"Once my dad came to the Roundhouse, your ma and Middy saw to it that I had plenty of mothering."

Angie moved to a picture of a ten-year-old Giff standing between Buck Gifford and her father. She reached out and gently touched her father's face. "I still miss Daddy so much. Sometimes I think I'll choke to death from the pain of it."

"It's like any wound, Angel. Eventually it'll heal over, but a scar remains to remind you of the ache."

She smiled her thanks at his comforting words. Then she moved on to another photograph. "Oh, my goodness!" she exclaimed. "That's got to be me or one of my sisters."

"It's you."

"Wherever did you find this old thing?"

"In one of my father's trunks." Actually, Giff had always kept the picture in his top drawer and had hung it up last year after she went off to school.

"I couldn't have been more than five or six when this was taken."

"It was taken on the day of your sixth birthday."

"I vaguely remember that pink dress I'm wearing. I think I had just gotten it as a birthday gift."

"That's right. You came running to show it to me and found me behind the barn kissing Cassie Bryant. She ran off when you started crying. I picked you up, dried your tears, and asked you why you were crying on your birthday. You told me it was because I was kissing Cassie."

"Did I really say that?"

"Yep. Then you told me you didn't want me

kissing any more girls because when you grew up, you were going to marry me."

"Oh, Giff, you're joking, aren't you?"

"No, I'm not joking, Angel. You were six and I was sixteen."

"I don't remember any of that at all, Peter Gifford. I think there must be more than just coffee in that cup you're holding."

They were a room apart, but the intimacy seemed to be shrinking the distance between them. Yet he hadn't budged, remaining motionless in the semidarkness, staring at her as he leaned against the counter, his long legs stretched out and crossed in front of him. His open shirt revealed the broad expanse of tanned muscle and dark hair on his chest, and the dim lighting kept his face and eyes shrouded in darkness.

For the first time in her life, she became aware of the pure male essence of him.

Shocked, she struggled with her confusing thoughts. Looking around uncomfortably, she said nervously, "Well, it's late. I better let you get some sleep."

"You know, Angie, we could try to make this marriage work."

Involuntarily her glance swung to the open bedroom door. "I can't, Giff. I'm just not ready for it; I'm sorry. It would be exchanging one lie for another."

He turned and put down his cup. "You can have the bed."

"Thanks, Giff," she said, relieved. "But I'll sleep on the floor in front of the fireplace."

"If that's what you want."

She hated the resigned tone in his voice; it made her feel like an overly indulged child.

Giff went over to a cedar chest, dug out a quilt

and blanket, then grabbed a pillow from the bedroom.

"Do you need anything else?" he asked after he finished making her a bed by the fire.

Angie shook her head. "Thank you, Giff. I'm sorry to be such a bother."

"Good night, Angie," he said, turning off the oil lamp.

"Good night, Giff."

He lay awake until he was certain she slept, then he got out of bed and went out to the other room. Trying not to disturb her, he lifted Angie into his arms. She opened her eyes and asked sleepily, "What are you doing, Giff?"

"I'm putting you in bed. Go back to sleep, Angel."

"Okay, Giff." She closed her eyes and fell instantly back to sleep.

Giff gently lowered her to the bed and tucked the quilt around her. For an instant he gazed down at her, sleeping peacefully. After all these years, how was he to convince her to look upon him as a lover—and not a brother? And could it be that she was still in love with that bastard Edward Emory? She had implied on the roundup that she wasn't. Was she trying to convince him or herself? These were issues that would take time to solve. Even though the desire to make love to her was becoming unbearable, he had to have patience. Besides, time was on his side. He couldn't help grinning: time plus Beth and Thia. He spun on his heel and left the room.

As he crawled into the pallet she had occupied, the faint fragrance of lavender emanated from the pillow. He buried his nose in it and fell asleep.

Chapter 9

Angie stretched languidly from the tips of her toes to the ends of her fingertips; then smiling, she relaxed back into a sleepy euphoria. She felt secure, totally at peace. She felt downright good.

"What an encouraging sight, to see a wife sleeping docilely in her husband's bed."

When Cynthia's voice suddenly invaded the snug cocoon, Angie opened her eyes to see her two sisters smiling at the foot of the bed.

It took a few more confused seconds for Angie to realize the bed Cynthia was referring to was Giff's bed. Jolted fully awake, she sat up.

What was she doing in Giff's bed?

As the events of the previous night flashed through her mind, the last thing she remembered was falling asleep in front of the fireplace.

How had she gotten in Giff's bed?

"Good morning," Beth said cheerily. "You aren't still angry with us about last night, are you?"

"I haven't made up my mind yet. But my instinct tells me I should be." Angie had greater problems on her mind than her sisters' actions last night. Had she climbed into Giff's bed of her own volition? And what had happened after she got here?

"I'd say, considering how you overslept this morning, everything turned out for the best. You ought to thank us," Cynthia said.

"Where's Giff?" Angie asked, tying to ignore the beaming, self-satisfied smiles of her sisters.

"He and the boys are driving the cattle to the station. There's a train coming in and they'll be loading them into stock cars today."

Angie got out of bed and grabbed Giff's maroon robe lying across the foot of the bed. She was befuddled as to when and how *that* had gotten there, since she remembered removing the robe in the other room just before lying down.

"I've got to get dressed. Why didn't someone wake me?"

"We just did," Cynthia said. They followed Angie out of the bedroom.

She threw a covert glance at the fireplace. There was no sign of the quilt and blanket. Giff had obviously been very busy before leaving that morning. Thank God, or the Lord only knew what her sisters might have tried next if they thought she had slept on the floor. She *had* slept on the floor, hadn't she?

It was clear to Angie that she could not remain at home under the watchful eyes and prying questions of her sisters. Once dressed, she headed for the stable. If she had expected to evade them, she soon found out differently.

"Where are you going?" Cynthia asked when Angie began to saddle Calico.

"I thought I'd ride to the station and give the boys a hand loading the cattle."

"That's a good idea. I think I'll join you," Cynthia said.

"What about David, Thia? Are you going to leave him here alone?"

"Oh, he rode out with the boys earlier. He's not one to sit around for too long."

"I might as well go with you," Beth said. "A few hours away from business will do me good."

"Don't you two have to plan Saturday's barbecue?" Angie reminded them hopefully.

"We did that this morning while you were asleep, Sleeping Beauty."

"In your husband's bed," Cynthia added. She met Angie's forced smile with a wicked grin of her own.

"Besides," Beth said, "just because Thia and I don't embrace the life of ranching with your verve doesn't mean that we're strangers to hard work. I'm sure they could use a couple extra hands."

"I'm sure they can, sisters dear," Angie said, more amused than disgruntled. They weren't fooling her for a moment—they were just coming along to ask more questions.

Angie suddenly became inspired. Up to now, she had been evasive with them, and in so doing, had fired their curiosity. It was time she became as aggressive as they were. She'd match them at their own game.

The station was a hub of activity and noise. The rasp of wheels on rail, the grind of train gears, the hiss of steam, and the toot of the train whistle played a discordant symphony in accompaniment with the disgruntled mewling of the cattle, the clatter of hooves against wooden ramps, and the shouts and whistles of the four men herding them into cars.

Putting her plan in motion, Angie rode up to Giff. "Good morning, darling," she said loud enough to carry to the ears of the curious. Then she whispered, "I'm sorry, Giff, but my sisters are watching." Leaning over, she kissed him on the lips.

It was an unexpectedly pleasant sensation, but she was too absorbed in enjoying the reaction of her sisters to do any more than smile into his startled eyes. Wheeling her horse in time to see Elizabeth and Cynthia exchange baffled expressions, Angie felt exhilarated. "Time to get to work, ladies," she said gaily, and rode in to join the men.

Cynthia held back and swung her gaze to her husband, hard at the task. "Just look at the darling, Beth. No matter how he denies it, Dave isn't happy unless he's being challenged mentally or physically."

"Then he sure married the right woman; I imagine you give him plenty of both. But where'd he learn to herd cattle?"

"He probably read how in a book. He never forgets one word he reads." She sighed. "He's so beautiful, Beth. I don't know what I've ever done to deserve him. I love him so much."

"I'm truly happy for you, Thia. I can't think of any two people who balance one another more beautifully. You're like salt and pepper: as different as day and night, yet together you're a delicious blend."

"Thanks, honey. So are Angie and Giff," Cynthia said, "but something's not right there. What do you think it is, Beth?"

"I know what you mean. They're keeping something back, but whatever it is, I know they'll work it out. They're so perfect for each other."

"Well, no sense in stalling any longer. I suppose we should lend a hand."

"I just wish I could embrace ranching with the same enthusiasm as Angie," Beth said. "Look at her."

They turned their attention to Angie. Lariat in

hand, she was laughing with String as they hazed the cattle attempting to stray from the herd.

"Giddap, horse," Cynthia said with less exuberance than she usually brought to most tasks.

Angie didn't make the train ride to the Denver stockyards with the men. To avoid a recurrence of the previous night, she was waiting for Giff in his house when he returned later that evening.

His surprise was evident. "Locked out again?"

"No. We've got to talk, Giff, but it seems like we're never alone. You know, you could make things so convenient if you'd move to the big house."

"Convenient for who?" he asked. He plopped down in a chair. "I'm beat, Angie. Can't this talk wait until morning?" Exhausted, he started to pull off a boot.

"Let me do that for you." She straddled his leg and pulled off the boot. Bent over, she straddled his other leg. He put his stocking foot on her rear and shoved lightly to offer assistance. The boot gave and slid off his foot.

"You shouldn't bend over like that; I'm tempted to kick that little butt of yours across the room. How long do you figure you can keep up this deception? Your sisters aren't fools, Angie." He got up and headed for the bedroom, tossing his vest aside as he did.

"That's what we have to talk about, Giff," she said, following him.

"I'm listening." Shedding his shirt, he went back into the other room. "Don't suppose you made coffee?"

"Yes, I did. I knew you'd want some when you got home."

"You want a cup?" he asked, filling a mug.

"No. Will you please sit down so I can talk to you?"

"If I sit down, I'll fall asleep. Say what you came to say, so I can get to bed."

"Giff, we have to figure out what to do about our marriage."

"I've got a great idea—tell the truth," he said sarcastically.

"I told you last night my reason not to. You agreed to it, Giff. Thia and Dave will be leaving right after the barbecue. We only have to keep up a pretense for two more days."

"Oh, and that ends it, huh? Is Beth leaving the country? And Middy? String and Red? How stupid do you think people are, Angie? You want a solution to the problem? We start living as husband and wife."

"You mean sharing a bed."

"I've been told that's customary for a married couple," he said evenly.

Giff watched her struggling with the idea. She walked over and stared into the fire. His heart ached for the torment she was suffering, but he had his own struggle: He wanted her. Loved her. He didn't want to pretend; he wanted to really live as husband and wife. He wanted her to carry his baby—the way she had been willing to carry another man's.

But was he cutting off his nose to spite his face? Maybe it was a mistake to resist her idea of moving into the big house. Maybe the closer proximity would work in his behalf—especially in front of her sisters. If she wanted to put up a loving appearance in front of them, he'd sure make the most of it. *That*, he could have fun with! He'd have to control his passion, though—remain patient and break down her resistance gradually. The more he thought of it, the more he liked the idea.

Walking over to her, he put his hands on her shoulders. "Okay, Angel, I'll do what you want."

She spun around, her eyes round with hope. "You mean it, Giff?"

"Yeah. I'll move into the big house first thing in the morning."

"Oh, thank you, Giff. Thank you," she cried joyously, throwing her arms around his neck.

Giff slid his arms around her waist and pulled her closer. Instinctively he lowered his head to kiss her.

Wisdom overcame impetuousness, though, and he brushed his lips across her forehead just as the door flew open.

Cynthia stood in the doorway, her quick perusal taking in the embrace and his state of semiundress. "Oops! Did I interrupt something?"

Giff dropped his arms and Angie stepped away. "Thia, did you ever hear of knocking?"

"Sorry, Giff. I was sent over to find out if you two are coming back to the house. We've decided to have a nightcap and we want you to join us."

"We were just co—"

"Tell them we'll be over in the morning," Giff said, cutting off Angie.

"Okay. Have fun, you two." She departed as swiftly as she had arrived.

"Why did you stop me?" Angie asked. "Didn't you just agree to move into the house?"

"You're concerned about impressions, aren't you? What impression do you think this made on Thia?"

Angie thought for a moment and began to giggle. "She'll think we wanted privacy tonight."

"And you know damn well Thia won't hesitate to tell them that."

He dug into his pants pocket and pulled out a coin. "I'll flip you to see who gets the bed."

*   *   *

The next morning the preparations for the following day's barbecue began. While Middy mixed gallon crocks of potato salad, pickled beets, and corn relish, Beth and Angie combined their skills to bake pies: Beth rolled out the crusts while Angie soaked peaches and peeled apples. Cynthia devoted herself to mixing the batter for a half dozen sponge cakes and then matched the effort with six cherry cobblers.

At midday Angie and Cynthia carried out a basket of cheese sandwiches and ice-cold lemonade to the men, who had not been idle themselves. The barn had been cleared out and cleaned for dancing, and the yard was now lined with long tables consisting of sheets of wood supported by sawhorses.

Seeing Giff stretched out in the shade of a fifty-year-old oak, Angie carried over a sandwich and a glass of the cool drink.

"Tired, Giff?"

"Yeah." He opened his eyes, reached up lazily, and pulled her down, capturing her mouth in a kiss.

"Wh . . . why did you do that?" Angie gasped, clearly shaken.

"Thia was watching," Giff said innocently, and sat up. "Impressions, you know."

Angie glanced over and saw Cynthia absorbed in talking to Dave. "Oh," she said, still slightly befuddled. "It doesn't look to me like she's watching us."

"She was. Why else would I kiss you? This is sure a lot of work for a one-day celebration."

"But now that the herd's been moved to the south pasture for the summer, and the rest of them have been sold, you can lie back and relax for a few months."

"And now that I've agreed to move into the big

house, just what bed do I lie back and relax in?"

"My sisters insist we take Daddy's room."

"There's no way I'm sleeping in the same bed that the Chief died in, Angie."

"Then we'll use my room, even though it's much smaller."

"You planning on sharing the bed, or were you thinking of flipping a coin every night?"

"Desperate times call for desperate measures— or something like that," she said. "I know you said the problem is some kind of a man thing, but when I think of how often we stretched out side by side on roundups, I don't understand why doing the same thing in a bed should make a difference."

"Okay—but I'm not making any promises. Just remember I warned you." He finished his sandwich. "I see String and Red are through filling the wagon for the hayride, so I guess I'd better set up the spit for tomorrow."

Her eyes flashed with devilishness. "You mean digging the pit for the spit."

Giff chuckled. "Or the bough for the cow."

"The heat for the meat."

"The bier for the steer," he shot back.

They both burst into laughter. "Oh, God, Giff!" Angie said, wiping away her tears of laughter. "I almost forgot how much fun we used to have making up those silly expressions. There's been so much misery since then."

"The misery's behind us, Angel. From now on there's only good times ahead for us."

"I'd like to believe that." For a long moment they looked deeply into each other's eyes, as if each were trying to gauge their commitment to one another.

"I'm glad to hear that you two have found something to laugh about," Dave called over to them. "I want to go on record as announcing that next year somebody else can clean out the horse stalls and *I'll* pitch the hay."

"How often in your line of work do you get to muck out a horse stall?" Giff yelled back. "We thought we were doing you a favor: not quite as boring as laying rails."

"And much more aromatic," Cynthia added with a dimpled smile.

"Thank you for the reminder, my love," Dave said. "Time to get back to my labor. The manure grows odoriferous while I laze here idle-if-erous."

Cynthia cringed in pain. "Idle-*if*-erous? Oh, Dave, that's terrible! I doubt there is such a word. And even if there were, the proper grammar would be 'idleiferously.'"

"But that wouldn't rhyme, Miz Schoolmarm, would it?" Dave pulled her to her feet.

"You see, Angel," Giff remarked, affectionately rumpling her hair, "everyone's a poet at heart. Oops, Thia's doing it again!" He pulled her into his arms and kissed her.

"Giff, you've got to stop that," she hissed when he released her. Smoothing out her hair, she glanced toward her sister and brother-in-law walking away hand in hand. Frowning suspiciously, she turned back to his open-palmed shrug, his blue eyes wide with innocence.

That night long after the women had gone to bed, Giff and Dave sat up absorbed in a chess game. When they finally finished and went upstairs, Giff opened Angie's bedroom door cautiously. A bed lamp was burning, but she had fallen asleep reading. He eased the book out of her hands, then gently lowered her head to the pillow and tucked her in.

The day will come, Angel, when you'll be awake and waiting for me in our bed. Not your bed; not my bed. Our bed.

He extinguished the lamp and, after stripping down to his drawers, lay on top of the counterpane. His last conscious awareness as he drifted into slumber was the sweet scent of lavender.

Chapter 10

The dry, splintered wood creaked as Billy Bob Walden swung his feet up on the table and tipped his chair backward. Unmindful that his bulk might be sorely testing the back legs of the rickety old chair, he clasped his hands behind his head and broke into a toothy grin.

Almost one hundred dollars stashed for the grubstake, he thought contentedly.

One hundred dollars! That was more money than he and the boys had earned in prit near a whole year since getting out of prison. All the way from California to Colorado, holding up freight trains and slow-moving coaches, rolling hombres drunker than themselves, dealing cards from the bottom of the deck, and even sticking their hands in ladies' underdrawers—whenever they got the chance—had kept them one step ahead of the law.

But lately life had been much better for the Walden gang. Even though the roof leaked, this abandoned cabin had kept them warm and dry ... mostly. Good hideout too, and not so far from the mill where he had hornswoggled the boys into working—temporarily, he'd told them.

Of course, he himself had not done a lick of work because he had to stay at the cabin and think. After all, he *was* the boss and the brains of this outfit. Yep, if he could just keep the boys working, another hundred dollars ought to do it. Then they'd ride off into the sunset and . . .

Well, he hadn't exactly worked out the details yet, but he was in no hurry. Since he'd come across Clarabelle over at the cathouse, he had something more interesting to think about right now.

"What yuh grinnin' at, Billy Bob?" Curly Ringo asked as he dumped an armful of twigs into the fireplace. "Are we fixin' to leave soon?"

"Ain't tellin' nobody nothin' yet, Curly. Yuh jest git a hustle on boilin' that pot," Billy Bob answered, annoyed. He didn't want Curly to intrude on his thoughts concerning last Saturday night with Clarabelle. Of course, he'd had a couple drinks too many to know exactly what *had* happened that night. But as usual, his lively imagination conjured up the ripe and juicy parts he couldn't exactly recollect.

"Yuh thinkin' about yer secret plan, boss?" Curly ventured again as he squatted in front of the fireplace trying to start a fire.

"Yep! That's what I'm thinkin' about, all right. My secret plan," Billy Bob lied.

"Well, I'll be mighty glad to hear about it, boss, 'cause we've been holed up in this shack long enough. Sure hope that secret plan of yers gets us a mighty sweet pot." Curly stood up and faced him. "It's time for the Walden gang to ride again, 'cause me and the boys are plumb tired of workin' at that dad-blamed sawmill. Shet!" Curly grumbled as he began to splash water from the bucket into the pot over the stale, wet coffee grounds. "The two bits yuh give us a day don't buy nothin' in town at night. What are we doin' here, anyway?"

"Dammit, Curly!" Billy Bob shouted, asserting his authority. Angrily he bumped the front chair legs with his feet, and the decrepit chair collapsed, slamming Billy Bob to the floor in a backwards somersault.

"There you go, changin' the subject agin," Curly accused while his dazed boss struggled to get up.

Billy Bob squinted up at his comrade-in-arms. "Like I told you—what we're doin' here is jest *tem . . . por . . . ary*," Billy Bob said with exaggerated patience.

"Tem . . . por . . . ary 'til *when*?" Curly said, squinting right back at his boss.

Rubbing his sore backside, Billy Bob limped over to another chair and plunked himself down. His eyes darting from side to side, he began to think in earnest.

"Well?" Curly asked, picking up the pieces of the broken chair and stacking them by the fireplace.

Stalling, Billy Bob stroked his long mustache, pursed his lips, and slowly clucked his tongue. But he said nothing.

Suddenly Curly strode to the back of the shabby cabin, to where Hank had etched a neat row of closely spaced lines on the wall to mark the days. He started to count, tracing each mark with his forefinger. "One, two, three, four, five, six . . ."

Billy Bob rolled his eyes and, drumming his fingers on the table, listened to Curly's slow drone.

". . . seventeen, eighteen, nineteen."

Frustrated, Billy Bob grabbed his tin cup off the table, and without looking, hurled it over his shoulder. Bull's-eye! The cup struck Curly's head with such force that his nose slammed into the wall.

"Dammit, Billy Bob! Why'd yuh go and do that for?" Curly asked, rubbing his bald pate and gingerly feeling his nose. "Now yuh made me lose my place."

Certain of what Curly would do next, Billy Bob clenched his teeth and fumed.

Curly slowly began again. "One, two, three, four, five, six . . ." In a short time, he neared the end of his count. "Thirty-one, thirty-two, thirty-three, thirty-four, and today makes . . . ah . . . thirty-five. So there, too!" he said defiantly. "The rest of us been workin' our butts off at that mill for thirty-five days, and whatta yuh been doin' all that time, boss?"

"Now, don't go gittin' yerself riled up over nothin', Curly. Shet! I told yuh a hundred times, I do the hardest work of all. I've been sittin' here for all them thirty-five days thinkin' about how we kin git our hands on more gold than yuh ever knowed existed. *That's* what I've been doin'," Billy Bob said emphatically. Leaning back, he crossed his arms over his burly chest. " 'Sides, somebody's gotta stay here and guard this place."

"Guard this place!" Curly said in amazement. "Yuh thinkin' someone's gonna come along and steal this shack?"

Billy Bob gave the notion a moment's thought, then shook his head. "Naw, ain't likely nobody wud do that, Curly." Then he whispered, "But jest s'posin' I wuz workin' at the mill too, and we're moseyin' back from work one day. And jest s'posin' a bunch of hombres wuz layin' in wait to bushwhack us at the cabin. What would happen if I wuzn't stayin' here to surprise 'em afore we got back here?"

Curly scratched his head. "Oh, yeah, I didn't think of that." Nodding, he turned toward the fire-place, then suddenly spun around. "No yuh don't, boss!"

"What now?" Billy Bob asked, exasperated.

"Yuh didn't answer my question. I asked yuh, *what* are we doin' here?"

Billy Bob groaned. Squinting at Curly, with all the patience he could muster, he said, "Like I told yuh boys *afore*, we're stayin' here 'til we save up enough grubstake fer my secret plan."

"But, boss, we're s'posed to be outlaws," Curly shouted. "Ain't no outlaws I ever hear'd of needs a grubstake!"

Fortunately for Billy Bob, just then a loud, yelping holler came from outside the back of the cabin. The two men rushed out, but stopped in their tracks and started to laugh when they spied Jeb Bloomer in one of his usual predicaments.

Waving a hammer in his right hand, the tall young man was jumping up and down while sucking on his left thumb and forefinger.

"What's the matter, Jeb Boy, some little gal bite your wanderin' hand?" Billy Bob teased.

"Naw, he most likely's gotta piddle awful bad," Curly said.

"Either way, he's still got one good hand to take care of business," Billy Bob taunted.

"Ah, shucks! I mean, ah shet!" Jeb corrected himself, around a mouthful of fingers. "How come I got to do more work than anybody else, and then when I bang my—"

"What's all the hollerin' about?" Hank Withers came running from a nearby copse of trees. Stew Potts followed behind him, dragging a small tree trunk that they had just cut down for Jeb's carpentry.

Mouth agape, Hank Withers stopped when he spied Jeb sucking his fingers. "On second thought, *don't* tell me about it," he said, shaking his head in disgust. He spit out a chaw of tobacco and then rammed a fresh wad into his mouth.

Stew, a tad more curious and compassionate than Hank, dropped the tree trunk. "What's the matter, Jeb, slam yer fingers agin?" Without waiting for an answer, he took a bite from a piece of beef jerky and turned to follow the others back to the cabin. "Don't forget to fetch some water afore yuh come in. Better hustle, it's gettin' kinda dark."

Jeb wiped his hand on his pants and gazed after the older, more experienced members of the gang. Then he looked back at the outhouse, which had collapsed in a heap the week before.

"One wall up and three to go," he said aloud. At least the hole looked to be in pretty good shape. Picking up a pail, he stuck his two swollen fingers back into his mouth and headed toward the river. On his return, he spied Curly tending to the horses.

"Don't be glum, kid. You'll mend," Curly said cheerfully. "Anyway, we're gonna be ridin' outta here soon, I 'spect."

Jeb looked perplexed. "Zat so? Ridin' out, huh? Then why am I fixin' that dad-blamed outhouse fer?" he grumbled.

Curly gave him a sharp look, then hung his head, digging at the ground with the toe of his boot. "Well, I reckon it's only fer temporary, but yuh know Billy Bob. Best to keep him happy," he warned, gently touching his sore nose. "Jest 'tween yuh and me, kid, with Billy Bob's poor eyes and bowed-out legs, that one-holer is a mite more comfortable target fer him than squattin' in the bushes."

"But we can't take the outhouse when we go, so—"

"Never mind that, kid, jest fix it. Nobody ever questions Billy Bob Walden," Curly said with pride. "He says we're gonna git so much gold, we kin do anythin' we want. Maybe we kin even retire from outlawin'," he added with a faraway look in his eye.

"Retire?" Jeb said, mystified. "But I jest got started, Curly!"

"Don't worry, kid. Yuh can't retire from some-thin' yuh never got the hang of in the first place. C'mon. Let's go eat," Curly said, shoving Jeb to-ward the cabin door.

As soon as they finished Curly's best offering—beans, hardtack, and stale biscuits—the gang sat down to play cards and drink whiskey. It wasn't long before Jeb lost the most money—and got the drunkest.

"That's enough, Jeb Boy," Billy Bob said when Jeb slumped in his chair and keeled over onto the floor. "Best yuh git some sleep. 'Sides, losin' all yer money playin' cards jest ain't the best way to spend it."

Bleary-eyed, Jeb sat up. "Ah, shucks, boss. I ain't broke and I ain't tired either. I jest wanna . . . go see . . . Emmy Lou." His voice trailed off and Jeb fell backwards, his head clunking on the floor.

"Will yuh look at that!" Curly said. "The kid's out cold."

"Yeh. It figures," Hank grumbled. "He can't hold a nickel's worth of liquor, and he's so dumb, he's always gettin' hisself into some kind of fool-ishness."

"Oh, yeah? Today at the mill wuz *yer* fault, Hank," Stew said defensively.

"Wuzn't either." Hank started dealing out the cards nonchalantly. "I jest gave him a li'l nudge when he started talkin' stupid, that's all."

" 'Tweren't no nudge. Yuh downright *pushed* him into 'em stacks of lumber, and he spent prit near the whole afternoon pilin' 'em up agin. The boss man wuz mad as hell."

"What do yuh mean he wuz talkin' stupid?" Billy Bob asked, his eyes glinting with suspicion.

"Oh, he's got a fool notion 'bout goin' to a party

with some dumb gal he wuz talkin' to when we wuz in town."

"Party? What party?" Billy Bob pressed.

"I dunno. Tomorrow, I reckon. Told her he had a couple brothers and got a invite fer all of us, but I set him straight."

That was enough for Billy Bob. He reached over, grabbed the water pail, and poured it over Jeb's head. Sputtering, Jeb sprang up and then slowly leaned back on his elbows.

"Come on, Jeb. Wake up. What's this 'bout a party, boy?"

Dazed, Jeb shook his wet head and stared up at Billy Bob. "What? Oh yeah, the party. It's tomorra. Kin we go, boss? There's gonna be a lotta food and—"

"Food!" Stew said, his interest picking up considerably.

"Likker too?" Curly asked.

"Dunno . . . maybe." Jeb struggled to think. "But she told me how to get to some ranch where the party's at. Kin we go, boss?"

"She? She who?" Billy Bob asked.

"Emmy Lou. She and her sis hired out to help with the cookin' there tomorrow. I kinda bumped into her at the bank today and we got to talkin' and—"

"Bank!" Billy Bob shouted. "What yuh doin' in a bank, boy?"

"Savin' up my money yuh let me keep," Jeb answered innocently. "Shucks—I mean, shet! I got nowhere to spend it, and Hank won't let me near the cathouse. He says the cathouse is jest for grown-ups and old men."

Billy Bob's eyes bulged out.

Zinging his cud toward the open door, Hank spoke up quickly. "Yuh silly greenhorn. S'posin' the bank got held up. Yuh'd lose all yer money."

"Wud not," Jeb said confidently.

"How do yuh figure that?" Hank fired back.

"Well, 'cause . . ." Jeb hesitated. " 'Cause no one around here wud likely rob the bank 'ceptin' us. And if we did, I'd get my money back."

"Now, that makes real sense to me, Jeb Boy!" Billy Bob said, astonished. "Who said this kid wuz dumb! The hell you say, Hank!" He squinted one eye shut and began stroking his mustache, plotting yet another crafty scheme. "Furthermore, goin' to that party strikes me as a right good idea, too."

"Who wants to go to some dumb party?" Hank said. "If we could jest grab the grub and run, it might be okay, but we'd have to stand around and talk so we wouldn't look suspicious."

"Hell no, Hank. We won't look suspicious. We got a invite, didn't we?" Billy Bob argued. " 'Sides, no harm in stickin' around fer a while. We might be able to grab more than food, if yuh get my drift."

"Yeah, like maybe some women that won't cost us nothin'," Curly said eagerly.

Curly's smile faded when Hank gave him the steely eye. Then Hank looked thoughtfully at Billy Bob. "You thinkin' there might be a loose gold bauble or two jest ripe fer pickin', boss?"

"Maybe even a cash box," Billy Bob said, his eyes widening.

"Well, it *might* be worth the ride," Hank conceded.

"Sure might. But remember," Billy Bob cautioned, "we cain't be too careful when we git there. Jest be real friendly like, tell the folks what a nice spread they got, and smile a lot, too. That'll throw off any suspicions they might be havin'."

"Yessiree!" Billy Bob said, gleefully rubbing his hands. "Come tomorra, boys, we'll climb on our horses and head out for that there party. The Billy Bob Walden gang will ride agin!"

Chapter 11

Rays of sunlight streaming through the east window made Angie's eyelids flutter. Then the awareness that she was not alone in the bed popped them wide open. Angie turned her head to gaze at the wheat-blond hair on the pillow and the long, muscular body of the sleeping man stretched out on the top of the quilt next to her.

When had he come to bed? Either she slept too soundly for her own good or he was part cat.

Her gaze traversed the long length of him, naked except for his drawers. He had the most beautifully proportioned body. Even in repose, bronzed and muscular, it emanated a vibrancy. She shifted her gaze back to his face. Shadowed by whiskers, the rugged jaw added to the aura of total masculinity.

Asleep, he looked like an innocent, but awake, he was a devil. She smiled tenderly. Kissing her whenever he claimed Cynthia was watching them—he wasn't fooling her one bit! He was just having a good joke at her expense. Though, actually, they weren't altogether that bad. As a matter of fact, they were rather pleasant . . . Matter of fact, she was beginning to enjoy them. Much more exciting than she'd ever have imagined . . .

Jolted awake by the direction of her thoughts, she tried to sit up, but the quilt kept her bound. It had been tucked firmly under the mattress on her side, and Giff's weight held it down on the other side. She wanted to be out of the bed before he woke up, but she was literally pinned to it.

Well, she'd just have to try going over the top of the quilt. She managed to slowly inch herself upwards until she bumped her head on the headboard. Restraining the curse she was too ladylike to utter, she leaned her upper torso over the top of the quilt and proceeded headfirst to inch herself out of it. She heaved a sigh of relief when she freed her hands and then her legs, and on hands and knees she crawled toward the foot of the bed.

Giff rolled over, opened his eyes, and was greeted by the delightful nightie-clad derriere of his wife. Unable to resist the temptation, he gave it a playful swat.

Wide-eyed and mouth agape, Angie turned her head and stared at him. "You hit me!"

"I gave you a husbandly love tap."

She scrambled off the foot of the bed, and eyes flashing with fury, she rubbed her posterior. "I bet you wanted to do that for a long time!" she accused.

He grinned. "It's crossed my mind a time or two."

"Peter Gifford, as long as I've known you, you've never touched me in that area."

"That doesn't mean it hadn't crossed my mind . . . a time or two," he replied with the same infuriating grin.

"What is *that* supposed to mean?"

"Are you trying to say that pert little rear end of yours didn't draw Edward's attention a time or two, also?"

"Oh, I see," she declared with arms akimbo. "It's

another one of those uncontrollable *man things*. Is that right?''

''Sad but true.''

''Just how many more of those *man things* will be coming up?''

He almost choked. Considering the swelling in his loins at the moment, he knew *exactly* what was coming up. She had no idea of the effect she was having on him, with her hair all messed up like a wild vixen and that thin nightgown that left little to his imagination.

''If you aren't planning on getting dressed, I'll be glad to show you.''

Her blush looked hot enough to spark a fire. Rushing over to the dresser, she quickly pulled out some underclothes. ''I'm going to take a bath.''

''You better hope Dave's not out in the hallway and sees you in that nightgown. I reckon he most likely suffers with those *man things*, too, you know.''

''Oh, you sound like a pervert!'' she said, irate, opening the door. Despite her anger, she paused, poked her head out the door, then raced down the hallway.

Giff lay back and laughed.

As Angie and Cynthia covered the tables with red and white checkered tablecloths, Angie glanced over to where Giff and String were roasting a calf on the spit.

''What's wrong, Angie?'' Cynthia asked. ''You've been glaring at Giff all morning.''

''The man's a brute and a pervert.''

''My goodness! And right in our own household, too! When did you come to this conclusion?''

Her obvious amusement only added to Angie's disgruntlement. ''This morning.''

''A brute and a pervert, huh? Hmmm,'' Cynthia

pondered, "sounds pretty serious. How long have you known Giff, Angie?"

"That's a stupid question, Thia. You know as well as I do."

"So you're saying you discovered this morning that this man you've known all your life is a brute and . . . a pervert to boot! Good heavens, what did he do?"

"I'm not saying. I can see where your loyalty lies. Giff can do no wrong in your eyes."

"If I hadn't just heard that with my own ears, I'd believe you were describing yourself more than me. Hey, Giff," Cynthia called, "what did you do to Angie to make her so mad?"

"Did you have to do that?" Angie declared, folding her arms across her chest.

Giff shoved his hat to his forehead and sauntered over. "I didn't do anything. She just got up on the wrong side of the bed this morning."

"Is that right, Peter Gifford? If you remember, I couldn't get up from *any* side of the bed this morning." Before Cynthia could pursue that puzzling statement, Angie remarked, "If you must know, he hit me."

Until then, Cynthia had been amused. "You hit her, Giff?" she asked gravely.

"Hit you! What the hell are you talking about, Angie?" Giff asked, as shocked as Cynthia.

"Oh, don't act so innocent, Mr. Peter Gifford. You know as well as I what I'm talking about."

"Good Lord! You don't mean that swat on your butt?"

Angie smiled victoriously at Cynthia. "See— what did I tell you? Of course, *he* called it a husbandly love tap."

"And that's exactly what it was. C'mon, Angel, I didn't mean anything by it. Let's kiss and make up."

This time she anticipated his move. When he reached for her, she quickly backed away and managed to evade him. "No, you don't. Not this time!"

"If that's the way you want it." Giff spun on his heel and returned to the spit.

Cynthia could barely keep from laughing. "Pumpkin, we've got to talk. Don't you know that men think up all kinds of reasons and ways to touch the woman they love? It's a kind of uncontrollable urge with them."

"Oh, you mean it's a *man thing*."

"Exactly!" Cynthia grinned broadly.

"I should have known better than to expect any sympathy from you, Thia. You always took Giff's side in any argument." Angie flounced back to the house, passing Dave on the way.

"Good morning, Angie. We couldn't ask for a better day for the barbecue."

"That's what you think," she snapped, and continued on to the kitchen.

Perplexed, Dave joined Cynthia. "What's Angie so upset about?"

"I think the honeymoon's over," Cynthia said. "You want to give me a hand covering these tables? Looks like I lost my helper."

The annual Roundhouse spring barbecue was as popular an event as the ranch's holiday party at the end of the year, and drew friends and families from Denver and all the surrounding ranches. Once the desserts and salads the women had prepared were set out on the tables, they were relieved of any more kitchen responsibilities. With the yard and barn in order, the steer roasting on a spit since daybreak, and a barrel of beer tapped and set in an iced tub, the men were free to seek their pleasures.

Giff usually mixed with the crowd, Red always took the young children for a hayride, and String would hold court around the beer barrel with Slim Collins beside him. Today was no exception. By midday the yard and barn abounded with the sound of male voices, chatting women, and the gleeful cry of scampering children chasing one another.

The day had begun right after dawn for Emmy Lou and Prudy O'Shea. Now, in the hustle and bustle of their duties, the two serving girls could scarcely contain their excitement as the guests continued to arrive. And with every arrival, another tasty salad, pie, or cake found a place on one of the long tables.

"Oh, Emmy Lou," Prudy said, scurrying back into the kitchen, "you should just go outside and see!"

"Yes, yes, I will, Prudy." Emmy Lou motioned impatiently. "But help me get this coffee done first."

Chatting nonstop, the girls made coffee until the big urn was filled, then hurriedly donning fresh aprons, they carried the coffeepot to a table outside.

"There, that's done." Emmy Lou sighed with relief and turned around. Standing on tiptoe, she began to search the crowd, some of whom stood gathered in clusters while others were already seated on many of the numerous chairs.

Prudy glanced at her sister from the corner of her eye. "Well, do you see him?"

"See who?" Emmy Lou said indifferently.

"*Him*, of course. The tall, handsome stranger who knocked you down at the bank yesterday."

"Honestly, Prudence O'Shea! For the life of me, I can't understand why certain people have such trouble minding their own business."

"Pardon me, Your Highness." Prudy grinned. "So how come certain other people talked about him from the time you got home yesterday 'til the time we went to bed?"

"But I didn't mean to..." Emmy Lou was clearly rattled.

Savoring the moment, Prudy broke out in sing-song, "I know a secret that I can't keep; there's someone here who talks in her sleep."

"I did *not!*"

"You didn't what?" Middy asked, approaching them from behind.

"It's nothing, Middy. Emmy Lou's just fussin' 'cause she can't find her beau," Prudy announced.

"Bow?" Middy eyed Emmy Lou's thatch of unruly red curls. "'Pears to me there ain't room in that mop for no bow."

The girls exchanged amused glances and began to giggle. Mystified, Middy threw up her hands, then laughing along, hugged them both in one sweep of her arms.

"Now get on with you, young'uns, and enjoy yourselves. But mind you, now, see to them dirty dishes when they start pilin' up, 'cause folks'll be chowin' down clear up to their leavin'."

"Oh, Emmy Lou," Prudy said, after Middy walked away, "I'm so excited I can hardly wait. Tell me again, do you suppose your fella works at the bank—or maybe even *owns* the bank?"

"Well . . . I don't think so. At least he didn't say as much. Anyway, he looked more like he worked outdoors. You know, like a cowboy."

"Oh-h-h, maybe he owns a ranch," Prudy said, impressed. After pausing for a long moment, she casually asked, "By the way, did he tell you anything about his brothers?" While her tone seemed nonchalant, she could not disguise the gleam in her eye.

"Why, Prudence O'Shea, you're too young to be asking questions about complete strangers!"

"You're just two years older than I am, and it seems to me," Prudy said haughtily, "it's a sight smarter to be asking questions than handing out invites to complete strangers."

At her sister's threatening glance, Prudy ran as fast as she could toward the kitchen, but Emmy Lou was only one step behind her.

While tending to their chores throughout the day, the girls still took every opportunity to mingle with the guests. But as the sun's lingering glow faded into an evening sky—and String and Red Bean had lit a large bonfire, Giff and Dave had staked several torches to light the yard—there was still no sign of Emmy Lou's young man.

She and Prudy were just about done lighting the lanterns on the tables when Emmy Lou suddenly stopped and looked toward a tangle of shrubbery.

"What is it, Emmy Lou?" Prudy asked.

"Nothing, I guess. Just thought I heard something in there."

"Well, I didn't hear anything. Too much noise going on around here. Anyway, a party's no time to get spooked by night critters in the bushes," Prudy said, laughing. Turning around, she pointed in the direction of the food tables. "Look over there. Could that be your young man?"

Emmy Lou whirled around and immediately sighed in disappointment. "Gosh no, that's not him."

"Well, it's a good thing," Prudy said, amused. "I swear I saw him stuffing food in his pockets. And it sure isn't likely for a banker or a rancher to be swiping food. Think I'll just go have a closer look."

Prudy wandered off, and when Emmy Lou returned to lighting the lanterns, once again she heard a noise—a definite sound this time.

"Pssst . . . pssst."

Standing tall, she put her hands on her hips,

faced the bushes, and challenged the unknown prowler. "Okay, will whoever's in those bushes please come out and identify yourself," she demanded, struggling to sound serious.

Stammering, Jeb crawled out of the bushes. "Shucks, ma'am, it's only me, Jeb Bloomer. Remember?"

"Why, gracious me, Mr. Bloomer! Whatever are you doing in there?"

"Shucks, ma'am, yuh invited me, didn't yuh?"

"Of course, but I didn't expect—"

"Well, Billy Bob says a man can't never be too careful 'bout protectin' his backside," Jeb said, rising to his feet. "So I figured I'd hunker down 'til I'd seen yuh. Then I'd know fer sure we wuz in the right place."

Gazing up at the tall young man she had longed to see again, Emmy Lou was too mesmerized to quibble about the lateness or strangeness of his arrival. "Well, that was right smart of you, Mr. Bloomer."

Jeb, too, was agog. "Zat so? Shucks, no one ever called *me* smart afore." He stared down into her big blue eyes. "Say, yuh reckon yuh might wanna be callin' me Jeb?"

"Oh yes, Jeb. And you call me Emmy Lou."

"Shucks, no one as purty as yuh's ever called me Jeb afore 'cause . . . I ain't never seen anyone so purty as yuh afore."

Emmy Lou blushed and quickly slipped her arm into his. "Why, thank you, Jeb. C'mon, I've got someone I want you to meet."

Chapter 12

◦─────◦◯◯◦─────◦

A cross the yard, Prudy tiptoed up behind the man with stuffed pockets and jabbed her finger in the small of his back. "Okay, partner, stick 'em up."

Immediately his arms shot straight up in the air, his fists still clenching squashed pieces of cake. "Don't shoot. I . . . I'm real friendly like, ma'am." Crumbs floated down on his shirt as he slowly turned around. Then he laughed as he lowered his arms. "Why, yer no ma'am. Yer just a kid!"

"Am not!" Prudy declared, stamping her foot in anger. "I'm sixteen, and I've got more manners than you've got." Shaking her gun finger at him, she scolded, "Shame on you, squirreling away our party food."

"Hold on there, li'l lady. I wuz jest gonna set at that table right over there and wanted to be savin' myself some trips back and forth."

"Saving yourself?" Prudy asked incredulously. Reaching behind him, she scooped up two plates and some silverware from the piles at the end of the table and shoved them at his chest. "That's what dishes are for. You ever hear of them, stranger?"

"Shoot, I ain't no stranger," he said indignantly. Then, trying to brush the crumbs away with his chocolate-smeared hands, he added, "And I reckon I've heard 'bout dishes a time or two afore. But I ain't no stranger, no siree, girl. I got a invite here," he said proudly. "And what's more, if yuh'd asked me real polite like, I'da told yuh my name."

She looked askance at him. "Which is what, may I ask?"

"Steward Leon Potts, at your service, li'l lady." He made a slight bow. "But," he drawled, "iffen yuh mind yer manners, yuh kin call me Stew."

"Well, Steward Leon Potts," she said, articulating each syllable as she put the dishes on the table, "I guess I could call you Stew if . . ." Prudy paused for a second, then her haughty expression changed to one of surprise. "Your name is *Stew . . . Potts*? I don't believe anyone in the whole world has the name stew pots!" She began to giggle and soon there were tears in her eyes.

Looking down, Stew shifted from one foot to the other and started to poke the ground with his toe. "Oh well, no matter," Prudy said, taking pity on him. "Whatever your name *really* is, Mr. Stew Potts, you'd better get those sticky fingers washed. C'mon, there's a pump in the kitchen."

As Prudy and Stew walked toward the house, Emmy Lou called out to her. "Wait up, Prudy." Pulling a tall young man by the hand, Emmy Lou ran up to them. "I want you to meet Mr. Jeb Bloomer. Jeb, this is my sister Prudence."

"Pleased to meet yuh, ma'am," Jeb said politely.

"Same here." Prudy gawked up at him. "Oh, and this here is, ah . . ." She hesitated, looking doubtfully at Stew.

"Shucks, Miz Prudence, I knowed him. That's Stew Potts. He's one of the boys."

"Boys?" Emmy Lou asked innocently.

"Well . . . ah . . . yeah. Least Ma always called us boys. Bein' as how me and Stew are brothers, sort of. Ah . . . you see," Jeb stammered, struggling with his lie, "I'm a Bloomer and Stew's a Potts, 'cause we all had the same ma, but different pas. Ain't that right, Stew?"

"Sure is, brother Jeb," Stew agreed glibly. "The thing is, Ma kept turnin' up widowed every now and agin."

"Oh my, how sad." Emmy Lou gazed wistfully up at Jeb. "Are any of your other brothers here tonight?"

"Sure are, Emmy Lou." Jeb pointed to the beer barrel. "See them two leanin' up agin' that there beer barrel? That's brother Curly and brother Billy Bob. Brother Hank is here, too, but I don't see where he's at right now." Jeb shook his head thoughtfully. "Yuh never kin tell what brother Hank is up to. He's kinda surprisin', even peculiar like, sometimes."

"Really? I suspect it *could* run in the family." Prudy impatiently grabbed Stew's arm. "C'mon, let's get you cleaned up before the dancing gets started."

"Okay, Prudy," Emmy Lou said, grinning. "We're going to eat now. See you later."

Curly watched Stew being led into the house. He straightened up and nudged Billy Bob.

"Hey, boss, did yuh see that?"

"What? Where?" Billy Bob squinted hard.

"Over there," Curly gestured. "I swear I jest saw Stew goin' inta that house."

"Oh yeah? I mean, *sure*, I seen him," Billy Bob lied. "Shet, Curly, iffen he kin get in, so kin we. Let's go."

Slightly tipsy, the two weaved their way toward the house and boldly entered by the front door—

only to be taken aback when they saw Hank in conversation with a tall blond man.

"Howdy, strangers." The man smiled, extending his hand. "I'm Pete Gifford. Most folks call me Giff."

"Well, howdy to yuh too, Giff. Glad to see yuh so friendly like," Curly said, shaking the man's hand. " 'Cause we're right friendly too, and any friend of Hank's is a friend of—"

"This here is Curly and that there is Billy Bob," Hank interrupted. With a pointed glare he said to them, "Giff is the foreman of this here spread. It's called the Roundhouse."

"Foreman! Well, if that don't beat all!" Billy Bob exclaimed, stroking his beard. "Say, Giff, exactly how big a herd you got to—"

"Billy Bob," Hank interrupted, clearing his throat, "I wuz just tellin' Giff that we're in the lumber business ourselves."

"We sure are," Curly offered in slurred speech. "Piles and piles of it. Yes siree . . . and every day, nothin' but sawdust, clear up to our balls—"

"*Eyeballs,* that is," Hank said, giving Curly a shove. "Giff, I reckon my buddy could use a li'l coffee 'bout now, so—"

"You bet, right this way." Turning toward the door, Giff grinned to himself.

"Hey, wait a minute, Hank," Curly blurted out. "I ain't wastin' no time sluggin' no coffee, less'n I git some . . . Say, mister," he said, looking at Giff, "yuh got somethin' to amuse a fella around here?"

"Sure do, Curly. How about a brand-new deck of cards?" Giff opened the top drawer of a nearby chest.

Curly looked befuddled. "Cards?"

"Cards'll be jest fine, Giff," Hank said quickly. He peered into the drawer while Giff searched for the deck.

"Here they are." Giff hesitated when he saw Hank staring at something in the drawer. Following Hank's gaze, he smiled. "Oh, that. Isn't it a beauty?" Reaching in, he retrieved a shiny object. "It belonged to my father. Even has his name engraved on it, but I never got the hang of it myself. By chance, are you a musician, Hank?"

"Him!" Billy Bob spoke up loudly. "Shet, he was the best mouth organer I ever hear'd, 'til some snake in the grass went and stole it."

Bleary-eyed, Curly blundered in. "Yeah, some low-down sidewinder stole it when we wuz in the caboose."

"*Railroad* caboose, he means," Hank corrected quickly, taking the harmonica from Giff. "You see, we wuz workin' with a rough bunch on the railroad a while back and . . . we spent a lotta time in the caboose."

Before another word could be spoken, Hank put the instrument to his mouth and began an intricate rendition of "I've Been Working on the Railroad."

Giff looked astonished by the performance—until Billy Bob and Curly broke into a boozy, off-key sing-along. "Okay, boys, I'm convinced." Smiling, Giff said, "You sure can play that thing, Hank."

Taking a last lingering look at the harmonica, Hank handed it toward Giff. "That's a mighty fine organ you got there, Giff."

Giff caught the yearning in Hank's eye. "Tell you what—Why don't you hang on to it for now. I just might be asking you for a tune later on." He slapped them on the shoulder and ushered them out of the house. "See you later, boys."

Soon after, Prudy and Stew rejoined Emmy Lou and Jeb in the yard. "C'mon, fellas, let's help move a few of these chairs over to the barn," Prudy said, suddenly whisking away Stew's plate of cookies.

"What fer?" Stew grumbled, grabbing a sandwich from the table.

"The barn dance will be starting soon, and we'll be needing more chairs in there. C'mon, hurry up."

Frowning, Stew looked at Jeb. "Now look what yuh got us into. Yuh got any idea what them gals'll be expectin' us to do next?"

Jeb shrugged. "Nope. But I'll bet yuh a whole dollar it'll be more fun than buildin' a outhouse." Scooping up a couple chairs, he eagerly trotted after the girls.

Scratching his head, Stew stood there for a moment. Then, jamming a few cookies in his mouth, he imitated Jeb's shrug, picked up some chairs, and followed.

By this time, Billy Bob and Curly had found their way back to the beer barrel. Their card game hadn't lasted too long. First off, the two ranch hands called String and Red, who had joined them in the game, began by insisting on some sort of rules; and soon after, the game came to a roaring, fifty-two-pick-up halt when Curly started counting the spots on the cards out loud.

"Shet, Billy Bob," Curly said as he slurped another swig of beer. "I wuz jest tryin' to distract 'em for yuh, boss."

"Hell, I knowed that! We shouda knowed better then ta set down with 'em varmints in the first place."

"Yer right, boss," Curly responded automatically. Yawning, he began slowly sinking downward until his rear end touched the ground.

"Just goes to show yuh, Curly, never trust a honest varmint," Billy Bob noted philosophically. "How many times have I told yuh that afore?"

"I forgit, boss."

"Well, it don't matter none. We didn't come here

to git cheated outta our game by no cardsharpers. We gotta stick to business and git ourselves back into that house."

"Yep, yer right, boss . . ." Curly's voice trailed off.

"Hmmm, folks seem to be driftin' over to that there barn," Billy Bob observed, stroking his beard. "We oughta be able to sneak back . . ." Pausing when he heard an all-too-familiar sound, Billy Bob looked down. "Aw, shet, Curly, this ain't no time to be taking no snooze!"

When the sound of music filled the air, most of the guests had already assembled for the barn dance. Colorful decorations in red, white, and blue, along with glowing lanterns and candles, gave the yawning space a warm and festive atmosphere.

Hand-painted lanterns hung from the rafters, while streamers and bunting seemed to be everywhere. Covered with red and white tablecloths, bales of hay scattered on the periphery served as tables, adorned with painted glass candleholders and vases of dried flowers.

"Do-si-do and around the bend, change partners and back again," the fiddler called out from the platform as another fiddle, two guitars, two banjos, and a lone harmonica embellished the rousing tune at a frenzied tempo.

But the barn's finery escaped the notice of Jeb and Stew, who had neither the time nor presence of mind to heed anything except the scramble to follow their partner. Having been hastily coached by Emmy Lou and Prudy in a few steps outside the barn, the two men bowed, whirled, slid, and stomped around the floor awkwardly. Jeb fared better than Stew, but by the third dance, they had improved.

When the dance ended Emmy Lou said breathlessly, "I declare, Jeb Bloomer, that was more fun than a gallop across the range and down the hill."

"Zat so? Wahoo!" he shouted, lifting her up and swinging her around—until he lost his balance and they went sprawling to the floor.

Giggling and exhausted, the couple walked hand in hand as they retreated to the sideline, where they found Prudy and Stew already seated at a table.

Prudy offered to fetch some refreshments. As she walked by the open barn door, she was distracted by something outside. Pausing to peer over at the corral fence for a moment, she shook her head and moved on.

"Hey, boss, do yuh think she saw us?" Curly whispered.

"Shet, how the hell wud I know?" Billy Bob said, disgruntled as he crawled farther into the corral. "Jest stay down and keep yer goldurn mouth shut."

Soon after, they got up on their haunches and waddled forward, encumbered by their awkward burdens. Billy Bob struggled with a heavy wooden chest, and Curly toted a dozen tools under one arm and a large, unwieldy painting under the other.

Finally clear of the light from the barn, they stood halfway up, moving ever faster in the darkness.

Suddenly Billy Bob slipped. Letting go of the heavy chest, he grabbed Curly, and they both ended up on their rear ends in a soft, squishy mire. Spattered clumps of wet dirt and bits of straw clung to the men and their loot.

They looked at each other aghast, and when a telltale odor soon reached their nostrils, they simultaneously let out a holler, *"Horse shet!"*

"Of all the goldurn messes yuh ever got us into, Curly, this one is the worst," Billy Bob ranted as they scrambled to get out of the manure.

"Me? What are yuh talkin' about, boss? This shet weren't none of my doin'."

"The hell you say, Curly Ringo! Iffen yuh'd helped me carry this box 'stead of draggin' along that shet yuh've got—"

"Shet? This ain't shet, boss. This is good stuff!"

"Oh yeah! Well, I'm tellin' yuh that a bunch of rusty tools and a picture of some dumb gal in a wig is *pure shet*."

"But, boss—"

"Never mind yer excuses. Yuh jest better be thinkin' pretty damn quick 'bout how we're gonna get this stink off us or I'll—"

"I've got it, boss. I saw a couple rain barrels over by the barn—"

"*Rain barrels!* Shet, yer dumb, Curly. Yuh better come up with somethin' bigger than that, or I'm gonna give yuh two rain barrels right on the head."

"Bigger? You mean like the stream, boss?"

"Stream? What stream?"

"The stream runnin' by the tree we tied the horses to."

"Oh, *that* stream. Good idea, Ringo. C'mon, we gotta get the shet outta here. Pick up yer loot and let's go."

After returning to the table with a pitcher of beer and a plate full of sandwiches, Prudy glanced toward the bandstand where several couples had gathered in front of the makeshift platform, listening attentively to the melodious sound and silvery overtones of a solo harmonica. "Gosh, that's one of my favorite songs."

Emmy Lou and Jeb followed her gaze, and suddenly Jeb stood up and poked Stew in the arm. "Hey, Stew, look over there."

"Don't bother me, kid. I'm eatin'."

"But, Stew, it's Hank up there."

Stew glanced up. "Yep, that sure is him, all right. Wonder where he picked up the 'monica."

"Picked it up? Where in tarnation did he learn to *play* it?" Jeb asked, amazed.

Stew chuckled. "Hank? Oh, he's a regular pied piper. At least he *wuz* 'til one of them rats stole his pipe when he wuz in the cab . . . California."

Stew gulped another sandwich, washing it down with a slug of beer. "That wuz some time ago, afore you wuz aboard, Jeb. But I guess he'd been foolin' around with it since he wuz a kid."

Frowning, Prudy looked at Jeb. "But if that's your brother, how come you didn't know that he plays—"

A sudden burst of applause interrupted her question, and before she knew it, Stew had pulled her over to the dance floor.

"Time for another hoedown," he said, smiling just as the fiddler stomped his foot and began to play.

Over at the platform, Cynthia motioned from the side to get Hank's attention. "I just wanted to tell you how much I enjoyed your music."

At the sight of her, he instantly recalled the painful episode at the railroad tent town in New Mexico. "Thank you, ma'am. Ah, Giff talked me into it. Even lent me his harmonica," he added, glancing around for a means of a quick escape.

"Then I guess we are indebted to him, too. I'm Cynthia Kincaid." She smiled, extending her hand. When he did not respond, she looked at him quizzically. "You look familiar, but I'm sorry, I don't remember your name."

"I'm Hank . . . ah, Witherspoon," he lied. Stoically he took her hand. "Pleased to meet yuh, ma'am. Best I get back to the band now." Wiping the mouth organ on his shirt, he turned and walked away.

Eyeing the crowd from outside, Hank spied Jeb looking his way, and motioned him over.

"Say, Hank, I sure as shootin' never knowed that you—"

"Button it up, kid. We gotta get outta here."

"Ah, shucks, Hank," Jeb whined. "How come?"

"Jest met one of 'em bitches who wuz at that tent town in New Mexico that we hit."

"So what?"

"Think we best git out of here afore she remembers where'd she met me." Looking past Jeb, Hank caught a glimpse of Stew. "Go get Stew. I'll look for the boss and Curly. Meet you by the horses."

Totally dejected, Jeb returned to the table.

"Why, Jeb Bloomer, whatever is the matter?" Emmy Lou asked soulfully.

"Shucks, Emmy Lou, sometimes my brothers are a pain in the . . . neck. 'Pears like we gotta go now."

"Oh no, Jeb. Whatever is the matter? Will I ever see you again?"

"Emmy Lou, you jest tell me where you live and wild billy goats cudn't keep me from your door."

After the boys left, the two girls sat at the table and talked about their exciting evening and the brothers' sudden departure.

"Well," Prudy concluded, "they really seemed sort of nice. But maybe we just got dew in our eyes. In a way, they looked and acted kind of strange."

"But, Prudy, don't judge everyone by what you see. Like Middy's always telling us, it's what's on the inside that counts."

"Yeah, well, that's what worries me most."

When Hank left the barn, he searched everywhere for Billy Bob and Curly. He even took a quick look around the house. Disgusted, he hurried back to the stream where the horses were tied. Hearing Billy Bob's voice, he ran over to the water's edge. There he saw Billy Bob and Curly each sitting on a rock in their drawers.

"What in the hell is goin' on?" Hank asked.

Almost falling off his rock, Billy Bob exclaimed, "Shet, Hank! You oughtn't to be sneakin' up on a man like that."

"Me and the boss took a little swim and we wuz jest wringin' out our duds," Curly said as he and Billy Bob struggled to get their wet pants back on. "Lookit here at our loot, Hank. *We* didn't come away empty-handed. What'd you git?"

Just then, Jeb and Stew came running up.

"I still don't see why we're leavin', Hank," Jeb said. "Me and Stew wuz havin' such a good—"

"Leavin'?" Billy Bob snarled. "The hell yuh say, Hank. We're goin' back to that house and—"

"Can't, boss. I think someone might be on to us. Let's git outta here, and we better hurry. No point in draggin' along that junk yuh got there," Hank said.

"I'll be tarred and feathered if that ain't all! Who made yuh boss? We're takin' every bit of this loot with us. You *hear* me?" Billy Bob shouted.

"Yeah, and so will everyone at that dance if yuh keep up that bellowin'," Hank grumbled.

"We've got good stuff here, Hank," Curly said.

"What? Bet yuh don't even know what's in that box, and yuh couldn't give them tools away." Shaking his head in disgust, Hank picked up the waterlogged picture. "And jest what the hell is this?"

Curly grabbed his treasure defensively. "This here frame is real gold."

Hank laughed scornfully. "Why, that ain't nothin' but yeller paint slopped on wood."

"It is?" Scratching his head, Curly looked at the frame. "Are you sure?"

"No, he ain't sure," Billy Bob snarled angrily.

"Well then, Hank Withers, I bet yuh two bits the lady in the wig is fer damn sure worth somethin'. So shut up."

Finally, all dressed, packed up, and mounted, the Walden gang rode off into the night once again: Billy Bob, still the triumphant leader; Curly, his ever-loyal comrade; Hank, a defiant but secretly contented man with a shiny new possession in his pocket; Stew, an exhausted and hungry sojourner; and Jeb, the sorrowful, lovesick kid.

Of course, Stew and Jeb had to ride double. The fifth horse, led by Billy Bob Walden himself, pranced along bearing the fruits of their hard day's labor: a wooden chest, a batch of tools, and a picture of a lady in a wig that was "fer damn sure worth somethin'."

Chapter 13

❧

Giff had found a secluded corner and for the last fifteen minutes had been watching Angie pass from one partner to another. He never tired of looking at her, especially when she was unaware of it. She was so beautiful. His insides were on fire; he ached from wanting to touch her. Throughout the day he couldn't shake the image of waking up that morning and seeing her in that thin nightgown. The blue dress she was wearing now didn't help his situation either. He loved her in blue—it made her eyes glow like sapphire jewels, and her skin . . . her skin glistened like satin in the glow of the lanterns. He grimaced when Jamie Skinner became her partner and grasped her around the waist. How could she smile at him?

"Look at that pile of horse shit," he mumbled when Dave joined him. "If that bastard's hands slip any lower on Angie, I'm booting him out of here so hard that he'll be halfway to Denver by the time he lands."

Dave took a long look at the dancing couple. "Giff, I think it's part of the dance. Looks like the other fellas are holding their partners the same way."

"Just the same, I don't like it!" Giff grumbled.

Nudging Giff's arm, Dave nodded toward Cynthia and Beth standing against the wall with their heads bent together in deep conversation.

"I've been around this family long enough to know that can only mean trouble for somebody."

"Speaking of trouble, here it comes right now," Giff said as an attractive blond woman approached them. "Her name is Diane. She's Melissa Cranshaw's widowed cousin—looking for a husband. For some reason, she's taken a liking to me. I sure as hell haven't encouraged her."

"Did you tell her you were married?"

"Not yet. I've been kept busy trying to avoid her all day."

"Well, I think this is a good time for me to find out what my wife's up to." Dave walked over to the two women and slipped his arm around Cynthia.

"How long do you think they'll stay mad?" Beth asked him.

"Will who stay mad?"

"We're concerned about Angie and Giff," Cynthia said. "They haven't been near each other all day. How can we announce the big news about their wedding when the bride and groom aren't even talking to each other? It's time we do something about it."

"Cyn, stay out of other people's business," Dave warned.

"This is family business, Kincaid, so we're all involved. Fortunately, I am an expert at such matters as this, so here's what we'll do: Beth, you tell the band to play a sweetheart waltz, and I'll grab Giff. You, Dave, will ask Angie to dance. At the appropriate time, we'll change partners." She glanced up and saw Angie approaching. "Here she comes now.

Remember what you have to do, Dave. Beth, get to the band."

Beth nodded and hurried away.

"Cyn, why don't we stay out of this?"

"David Kincaid, if you don't help out here, Angie and Giff won't be the only couple not talking."

"You're going to owe me for this, Miz Sin," Dave said. "Angie," he greeted, "I haven't danced with my little sister-in-law yet. The next dance is mine."

Angie looked at him in surprise. "I thought you didn't know how to dance, Dave."

"Oh, he can dance," Cynthia said. "He just doesn't do it well."

"Shades of Willard Hepplewhyte!" Angie groaned.

Cynthia looked around until she spied Giff, just as the music began. "Well, since it appears I'll be without a partner, I guess I better go and find one. 'Bye, you two."

Angie shook her head. "Excuse me for saying so, but I've never seen Thia surrender a man so willingly. Is your dancing that bad, Dave?"

" 'Fraid so, Angie," Dave said, grabbing her hand.

Giff was being towed by the hand toward the dance floor when Cynthia stopped them and took his arm. "Oh, sorry," she said sweetly, "but Giff promised me this dance." Relieved, Giff slipped his hand out of Diane's grasp.

"That's your hard luck, darling, because, as you see, I have him." Diane yanked back Giff's hand.

"Not for long, *darling*," Cynthia said with a syrupy-sweet tone. "Oh, Willard," she said to the pudgy man who had just approached them, "this lovely lady is without a partner. Would you be kind enough to dance with her?"

"My pleasure, dear lady," Willard said, offering a courtly bow.

"You'll love him, *darling*. Willard Hepplewhyte is the best dancer in the county." With that, Cynthia gave a firm tug and pulled Giff away from the woman.

With a backward glare over her shoulder, Diane allowed Willard to lead her to the dance floor.

"My goodness, for a minute there I thought I'd have to Indian-wrestle her. Who is she, Giff?"

"Her name is Diane Divine. She's Melissa Cranshaw's cousin from Philadelphia. Spent the summer here and is staying through the wedding next week."

"How divine," Cynthia said. "Does she live up to her name?"

He looked at her and grinned. "How the hell would I know?"

"Well, she seemed determined to dance with you."

"Almost as determined as you. Now that the two of you managed to yank my arms out of the sockets, mind telling me what this is all about?"

"Are you still angry with Angie?"

"Of course not, but she's still mad at me."

"This is a sweetheart waltz, you know."

"And I'm waltzing with a real sweetheart," he said.

"That's so *sweet*, Giff." Cynthia glanced over his shoulder and nodded at Dave. "But I'd rather be waltzing with my sweetheart. Time to switch partners."

She stopped abruptly and stepped aside as Dave shoved Angie into Giff's arms. Cynthia and Dave then waltzed away.

Giff smiled down at Angie as they began to move to the music. "You still angry with me, Angel?"

"No. I thought you were angry with me. You've been avoiding me all day."

"Believe me, Angel, it's not you I've been avoiding."

The music ended, and following Beth's instructions, Red stepped up to make an announcement. "All right, everybody listen up. This here wuz a sweetheart waltz and yuh'll know what that means. Sure hope you're dancin' with yer sweethearts, 'cause I wanna see all you little ladies out there give them partners of yers a big kiss."

Giff looked down at her, amused. "Well, I'm waiting for my kiss, sweetheart."

Angie rose up on her toes and kissed his cheek.

"*Darling*, that is no way to kiss a sweetheart." The remark had come from Diane Divine, who had ended up next to them when the music had ended. "You must let me show you how it is done properly."

Nudging Angie aside with a hip, Diane locked her arms around Giff's neck. Before he could move, she proceeded to kiss him passionately.

"Hey, that woman's trying to steal my act," Cynthia said, suddenly appearing beside them. "She's acting more like me than I am."

"Yeah, but you were much better at it, Miz Sin," Dave said, hugging her to his side.

"That's your husband she's kissing, Angie. Are you going to let her get away with it?" Cynthia declared.

"I certainly am not."

Aware of the conversation around him, Giff suffered through Diane's kiss. She had a lock on his lips as strong as the one around his neck and he couldn't break away.

Angie tapped Diane on the shoulder. "Excuse me, Miss Divine," Angie said, yanking Diane out of Giff's arms. "I think I've got the idea now."

Suddenly Cynthia's actions became clear to Giff. Bless his beloved sister-in-law! This was an opportunity too good to pass up. When Angie put her arms around his neck and raised her head, he met her halfway. Her lips parted beneath his as their mouths met—a perfect fit, as if made for each other. Slipping his arms around her waist, he gathered her closer, deepening the kiss hungrily, any pretense of casualness obliterated by the first touch of her warm, sweet lips. Desire coursed through him with the intensity of a shock wave and he increased the pressure of the kiss, devouring the softness of her lips and demanding a response.

At first her response was hesitant, as if she were resisting, but his passion overrode her reserve and she surrendered to the pleasure of the kiss.

Raising his head, he gazed into her eyes and saw her shock and confusion. Yet now he knew for certain that a kiss could never be enough.

A burst of whistles and applause resounded, and Giff discovered they had become the center of attention. Looking around at the circle of faces, he saw the pleasure on Cynthia's, a grin on Dave's, and hostility on Diane's.

Beth was calling for attention and the barn quieted to listen.

"Friends and neighbors, as you all know, my family has always celebrated the completion of the spring roundup. This year we MacKenzies have a greater reason for celebrating. With great pleasure and deep affection, we would like to announce the marriage of Angie to Pete Gifford."

Angie spent the next hour at Giff's side accepting people's congratulations and well wishes for the future, still stunned by Giff's kiss. When the opportunity finally presented itself, she stole away to her room for the night.

Once in bed, she lay for a long time thinking about Giff's kiss. Her response to it had shocked her. Whatever had aroused such passion in her? And what must Giff be wondering?

She supposed it felt perfectly normal to him. If a woman kissed him, it would be natural to kiss her back—especially a woman like Diane Divine. *Another one of those man things, no doubt!* Her eyes began to droop. Was marriage to her preventing him from pursuing the eastern temptress? They certainly appeared to be taken with each other.

I wonder how often he's kissed her.

When she awoke in the morning, she saw that the bed beside her had not been slept in. Giff obviously had spent the night in his own house.

The thought was quickly shoved to the back of her mind upon seeing suitcases set in the foyer. She hated to see Cynthia and Dave leave. No matter how dismal a situation was, Cynthia always managed to take the gloom out of it.

Her sisters and Dave were in the kitchen finishing their breakfast. To her disappointment, Beth was dressed for traveling, too.

"You and Giff are on your own, Angie," Beth said. "Charles Reardon and I are going to Washington, D.C., to try and raise some capital. And Middy is gone, too. The poor dear worked so hard preparing for the barbecue that I thought she needed the day off."

Dave took a final swallow from his mug, and got to his feet. "If she'd stop fighting with the cooks, she wouldn't have to work so hard. Sorry, ladies, we have a train to catch." He paused and gave Angie a peck on the cheek. "Can't tell you how happy I am for you and Giff."

"Thanks, Dave," Angie said, wondering how or when she could ever tell the whole truth to these people she loved so much.

As Dave left to load the luggage, Beth followed

him, but Cynthia lingered behind. "Come on, Cyn," Dave yelled, "time and trains wait for no one."

With their arms around each other's waist, Angie and Cynthia walked outside. Giff was waiting in the buckboard, but Angie avoided making eye contact with him.

"Good-bye, Pumpkin. Take good care of Giff. I know the two of you will be as happy as Dave and I."

"I don't think anyone could match you and Dave, Thia."

" 'Bye, Angie," Beth said, giving her a hug and kiss. "I don't know how long I'll be gone. You know those Washington bureaucracies."

"I understand," Angie managed to say before being pulled into Cynthia's bear hug.

"Good-bye, Pumpkin. I'll miss you."

"I'll miss you, too, Thia. I don't see why you can't stay longer."

"Dave has to get back to work."

"Well, that doesn't mean you couldn't stay."

"Pumpkin, my place is with my husband."

"Cyn honey, I'm sorry, but we've got to go," Dave said, hurrying back to them.

"My master's voice," Cynthia whispered. She kissed Angie hurriedly and gave Dave her hand. He helped her into the buckboard and climbed up into the seat beside Giff.

"Good-bye," her sisters called out, waving.

Desolate, Angie turned and walked back into the deserted house.

Even though she felt uncomfortable about the passionate kiss they had shared, Angie knew she couldn't keep avoiding Giff. When he returned an hour later, she decided the best thing to do was to face him and get it over with.

As she walked to the barn, she saw Giff ride off on his stallion in the opposite direction. Angie approached String, who was in the barn pitching hay into the horse stalls. "Where did Giff go, String?"

"He rode out to work on the house he's buildin'."

"He's building a house?" she asked, surprised.

"Yep. On the spread yer pa left him. Ain't he told yuh?"

"Not a word." Angie was flabbergasted. "How long has he been building it?"

"From the time the Chief left the spread to him. Reckon he's plannin' on surprisin' you."

Considering the circumstances, Angie knew Giff hadn't been building the house for her. Horrified, she wondered if he had been planning on marrying someone else when he came to St. Louis. Had he abandoned those plans to help her out of her predicament?

"I think I'll ride out and see it for myself."

"Sure hope I ain't let no cat out of the bag," String said worriedly.

"I won't say a word, String," Angie said as she saddled Calico.

Chapter 14

⌒⌒∽∞∽⌒⌒

Willow Range was only a twenty-minute ride from the house and contained within its sprawling limits some of the best grazing land on the ranch. Splashing across the river that gave the area its name, Angie paused on the bank to allow Calico a drink. Then she followed the sound of a hammer's ring and drew up when she saw the house.

Set back several hundred feet from the Willow River, the house stood in a stand of willow and pine. She was surprised to see that the four walls of the structure were already erected. Spying Giff pounding rafters on the roof, she goaded Calico to a slow trot.

Giff was shirtless, his tanned back and shoulders glistening with a sheen of perspiration. Mesmerized, she watched the muscles across his shoulders and arms expand and contract with each blow of the hammer. Her gaze followed the slope of his shoulders, across his back, and down to his narrow waist and hips.

He has a beautiful, symmetrical body. I'd like to paint him just as he looks now, she reflected.

Brick's welcoming neigh to Calico alerted Giff to her presence. He turned his head and saw her.

"Hi," Angie said.

"What brought you out here?" he asked, climbing down from the roof.

"Just out for a ride." She dismounted and joined him in the shade. "So you're putting up a house out here. Does that mean you're planning on leaving the Roundhouse?"

He shoved his hat to the top of his forehead. "The thought has never entered my mind."

"Then why are you building a house?"

"At one time I figured if I ever got married, my wife might want a place of her own instead of living on the Roundhouse. But leave the ranch?" He shook his head. "The Roundhouse is my life, Angel. It always has been."

"That's because you're so good at what you're doing. You're fortunate, Giff. I wish I were that good at something." Angie hesitated, then questioned, "Giff, if I ask you something very personal, will you be honest with me?"

He picked up a canteen lying nearby and uncapped it. "Reckon so," he replied guardedly, and took a deep swig from it.

"At the time you came to St. Louis, had you already planned to marry someone else?"

He chuckled warmly. "How could I do that, when a long time ago a six-year-old, curly-headed moppet with dark hair and sapphire eyes already staked a claim on me?"

Angie looked at him and smiled. "I'm serious, Giff. Did you change your marriage plans because of me?"

"No, Angel. I have never changed my marriage plans."

"Why are you continuing to build this house then?"

"I guess one day it'll be someplace to call my own. I've been living in somebody else's house all my life. Someday I'll have to turn the reins of the Roundhouse over to someone else."

"Giff, you're scaring me with that kind of talk. The Roundhouse is yours as much as anyone's. No one knows the ranch as well as you do. Without you, what would become of it?"

"You could run this ranch if you had to."

"I doubt that," she scoffed. "Regardless, I don't want to."

"What do you want, Angie?"

"I don't know." Frustrated, she declared, "I don't know what I want. After studying the great Masters, I know now I'm no artist."

"What about the stage?"

She rolled her eyes. "*That* was a disillusioning experience."

"So what's ahead for you, Angie?"

"I haven't taken the time to think it out, but I guess one of these days I'll have to sit down and decide what I want to do about my life . . . and our marriage."

"I see." He stood up abruptly and she sensed an anger in him. "I might as well make the most of the daylight and get back to work."

It was a clear dismissal. Puzzled, she mounted Calico. "Will you be back to the house for dinner?"

"Yeah," he said. "Come to think of it, it'll be the first meal my wife has cooked for me."

"I cooked for you on the roundup."

"You did that for me *and* the boys."

Angie couldn't see the distinction, but she dropped the issue and rode away.

Upon returning to the house, she checked the smokehouse and, disappointed, moved on to the chicken coop. By the time Giff came through the kitchen door that evening, Angie had dinner waiting.

"Sit down, Giff," she said. "I thought since there's only two of us, we could eat right here in the kitchen."

"Fine with me. I'm more comfortable in here than in the dining room anyway."

For several minutes they ate without any attempt at conversation until Giff broke the silence.

"This stew tastes as good as Middy's," he said, spearing a piece of chicken.

"It should; it's Middy's recipe. I figured you had enough beef yesterday."

"I bet she made this for Slim tonight, too. It's his favorite."

"Slim! Is she with Slim?"

"Sure. She left with him last night." Giff picked off one of the biscuits baked on the top of the casserole, cut it in half with his fork, then popped a piece into his mouth.

"Slim Collins! The same Slim Collins who worked here on the ranch?"

"Yeah." He glanced over at her. She knew she looked befuddled. "They've been seeing each other for years."

"I can't believe it."

"You mean you didn't know?"

"Anything that strange never entered my mind."

"What's so strange about it?"

"Well, their ages for one thing, Giff. It's pretty ridiculous to think that people their age are *court-ing*."

Frowning, he put down his fork. "You saying there's gotta be some age limit when people just stop caring and feeling?"

"Don't get angry about it, Giff. I just meant that dating makes it sound romantic. I'm sure it's more of a companionship thing."

"So you think they're too old for romance? No kissing—no making love?"

"Kissing! Making love! I can't even imagine it. Good heavens, Giff! Middy and Slim have been friends since before I was born. Good friends don't sleep together—they don't kiss romantically."

He tipped back his chair, and his blue-eyed gaze bored into hers. "What about that kiss between us last night? That was no peck on the cheek."

The heat of her blush could have boiled water. She had been tiptoeing around him, hoping to avoid any mention of that kiss last night, and now she had opened the door for him to barge right in with it.

"Well . . . ah . . . that was different. It was just for everyone's benefit because . . . ah . . . Diane Divine made such a spectacle of herself."

"Are you trying to say you didn't feel that kiss? Well, I sure as hell did, and it sure wasn't what's meant by *as much fun as kissing your sister*!"

"That's probably because of that man thing you suffer from." She got up hurriedly and carried some dishes to the sink.

Angie could feel his stare in the middle of her back. She had no explanation for the way she'd responded to the kiss. Was it the situation she had been in? Her resentment of Diane's publicly embarrassing her? Was it the actual excitement of the kiss? Whatever the reason, she had responded and she had enjoyed it.

She heard his chair scrape on the floor as he got up, but she didn't turn around, didn't dare look at him. Giff could always read what she was thinking.

As she busied herself at the sink, she knew that he was behind her. She could sense his nearness, could feel the warmth of his body.

"I could kiss you now, Angel. There's no one here. No one to impress. Just the two of us—alone in this house. And I could draw the same response from you as last night."

His deep voice was mesmerizing—a drug on her senses. She fought the urge to turn around, because she knew she'd end up in his arms. How could that be? Why should she feel such emotions? Was what he said about a man and woman true, that romantic feelings weren't important? Could it really be possible that whatever each of them was feeling at this moment was only a male and female attraction? It had never existed between them before; why should she be aware of it now? It was against all common sense or reasoning.

"How much longer can we go on pretending? I want you to think long and hard about us, Angie, because we can't go on like this. If we're going to give this marriage a chance, we have to start living as man and wife. Good night, Angel."

She waited until she heard the door close, then she slumped in relief. Her legs were trembling and so were her hands. Frightened and confused, without conscious thought she entered the library and found herself in front of her father's portrait.

"Why, Daddy?" she asked, looking up to it for guidance. "What's happening to me?"

Tossing restlessly, Angie threw off the bedsheet. *How much longer can we go on pretending?* There had been anguish in his voice when he issued that challenging question.

She closed her eyes, remembering the excitement of his kiss. Her response to it. And the reality was that she had wanted him to kiss her again tonight. Her nipples grew taut with arousal and she bolted out of the bed. How, after all the years they'd been together, did his touch, the scent of him, even the sight of him, become such a distraction? How could she have naively believed they could marry and not share a bed?

How much longer can we go on pretending?

Walking to the window, she glanced at his house and saw a dim light gleaming from his bedroom window. He was probably agonizing with the same thought this very minute. Should she go to him? She folded her arms across her chest to fend off her trembling.

This is madness!

Turning away, she rushed back to her bed.

After spending another miserable night, Giff had eaten breakfast in his own house. Now, sipping his coffee as he stood in the doorway, he watched Angie at the corral feeding an apple to Calico. All night he had cursed himself for being ten times a fool for not taking advantage of the situation. They had been alone in the house, and he couldn't have hoped for a better opportunity to tell her what he was really thinking. From the time he had found her in St. Louis, he'd been listening to her tell him how she felt, and had held his tongue to keep his true feelings to himself—the way he had always done in the past three years. When he'd asked her to marry him, he had acted out of a desire to help her and the baby. Now the situation was different, but one fact still remained: he was married to the only woman he'd ever loved—would ever love— and he would never let her walk out of his life again.

Until the night of the barbecue, he had intended to honor their asinine agreement not to share a bed until she was ready. He'd told himself that it was worth it, just to have her near and know she was safe. She had convinced him that she could never feel anything but friendship for him, and he had believed he could settle for that. Then he had kissed her—and her response had blown the hell out of that belief.

Right now Angie was running scared, confused as hell about her feelings. She wasn't about to admit the truth to him, much less to herself. But for the first time in years, he knew there was hope. It would just take time for her to recognize it, too.

Right now he had the fight of his life on his hands. He'd woo her. Court her. And somehow convince her that her happiness lay right here at the Roundhouse.

His gaze lingered on the beauty of her face as she lifted her head and turned it toward an approaching buckboard. Giving Calico a parting pat, she walked back to the house to greet the unexpected arrivals.

Putting aside his cup, Giff returned to the doorway to study the new visitors. He had a good memory for faces, and was certain he'd never met the driver of the buckboard or the woman who sat on the seat beside him.

Curious, he glanced at Angie and instinctively stepped forward. She had turned pale and was staring in shock at the man who had climbed down from the rig.

Chapter 15

"**E**dward!"

Edward Emory grasped Angie's hand and brought it to his lips. "My dearest Angeleen," he said, looking deeply into her eyes. "How I have missed you."

"Edward, what are you doing here?" she asked uneasily. Angie glanced toward Giff's house and saw him taking in the whole scene.

"Why, I have been searching for you, of course. I have had a terrible time tracing you, my dear."

"And why have you brought Miss Crawford with you?"

"When I told the dear woman about your plight, she insisted upon accompanying me."

"Oh, you poor girl," Stella Crawford gushed, having joined them. She flung her arms around Angie, engulfing her in the scent of a cheap perfume. "When Edward told me of your delicate condition, I insisted he return to you at once."

Angie saw that Giff was now walking toward them. She didn't want to introduce the couple to him. The Lord only knew what his reaction would be to Edward.

163

"Shall we go inside and sit down?" she said. Turning hastily, she went into the house and they followed her.

After seating them in the parlor, Angie went out to the kitchen and asked Middy to serve tea. On her way back, she stole a glance out the window and was relieved to see that Giff had altered his course and was now down at the corral. When she entered the parlor, Stella put down the porcelain figurine she had been examining.

"How charming," she said. "I've never seen anything like it."

"It was made in England. That particular figurine was one of my mother's favorites."

"And when will we have the pleasure of meeting your mother, Angeleen?"

"Both of my parents are deceased, Miss Crawford."

"Oh, that's too bad," Stella intoned, with an avaricious glance around the room. "Then this house and ranch is yours."

"And my sisters'."

"Edward said your family is in the railroad business."

"Yes, we own a line called the Rocky Mountain Central."

"My goodness, with all this wealth, whatever induced you to hire yourself out as a chorus girl on a riverboat?"

"I haven't quite figured that out myself. In retrospect, I'd say sheer stupidity, Miss Crawford."

"Do call me Stella, hon. We're among friends here."

Middy appeared with the cart containing the tea service and a silver salver of small sugar cookies. As soon as she left, Stella helped herself to one of the cookies and munched on it greedily while Angie poured the tea.

"Actually, I'd have liked coffee more," Stella said when Angie handed her a cup. "Tea ain't . . . isn't . . . to my taste."

Apparently the cookies are, Angeleen thought as Stella snatched another cookie from the tray. "Oh, I'm sorry. I'll have Middy bring us a pot of coffee."

"That won't be necessary, Angeleen," Edward said, frowning at Stella. "I am sure you will find the tea just as refreshing, Stella dear."

"Yeah, sure," Stella said, settling back in her chair after taking a couple of more cookies.

"I apologize for my negligence," Angie said. "I should have asked your preference. Would you prefer Middy bring sandwiches?"

"No, if course not," Edward said quickly. "We ate in Denver." This time he gave Stella a scathing look. "Isn't that right, Stella?"

"Yeah. These cookies are fine," she said, brushing crumbs off her ample bosom.

Pouring herself a cup of tea, Angie sat back and relaxed. "I can't tell you what a surprise it is to see you, Edward. Why exactly have you come here?"

"First, I must apologize for my hasty departure from the *Mississippi Belle*," he said.

"It was rather abrupt, wasn't it?"

Angie was amazed at her own impassiveness. Looking at Edward now, away from the aura and glamour she had once associated with the stage, she could see he was a very ordinary man. He was handsome enough—for an older man—but her own father had been handsomer up until the time he had become ill.

She wondered why she had never noticed how pale Edward's skin appeared in the bright light of day. Why, compared to Giff, Edward even looked pasty. And effeminate. Yes, quite effeminate. How could she ever have believed that she was in love with Edward Emory? Compared to Giff, he was . . .

She cut off the thought. She must stop making comparisons to Giff. It wasn't fair. After all, Giff was a much younger man, with a body conditioned by rugged living and hard work. But Edward failed miserably in a comparison with her father, also.

Her mind began scrambling to dredge up an image of someone with whom to compare Edward. Dave Kincaid? Hardly—that would be the same as comparing Edward to Giff. Charles Reardon? Their ages might be similar, but Charles exuded a sense of authority and competence; Edward had a more suave and guileful presence. String and Red? She smiled. String and Red were a precious species all their own.

Then a light flashed in her mind: Jamie Skinner! Of course. Jamie had the same glint in his eyes and many of the same characteristics. He lacked Edward's smoothness and polish, but give the toad a few more years, she reflected, and Jamie would be able to pass as Edward's brother.

Turning her open stare on Edward, she couldn't imagine how she had ever been naive enough to have fallen for his false charm. She wanted him and his paramour out of the house as quickly as possible. As soon as Edward said what he came to say, she would show him the door.

"Well, Edward, I am waiting." Now that she recognized the man for the bounder that he was, she no longer felt intimidated by him.

Edward put down his cup and clasped her hand. She held her own stiffly in his grasp. "My dearest Angeleen, I have thought of nothing else but you since the night I left the riverboat." At her look of skepticism, he continued. "Whatever you may have thought at the time, I can assure you there is an explanation for my actions."

"And what would that be, Edward?"

"When I left your cabin that night in St. Louis, I

was ecstatic to hear that I was to be a father. I wanted to share the good news with Stella. After all, she was my partner, and as such, we were extremely close."

"I'm sure you were . . . are," Angie said. Strange how much clearer she could see things now than she had at the time.

"Unfortunately, Stella's condition had taken a turn for the worse. You do remember I had mentioned that she was slightly under the weather that evening."

Angie nodded. "Yes, I remember." She wished he would get to the point and stop acting like a weasel. Glancing at Stella, she saw the woman appeared not to be listening as she strolled around the room examining art pieces while munching on a cookie. Angie could already hear Middy's complaints about the crumbs scattered all over the room.

"It was clear to me that Stella needed a doctor," Edward said, continuing his story. "She asked me for help and I could hardly refuse."

"So rather than summon a doctor to the boat, you packed up all your clothes and left," Angie said indifferently. "That makes sense."

"I understand your skepticism, my dear. I would feel the same way in your position."

"I doubt you understand how I feel, Edward— or how I felt when I heard the news that you and Stella had left."

"Dear Angeleen, I have agonized imagining that moment. And so has Stella. Isn't that right, Stella?"

Startled, the woman put down the crystal sculpture she had just picked up. "Oh, yes, of course. Agonized."

"That is most kind of both of you."

"In the weeks that followed, Stella's condition required my constant attention. I dared not leave her side."

"Not even long enough to post a note or letter to me in explanation," Angie added.

"Now, why didn't I think to do that?" Edward said, appearing bemused. Angie merely raised a brow in response. "But look at you, my dear. You look ravishing. You weathered the crisis magnificently." With a dramatic sweep of his arm, he declared, "And as the Bard would say, 'All's well that ends well.' For now I have found you again, my love," he declared, clasping both of her hands to his breast. "We can wed at once and await the arrival of our child. How I look forward to that blessed event."

Angie had recognized his lack of singing ability a long time ago, but until that moment, she hadn't realized what an atrociously bad actor he was—as well as liar. For the first time since the disappointment of her mistaken pregnancy, she felt absolute joy in knowing she was not carrying this man's child.

"I am not with child, Edward."

The statement appeared to have no immediate effect on Edward, but it clearly caught Stella's attention. She spun around in surprise, and the women's gazes met and locked while Edward continued to ramble on about the forthcoming joy of parenthood.

"Oh, shut up, Eddie!" Stella hissed impatiently. "Didn't you hear what she said?"

Edward stopped speaking abruptly. "I don't understand."

"I said that I am not with child, Edward."

He looked dumbstruck. The loss of composure only made him look older and more ridiculous to her.

Stella had a much faster recovery time. Hand on

hip, she walked over to them. "Oh, I get it, hon. You figured you could trap Edward into marrying you by making him think you were having a baby."

"No, dear, I'm afraid you don't *get* it at all," Angie said. "At the time, I believed I *was* having a baby. I was quite devastated when I found out that I had been wrong. However, I do admit that at the time I wasn't seeing or thinking clearly about anything."

"The important thing, my love, is that throughout our separation I have never stopped thinking about you. And now that dear Stella is well and back on her feet, you and I are free to marry."

"I can't do that, Edward. I'm . . ." Angie was about to tell him she was already married, but she was enjoying watching him squirm too much to put him out of his misery. Revenge was sweet.

Yet he had come to do right by her; she shouldn't consider revenge—even though she didn't believe his explanation for a moment. Why did he have to lie to her? Why didn't he just admit that he had deserted her when he thought she was carrying his baby!

Still, he had come back to do the right thing. Her father had often said that forgiveness was one of the hardest qualities for a human being to exercise, but when given sincerely, it represented a great growth of character. This situation called for her to practice forgiveness and not seek the temptation of revenge.

"It's too late, Edward."

"Nonsense. I shall have to apply my persuasive powers to convince you differently, my love." His air of cockiness was difficult to bear, but she told herself she must concentrate on her character growth.

For the next hour she did just that, putting aside

her previous bitterness toward Edward. By the end of the hour Angie had convinced herself that his intentions were sincere, because there was no other reason why he would have followed her to Colorado.

Just as they sat down to eat lunch, the sky clouded and it began to rain. The storm developed into a full-scale torrent, and unable to turn them out in the downpour, Angie extended an invitation to stay for dinner.

By the time the dinner hour approached, the storm had moved to a distant rumble in the higher elevations. Giff still had not joined them, so Angie asked Middy to delay dinner until he arrived. She needed to talk to Giff before introducing him to the couple.

"Stella, why don't you entertain us with a song," Edward suggested. "I am sure Angeleen would be happy to accompany you on the piano."

"Of course, I would love to."

"Well, if you insist," Stella said, clearly pleased.

As Stella rummaged through the sheets of music, Angie said apologetically, "It's not like Giff to keep dinner waiting. He's very considerate."

"I would say you are the considerate one, Angeleen, for being so tolerant of a mere hired hand."

"Giff is much more than just a hired hand, Edward."

She couldn't have asked for a more ideal lead-in to tell him she was married to Giff. "Giff is . . ." The words lodged in her throat when she glanced over and saw Giff standing in the doorway of the parlor. From his expression, she knew he had overheard Edward's pretentious remark. "Oh, here he is now! Come in, Giff," she said, jumping to her feet.

"Sorry I'm late. Storm held me up."

She could tell by the set of his shoulders that he

was angry. "Stella and Edward, this is Peter Gifford, the foreman of the Roundhouse." She smiled nervously. "Miss Crawford and Mr. Emory are joining us for dinner, Giff."

"How do you do, Giff," Stella said. Her eyes were gleaming with interest as they swept him from head to toe. "You don't mind my informality, do you?"

"We don't stand on airs around here, Miss Crawford."

"Oh, you must call me Stella."

Giff turned a cold-eyed glare on Edward. "Edward Emory?"

"Yes. How do you do," Edward replied, just as icily.

Neither man offered his hand; they eyed each other like two rutting bulls about to clash over the same heifer. Angie felt uncomfortably like that cow. She stepped between the two men before they could spear each other to death with their pointed glares. "Sit down, Giff. Stella has consented to sing for us before dinner."

"You could say I'm singing for my supper," Stella tittered, batting her lashes outrageously at him.

Angie seated herself on the piano bench. When Edward sat down beside her, Giff walked over and poured himself a drink from a crystal decanter.

"Fellow makes himself right at home, doesn't he?" Edward said with disdain. Despite a mild effort to speak softly, the remark had to have carried to Giff's ears.

"Edward, this *is* his home. Giff was raised on the Roundhouse the same as I."

Remember your character growth, she reminded herself as she pounded out an attention-getting chord on the piano. Flipping over the cover page of the music sheet, she began to play the strains of

"Silver Threads Among the Gold." Most apropos—
she had begun growing older by the minute.

True to form, Stella managed to hit enough sour
notes to make the hair stand up on Angie's nape.
Instead of calming people's tempers, she was certain Stella's singing was aggravating the tension.
Angie couldn't help smiling when she glanced at
Giff, who looked like he was ready to bolt from the
room.

As Stella continued the song, Angie saw Middy
in the doorway waiting to announce dinner. Knowing the woman's proclivity toward outspoken can-
didness, Angie felt a rising panic. *Don't you dare say
what you're thinking, Middy McNamara!* she warned
in a silent command.

"Superb, dear Stella! Superb!" Edward exclaimed when the song ended. "Do sing another
song for us."

"Dinner's ready," Middy announced at the doorway. "And the food ain't gettin' any warmer waitin'."

"Thank you, Middy." Angie was relieved that
her comment focused on food and not on the quality of the singing. Rising, she said, "Shall we dine?"

"I declare, Angeleen, your hired help is the most
insolent I have ever encountered."

"Edward, please. Middy is a beloved member of
this household. She practically raised me."

"Then it's remarkable you fared as well as you
have."

"Take my advice, Emory. You'd be a fool to
make an enemy of Middy," Giff warned.

Edward gave him a long, contemptuous look.
"Your advice, Mr. Gifford? I am sure your advice
is better directed toward the collection of cows."

"Since you've raised the issue of livestock,
Emory, and appear to be the expert, have you ever

wondered why there are more horses' asses in the world than there are horses?"

Stella broke into loud laughter.

Edward took Angie's arm. "I can't believe how you continue to permit such insolence from your domestics, Angeleen."

"I think that was meant for you, Eddie," Stella said.

Ignoring Stella, he said to Angie, "You must speak up, Angeleen, or these servants will continue to take advantage of your sweet and loving nature."

"Like you did, Emory?" Giff asked, passing them on his way to the dining room.

Angie had had unpleasant meals before, but nothing compared to the one she was suffering through at the moment. Edward carried on an endless flow of inane conversation while Giff sat silently at the end of the table glowering at her throughout the meal. Oblivious to it all, Stella simply gobbled down food as quickly as she could raise it to her mouth.

"How long are you planning on remaining in the Denver area, Edward?" Angie asked during a temporary lull.

"That will be entirely up to you, my dear Angeleen," Edward said. "I intend to remain until I can convince you of my sincerity."

She stole a glance at Giff. If possible, his glower had deepened and darkened.

"Edward, we've already discussed this. I forgive you. So there is nothing more to detain your departure in the morning."

"That's what you think."

The curt retort had come from Giff. Startled, they all turned their heads and looked at him.

"A mud slide's closed the road—at least to carriages. That's what held me up. A horse and rider can skirt it, but until we clean up the mess, you can't get a buggy or buckboard past it."

"Oh no, how long will that take?" Angie asked.

"A couple days."

"Well, my dear, it appears that we'll have to prevail upon your hospitality for the night. You see, my beloved, those are not raindrops falling from the heavens. Divine fate has wept tears of joy to intervene in my behalf," Edward said.

Angie smiled weakly. "So it seems you will be remaining after all, Edward. I hope you came prepared for this unexpected turn of events."

"My dear, I came prepared to remain forever," Edward said dramatically. "Nothing will deter me from my goal of making up for the heartbreak I've caused you. I can't tell you how it wounds me to think of the distress I've brought to that precious heart of yours."

He suddenly leaned forward and lightly brushed a speck off her mouth with the tip of his napkin. "Away, thou errant crumb, for those luscious lips are mine alone to rest upon."

Giff shoved back his chair. Shaking his head, he looked at Angie. "Either you tell this asshole the truth, or I will."

Throwing down his napkin, he left the room.

Chapter 16

◈◈◈

Giff settled down into the hot tub of water, then took a swallow from the whiskey bottle. Setting it down beside the tub, he leaned back, closed his eyes, and settled his Stetson over his face.

He had to get a hold on himself. Until today, he hadn't tried to visualize the man Angie had given herself to. From the time they came back from St. Louis, he had lived with the fear that she was still in love with Edward Emory. Now, having met the man, he couldn't believe she had been addle-brained enough to let him seduce her. The thought of Angie—his Angel—in bed with that man . . . He shoved up his Stetson, reached for the bottle, and took another swig.

How could she have done it? Angie had always had a good head on her shoulders and her feet on the ground. Sure, she was confused right now about what she wanted in life. But that was because she was fighting her own natural instincts, and when a person did that, it was goldarn easy to get your thinking messed up. *But Edward Emory!* He reached again for the whiskey bottle.

175

The door slammed and Angie called out, "Giff, where are you?"

Leaning back, he covered his face again with his Stetson.

Angie barged into the bathroom. "I want to talk to you."

Giff lifted his hat and squinted up at her. "Do you mind? I'm taking a bath."

She snorted in contempt. "In whiskey, no doubt."

He responded by raising the bottle to his mouth and taking another swallow. "Shouldn't you get back to your guests before they steal everything that isn't nailed down?" Leaning back, he closed his eyes.

"Oh, you're drunk! There's no sense in trying to talk to you." She marched out of the room.

"I am not drunk." He stumbled out of the tub, stubbing his toe in the process. Wrapping a towel around his waist, he hopped after her, dripping water. "What do you want?"

Angie stopped and spun around, her blue eyes blazing with fury. "I came to tell you your conduct tonight was reprehensible, Peter Gifford. Edward was only being sociable, and you were nasty and vindictive. You had no right to insult poor Edward the way you did."

"Poor Edward?" he shouted, so loud she clamped her hands over her ears. "Is he the same *poor Edward* who ran out on you when he thought you were carrying his kid?"

"Well, thank you for that! Couldn't you have shouted a little louder? Someone in Denver might have missed hearing it."

"I'll do more than shout if that slimy bastard touches you again."

"At least he came back to do right by me."

"Hah!" he said, shoving his Stetson to the top of

his forehead. "If the bastard wanted to do right by you, he'd have kept his hands off you to begin with. Good God, Angie, he's old enough to be your father."

"It's my choice to make, not yours. What difference should that make to you?"

"I'll tell you what difference it makes! From the time you grew up, I didn't touch you, lady. I didn't put a finger on you no matter how many times I wanted to, because I thought I was too *old* for you. That I'd be making a fool of myself because you'd prefer a younger, good-looking fellow and not some broken-down old cowpoke like me. You sure fooled me, lady. The first thing you did when you were on your own was get yourself messed up with some lecher old enough to be your father. And if that's not bad enough, he's the worst boot-licker I've ever met."

She thrust her chin up defiantly. "I wouldn't expect you to appreciate a man with Edward's sensitivities and delicate tastes."

"Delicate tastes? What a crock of crap! Do you think that redhead's traveling with him to soothe Grandpa's *delicate tastes*?"

"If you're through with your vulgar ranting and childish insults, Peter Gifford, I'll return to my guests."

"Guests—that's another joke. You can't even recognize a deadbeat when you see one. It's a damn shame your father isn't alive: the Chief wouldn't have let the son of a bitch through the door."

"Keep my father's name out of this. I don't need you to remind me he's gone—any more than I need you to take his place. I've had my fill of you telling me what I can do and what I can't! You're not my father, Giff, so you can get that fool notion out of your head." She spun around to leave.

He grabbed her arm and pulled her back. "That's

right; I'm not your father. And I'm not your *brother* either. So you can get *that* fool notion out of *your* head. *I'm your husband!*"

He pulled her into his arms and crushed her against his chest. "All promises are off, Angie. From now on, I start acting like one."

She could feel the contained power and anger in his hands, and the hardness in the lips that covered hers with a bruising kiss, as punishing as it was angry. Blood pounded in her temples as shock yielded to fury, and she struggled to free herself from the fiery possession.

Breathless and choking, she broke away and delivered a stinging slap to his face. "How dare you! And you presume to judge another man's treatment of me! Don't ever dare to do that again, Giff. Whatever privilege you think you are entitled to as my husband does not include humiliation and abuse."

She saw a flicker of contrition in his eyes, but they still glowered with anger. If he felt any shame for his action, he covered it up with bravado.

"I mean it, Angie. Tell your lover that if I see him put one finger on you, I'll grind that smirking face of his into the dust."

"I don't understand what's gotten into you, Giff. Maybe you think you're right, or that I deserved to be treated like this. If so, you've had your revenge. But if you intend to remain on this ranch, you better not threaten me or any guest of mine again. Don't think for a moment that my sisters won't back me up on this if I tell them how you've just treated me like I'm a whore."

"Aren't you being a little overdramatic, Angie?" he lashed out. "All I did was kiss you."

"A kiss intended to humiliate and punish me. But you only humiliated yourself, Giff." She turned and strode out of the house.

*　　*　　*

Being angry with Giff was misery. She wanted to talk to him about their quarrel and hoped, since he did not trust her alone with Edward, that he would return to the house that night. It was the one time she wished he would, because after she retired, Edward knocked on her bedroom door with the intention of spending the night with her. Only her threat to call for Giff's help discouraged his amorous intentions, but just thinking about Edward's nerve made her mad. She would never admit it to Giff, but the sooner Edward and Stella were gone, the happier she'd be.

Edward and Stella had not arisen when she got up and dressed in the morning, so she hurried over to Giff's house and found it deserted.

The promise of a beautiful day lifted her bad spirits. Despite the early hour, bright sunlight offered the assurance of another hot day. Suspecting where she'd find Giff, Angie saddled Calico and headed south on the road toward Denver; there was only one spot she knew of where a slide could block the road.

Her suspicions proved true and she reined up a short time later when she saw Giff and the Bean brothers digging at the rock and mud that blocked the passage.

All three men had discarded their shirts, and perspiration coated their arms and chests like a second skin.

Giff stopped and leaned on his shovel when he saw her.

"How's it going?" she asked.

"It'll take a couple days to get the road open. Takes time to move all this mud."

"You don't have to try to do it all in one day."

"The sooner, the better. It's not as bad as it

looked last night. Besides, I'd hate to delay your guests' departure. What are they up to this morning?"

"Actually, they're not up at all. They were still in bed when I left."

"That figures."

"It is a little early, Giff. After all, they are city dwellers."

"I see you're still making excuses for them."

"Not everyone gets up at the crack of dawn the way you do. You have to make allowances for them." She looked at him hopefully. "Giff, please, let's not argue again. I'm miserable when we're on the outs."

"So am I, Angel. I'm sorry. Not for what I said about Emory, but I'm sorry about the kiss."

"Well, I kind of overreacted myself." She grinned at him. "You sure looked silly last night standing there dripping wet wearing only a towel and your Stetson."

"It could have been worse, Angel: I might have been wearing only my Stetson."

"I was hoping, since Edward and Stella are unable to leave, you would give them a tour of the ranch. It would be something to keep them occupied."

"What do you need me for? You know the ranch as well as I do."

"I would just prefer if you'd accompany us. Do you think the boys can handle this without your help?"

"Reckon they could, but three of us can get the job done faster. And I'm happier not being around Emory."

"Oh, all right. Forget I asked," she said, disappointed. "I better get back to the house." She wheeled Calico to leave.

Giff grabbed the halter. "Hold up, Angel. Give

me a couple minutes and I'll ride back with you."

"Thanks, Giff," she said, relieved.

Angie watched him as he walked back to String and Bean. He did everything with such an easy motion. Riding. Walking. Unlike the awkward gait of many cowboys, who were more used to being on horseback than afoot, Giff had an easy, long-legged stride. After a couple minutes of conversation with the boys, he grabbed his shirt and mounted his gelding.

As they rode back to the homestead, Giff glanced askance at her. "You figure those friends of yours can sit a saddle well enough to show them the spread?"

"I never thought about that. You may be right; we might have to take the buckboard."

He veered off the road and headed for a nearby waterfall, one of many that fed the stream that wove through the ranch. "Hold these for me," he said, handing her his shirt and Stetson.

Angie waited on the bank as he rode under the waterfall, the cascade of water pouring over rider and horse. He came back dripping wet, shaking the water out of his wheat-colored hair. Slicking it back with his hands, he slapped his Stetson back on his head.

"Feels good to get rid of that sweat."

"You could have used the shower at the ranch." She handed him his shirt.

"This way's much faster." Grinning, he slipped on the shirt. "Bit colder, that's all. Have you forgotten how you used to like it?"

"I've outgrown showering under waterfalls, Giff."

"That's a shame," he said. "It's still as much fun as it used to be."

When they rode up to the house, Middy came outside to meet them. "Hey, Giff, where'd you haul the trash I lugged down from the attic, that I had piled up in the back hallway? I have more to add to it."

"What trash, Middy?" Giff asked.

"Oh, there was an empty chest, some rusty old tools, and that cheap picture the Chief won at that carnival years ago."

Giff shook his head. "I didn't touch it. I doubt the boys did, either. They never remove anything from the house without asking."

"Maybe Beth had them do it. Sure glad it's out of the way. But I've got more to go now."

"Good morning, Angeleen," Edward called out, stepping outside. He ignored Giff completely. "My goodness, you're up early this morning."

Angie dismounted. "Good morning, Edward. We've been checking on the road. The boys have started shoving the debris over the side. They should have the road open in a day or two."

Much to Angie's chagrin, Middy went back inside and Giff took Calico's reins and rode on down to the barn, leaving her alone with Edward. He followed her into the house, and once inside, pulled her into his arms. "How I've missed you, my love."

When he tried to kiss her, Angie turned her head so the kiss fell on her cheek. Shoving him away, she said angrily, "Edward, I have made my position clear. I do not love you and I insist you stop trying to force your affection on me."

"Love doesn't die that swiftly, my love."

"You'd be surprised how swiftly it dies, Edward. Especially when one is alone and faced with a crisis."

"You're still angry with me because I left you in St. Louis. I beseech you, my love, to forgive me for that dastardly deed. I explained to you that I was concerned with Stella's welfare at the time."

"I am not angry with you, Edward. In fact, your

departure kept me from making a horrendous mistake. And please believe me, I am not in love with you either."

"It's that cowboy, isn't it? I've seen how he looks at you. Surely he couldn't usurp my place in your heart."

The opportunity was too good to let it slip past. "Well, he has."

Edward snorted derisively. "Do you believe for a moment I will surrender you to the vulgar pawing of that cretin, my dear Angeleen?"

She arched a brow. "I really don't think you have anything to say about it, Edward."

Angie hung her hat on the rack. Glancing in the mirror, she fluffed up her hair, then turned back to him, smiling and composed. "Have you eaten, Edward?"

"Yes. Stella and I ate while you were gone."

"Where is Stella?"

"She felt indisposed and has taken to her bed."

"What a shame. I had hoped to show you the ranch today."

He smiled. "There is no reason to change your plans. You and I can still do so."

"We couldn't think of leaving poor Stella alone if she's feeling indisposed."

"I'm sure it's nothing serious, Angeleen. The woman takes to her bed more often than a newborn babe."

"Why, Edward, how ungallant of you," she said, amused. "We can postpone the ride until tomorrow. Besides, I am sure Giff would prefer to get back and help the men."

"What difference can it possibly make to him?"

"Why, he would be coming with us, of course." She took a brief moment to enjoy his displeasure. "I'm hungry. I think I'll have a bite in the kitchen. Would you care to join me, Edward?"

"Good Lord, in the kitchen! With all those offending cooking odors and such? I think not, my dear. I'll take the opportunity to check on dear Stella."

The ends of her mouth curved into a faint smile. "That's an excellent idea, Edward. Do take the opportunity to check on dear Stella."

Giff was straddling a chair when she entered the kitchen. "Middy, is there a piece of that coffee cake left that I smelled baking this morning?"

"Yeah, I managed to save you and Giff a piece before that redheaded scavenger could sink her teeth into it."

Angie sat down at the table, and Middy placed a plate in front of her. "Better eat this fast afore she sniffs it out and comes in to peck at the crumbs."

Angie winked at Giff. "I have noticed how much Miss Crawford does enjoy food. It must be your good cooking, Middy. But I guess I'm safe; she's ill and has gone back to bed. By the way, Giff, that means we won't be taking that tour of the ranch today."

"Ain't no surprise to me that she's ill," Middy grumbled. "I ain't never seen a woman eat as much as her."

"Middy McNamara! Aren't you the one who's always complaining that we don't eat enough around here?"

"Well, it's true. You and your sisters don't eat enough to keep a bird nourished. But if that Miz Crawford stays around here much longer, there ain't gonna be enough slop to feed the hogs."

Angie glanced at Giff. His expression was inscrutable. Whatever he was thinking, he obviously intended to keep it to himself. They made eye contact for a few seconds, then he raised the mug to his mouth.

Angie stared at his free hand, draped casually

over the back of the chair. The sleeve of his shirt was rolled up to his elbow. Her gaze moved down his muscular arm, bare except for the light, silky hair barely discernible against his bronzed forearm. Giff had nice hands, too: tanned and long-fingered, the nails always clean and clipped short.

Last night during their argument, she had found the strength contained in those hands and arms frightening; today she found it fascinating. Recalling the night he massaged her, she thought of the strength in his hands, the warmth of them . . . the feel of them on her flesh. She blushed, and glanced up guiltily to discover him staring at her. Good God! Was he reading her mind again? He always could.

Giff stood up, turned the chair around, and shoved it back under the table. "Well, as long as the plan's been changed, I might as well get back and give the boys a hand clearing that road." He walked over to her and bent his head down. "Think about me while I'm gone, Angel."

Dammit! The man was uncanny. He had read her mind. She had no defense against him!

"Matter of fact, I was just thinking that I should be riding out and giving you fellas a hand."

He shoved his Stetson to his forehead and put his hands on his hips. "Is that right? What about your houseguests?"

"What about them? I have prior responsibilities, don't I?" She thrust up her chin spunkily. "Or are you reneging on our arrangement?"

"What arrangement?"

"I thought you hired me as a hand on this ranch."

Chuckling, he said, "Oh, *that* arrangement! I thought you were referring to the other one."

"What other one?"

"Our marriage. You've been warned, lady, I'm

definitely reneging on those arrangements."

She motioned toward Middy, whose back was turned to them. "This is not the place to discuss it, Giff," she muttered through gritted teeth. "I'll get my hat."

"What time will you be back for dinner?" Middy asked, following them out to the hitching post.

"About six," Giff said. He swung up on his gelding.

Angie mounted Calico, and side by side, they rode away.

"Hope I can stomach another meal with your friend Edward, because from what Middy said, sounds like I'll have my hands full just wrestling a bone from the redhead."

"Or wrestling with the redhead," Angie said. "I noticed she had her eye on you, Giff."

"Not a chance, babe. My tastes run strictly toward gals with dark hair and blue eyes."

She tried to conceal her pleasure. "What makes you think there might not be dark hair under all that red dye?"

"I never thought about that. Could be worth checking out after all." He goaded his horse to a gallop.

"Let's take him, Calico." In a burst of speed, Angie spurted past him.

They raced to the site of the mud slide.

Chapter 17

～⌒◯◯⌒～

With faces and clothing coated with mud, the four people toiled throughout the afternoon in the slippery muck. Other than simply shoving the huge mound of mud over the side, there was nothing much more that could be done to remove the obstruction that had blocked the road. Less than half of the pile remained, but the road was still impassable.

Were the mudslide not preventing Edward and Stella from departing, the task could have been done at a more leisurely pace; but both Angie and Giff, in an unspoken alliance, were determined to get rid of the couple as soon as possible.

"We're jest movin' this pile of dirt from one spot to another," Red grumbled, wiping his brow.

"Gotta get the road open, don't we?" String declared. "Ain't much more we can do with it. Whatta you think we should do—try packin' it back where it come from?"

"I'm a wrangler, not a goldurn ditch digger," Red declared, tossing another shovelful of mud over the side.

"Quit yer grumblin', Red. You don't hear Miz Angie complainin', do yuh?"

Listening to the brothers' eternal spatting, Giff leaned on his shovel and winked at Angie. "You getting tired, Miz Angie?"

"No, but I think there's more mud on me than there is on the road. I'll probably have to burn these clothes when I'm finished."

"You look durn cute, Miz Angie, all that mud on you and all," he teased.

"And you must be durn crazy, Mr. Giff!" She shook her head in disgust. "To think I once thought mud fights were fun!"

As she tossed another shovelful over the side, her foot slipped in the mud. "Giff!" she cried out as she began to fall backwards.

At the same time she reached out in desperation and grasped his shirtfront, Giff pulled her into his arms, but too late to stop her fall. Together they tumbled over the side into the pile of muck. After sliding several feet, they came to a stop with Angie flattened beneath him.

"Angel, are you hurt?" he asked worriedly.

"No." She started laughing. "But you should see yourself. You're covered with mud."

Giff joined her laughter, his wide smile cutting a white swath across his mud-splattered face. "I can't look any worse than you."

"You two okay?" String called from above, he and Red peering cautiously down at them.

"Yeah, we're fine," Giff yelled back. His face settled into a crooked grin as he stared at her. Reaching out a muddy finger, he brushed aside a sodden strand of hair hanging over her eye.

Angie looked into his eyes, more conscious of the feel of him on her than the murk she lay in.

"Giff, get off me. I'd like to get up." He didn't budge, but continued to stare at her. "Giff, I said get off me."

His gaze had turned to naked passion, and she

blushed under his intense stare. Mesmerized, she watched the slow descent of his head, closing her eyes when he covered her mouth with his own.

She parted her lips under the warm pressure and he slid his tongue past her lips. Unlike last night's bruising kiss, this one was slow and seductive. The tantalizing sweeps of his tongue thrilled, instead of burning, causing a delightful warmth to radiate from her loins and creep throughout her body with a sensation so sweet that she lost awareness of all but the exquisite pleasure building within her. It took her several seconds to realize the kiss had ended, because her body was still reacting to it.

Opening her eyes, she found his unwavering gaze on her face. Forcing a quivering smile, she asked, "Why did you kiss me, Giff? String and Red aren't watching."

"Because I wanted to," he replied in a husky murmur.

She sucked in a breath, unable to think of a response.

"Let me up, Giff." She shoved feebly at his chest.

When he shifted to a sitting position, she crawled away on hands and knees. Once at the top, she stood up, shook off the mud clinging to her arms and hands, then glanced down at him.

He was sitting in the same spot, staring up at her.

Angie was more confused than ever. She was ashamed to admit how exciting Giff's kiss had been—but her insides still churned from it. She needed to get away, to clear her head.

Angie reined in when she reached the swimming hole. "I can finally get rid of this mud, Calico," she said, dismounting.

Fully clothed, Angie waded to the waterfall. Lifting her face, she let the cool water pour down on her as she continued to wrestle with her thoughts.

Could Giff be right? Even if she didn't love him, could they share a bed and make love? If today was any indication, it wouldn't be too difficult. And it certainly would put an end to all the existing problems. They could start living as husband and wife the way Giff wanted to.

As she rinsed the mud out of her hair, she thought of his words: *all promises were off.* He'd as much as declared that he intended to take her to bed. The thought of it set her heart hammering in her chest. Was she really ready for that? They'd have to sit down and have a long talk before she'd consider such an arrangement.

Free of the grime, Angie waded out of the water, and after wringing out her hair, she shoved it behind her ears and put on her Stetson.

"That's what I'll do, Calico," she murmured, swinging into the saddle. "Tomorrow, as soon as I get rid of Edward and Stella, I'll sit down and have a long talk with Giff."

Angie rode away from the swimming hole, her spirits as refreshed as her recently cleansed body.

As soon as she disappeared, Giff stepped out of the trees and waded into the cool water. It helped to soothe the ache in his loins. As he had watched her bathing, it had taken every ounce of his self-control not to approach and make love to her.

If only they'd been alone. If only they hadn't been lying in a mud pile. If only String and Red hadn't been due to come down the road at any minute. If only that damn Emory weren't at the house. If he had any mettle, he'd follow her home and finish what had begun on that hillside. If! If! If!

One thing was for certain: the kiss they had shared. There wasn't one nuance about Angie that he didn't recognize, and she'd no longer be able to deny that his kiss and touch excited her.

But as much as he wanted to, he wouldn't press the issue tonight. He'd let her think some more about that kiss. Then tomorrow, after Emory was gone, there'd be just the two of them.

He lifted his face to the cascading water. *After tomorrow night, there'd be no more ifs!*

After successfully avoiding the couple for most of the day, Angie could not avoid joining them in the evening. Dinner was an uncomfortable repeat of the previous night: forced conversation, Edward fawning over her, Giff glowering at the end of the table, and Stella ignoring them all to gorge uninterruptedly.

"We'll have the road open by midday, Emory; that will allow you plenty of time to return to Denver tomorrow," Giff said pointedly.

Since it was the only time he'd spoken directly to Edward throughout the meal, the remark caught Angie by as much surprise as it did Edward.

"That's most enlightening news, Gifford, but Stella and I have no intention of leaving tomorrow. Angeleen has offered us a tour of the ranch."

"I don't think that will be necessary now that the road will be open."

"Really!" Edward regarded Giff with a look as disdainful as the tone in his voice. "My good fellow, your opinion on the matter is neither sought nor a consideration."

In the hope of warding off an explosion, Angie literally jumped to her feet. "I'll have Middy serve our coffee in the parlor."

"Tell her to bring some more of those little sugar cookies if she has some," Stella said.

"For heaven's sake, Stella, you just ate a large slice of pie," Edward lashed out, taking his frustration with Giff out on the startled woman.

As they entered the parlor, Angie slowed her step to allow Giff to catch up with her. "You promised no trouble, Giff," she whispered.

"No wonder Stella gets ill—Emory's a real stomach turner."

"Remember your promise," she warned. As the others entered, she asked, "Perhaps some cards?"

"I would love to hear you play again, my dear Angeleen. I had no idea how talented you are."

Willing to do whatever she could to soothe the tension in the room, Angie sat down at the piano and began to play a pleasant Beethoven sonata in the hope of calming some of the taut nerves. After all, according to Congreve, "Music has charms to sooth a savage breast." She glanced at Giff's fuming figure leaning against a nearby wall, arms folded across that savage breast, looking ready to explode. In a silent plea her gaze met the menacing scowl in his blue eyes. *Please, Giff, no trouble tonight.*

Giff knew what was on Angie's mind. If he was going to keep his word to her, he had to get away for a few minutes for some fresh air. Slipping out of the room, he went onto the portico.

He could use a smoke and wished he had the makings with him. However, the stillness of the night and the warm breeze ruffling his hair had a calming effect on him.

For Angie's sake, he would hold his temper and tongue one more day, and then he'd be rid of them. Preparing to go back inside, he drew another deep breath.

"I thought maybe you'd like some company." Stella Crawford sidled up to him out of the darkness. "Aren't you lonely out here by yourself, good-looking?" she asked, smiling up at him coquettishly. He observed that moonlight cast a much more flattering light on her than the bright glow of the indoor gaslights.

"Actually, Miss Crawford, I was just coming back inside."

Her lips curved into a pout. "Miss Crawford! That sounds so formal." She put a hand on his chest. "Do call me Stella, Giff." Her hand crept up his chest. "You feel as tight as a wound up coil, honey. You need the touch of the right woman."

"You've got that right, lady."

"I could be that woman."

"I don't think so."

"Why don't you try me and find out?"

"No thanks, Stella, but I appreciate the offer."

For a second her eyes glinted with anger, then her mouth curved into a scornful smile. "I know why you're turning me down. It's because of precious little Angeleen, isn't it? You're wasting your time, good-looking. The girl's in love with Edward; can't you see that? And Edward can be very persuasive."

Giff arched a brow. "So where does that leave you in that triangle?"

"Right at the top, honey. Stella always ends up right at the top. You can be sure of that."

He removed her hand from his chest. "You know something, Stella? You're talking to a guy who doesn't come up a loser himself. Better warn your boyfriend about that. Shall we join the others?"

Returning to the parlor, Giff saw that Emory was now seated beside Angie on the piano stool. Giff sat down, and to his further disgust, Edward began to sing a love ballad to her. He couldn't believe how a man could continually make such a complete ass of himself.

"Thank God," he mumbled when the song finally ended.

"Bravo, Edward! Bravo!" Stella exclaimed, applauding. "And so romantic. You've never been in better voice."

"Yes, Edward, that was very nice," Angeleen said, darting an apologetic glance in Giff's direction.

"Thank you, my dear Angeleen, and I meant every word of the song for you." He leaned forward and it appeared he intended to kiss her.

Giff bolted to his feet. In seconds he covered the distance to the piano, clamped a hand on the neck of Edward's jacket, and yanked him off the stool. The startled and quivering man could only stumble along beside him as Giff forced him over to a chair.

"Sit *here!*"

"Why . . . why . . . of all the nerve," Edward stuttered. "Your conduct, sir, is uncivilized."

"Sorry, old man," Giff said cordially. "You were blocking my view of Angie. And I don't like anything or anyone getting between me and my wife."

Stella started to choke on the piece of chocolate candy she had just popped into her mouth. Giff walked over and slapped her on the back, while Edward stared in shock at Angie.

Smiling, Giff returned to his seat and sat down. "Do continue, my dear Angeleen."

Angie glared at him, then proceeded to pound out a Chopin polonaise.

He had made his point without throwing a punch, and rendered Emory speechless in the process. Very pleased with himself, Giff leaned back in his chair.

Chapter 18

Angie sketched the terrain from her perch in the hayloft. The profusion of color was breathtaking. She regretted she had brought charcoal instead of her oils. Spring, as always, had rejuvenated the countryside with yellow wildflowers. Pink and white blossoms decorated the fruit trees, and birch and mountain oak added their leafy shades of green to those of the towering aspens and pines. Melting snows had created waterfalls cascading from the granite peaks. By the end of summer most would be reduced to thin trickles, but now they sparkled with rainbow hues in the sunshine as they dropped in majestic splendor into the rivers and streams below.

The hayloft also offered a safe haven from Edward. After Giff had launched his missile last night, then had the audacity to leave a short time later, the situation had grown progressively worse. If Giff had kept his mouth shut, she could have sent Edward and Stella on their way without any complications.

But Edward's vanity was inconceivable. He now believed, more than ever, that she was still in love with him! He'd even accused her of not loving Giff, but of simply marrying him to give the baby a name. True, he was right about the wedding—but there was no convincing Edward that she no longer loved *him*. Moreover, he accused her of lying about the baby, and believed she was still carrying his child. The whole ugly scene could have been avoided if only Giff had kept his temper in check and not told Edward and Stella they were married. *Is that so much to ask of a man?*

Of course, she had to place some of the blame where blame was due. She had made a real mess of the unfortunate situation by not informing them she was married the minute they showed up at the door. But she had enjoyed giving the pefidious man a taste of his own medicine.

Hearing a noise below, Angie peeked over the edge of the loft and saw that Giff had entered the barn, leading Dolly, one of the harness mares. He fired up the kiln, then removed his shirt and hung it up on a peg.

"Let's get that shoe off you, Miz Dolly," he said, and set to the task of prying a rear shoe off the horse.

Well, she had a word or two to say to him about last night. Then she thought the better of it. He certainly had borne enough of Edward's sarcasm as it was, so why should she and Giff continue to argue over Edward Emory? She wouldn't even bring up the subject of last night with Giff.

Angie was about to call a greeting down to him, but ducked back when Stella sauntered into the barn. "Good morning, good-looking."

"Hi," Giff said, glancing up with a grin.

"What are you up to?" Stella asked.

"Putting a new shoe on Dolly here before we leave this morning."

Stella laughed loudly. "Sure is an odd name for

a horse. What would you name me if I was a horse, honey?"

"Why, Miz Crawford, I could never think of you as a horse," Giff replied gallantly.

Even though you eat like one, Angie thought spitefully. *Sorry, Daddy, but after last night, I've abandoned working on my character growth.*

"Gotta say you look even better with the shirt off, honey. Guess it must be all that sweat . . . and bulging muscles. It's enough to set a poor woman's heart to fluttering."

"Now, why do I think it doesn't take much to set that heart of yours to fluttering, Miz Crawford?" Giff reached for his shirt and slipped it on.

Disgusted, Angie rolled her eyes. *Yeah, a cookie on a platter will do it.*

"Why'd you go and do that for? You've spoiled my view, honey. This is a good spot to pick up where we left off last night on the porch." She shook her finger at him girlishly. "You naughty boy, you didn't tell me you were married then."

What does Stella mean? What happened between them on the porch last night? Angie's breath knotted in her throat, the way it had done the night of the barbecue when she saw him kissing Diane Divine.

"Married or not, Miz Crawford, my answer's the same as it was last night. I'm not interested."

Good for you, Giff—that's telling the brazen hussy! Now tell her to get out of here and leave you alone!

As if she had transmitted her thoughts, Giff said, "Well, you'll have to excuse me. I'd best get back to shoeing this horse or we won't be going anywhere today."

"You're no fun, good-looking," Stella said, and sauntered out as unruffled as she had entered.

Angie was too embarrassed to let her presence be known now. She knew he would wonder why she hadn't spoken up sooner, so she remained silent.

Giff returned to scraping and fitting the shoe. Perspiration dotted his forehead and he pulled off his shirt again. Stella was right about one thing: his body was exciting to behold.

Angie reached for her pad and pencil. She had thought of sketching him like this, and realized she'd never have a better chance since he was unaware of her presence.

Her hand moved rapidly over the paper, drawing the powerful set of his shoulders, the knotted sinew of his arms. As he hammered out the iron shoe, she captured with deft strokes the ripple of his supple muscles, stretching and contracting with rhythmic flow.

When she finished, pleased with the end result, she got up and started to back away from the edge of the loft. Then she squealed involuntarily when she stumbled backwards against the wall, dropping her pad and pencil.

"Who's up there?" Giff called. "Is that you, Angie?"

"Yes." To her distress, the upper back of the right sleeve of her blouse was caught on a nail, and she tried to twist enough to reach it and release herself. Failing in the attempt, she realized she had just made it worse and now needed his help.

"Giff, will you help me for a minute?"

"What are you doing up here?" Giff asked when he climbed up.

"I've been sketching."

"In the hayloft?"

"Yes. I get a more extensive view of the terrain up here." She didn't want to admit that she'd shifted to him as a subject.

"Oh, I see. How long have you been up here?"

"A couple hours," she said casually.

"Why didn't you say something? You must have known I was right below."

"I've been busy. When I'm drawing, I shut out everything except the view I'm sketching." She sounded too defensive to make it believable.

"Is that so," he said. "Who are you hiding from up here, Angie? Me or lover boy?"

"Hiding! Don't be ridiculous, Giff. Why should I hide from either of you? I told you, I came up here to draw because of the view."

He stooped over and picked up the drawing pad she had dropped. "What's this? This doesn't look like any landscape."

"It's nothing," she said, attempting to grab the pad away from him. But the nail held her in place.

"Rein up a minute." He held the pad out of her reach and studied the drawing. "This is me." Perplexed, he looked at her. "Why did you draw me, Angie?"

"I got sidetracked when you came in and started to shoe Dolly. I've never been very good at drawing the human anatomy, so I decided to practice. Now, will you help me? I'm caught on something. I think it's a nail."

"Why didn't you say so?" He closed the distance between them and reached behind her. "So why me?" he asked as he fumbled to release her. "I'm sure your guest would have been willing to pose for you. Or don't you draw *still life*?" Amused at his own joke, he started to chuckle.

"That's very humorous, Giff." He was standing so close, she could feel the heat of his body, and the musky scent of him permeated her senses, eliciting an intoxicating awareness of him. "What's taking you so long?"

"You've really got yourself snagged up here. Let me try this." He grasped her around the waist and slid her up the wall. With one hand and the pressure of his hard thighs, he held her suspended as he worked to free her with his other hand.

His nearness, his hips pressed to hers, the scent of him, were overpowering. Her heart hammered in her chest and she feared he could feel it, too.

"You're not making this any easier," he said. "Would you mind holding on so I can use both hands?"

She trembled as she gripped his shoulders. His flesh felt hot against her fingertips. She fought a bold urge to slide her hands along the muscular span of his broad shoulders, to curve her hands and follow the slope of them into his firm, hair-roughened chest. Enmeshed in her desire, it took her a long moment to realize he had stopped what he was doing and was staring at her.

"What about it, Angie?"

"Wha . . . what?"

"The blouse. I told you, either you need to take it off, or I'll have to rip the sleeve to free you. Which do you want to do?"

"Take it off," she said.

"You want *me* to take it off you?"

She suddenly realized that her feet were on the floor again but she was still clutching his shoulders. "No. No, I can do it," she said, lowering her arms.

With trembling fingers she released the buttons of her blouse. He helped her shrug it off her shoulders and manipulate the sleeve so she could slide her arm out without tearing it. Unfortunately, the effort required more body contact than was comfortable to her already heightened awareness. Once finished, she remained looking up at him, her eyes round and liquid as his yearning gaze searched her face.

"Angel."

"Yes, Giff?"

"Angel, I . . ."

His words were choked off as he pulled her into his arms, his mouth covering hers hungrily. Ever since yesterday's indelible kiss, she had coveted this moment, and she parted her lips eagerly under the firm pressure. His arms tightened, crushing her breasts against his chest, the warmth of his flesh fueling her rising passion. This sweet assault was too exquisite to resist—her body pulsed with shocks of glorious sensation energized by her awakened sexuality.

"Angel. Oh God, Angel!" The murmur was more of a plea than a whisper as he covered her cheeks and eyes with quick kisses before returning to claim her lips.

This time his kiss was demanding, and she slid her arms around his neck, responding with the urgency of her own aroused hunger. She breathed his name into his mouth, arching against him, seeking closer, greater, contact.

The mere touch of his hand sent a flood tide of passion swirling through her, sweeping away any resistance. It was strange to have Giff do these things to her, unreal to be in his arms, her body throbbing for his kiss—his touch. But there was nothing imaginary about the erotic sensations his kisses and touch created. Heat swirled inside her head, blinding her vision, robbing her breath. All reason slipped away in the exquisite siege on her senses.

Mouth to mouth, they sank into the straw. His probing tongue elicited fluttering moans of pleasure from her.

The sensual sound drove him wild. Slipping his arms under her, he crushed her tightly against him. He couldn't get enough of the feel of her. Sweeping his hands down her spine, he cupped the firm cheeks of her derriere.

"Giff, we have to talk," she whispered in a throaty plea.

"Later, Angel," he murmured.

Too long, he had fought to resist this inevitable moment. He knew he should slow down, but the hard-fought battle had erupted into a total rout. He was out of control.

Raising his head, he managed to release the six tiny pearl buttons on her camisole without ripping any of them off. Shoving aside the folds of the garment, he reveled in the sight of her naked breasts. Hot blood pounded at his temples. God, they were beautiful! Lowering his head, he closed his mouth moistly over one of the taut crests.

Pushing up her skirt, he slid his hand along the inside of her thigh. He covered her throbbing core and felt the heat of her through her thin drawers. Slipping his fingers into the garment, he began to massage her.

"Oh, sweet heaven, Giff!" She clutched at him, her nails biting into the corded muscle of his shoulders.

He tore his mouth away from her breasts to cover her lips with his own, and drove his tongue into the chamber of her mouth. Under the escalating demand of his own passion, the rhythm of his hand quickened.

She began to writhe beneath him, and when he felt her tremors, he knew his own climax was imminent. He reached for the top of her drawers to pull them down—and froze at the sound of a shout.

"Angeleen!" It was Edward Emory.

Giff raised his head. *Son of a bitch!*

Angie heard it too. She opened her eyes and stared in wide-eyed shock at Giff. He brought a finger to his lips, warning her to silence.

"Angeleen!" The shout was repeated, this time directly below them.

"I see the cowboy's gone, too," Stella said. "He was here a short while ago. Looks like he left in a hurry."

"Where in the world can she be?" Edward complained, irritated.

"Try the loft." Stella snorted in derision. "Maybe they decided to have a roll in the hay, Eddie."

"Oh, don't be so crude, Stella. The girl is naive, but she isn't *that* unrefined."

"Yeah, well, that cowboy's a lot of man. She must have figured out by now how to keep him happy."

Their voices began to fade as they moved out of the barn. "The cretin obviously married her for her money."

"So what? Ain't that what you had in mind too?"

"Let me up, Giff," Angie said after a moment.

It was plain that any thought of lovemaking was now the furthest thing from her mind. He shifted off her, and she sat up. Clutching the sides of her camisole together, she began self-consciously to button it.

Giff stood up and went over to release her blouse. By the time he returned, she was on her feet and trying to restore some order to her disheveled hair. He held out the blouse. "Here, no damage done."

She snatched it out of his hand and quickly donned it, then began to search the straw. Seeing the sketch pad and charcoal pencil near his feet, he picked them up. "Are these what you're looking for?"

"Yes. Thank you." Without making eye contact, she took them from his hand.

"Angel, I think we should talk about this," he said gently.

"There's nothing to talk about, Giff. Just forget it happened." She passed him to leave.

"Like hell I will!" Although he was sensitive to her embarrassment, he resented her trying to dismiss the whole incident—the first major breakthrough in their relationship—as if it had never happened. Grabbing her arm, he swung her around to him. "I *want* to talk."

"I'm not ready to talk about it. This whole thing has been very humiliating to me."

His resentment flared into anger. "Humiliating! Why? How were you humiliated? Frankly, I was enjoying it, and don't try to say that you weren't, too! What happened—or almost happened—was a perfectly natural occurrence between a husband and wife."

"That may be, but we don't have a normal married relationship."

"Through no fault of mine. You're the one preventing it. But you sure as hell weren't repulsed by my kisses or my touch, so I don't like your acting like I forced myself on you."

She hadn't meant to imply he was at fault; he'd misunderstood everything she was trying to say. Edward's remark had struck a chord. Now that the passion of the moment had cooled, she felt there *had* been an element of crudity about their actions. "I'm not accusing you; I humiliated myself."

"What the hell is *humiliating* about making love with your husband? And enjoying it! Or was Emory right? Maybe you do believe that a roll in the hay is beneath your dignity—too *earthy* for your refined tastes. After all, as you reminded me a couple nights ago, I *am* just another hired hand around here."

"Now who's talking childishly, Giff? You're no more a hired hand than I am."

"Then why couldn't you admit to Emory that we're married?"

"Because I was enjoying watching him grovel," she lashed out defensively. "I thought it'd be a sweet revenge." Having admitted her motive, she was ashamed of her pettiness. She had never considered herself vindictive, but her actions had proven her wrong.

"Are you sure about that? Maybe you regret that it was me in this hayloft and not Emory."

"I swear that's not true, Giff." She felt a rising desperation. "I just feel embarrassed it happened . . . the way it happened. I thought when—and if—we ever made love . . . " She shook her head. "It was just not how I visualized it. I don't understand how it happened."

"You don't have to understand it, Angie. You just have to enjoy it."

"I see! Pleasures of the flesh! Maybe that's enough satisfaction for you, but I feel that desire without love is too impersonal—too dehumanizing. I'd like to believe we're more than rutting animals!"

She looked at his pain-glazed eyes and felt her heart constrict with anguish.

"I believe we are, Angel. But I think it's time you grew up and faced a few realities about life . . . and yourself." He strode to the ladder. "Count me out of your grand tour of the Roundhouse. I've seen it before."

She sank down in the hay and buried her head in her hands. Everything she said and did seemed to complicate her life. Giff was right about one thing: she had to grow up.

Hearing the sound of hoofbeats, she went over to the loft doors and saw Giff riding away. She had hurt him again. She hadn't meant to, but in her own self-absorption, she had hurt him again. Desolately she climbed down the ladder.

Chapter 19

Edward hurried out of the parlor as soon as Angie entered the house.

"Angeleen, where have you been?"

"Is there a problem, Edward?"

"I've been looking everywhere for you."

"Apparently not *everywhere*, Edward." She deliberately picked a piece of straw out of her hair, and smiled serenely at his appalled look. "By the way, the tour of the ranch is off. So there's nothing to keep you and Stella from leaving."

He gave her a long look as if sensing her belligerent mood. "I have a business proposition I'd like to present to you before we leave, Angeleen."

She was in no mood to talk to him. She had a lot of thinking to do involving Giff, her future, and the Roundhouse. But if giving him ten minutes now would get rid of him, she was glad to do it. "All right, Edward. Let's go into the parlor."

Once seated, Angie folded her hands on her lap and waited for him to speak. With theatrical flourish, Edward put a hand on his chest and began to pace the floor.

"Edward, since there is only me for an audience, feel free to sit down and relax."

"My dear Angeleen, ever since the events of last night, I have thought deeply about our situation. The shock of your marriage was so distressing that I admit I spoke in haste. I regret my accusations, although I find it confusing why you'd choose Gifford over me. Despite this, I believe I have reached another solution that would be advantageous to both of us."

"Get on with it, Edward. You still have a long trip back to Denver. I'd hate to see you get lost on one of these mountain roads."

Edward cleared his throat and resumed his pacing. As she watched him, he appeared more and more ridiculous to her. How could she have once believed that she loved him? He was everything Giff had accused him of being: pompous, vain, snobbish—and worthless. On top of all his other frailties, he didn't even have a sense of humor! As for his ability as a lover, Edward had never raised her passion to a smidgen of the fevered pitch that Giff's kiss could evoke from her.

"Angeleen!"

Startled, she opened her eyes. She had been so deep in her daydreaming that she hadn't been aware of closing her eyes. Looking distressed, Edward stood over her.

"Are you ill, Angeleen? You're quite flushed."

"No, I'm fine. I'm sorry, Edward, what were you saying?"

"I said that I thought it would be a wonderful idea to open a repertory, a theater for performing arts, right in Denver. Not only could we offer live performances, but we could encourage young performers to enroll—for a fee, of course."

"That's a very ambitious idea, Edward."

"I realize, of course, that we could not present operas, but we could do dramas and offer musical selections to which you could lend your pleasing talent."

Despite her dislike of Edward, the idea did have some merit. And the thought of performing on a legitimate stage without having to wear trashy red tights was appealing.

"I would think it would be quite costly."

"That is true. I would need you to make a substantial contribution to get us started."

"How much of a contribution?"

He hesitated. "Perhaps five thousand dollars," he said cautiously. When she didn't flinch, he added slyly, "Or conceivably even ten thousand."

She did have the inheritance from her grandfather MacGregor. She'd offered the money to Beth to put toward the railroad expansion, but her sister had refused to take it, insisting Angie keep it for something she'd want for herself.

Perhaps she should attempt a theatrical career again. The question was whether she dared trust Edward. His livelihood did depend on performing on the stage, and a permanent theater, instead of a riverboat, would have to be as appealing to him as it would be for her.

"I do like the idea, Edward. I'm going to think about it, and talk it over with family members to get their opinions."

His lip curled up in disdain. "I hope you don't mean your husband, my dear Angeleen."

"Of course my husband, as well as my sister Elizabeth, who is the businesswoman in the family. She's been in Washington, D.C., but should be returning in a day or two."

"I am delighted to hear your enthusiasm, dear lady." He rubbed his hands together. "I can't wait to get started on the project."

Angie stood up. "I'll contact you when I've made a decision. In the meantime, I'll ride down to see if the road is open sufficiently enough to get your carriage through. I'll be back in a quarter of an hour."

"I'll accompany you, Angeleen," Edward said agreeably.

"Do you ride, Edward?"

"No, but can't we take the buggy I drove when we arrived?"

"I suppose we can," she said unenthusiastically. Then a welcome thought crossed her mind. "As a matter of fact, Edward, bring your luggage along. I'll have Middy pack you a lunch, and you and Stella can continue on."

"Stella's not here. She decided on a walk. She was curious to see the site of the mud slide."

"Then you can pick her up there and keep right on going."

Her sudden rush of plans clearly caught him by surprise, and he had no choice but to go upstairs to get the bags. Angie hurried into the kitchen and told Middy the news.

"And good riddance it will be, I'm thinkin'," she said. "What a pair they are: him with his long nose so high in the air, 'twas a wonder he didn't trip over the crumbs the other one kept scatterin' all over the house. As though I ain't got nothin' to do but follow her around with a broom."

"They'll be gone soon."

Middy glanced askance at her. "What did Giff ride out lookin' so cross about? Are the two of you fussin' again?"

"That's none of your business, Middy McNamara."

"I swear you two have had more spats since you married up than you did the whole time you was a-growin'."

Her spirits buoyed, Angie hugged the housekeeper. "I think it's got something to do with that *man thing* men suffer from, Middy dear," she said, and headed for the door.

"Yeah, that'll do it every time," Middy said profoundly.

The remark brought Angie to a dead stop. Turning her head, she saw that Middy had started slicing bread for sandwiches. *Middy, too! Am I the only woman who doesn't understand exactly what that stupid expression means?* Then she raced out the door, headed for the barn.

After harnessing Edward's carriage, Angie put a saddle on Calico. Middy came out and put a lunch basket in the buggy as Edward loaded his and Stella's luggage.

"Where's that redhead? Hope he ain't plannin' on leavin' her behind," Middy grumbled.

"She went for a walk. Rather than waste time waiting for her to return, I'm hoping we'll meet her on the road."

"Humph!" Middy snorted. "Did you try the smokehouse? She could be in there gnawing on a ham hock."

"Middy, if Giff shows up, tell him I have something important to talk over with him," Angie whispered when Edward was prepared to leave.

"You gonna kiss and make up with the darlin'?" she asked hopefully.

Angie winked at her, then swung up into the saddle.

The idea of riding Calico was sheer inspiration. The arrangement discouraged any attempt at conversation by Edward, especially when she rode ahead of the buggy as she was doing now. Secondly, it gave her the chance to try and think of an appropriate apology for what she said to Giff this morning.

Not that she needed an excuse to dwell on the morning, for it seemed as if no matter who she was with, or what she was doing, her thoughts always slipped back to those moments in the hayloft when he had made love to her.

Maybe it was time for her to face the reality that she and Giff were man and wife. He was no stranger to her—no man knew her as well as he did. They had always loved and respected one another. Anything he did to her, be it adjusting her stirrups, scolding her for not listening to him . . . making love to her . . . was always done in loving care. What a hypocrite she must appear to him. He knew she had willingly gone to Edward's bed, but shunned his—the man who had looked after her welfare from the day she was born. No wonder her words had hurt him. She had implied *their* relationship was the sordid one! God forgive her, she had even compared them to rutting animals! She had a lot to make up to him. And if sharing his bed meant that much to him, it was time she started thinking about his needs and quit considering only her own.

Angie grinned to herself. It would still be a coin toss to decide whose bed they slept in.

Oddly, Edward's idea for a repertory was appealing to her, as well. As much as she'd like to see the last of him, it would be exciting to be part of a repertory. Perhaps on rare occasions she *would* perform on the stage—just to satisfy that unfulfilled artistic side of her.

Yes, her life was beginning to take on a rosier glow. Maybe she hadn't fouled it up as badly as she feared.

Now she couldn't wait to get rid of Edward and Stella, to find Giff and convince him she was willing to be the wife he hoped for.

As they passed the waterfall, she heard a woman's laughter coming from the swimming hole. It could only be Stella, and she veered off the road to investigate. Edward also must have heard the sound, because he didn't hesitate to follow.

Approaching the riverbank, she saw Giff's chestnut tied to a tree. A pile of his clothing was lying on the ground, next to the heap of Stella's clothes.

Angie raised her head and looked at the water. Her heart seemed to leap into her throat when she spied them in midstream. Submerged in the water up to their necks, Stella had her arms locked around Giff's neck and she was laughing up at him.

They stood up when Angie trotted into the water on Calico, but Stella didn't lower her arms.

Although relieved to see that Giff was still in jeans, Angie noticed that the one-piece undergarment clinging to Stella's curves did little to disguise her God-given endowment. Angie saw red.

"Stella thought she saw a water snake," Giff explained, grinning sheepishly.

"A water snake! This far north?" Angie snorted. "The only snake in these waters has red hair." Leaning down from the saddle, she grabbed a fistful of Stella's hair and yanked her away from Giff. "Take your hands off my husband!"

"Why, you little bitch!" Stella shouted, clutching at her head with both hands. "That hurt."

"And I'd be happy if you'd get out of the water before you poison all the fish with that red dye." Angie wheeled Calico to head back to the riverbank.

"That does it!" Stella screeched. "I think you could use a swim to cool off, dearie."

Stella lunged at her from behind, grabbing a fistful of Angie's skirt. As she started to slide, Angie jerked the reins, causing Calico to rear up on his hind legs. She tumbled into the water, landing on top of Stella. Calico trotted out of the water as Stella came up sputtering vile expletives at Angie.

"It's a shame I don't have a bar of soap to wash out that dirty mouth of yours," Angie declared. Wiping the water out of her eyes, she started to wade back to the riverbank.

"What's the matter, *dear* Angeleen—afraid of a fight?"

Angie turned around slowly. "What did you say?"

"You heard me, you skinny-ass bitch."

Giff was gaping in disbelief. Hoping to ward off any further argument, he said, "Okay, that's enough, ladies."

His words came in vain. Angie lunged at Stella and the two women began pulling each other's hair. Avoiding their elbows and hands, he finally succeeded in separating them. Then, locking an arm around Angie's waist, he lifted her out of the water. Squirming and shouting for him to set her free, Angie tried to kick free of Stella, who had a hold on her legs. Giff tried to ward off Stella with his free hand, but the redhead gave him a shove that knocked him off balance. Angie slipped away from him as all three of them went under. When he regained his footing, he saw that Stella was holding Angie's head under the water.

"Let her up," he shouted. Pushing Stella off Angie, he once again got a firm hold around Angie's waist. "I said that's enough!" he shouted angrily.

"Says who?" Stella shouted back. Snarling like a cornered she-wolf, she pounced on him and began pounding him with both fists. Forced to release Angie to ward off Stella's blows, he shoved Stella away just as Angie let go with a punch that landed on his chin instead of Stella's. As he started to fall backwards, he reached out and grabbed Angie for support, and they both went under.

Snorting with pleasure, Stella turned for shore.

Still full of fight, Angie moved to stop her, but

Giff restrained her as Stella marched dripping out of the water. Raising her arms above her head, Stella clenched her fists together like a victorious boxer, claiming victory over both of them.

Furious, Angie slapped Giff's hands aside and glared at him. "If you hadn't interfered, I'd have won."

"That's questionable."

"There's something else that's even more questionable: just what were you and that redheaded witch up to when I rode up?"

"I was on my way back to the house when I heard her screaming that there was a snake in the water."

"And you jumped in to wrestle it."

"That's right."

"I must say that was some big snake you were wrestling when I rode up. The two of you sure made a fine sight for anyone coming along to see."

"What the hell difference does it make?"

"I'm only thinking of what people would say. You're my husband, remember?"

"It's amazing how you fall back on that when it's convenient—but I noticed you had trouble remembering it when your boyfriend was slobbering all over you." He looked at her grimly. "I've had enough of this childishness, Angie. I've got better things to do with my time."

He waded back to the riverbank, pulled on his boots, then snatched up his hat and shirt from the ground. Climbing on Brick, he rode away without a backward glance.

Upon reaching the riverbank, Angie shook herself off and then mounted Calico, who was chewing docilely on a nearby patch of grass. She rode over to the buggy, where Edward had remained throughout the whole fracas.

"I want the two of you off the Roundhouse at

once. If I ever see either of you on this spread again, I'll shoot you for trespassing."

Having donned her clothes, Stella tramped up to the buggy, tossed in her soaked undergarment, then climbed into the carriage.

"I see you're still spouting off at the mouth. Trying to get rid of all that water you swallowed, sister?" she taunted.

"Ladies, let's all just put this unfortunate incident behind us," Edward said. "We must all try to get along. After all, we'll soon be business partners."

"You can forget about that," Angie declared. "I'd go back to working on that miserable riverboat again before I'd enter into any partnership with the likes of you two."

"You told me you would be willing to invest in the repertory," Edward accused. "Are you going back on your word?"

"I did *not* give my word. I said I would think about it and give you my answer later. Well, I thought about it, all right. I had plenty of time to think about it while your girlfriend was holding my head under the water trying to drown me."

With a vituperative snarl Edward turned to Stella. "See what you've done now! Are you satisfied?"

"You're just lucky you had your bodyguard, sister, or I'd have finished you off," Stella threatened.

"Shut up, Stella," Edward grumbled. "If you'd kept your hands off her husband, we wouldn't have this problem."

"What did I do except defend myself? This lying bitch is the one who started the fight."

"I haven't lied about anything," Angie declared.

"Hah!" Stella's face twisted with scorn. "What about telling Eddie you were having a baby, hoping to get him to marry you? That's the oldest game around."

"Not quite, Stella. I believe *your* game has the distinction of being the oldest profession in the world."

Stella stood up with balled fists. "You accusing me of being a whore?"

"Oh, sit down, Stella!" Edward snarled. "Haven't you done enough damage for one day?"

"Get moving," Angie ordered. "And remember what I said: don't step foot on MacKenzie land again."

She gave their horse a swat on the rump. Startled, the animal bolted forward.

Clutching the reins, Edward fell back in the seat. Stella, who had been standing, somersaulted feet over head into the backseat. Angie grinned at the sight of the woman's legs and bare buttocks thrashing wildly in the air as she tried to sit up.

She watched the carriage continue down the road with the voices of the passengers raised in argument. As the buggy careened around a curve, Stella's screech of "Watch what you're doing, you mealymouthed bastard" floated back on the warm breeze.

Chapter 20

Billy Bob woke up with a start.

Bleary-eyed, he looked around the empty cabin. Trying to collect his thoughts, he wondered how long the boys had been gone. Then he remembered booting them out the door just past dawn that morning. *Couldn't of been much more than a hour ago*, he reasoned.

As he struggled to get up, he squinted against the bright sunlight coming through a window ... the window that faced the western sky.

"Shet! Sleepin' the day away wuz a plumb waste of a day." With the time he had left before the boys got back, he'd just have to do his thinking twice as fast. Yawning, he scratched his backside and went over to the fireplace.

He automatically picked up the cold coffeepot and poured the remaining black, grimy contents into his tin cup. Then in his usual rocking gait, he made his way to the table.

As he moved around the room, the eyes of the Lady, leaning against the wall, seemed to be following him, and when he sat down, he caught them staring straight into his.

Annoyed, he drummed his fingers on the table. If only she would look away, he could get some serious thinking done.

Ever since the other night, when he and Curly rescued the Lady from Hank, she had sat smiling from her yeller frame atop the sturdy wooden chest they had toted back to the cabin.

Both things had ended up a mite busted by the luggin', but it had been worth the trouble.

He looked down at the gaping doors of the chest and frowned. If only he had something valuable to stow away. Right now the chest stood mostly empty except for a few tin dishes and those dad-blamed useless tools.

Tweaking his mustache, he raised his cup in a silent toast as he squinted back at the Lady, trying to imagine what she would look like stripped na-ked—and without that wig on her head.

Taking a swig of coffee, he grimaced, then spit it out, wiping his mouth on his sleeve. "What me and you needs, Lady, is a good stiff drink."

Leaning forward, he peered at the Lady's rounded chest. Then he got up and stood above the painting, trying to see down the front of her dress. He soon sat back dejected. First off, the boys had drunk up all the likker last night. And secondly, there weren't much use in him gettin' all worked up over no gal that wuz stuck on a piece of card-board.

Jolted by an overwhelming urge for a drink, he grabbed his hat and gun, ran out the door, climbed on his horse, and galloped away. Within a few hundred yards he reined up short, wheeled his horse around, and galloped back again. He'd for-gotten to padlock the door.

Ten minutes later, Billy Bob tied his horse to the hitching rail in front of the saloon, and strode through the swinging doors with all the determination befitting a man intending on doing some serious drinking.

But to his surprise, nobody seemed to notice him.

With clopping heels and spurs jingling, he lumbered over to the bar. Squinting, he saw that the bartender was one of the men involved in a dice game at the end of the bar.

Billy Bob steamed with indignation. Tolerating being ignored had never been his long suit, and even though he lacked the hot temper of his murderous brother Charlie, the blood of the Waldens still coursed—if somewhat idly—through his veins.

No one brushes aside Billy Bob Walden, he thought angrily as he drew his gun. He'd just show that dad-blasted Jake a thing or two. Taking careful aim at the liquor bottles on the top shelf behind Jake, he cocked his pistol and closed his eyes, flinching as he squeezed the trigger.

Click!

At the unexpected sound, his eyes popped open and he looked incredulously at his gun. "Dammit to hell," he muttered under his breath as he banged down his gun and began wrestling with his gun belt in search of bullets.

Soon frustrated with the effort, Billy Bob decided to take the swifter, more direct approach. "Hey, Jake! Git the hell down here and gimme a snort of red-eye," he shouted.

"Be right there," Jake hollered back, rolling the dice once again. Eventually finished with the game, Jake sauntered down and poured Billy Bob a drink.

About an hour passed as the two men talked and guffawed, mostly swapping stories about their conquests at the cathouse.

When Jake asked where he and his friends had come from, Billy Bob quickly changed the subject by pointing to the back wall. "Is that clock right?"

"Far as I know. Why do yuh ask?"

"Jest waitin' for the boys. They oughta be here pretty quick now."

Just then the bar doors swung open and the men were distracted by a loud female voice.

"Aw, for Pete's sake, Eddie, don't start that again!" she whined.

"Hush up, Stella. People are looking." Annoyed, her companion grabbed her arm and hurried her over to a table.

Billy Bob turned to get a closer look, and his eyes immediately bugged out when he spied the woman's huge, bouncing breasts.

"Will yuh look at that!" he whispered, exchanging raised eyebrows with Jake.

"Sure's enough to burn down the barn door, ain't they?" Jake answered under his breath.

The couple took a table within earshot, and Jake called out, "What'll yuh have, folks?"

"A bottle of wine and a shot of whiskey," the woman bellowed, flopping a large velvet bag on the table. Making herself comfortable, she crossed her legs, the slit of her long, narrow black dress opening to the knee.

Jake served the drinks, doing a double take when she promptly rearranged them, grabbing the whiskey for herself.

Looking into the mirror behind the bar, Billy Bob squinted to watch her every move.

"All right, Stella, slow down," her companion said as she belted down the whiskey and then poured wine into her empty glass. "I've had enough of your drunkenness for one day."

"Drunkenness! What do you mean? I deserve a good stiff drink after brawling with that bitch!"

Intrigued, Billy Bob put down his drink and listened closely.

"What did you expect, messing around with Gifford like that?"

Gifford? Billy Bob thought the name sounded familiar. But where in tarnation . . . It had something to do with a mouth organ. Suddenly he remembered. This woman must have been messing around with that Gifford fella he'd met at that barbecue.

"Oh, shut up about Gifford," she snapped. "He's nothing but a dumb foreman on that wretched ranch. You know he's not my type."

"*Any* man is your type, Stella." He grabbed her wine and drank it down in one gulp.

"Well, fancy that! Any chance you're getting jealous, Eddie?" she said, rolling her eyes and fluffing her hair.

Slamming down the glass, he looked at her with contempt. "The point *is*, my dear, if you had kept your hands off Gifford, we'd still have a deal for ten thousand dollars. Instead, you got us kicked off the ranch and we got nothing."

"*Me?* Listen here, you two-bit swindler. Just stop blaming someone else for your own stupid ideas. That MacKenzie bitch had you buffaloed right from the start. And you know what else? Any fool but you could tell that there wasn't no way in hell you were ever gonna get one red cent out of that stinking MacKenzie ranch!"

MacKenzie! MacKenzie ranch! Stunned, Billy Bob jolted upright and stared pop-eyed into the mirror, his body rigid with fury. How could he have wandered into the clutches of the enemy without even smelling the stench of them dad-blamed MacKenzie polecats?

He grabbed his gun and angrily moved to spin around. In his haste, his foot got caught on the bar rail and he went crashing to the floor. Undaunted, he quickly got up and stomped toward the swinging doors as fast as his wobbly legs could carry him.

Barging into the general store, Billy Bob ordered the supplies he needed to implement yet another of his brilliant schemes—hastily conceived, perhaps, but nonetheless brilliant.

"Yesiree!" he mumbled gleefully. "This time them MacKenzie varmints are gonna pay for their misdeeds."

By the time his gang rode up to the saloon, Billy Bob was waiting for them.

"Hey, boss," Hank called out. "What's all that stuff yuh got there?"

"Never mind that, smarty britches. Yuh pokes just stay settin' 'em saddles 'cause we ain't got no time fer stallin'."

He tossed up a rope, a lantern, and a box of matches to each man, then quickly unhitched his horse.

"Where we goin', boss . . . and what's this stuff fer?" Curly asked, confused. "Shet, I already got me a rope."

"Ropes kin fray and we gotta be prepared. This time there ain't nothin' gonna be thwartin' Billy Bob Walden."

Scrambling onto his horse, he yelled, "Let's go."

Billy Bob charged away with Curly and Stew close behind.

Jeb tugged at Hank's sleeve. "Where we goin', Hank?"

Shaking his head in disgust, Hank spit out his cud of tobacco. "By the direction he's headed, I reckon that old fool musta found out that ranch we wuz at has somethin' to do with them MacKenzies he's always rantin' about."

"Zat so? How'd yuh know that, Hank?"

"I didn't say so afore, but I knowed that one gal, soon as I seen her."

"What gal . . . where?"

Hank poked Jeb in the arm. "At that barbecue yuh drug us to, stupid," he said, and took another chaw of tobacco. "Remember the li'l gal back at that railroad tent town in New Mexico, the one what chased yuh all out with a rifle and a passel of women throwin' spaghetti?" Jeb nodded sheepishly. "Well, that's the same gal I seen the other night right there at that there big doings. Come on, kid. Best we follow Billy Bob for now."

"Yeah, he's got all our money!" Jeb said, riding hard after Hank.

An hour later, the sun had just slipped into the horizon when Hank rode up alongside Billy Bob to signal a halt. After the two exchanged a few words, Billy Bob dismounted and the others followed suit.

Shielding his eyes, Billy Bob peered into the distance. "Now, yer damn sure this is the MacKenzie ranch, Hank?"

"Hell no, boss. But I *am* sure this is where we wuz at fer that party the other night."

"Shet! They're one and the same. I jest told yuh what I heard at the saloon. Now, let's see, where's that there ranch house?"

"We're not in sight of it yet. But I kin see their cattle grazin' over yonder on the hill."

"Sure is some mighty fine fencin' they got hereabouts," Curly said, kicking the wooden fence post.

"Good!" Billy Bob said, stroking his beard. "That's jest what we came for."

Looking confused, Curly ventured a question. "What do we need fencin' fer?"

"Not *fencin'*, yuh damn fool!" Billy Bob barked, smacking his hat alongside Curly's face.

"Well, *what* then? Yuh ain't told us nothin' yet, boss," Curly said defensively, putting a hand to his smarting nose.

"We're here to cause them no-good MacKenzies some all-fired miseries they ain't never gonna fergit. Yessiree, once and for all, the Walden gang is gonna make 'em wish they ain't been born. That's *what*, Curly."

"But how we gonna do that, boss?"

"By rustlin' them cattle, of course!"

The men looked at each other, dumbfounded, until Hank folded his arms and shook his head. "Boss, yuh gone loco or somethin'? We don't know nothin' 'bout rustlin' cattle."

Billy Bob wheeled around, standing toe to toe with Hank, and squinted up at him, eyeball to eyeball. "The hell yuh say! I suppose we didn't know nothin' 'bout train robbin' neither—'til we just went ahead and plundered that freight."

"Yeah, well, we didn't get exactly rich on that haul, boss."

"Confound it all, yuh stubborn mule! Yuh know damn well that weren't about money, and neither is this. It's about gettin' even with them dad-blamed MacKenzies. And as for rustlin' cattle, any fool kin do it—even you."

Hank stepped back as Billy Bob began poking him in the chest at each word. "Trouble with yuh, Hank, is yuh ain't got no imagination."

"I reckon yuh got enough for all of us, Billy Bob." Gently pushing Billy Bob's finger away, Hank thought for a few seconds and then hooked his thumbs in his belt. "Tell yuh what, boss. Iffen me and the boys help yuh git them cattle rustled, will yuh git us out of that dad-blasted mill?"

"Yeah, boss. It's time we used the money yuh got stashed for us and git goin' on yer secret plan to make us all rich," Curly enthused.

"Sounds like a good idea to me," Stew said, throwing a handful of peanuts into his mouth.

"Me, too," Jeb agreed.

Hank raised an eyebrow. "Then it's a deal, boss?"

Billy Bob smiled his toothy grin. "Damn tootin' it is, boys. Good as cash on the barrel."

Nodding in agreement, Hank zinged his cud against a fence post.

The men sat on the ground while Billy Bob rifled through his saddlebags. After dropping down several boxes of bullets, a long black whip, a tin of lantern oil, and a small saw before them, Billy Bob stood back, waiting for their approval.

The men stared silently at the objects on the ground. Disgusted that they didn't seem to appreciate his planning and resourcefulness, Billy Bob plunked himself down near Jeb.

"Jeb Boy, them cattle must be spread all over creation out there. So we'll have to rustle one bunch at a time through the hole in the fence."

"There ain't no hole, boss—less'n yuh mean between 'em slots."

Grimacing, Billy Bob slowly rubbed a hand across his face. "I swear yuh ain't got the brain to spit downwind." He held up the saw. "I'm gonna make a hole with this saw."

"Zat so? How yuh gonna know where to make the hole?"

"I won't know 'til I seen which way the cattle are headed. We'll probably need several holes. Can't really expect every bunch will run in the same direction. Best we start with a hole right here first off, so's we kin get in, Jeb Boy."

He walked over to the fence and began to saw one of the fence posts.

"Why don't we jest kick out some of 'em fence rails, boss?" Hank asked. He gave one a solid kick and the rail splintered.

"I thought to do that once I cut through it a mite," Billy Bob said quickly. "Well, don't jest stand there, kid. Start kicking!" he hollered.

Within minutes, they finished kicking out a large section of the fence, and sat down again. Billy Bob shoved a box of bullets in front of Jeb. "Take some extra bullets. I got a box for each of yuh."

Looking further confused, Jeb picked up the box. "What for? Shucks, boss, we ain't gonna be shootin' the cattle, are we?"

"Of course not, yuh nitwit, but we just might want 'em to go faster then they wanna be goin'. Take a couple shots in the air if they get ornery, and 'em critters'll git the idea, all right."

"Ain't yuh fearin' 'em shots might stir up the ranch folks, boss?" Hank asked.

"Who's gonna pay a mind to a couple shots at night?" Billy Bob scoffed. "Could be someone takin' a shot at a coyote."

"Don't figure there's too many of 'em up here in these mountains. Think they're partial to where it's warmer at night."

"A rabbit then," Billy Bob snarled, with a menacing glare at Hank.

"Who gits this black snake?" Curly picked up the whip to take a closer look.

Billy Bob grinned with pride. "Ain't that the best damn piece of cowhide yuh ever seen? That there whip is for me . . .'cause I'll be takin' up the rear. That's the hardest job of rustlin', taking up the rear, yuh know. I figger yuh and Stew kin ride along one side of the herd, Hank and Jeb kin ride t'other, and I'll be whippin' 'em from the rear with that there fine piece of cowhide."

Taking the whip from Curly, Hank examined it carefully and then gave Billy Bob a slow, sideward look. Billy Bob stared back, bracing himself against Hank's steely eye and sharp tongue, but Hank made no complaint. He merely tossed the whip to

Billy Bob. "Yep, that's a mighty fine piece of cow-hide yuh got there, boss."

"Okay now, everybody git some of this oil into the lanterns I gived yuh. I got 'nother tin in my saddlebags in case we run out. It'll be dark prit near soon, and with that slip of a moon we had last night, there ain't gonna be hardly any tonight."

"But, boss, why the lanterns? How come yuh didn't git torches?"

"Shet, Curly, use yer head! We can't go lightin' up the countryside like a string of cavalry on . . . on . . ."

"Parade," Hank filled in.

"Yeah, no parades. Sorry, boss, yer right." Curly took the tin from Billy Bob and began slowly drib-bling oil into his lantern.

"C'mon, Hank. Let's you and me ride up a piece alongside the fence to where yuh seen them cattle on the hill. We'll put a hole in the fence there-abouts, and that'll be our first drive through. It'll jest take a few minutes, so you boys be ready to ride when we git back."

Trotting alongside Billy Bob, Hank saw him loosely winding the whip on his saddlehorn. "Say, boss, I never knowed yuh to heft a long whip like that afore. Them's not easy to crack iffen yer not practiced."

"Yeah, well, I figger the only diff'ence between a greenhorn and an expert, like I'm gonna be, jest amounts to a snap or two. Like I always say, Hank, there ain't no sense in wastin' time."

"Uh-huh. And jest how you figger on ridin' yer horse, holdin' on to the reins, carryin' a lantern, and heavin' practice snaps with that whip at them movin' steers? Even *you* only got two hands, boss."

When Billy Bob kept silent, Hank added, " 'Sides, what yuh wanna go messin' up a fine piece of leather like that for, specially on a bunch of MacKenzie cattle?"

The tongue-in-cheek questions didn't rankle Billy Bob one bit; instead, they gave him the chance to confess a secret without the other boys around.

"Aw, shet, Hank! Now and again, yuh kin smoke a fella outta his hole better than anyone I ever knowed. Truth is, ever since I wuz a kid, I wanted a whip like this. Like I told yuh, brother Charlie used to beat the hell outta me and Beau, and most every livin' critter around. Well, he's long dead now, shot by MacKenzie bullets, and I sure ain't never gonna fergit that—even though Charlie was meaner than a passel of snakes in the noon sun."

Calming down, Billy Bob thought for a moment and then blew out a heavy breath. "Ever since Charlie bit the dust, seems like me and ole Beau jest up and got the peace we never had afore."

At Hank's sideward glance, Billy Bob got back to his secret. "Shet! Don't know what I'm yappin' on about that for. Anyway, when I seen this whip settin' in that store winda today . . . well, I still had the hankerin' for it, so I jest up and decided to git myself a . . . what do yuh call it?"

"A present?" Hank guessed.

"Yep. That's what yuh call it, all right."

"Zat so?" Hank replied in a squeaky voice, borrowing Jeb's perpetual question, and glanced wide-eyed at Billy Bob.

"Yep." Billy Bob grinned. " 'Cause yuh see, near as I can figger, today's my birthday. What do yuh think about that, Hank?" Goading his horse, he galloped away, leaving Hank alone to his own sharp-edged opinion—which he did not want to hear. He just wanted Hank to know, that's all.

Perplexed, Hank rode after Billy Bob. Maybe the boss was going loco, crazy like his brother Charlie. No, not like Charlie—Billy Bob always seemed just a little witless, at most. But the boss had been sad, funny, and angry—holding on to his whip like a kid with a toy, and mumbling about peace—all in the same short stretch. And buying hisself a present on his own birthday? Hank shook his head. He never even knew Billy Bob had a birthday afore.

Hank caught up to Billy Bob just in time to stop him from going too far. "Whoa, boss. The cattle are up yonder."

The two men dismounted and broke another hole in the fence. Then in silence, like the thieves in the night they aspired to be, the two cattle rustlers rode back to the rest of the gang.

After a few more instructions from their boss, the gang made their way through the opening.

"Okay, boys, stay close and follow me," Billy Bob hollered.

"It's getting too dark, boss," Hank said.

His warning came too late: Billy Bob thundered off with the cry, "Yahooo!"

At full gallop in the fading light, his horse sped past shrubs and bushes, over a small gulch, through a sparse clump of trees, and up the hill.

"Whoa, boss!" Hank suddenly called out, just as the horse, stumbling into a steer, lurched up on its hind legs with a frenzied screech, sending Billy Bob flying into a backward somersault. He hit the ground with a thud. Following close behind, Jeb's horse stopped abruptly, dumping Jeb on the steer Billy Bob's horse had knocked over. Jeb rolled off the cow and ended up beside his leader. Bellowing, the angry steer rose up and trotted away.

Fleeing the commotion, the herd immediately began to stampede through the broken fence. "Damn it all, go round 'em up," Billy Bob shouted.

Hollering and whipping their horses, the men rode after the cattle as the thundering herd surged down the hill.

"Let 'em go!" Hank shouted finally. "We best go and check on the boss and Jeb." After lighting their lanterns, the three men rode back up the hill to look for their fallen leader, following the string of howling curses, which they could hear from quite a distance.

Jeb had survived the fall with nothing more than a lump on his head, but Billy Bob's leg was bleeding. He had tied a bandanna around his wound and was hobbling around whistling for his horse. The horse finally came bursting out of the bushes, chased by an angry horned steer.

"Boss, best we clear out," Hank said.

"The hell yuh say, Hank! Why, that's jest a small, scraggly bunch. This whole ranch is full of steers, and I aim to drive off every last one. Now, help git me up on my horse."

"But that leg of yers might be worse than yuh think, boss. Maybe we better skedaddle like Hank says and—"

"None of that talk, Curly. Knowed for a fact I ain't hurt bad. Hope you boys ain't welchin' on our plan, are yuh?"

"Well, jest what *is* our plan, boss?" Curly asked, scratching at his bald pate. "Yuh ain't never told us."

"Yeah, boss, once we rustle 'em cattle, what are we gonna do with 'em?" Jeb asked.

"I wuz wonderin' 'bout that myself," Stew said innocently.

Billy Bob hadn't gotten that far in the planning of his great scheme for revenge. Backed into a corner, he had to think hard and fast.

"Shet, yuh boys are dumb! Don't know why I bother explainin' nothin' . . . nohow . . . never—to such a bunch of dad-blamed jackasses."

Putting his hands on his hips, he took a deep breath, and as his cheeks filled up with air, his eyes protruded. After a few seconds, Curly asked, "Yuh all right, boss?"

Billy Bob rolled his eyes toward Curly and his puckered lips noisily smacked against each other as he slowly exhaled. "Of course I'm all right. Let's see, where wuz I?"

As he stalled for time, his gaze fell on a nearby pile of fence slats and posts stacked under a tree. At least it looked to be like fence slats and posts. He grew excited as a hasty plan unfolded before his eyes. "Oh, yeah, the corral!"

"Corral? What corral?" Curly asked, with a quick sideward glance to Hank.

"A big corral like this'n. The one we're gonna make by that shack we're livin' in. Now, we gotta stop jawin' and start rustlin'."

"You sayin' we're gonna rustle cattle from all over this ranch, then drive 'em through trees, bushes, and a stream, to get them all the way to our shack—and all in the dark!" Hank said incredulously.

"Yep, that's what we're gonna do, all right! We'll haul back some of 'em posts in that pile, then we'll tie together all that rope we've got to make the sides of the corral. So let's start drivin' 'em rustled cattle."

"But we'd have to start all over agin," Curly blurted out.

"Start all over? The hell you say. What did yuh do with 'em?" Billy Bob looked at Hank.

Hank shifted nervously. "We rustled 'em right through that hole in the fence at the top of the hill, jest like you said, boss. That's what we did," Hank said.

"But all 'em damn cattle we drove out of the hole at the top of the hill ran down the hill and right back into the hole we made at the bottom of the hill," Curley said. "Ain't that right, Hank?"

Billy Bob slapped his forehead, closed his eyes, and wiped his hand clear down his face to the end of his beard. Then his eyes bugged out and his face turned red. "Yuh sayin' 'em rustled cattle is right back where they started from!"

Enraged at their stupidity, Billy Bob drew his gun and was about to fire it into the air, but Hank immediately lunged at his legs, taking him to the ground. The pistol flew out of Billy Bob's hand.

The other boys quickly pounced on the two of them, making it impossible to know who was exchanging blows. Thrashing and punching, the pile rolled around, unmindful of the lanterns they were knocking over.

Tiny pools of burning oil formed wherever the smashed lanterns landed. One lantern flew into the woodpile and the oil streamed out, followed by the flames gobbling it up. Within seconds, the pile of dry wood burst into an inferno.

The men's heads all popped up at the sound of the crackling flames. Fiery sparks had begun leaping off the burning pile, igniting nearby bushes and brush.

"Run for all yuh got," Billy Bob yelled.

Crashing and bumping into one another, the gang managed to mount their horses and galloped away.

When they had distanced themselves from the site, they stopped and looked behind them.

"Will you look at that," Jeb said, pointing in astonishment. The whole hillside was ablaze.

"Sure glad we ain't up there," Stew remarked.

"Let's get out of here," Curly said.

They goaded their horses and rode on, but Billy Bob remained.

"You comin', boss?" Hank asked, riding back to him.

"Heh! Heh! Heh!" Billy Bob guffawed. "I sure showed 'em MacKenzies this time."

"But, Billy Bob, we didn't make off with any of their cattle. Yer all bleeding and busted up; Jeb's dizzy with a big bump on his head—so how'd yuh figure you showed 'em, boss?"

"Wait 'til they find their fancy fences all busted up, Hank! It'll take 'em days to fix 'em. 'Bout time they learned there's no messin' with the Billy Bob Walden gang."

Pulling off his Stetson, he wheeled his mount, slapped the flank of his horse, and galloped off, laughing victoriously.

Chapter 21

❦

Angie sat on the swing in the dark, anxiously awaiting Giff's return. She couldn't wait to tell him the good news about Edward and Stella. She knew he'd be glad to hear she had ordered them both off the ranch.

She flushed, recalling her jealous reaction when she saw Giff and Stella in the water together. To have accused him of ... Oh, she had so much to apologize to him for. How she wished he'd get home!

More than likely he had ridden out to work on his house, but now that it was dark, he should have been back.

She cast a fretful glance in the direction of Willow Range. Seeing the glow in the sky, she stood up, alarmed. It was too bright a glow to be caused by a couple lanterns. Something was wrong!

Angie started for the bunkhouse, then remembered String and Red had ridden into town. Turning on her heel, she raced to the barn and saddled Calico.

She sped through the night, recklessly leaping over whatever was in her path. The nearer she got to Willow Range, the greater the glow. Soon the smell of smoke reached her nostrils and she feared that it was Giff's house burning.

The smoke was dense by the time Calico splashed across the river, and she rode into what seemed like a scene from hell.

Fire loomed everywhere. The fence and pile of posts had burned to ashes. Much of the scrub and brush were seared to the ground, and several of the trees were ablaze as the fire gobbled them up as it crept down the hill. Angie pulled her bandanna over her nose and mouth, but the smoke stung her eyes. Spooked by the fire, Calico fought the reins.

At least the fire was still a good half mile away from Giff's house, but where was he? Surely the inferno would have attracted his attention. Fearing the worst, Angie picked her way through burning patches, the darkness and smoke limiting her vision, worried that he was hurt and unconscious.

After searching for several minutes, she began to panic. Oh God, where was he? What had happened to him? The sound of bawling cattle added to the nightmare, and with every moment her anxiety increased. The fire, the smoke, and her mounting panic brought back the horrendous memory of the night she was trapped in the cabin on the riverboat. Giff had saved her then.

Dear God, please don't let me be too late to help him now.

"Giff, where are you?" She continued calling out his name, over and over again, each cry louder with desperation. Seeing an object on the ground, she dismounted and picked up a long bullwhip. The crew had never used a bullwhip to drive the cattle, but there was no time to ponder it at the moment. She had to get a firm hold on her fears and stop reacting hysterically. She had assumed

Giff had come to Willow Range, but her common sense now told her he hadn't. In all probability he was sitting in Slim's saloon at this very minute, while she was wasting valuable time searching for him. And there was nothing she could do about the fire except hope that it would burn itself out when it reached the river.

She glanced down the hill and saw a new reason for concern: the herd at the bottom of the hill was in the direct path of the fire. At the moment the cattle were downwind of the smoke, but it would only be a matter of minutes before the fire reached them, and they'd never be able to outrun it. The only hope of saving the herd was to drive them across the river. And that would not be easy. Once the cattle hit that water, they'd want to stop and drink. It had been hard enough keeping them moving when they crossed the first time, and then she'd had Giff's help. There were a lot fewer steers now, but still too many to avoid losing some of them.

"Well, Calico, that's better than losing all of them." Reaching for the bullwhip, she galloped down the hillside.

When she began hazing the cattle, they initially wouldn't move. After several more cracks of the bullwhip, she finally got them turned and moving toward the stream. The smoke grew thicker, and the heat of the fire had intensified by the time they began to move slowly through a large hole in the fence.

Angie continued snapping the whip above their heads in an effort to get them to run. One of the steers in the water stumbled and went down, and the cattle around it began to jam up, slowing down those still behind them on the bank. The crack of the whip sent a fountain of water spurting into the air, and the milling steers finally surged forward, swerving around the downed steer. The fence behind them was already burning, and the pitiful wailing of an unfortunate cow caught in the midst of the flames added to the hellish spectacle. With flames licking at their heels, Angie drove the last steers into the water. Sparks leaped through the air, landing on the hides of the cattle, only to be quickly extinguished by the cool water as the cattle swam to the opposite shore, prodded by the relentless crack of the bullwhip above their heads.

By the time she got all the cattle across the river, Angie could barely raise the whip again. Turning her head, she looked back. The whole riverbank on the opposite side was burning.

Giff bolted up to a sitting position. Something out of the ordinary had woken him up. When he smelled the smoke, he bolted out of the bunk and ran to the door. A distant glow lit up the dark night like a sunrise. He couldn't tell at this distance what was burning, but it appeared to be in the vicinity of the house or depot. Within minutes, he had dressed and saddled Brick, and was racing toward the site.

He cursed himself repeatedly. He should have ridden back earlier. He'd genuinely intended to, but had lain down on a bunk in the line shack and dozed off. If Angie had been harmed, he'd never forgive himself for riding away in anger, leaving her in the hands of Emory and that crazy Stella. The Lord only knew what those two people were capable of doing!

With relief, he soon was able to tell that the site of the glow was not the main house. Veering toward the Willow, he goaded Brick, and horse and rider stretched out in a desperate run.

As he neared the Willow he could see the burning hillside, and by the glow from the fire lining the opposite bank, he saw the herd and the figure on horseback. He recognized Angie at once. Shouting her name, he galloped toward her.

Angie heard him call and saw him galloping toward her. "Giff!" she cried joyously. Any fear she had harbored was now put to rest.

He rode up to her. "Angie, are you okay?"

"Yes, and thank God you are, too."

"What happened here?"

"I don't know. I saw the fire from the house, so I rode out. I was afraid it was the house you're building." Suddenly she began crying. "And when I couldn't find you, I didn't know what to think. I was so frightened that something had happened to you."

He climbed down and lifted her off her horse. "Angel, I'm fine," he said, pulling her into his arms. She continued sobbing, and he held her closer. "Honey, it's okay. I'm fine. I was at the line shack and when I saw the fire, I rode over." He tucked a finger under her chin and tipped it up. "I'm sorry, Angel. I'm so . . ." The last word was smothered by the hungry press of his mouth on hers. Parting her lips, she returned his kiss, her emotions whirling with the startling realization of how much his kisses excited her. This time she knew that one kiss was not enough, and she gloried when he reclaimed her mouth in a slow, drugging kiss.

Breathless, she stepped back. "Oh God, Giff, I'm so happy you're here."

"Angel, we've got to talk."

"I know—but I don't think you mean here and now," she said, smiling at him through the tears glistening in her eyes.

"No, I reckon not." He glanced around. "Where's String and Red?"

"I'm alone. They rode into town earlier."

"You mean you drove that herd across the river in the dark by yourself?"

"I didn't have much choice, did I? We'd have lost the herd."

"Angel, that's amazing!"

"Does that mean I've proven that I'm a good enough hand to ride for the Roundhouse?" she asked with a puckish grin.

He hugged her to his side. "Angel, the job's yours for life. You've earned your pay for the year. Just sit down and relax while I bunch up these cattle for the night."

Angie took him up on the offer. She plopped down on the ground and leaned back against a tree and waited as Giff hazed the strays back to the herd. The fire on the other bank had burned itself out by the time he rode back to her.

"Angie, I've got to do something about my leg."

"What's wrong with it?" Then she saw his bandanna wrapped around his thigh. When she reached out and touched it, her hand came away bloody.

"A horn grazed it. It's bleeding pretty badly. I'm going to head for the line shack, since it's closer and there's some supplies there. You best head back to the house, honey. I'll ride in tomorrow."

"If you think I'm going to leave you out here alone with a bloody leg, you've got another guess coming, Pete Gifford. Let's get you to that line shack fast."

By the time they rode up to the tiny cabin, Giff's whole trouser leg was saturated with blood.

"Put your arm around me," Angie said as she helped him dismount. Her knees almost buckled when she took the full measure of his weight. She helped him hobble into the tiny cabin, to a chair at the table. "Sit down while I light the lamp."

She carried the lamp over to the table. "Let me

take a look at that leg." Kneeling on the floor, Angie untied the blood-soaked bandanna. After ripping through his jeans and drawers, the steer's horn had left an ugly gash on Giff's flesh. Angie glanced up worriedly at him. "You've lost a lot of blood, Giff. And you need some stitches to close up this gash."

"There's a sewing box on the shelf. Should be a needle and thread in it."

Her eyes rounded in shock. "You expect me to sew up your leg?"

"Reckon so, Angie. It's too far back to the house for Middy to do it. I'd probably bleed to death by then."

"Giff, I've never stitched up any wound before. I don't know if I can do it."

"Any hand worth his keep knows how to stich up a wound. Believe me, honey, it will hurt me more than it does you. Just make sure you clean it out good before you sew it shut. There's a roll of bandaging on the shelf and there should be a bottle of whiskey, too, unless String drank it all."

She folded the bandanna into a pad and stood up. "Press this against the gash and sit still while I get a fire going."

"It's gonna get damn hot in here with a fire going."

"I know, but I'll need hot water to cleanse your leg."

While she waited for the water to boil, Angie went outside and unsaddled the horses, stabling them under the lean-to. Giff was attempting to pull off his boots when she entered the shack.

"I told you not to move." Dumping the saddlebags and his rifle on the floor, she hurried over to him. "Sit back and behave yourself."

"What a bossy female. Maybe you should ramrod this outfit."

She knelt down and pulled off one of his boots. "I might have to, Pete Gifford, when you bleed to death." The second boot hit the floor and she stood up. "Pants next," she ordered sharply.

"That'll be a real interesting feat, since I've been ordered not to move."

"Giff, you aren't taking this seriously enough. You have a bad wound, so I have to get your pants off you. I'll try to be as gentle as possible, but you're a big man to handle."

"You know, Angie, coming from any other woman, those remarks would have intriguing implications."

"If you're referring again to that *man thing* you suffer from, I can assure you that's the farthest thing from my mind," she said, releasing his belt buckle. "And I can't believe at a time like this that your mind's on it, either," she sputtered.

He brushed aside her hands when she started to unbutton the fly of his pants. "I'm not quite dead yet, so keep your hands where they won't do any harm. You can help by threading a needle. I'll get my pants off by myself."

Disgusted, Angie went over to the shelf and found the sewing kit, a roll of bandage, and a half-filled bottle of whiskey. When she returned, Giff was seated in only his bloodstained drawers.

"Looks like I'll have to take off my drawers, too. How about getting me a blanket from one of the bunks."

Angie tossed him a blanket, then, turning her back, she went to the fireplace to check if the water had come to a boil. Giff had shed his drawers and had the blanket wrapped around him when she returned with the water. But the effort had taken a toll: his face looked drawn with pain and he appeared weak from the loss of blood.

"Let's just get this over with," he said.

His thigh felt firm and powerful beneath her touch as she rinsed away the blood with a strip of bandage that had been dipped in the hot water. He was no longer bleeding profusely, but blood still trickled from the ugly gash.

"At least the bleeding's slowed," she said hopefully. "That's an encouraging sign, Giff."

"Depends. It could be I'm running out of blood," he joked.

She cast a pointed look at him and returned to examining the gash. "Now that the blood's cleaned away, it doesn't look as bad as I originally thought." Reaching for the needle, she dipped the tip in the hot water, then worked out a tiny piece of blue denim lodged in the wound.

"Get it all out, Angel," he warned. "I don't want any infection."

Perspiration glistened on his forehead by the time she worked several more threads to the surface. "I think I've got it all, Giff." Picking up the bottle of whiskey, she hesitated. "This is going to sting."

"Just get it over—"

He sucked in his breath as she poured the whiskey into the open wound. Glancing anxiously at him, she saw that his tanned face had turned gray. He reached for the whiskey bottle and took a long draft.

Struggling to build her courage, Angie drew a deep breath and closed her eyes. She gently pressed the jagged edges of the wound together and took the first stitch.

"I remember the time when Middy sewed up your arm," she said.

"So do I. You held my hand and cried until she finished."

"I know. If I remember, I was only ten years at the time. I felt every stitch she made."

With every pass of the needle, her hand became steadier. After ten stitches, she looked up and smiled tremulously. "I'm through."

Angie poured whiskey over the ligature, covered it with a compress, then wrapped several yards of gauze around Giff's thigh to protect the wound.

Her quavering smile had changed to one of satisfaction and pride. "What do you think?"

"You did great, Angel."

"You did pretty well yourself. But you didn't have to be so darn stoic, Pete Gifford. I wouldn't have thought less of you if you'd let out a groan or two."

He grinned broadly and she was relieved to see that the color had begun to return to his face. "I thought of it a time or two, but I figured you were suffering enough for both of us." Tipping up her chin, for a breathless moment he smiled down into her upturned face. "Thanks, Angel." Lowering his head, he placed a light kiss on her lips.

A swarm of butterflies took wing in her stomach.

"I think you'd better lie down," she chided. "I'll make a pot of coffee. Is there anything you need?"

"Not right now." Hobbling over to the bunk beds, he stretched out in the lower one, covering himself from the waist down with the blanket.

As soon as the coffee was done, Angie poured Giff a cup and carried it over to the bunk. He was sound asleep. The blanket had slipped off him and his nudity was exposed to her gaze. For a long moment she stared shamelessly at the beauty of his body: long, tanned, and muscular—a sinewy litheness that reflected strength, not merely size.

Strange—a few months earlier, the thought of a man's nudity had been distasteful to her. Yet now she could not absorb enough of Giff's nakedness. In truth, other than Giff, Armand Bordeau was the only naked man she had ever seen. Despite her in-

timacy with Edward, she had never actually observed him nude, because he'd always made love
to her in the dark.

Feeling like a voyeur, she covered him, then
turned away.

Chapter 22

❦

The fire had burned itself out by the time Angie finally finished washing Giff's jeans and drawers. She hung them to dry on two of the wooden pegs in the walls.

After checking on the horses for the night, Angie removed her boots, blew out the lamp, and climbed up in the upper bunk.

The fireplace had heated up the cabin, so she climbed back down and opened the window and door, hoping to catch some of the evening breeze. Still, unable to fall asleep, Angie continued to toss restlessly, trying to keep her mind off the man in the bunk below her.

"Trouble getting to sleep, Angie?" Giff suddenly asked.

"Oh," she said, startled, "I thought you were sleeping. Did I wake you?"

"No."

"How does your leg feel?"

"Like hell."

"I wish I had something to give you for the pain."

"I can't believe I let myself get gored by a steer."

"It could have happened to anyone," she said. "I wonder what started the fire? Maybe it was mischievous boys sneaking a smoke." Her eyes twinkled merrily. "You know, that man thing."

He grinned. "You're probably right, Angel. That could even explain that whip you found."

"At least the fire didn't reach the house you're building."

"Speaking of houses, do you think there'll be anything left at the Roundhouse when we get back?"

"Why wouldn't there be?"

"With you gone, your two friends have probably carried off everything they could tote on their backs."

"They aren't there, Giff. I ordered them off the ranch."

There was a long pause, then he finally asked, "How come?"

"Do you have to ask?"

"I thought you were in love with Edward," he said. His voice sounded guarded to her.

"At one time I believed I was. I know now I was mistaken."

"Are you sure, Angie?" This time he sounded considerably heartened.

"Cross my heart and hope to die," she said lightly. Then she added solemnly, "Yes, I'm sure, Giff. I've never been more sure of anything in my life. I don't know how I could ever have loved Edward Emory. I don't know what I was thinking."

"You're not the only one, Angel. Ain't too many people who keep their heads on straight when they think they're in love."

"Have you ever been in love, Giff?"

"Only once."

"Pete Gifford, I thought we were friends. How come you never told me?"

"Reckon I just never got around to it."

"Well, what happened?"

"Waited too long, I guess. She went away and fell in love with someone else."

"Oh, Giff," she said. "That's so sad."

Angie suddenly felt a tight drawing in her chest at the thought of him in love with some faceless woman—kissing her... caressing her the same way he had done to her in the hayloft. She felt a surge of jealousy and resentment. How could Giff do that to her? How could he fall in love with someone else? He was her best friend—he belonged to her. He'd always belonged... She stopped, realizing the selfish direction of her thoughts. She had no right to resent his actions. When had she given a thought to Giff when she was off pursuing her own whims?

And when had her feelings for him changed so radically? When he kissed her? In the hayloft?

Timorously she asked, "Are you still in love with her, Giff? Is that why you never married?"

"I'll probably always love her," he replied. "So what are your plans now?"

Her curiosity—and disheartenment—was fierce, but he obviously wanted to change the subject. Tucking her hands under her head, she stretched out and relaxed. "Edward actually had a great idea about opening a repertory in Denver, which appeals to me. You know, Giff, I've always had this fantasy where I see myself on a stage in front of a packed audience playing Chopin or Beethoven; and when I finish, the audience rises to their feet with shouts and applause."

"Sounds like you intend to see Edward again."

"Heavens, no. Even if I did pursue the idea of a repertory, it would not be with Edward Emory."

"What happened to your idea about going to the conservatory in Denver?"

"Are you suggesting I need a little more practice before I perform in front of an audience?" she teased.

The sound of his chuckle brought a smile to her mouth. "I thought a fantasy was something out of reach," he said. "That's why it's a fantasy. If you get to live it out, it ceases to be one, doesn't it?"

"Are you asking me or telling me?"

"Asking, I guess."

"I'd think it depends on what you're wishing for. Everyone's fantasy surely isn't out of reach. What's yours, Giff?"

"Who says I've got one?"

"Oh, there must be some fantasy, something you've dreamed of doing," she cajoled.

"Just one thing," he said in a voice rife with whimsy.

"What is it?" After several seconds of silence, she leaned her head over the edge of the bunk to see if he had drifted into sleep. His eyes were open and he lay staring into space.

"Come on and tell me, Giff," she said playfully. "I've told you my fantasy. What's yours?"

"Naw. You'd only laugh."

The moment had lost its frivolity. She sensed whatever he hesitated to say concerned her as much as it did him. Whatever secret he harbored, she knew with certainty that if he revealed it to her now, this moment of truth would be the closest one they had ever shared. Driven by an urgency that far exceeded curiosity, she climbed down and sat down on the floor beside his bunk.

"I won't laugh, Giff. What is your fantasy?"

Turning his head, he looked at her; his blue eyes stared clear and forthright into hers. "To make love to you."

A sudden jolt to her heart set her pulses pounding in her ears. She tried to assess his expression, so serious but unreadable. "Are you joking, Giff?"

A sadness crept into his face and voice when he answered. "I wish I were."

She felt a surge of excitement, an emotion that had nothing to do with feeling grateful or obligated to him. Female responding to male—a mating call as ancient as Adam and Eve and as recent as the attraction she had been fighting since their return to the Roundhouse.

Entirely swept up in the feeling, Angie finally acknowledged the truth to herself—*she was in love with him*. She didn't know how or when it had occurred, but right now she needed to act on it.

Angie rose to her feet and removed her clothing. Giff remained silent and still, his riveted gaze searching her face, dredging her soul.

Oh, God, Giff! Say something. Help me with this.

But he appeared to have no intention to do so. Whatever his thoughts, they remained concealed behind an inscrutable stare that shifted to her shoulders, her breasts, and then lower.

Angie moved closer until the edge of the bunk restrained her trembling legs. Then she reached out and swept aside the blanket that covered his nakedness. Her gaze swept his body, and her courage faltered when she reached his prominent erection. Every inch of him was raw . . . sensual . . . virile . . . male.

Was she woman enough for this man? What if she failed to live up to his expectations?

"I wish I were more experienced, Giff. I want to live up to your fantasy. To—"

Pulling her on top of him, he cut off her words with his mouth. She parted her lips beneath the possessive pressure of his, causing him to tighten his hold and crush her against the hard outline of his body. Surrendering to the arousing thrill of his kiss, she stretched out along him, engulfed in the pure male of him—muscle, strength, warmth, and an essence that drove her wild with the awareness of his masculinity. Certainly Edward had never exuded such a sensuality, and she rejoiced in her own femininity.

He shifted their positions so that his weight covered her. The heat of his body coursed down the length of her, enveloping her in a delightful warmth. His hand skimmed the curves of her body like the loving touch of a sculptor forming a work of art, and she moaned aloud with pleasure until his lips reclaimed hers, his tongue probing the moist chamber of her mouth.

She loved the mindless ecstasy of his kisses. Closing her eyes, she whispered her approval and pleaded with him to never stop.

Murmuring his name incessantly, she breathed it in sighs as he covered her face, her eyes, and her neck with quick, hungry kisses that fueled the fire he had ignited within her to a greater intensity.

"You're so beautiful, Angel. So beautiful," he whispered. "It seems like I've dreamed of this moment forever."

She parted her lips, drawing an instant response to the invitation. His feathered kisses drove her to a frenzied need for more. She searched for his mouth. "Kiss me again, Giff," she pleaded shamelessly.

He claimed her mouth with a wild fervor, plunging his tongue inside until she whimpered for breath. As soon as he freed her lips, she felt the loss and wanted more, but he had moved on to a new target.

As his hands and lips explored her body, each touch released a flood of sensations that escalated into a wave of passion washing through her with a feeling so exquisite that she cried out from the pure pleasure of it. Her body throbbed with a pulsation that threatened to erupt, and she responded explosively, arching against him with ecstatic moans.

Pressing a trail of kisses to her naked flesh, he followed the slide of his warm hand down to her stomach. Lowering his hand, he cupped the core of her femininity in his warm palm and his fingers stroked the sensitive nub in an erotic massage. She sucked in her breath, a surge of heat and divine sensation building until it exploded within her.

He held her until her rasping breath slowed to an even rise and fall of her chest, then he kissed her: a long, demanding kiss that set her heart pounding again. Shifting from under him, she sat up and straddled him.

"Am I hurting your leg?"

He chuckled, an unbelievably warm, sensual sound that sent a shiver of pleasure down her spine. Why hadn't she ever recognized that before?

"Angel, at this moment the pain in my leg is the farthest thing from my mind."

"And what of your fantasy? Is your mind free now of that, too?" She pushed aside the curtain of dark hair that draped across her face.

Giff reached out and wove his fingers into its thickness. Cupping her cheeks with his thumbs, he pushed her hair back. "Not quite; there's still more to it."

The ends of her mouth curved in a smile. "I suspected as much. It's my turn, isn't it?"

She caressed his wide shoulders, her fingertips tingling, tracing the slope to the muscular brawn of his chest. "Was this part of it?"

"What do you think?" he asked in a husky murmur.

Dipping her head, she pressed a kiss to the bronzed flesh, then lightly tugged on one of the nipples with her teeth. She felt more than heard the sharp intake of his breath, and raised her head. "Do you want me to stop?"

"Not in my fantasy," he managed to say.

She licked the nipple and his breathing quickened. His reaction excited her. Driven by her own escalating passion and the exciting timbre of his urging guidance, she continued to explore his body with her tongue and fingertips. He was hard and hot, his chest and shoulders glistening with a faint sheen.

Fighting to hold on to the control he had exercised for years, he reached out, clutching her shoulders. "Honey, I think we better cut to the chase," he rasped hoarsely.

Rolling over, he shifted her to her back and moved on top of her. His mouth and hands sought and caressed, arousing her again to a state of mindless rapture. She groped mindlessly for him. "Please, Giff? Now!"

He entered her, linking their bodies as one. For the briefest of moments he hesitated. "You're so tight, Angel. Am I hurting you?"

"Oh God, no," she moaned. "Don't stop. Please don't stop!"

"I couldn't if I wanted to," he whispered, claiming her lips in a fervorous kiss.

As hot passion swept through them, the tempo of his thrusts increased. He recaptured her mouth, swallowing her cry of rapture as together they rode the crest of that frenzied wave to a shuddering ecstasy.

Chapter 23

After dressing the next morning, the first thing Angie did was check Giff's leg. Much to her relief, the wound showed no signs of bleeding or infection, and the night's torrid lovemaking had not broken open any of the stitches, either.

"Looks good, Giff. How does it feel?"

"Stiff and sore, but I can ride," he said, pulling on his drawers.

"You shouldn't attempt anything strenuous. You don't want that wound to open." She moved to assist him.

He arched a brow. "Angel, if the stitches survived last night, I don't think we have to worry about it opening." A hot blush stained her cheeks. Grinning, he pulled her into his arms and she buried her face against his chest. "What are you blushing about?"

"Don't tease me, Giff. It's embarrassing."

"Why should it be? Angel, last night you were wonderful."

"I was wanton. I can't believe I behaved so outrageously."

When she tried to burrow deeper against him,

he stepped back. "Honey, I think we better talk about this. Why would you think you acted outrageously?"

"I was out of control, Giff," she said, and knelt down to help him pull on his boots. "I can't imagine what got into me. I've never felt such . . . carnal instincts before."

"That's good to hear. At least I get a better rating than Edward," he teased.

She jerked up her head. "That isn't funny, Giff. Remarks like that make me feel even cheaper than I do already."

He raised his hands in supplication. "You're right, Angel; my remark was in bad taste. I'm sorry. I was only trying to lighten your mood because I can't see why you feel so guilty about something so natural. We're married, honey."

She frowned in consternation. "I know that. That just complicates this whole thing more," she replied and stood up.

"Complicates it! I'd think it would resolve it. You're making it complicated by trying to decide if last night was a mistake or not," he said resentfully.

"Giff, you're not trying to understand my problem," she shot back immediately. "There are a lot of things I have to sort out."

He grasped her upper arms and looked down at her earnestly. "Then let's sit down and talk about them. We'll work them out together, Angel."

She worried her lower lip as she looked up at him. "Giff, I'm not trying to deny that what happened last night between us was the most exciting thing I've ever experienced."

"Then what's so complicated about it?"

She hesitated for a long moment, trying to decide whether to be totally truthful with him. But the moment called for the truth, and she decided the time had come to get it off her chest.

"I want you to sit down, Giff, and listen to what I have to say. Promise you won't interrupt me."

"All right." He sat down, leaned back, and crossed his right foot over his left knee. "Get it out, Angel."

"You were right when you said that I'm trying to decide if last night was a mistake, because now I have to make a choice: if I accept the role of your wife, then I must forsake my art and musical aspirations."

"I don't—"

"You said you wouldn't interrupt," she warned. He settled back again, and she continued. "I'm not certain if I'm prepared to make that choice. Giff, last night you showed me how incredibly thrilling it can be for us to make love; but there's more to being a wife than just sharing a bed with you. It means devoting all my time and energies to this ranch. It means bearing your children." She reached out and tenderly stroked his cheek. "And you'd make such a wonderful father." For the length of a breath, they gazed into each other's eyes. Then she continued. "I was reconciled to our making love. I even intended to tell you so, after I kicked Edward off the ranch. But I wasn't prepared for that all-consuming passion I felt last night. It scares the devil out of me, because I'm afraid *that*, more than anything, is what will affect the choice I make. A choice that affects your life as well as mine."

Hearing the sound of approaching riders, she glanced at the open door. Giff got up and walked to the doorway. "It's String and Red." He picked up his gear, then paused at the entrance. "Looks like we'll have to finish this conversation later, Angel." Then he limped outside, leaving her standing in the center of the floor feeling desolate—and frustrated. She finally grabbed her hat and followed him.

"We seen some smoke hangin' in the air this mornin'," String said, as Giff saddled the horses. "Middy got a mite worried and sent us out lookin' for yuh. 'Pears like about five acres burned. How'd it get started?"

"Kids, I guess."

"Damnation!" Red cursed. "Durn fool kids mighta wiped out the herd. Good thing you got it across the river in time."

"I didn't do it." Giff turned his head and looked at her. "My wife did."

Her pulses leaped in response to the pride in his eyes and voice.

String shook his head. "Drove 'em herself, did she? I swear that gal's got more mettle than ten twice her size." Ogling the huge rip in Giff's jeans, he asked, "What did yuh do to yer leg?"

"Took a horn in the thigh."

"You mean you let one of 'em steers get a horn into yuh like some greenhorn!" Red exclaimed in disbelief.

"Yeah, I got careless. Angie sewed up the gash."

String slapped his Stetson against his thigh. "I'll be dad-blame! I swear there ain't nothin' that gal cain't do when she puts a mind to it. Yuh sure picked the proper wife fer ranchin', Giff."

"Yeah, I sure did," Giff said.

"Since you fellas prefer talking around me like I'm not here, I'm going to ride back to the house," Angie declared.

"You mind riding back alone?" Giff asked. "I'm going with the boys to take another look at the damage."

"That's fine. I'll see you back at the house."

After she was mounted, Giff leaned against Calico and draped his arm over her thigh. "Remember, Angel, we've got a conversation to finish."

She lowered her head and they kissed lightly. "So long, boys," she said, waving as she rode away.

The ride gave her plenty of time to go over what she had said to Giff. He hadn't appeared angry, but he'd always been patient and understanding in the past—except about Edward; then he'd acted like a raging bull, snorting and kicking up dust at everything she said or did.

"What do you think, Calico? You know him as well as I do," she said as she rode up to the barn. After stabling the horse, she went into the house, yelled a greeting to Middy, then went upstairs to take a bath and wash her hair.

As she sat in the tub, drizzling water over her knees from a dripping sponge, Angie came to the conclusion that she needed a woman's advice about the whole situation: Giff, their marriage, and her indecision about what to do with her life. Someone with a wiser, more worldly eye—someone like Thia. Yes, Thia would know exactly what to do. If only she were still there. But she wasn't, Angie thought desolately, plopping the sponge into the water.

But what was preventing her from going to Thia?

Climbing quickly out of the tub, Angie donned a robe and hurried down the stairway to the den. Beth would surely have a train schedule. After rifling through several piles on the desk, she found what she was looking for. To her delight, she saw there was a freight train passing through in two hours. Racing back upstairs, she dressed and threw some clothing into a valise.

After considerable beseeching, Angie succeeded in getting Middy to drive her to the depot. It was a victory she couldn't celebrate, however, because throughout the whole trip, Middy complained how much she didn't like the idea of Angie leaving.

"Ain't natural to be runnin' off like this without a word to Giff. He's not gonna like it when he gets back and finds you gone. And he'll be blamin' me for being the one to help you."

"Just explain to him that it was necessary for me to speak to Thia. With any luck, I'll be able to catch the train back tomorrow."

"Pity you couldn't have done your talkin' while your sister was right here, missy."

"If I had, then you wouldn't have anything to complain about now, would you?"

"Watch your smart mouth," Middy growled.

"Thank you, dear," Angie said when they finally reached the depot. She kissed Middy on the cheek, climbed down from the buckboard, and grabbed the valise.

"Don't like you off alone like this," Middy said. "No tellin' what kind of strangers you might meet."

"I'll be traveling on a Rocky Mountain Central freight train. It doesn't carry passengers, so it's unlikely I'll meet any strangers on the way. And I'll be back soon."

Shaking her head, Middy flicked the reins. "Giff ain't gonna take kindly to this," she clucked as the wagon rolled away.

Angie put up the signal flag for the train to stop, then sat down and waited.

"Hey, Giff, hear that? Sounds like the train stopped at the Junction," Red said as the three rode near the depot on their way back to the homestead.

"Must be Beth getting back," Giff said. "Let's take a look."

Goading his horse to a gallop, Giff rode ahead. He reached the depot just in time to catch a glimpse of Angie stepping into the caboose of a train pulling out.

"Angie!" She turned and saw him. "Angie, where are you going?" he shouted, and began to race alongside the track.

"I left you a note," she yelled back.

All Giff could think of was her doubts and confusion that morning. If she was running away, he wanted to hear the reasons for it from her, not any damn note. Grabbing the railing on the train, he swung from his horse to the caboose.

"Take care of Brick," he shouted to the two startled ranch hands, who had already grabbed the dangling reins of his gelding.

"Giff, what are you doing?" Angie exclaimed.

"I could ask you the same question," he said, following her into the car. "Where are you going?"

"I'm making a quick trip down to end of track."

"What's wrong? Does Thia have a problem?"

"No, I'm the one with the problem. I need some answers and I want to talk it over with Thia."

"Dammit, Angie, I thought we'd agree to talk it over. I'm your husband, remember?" he snapped belligerently.

"Neither of us seems to be able to keep our emotions out of our thinking. Look at how angry you are right now. It seems like one or the other of us is always in a huff. How can we ever discuss anything rationally?"

He tossed aside his hat and came over to her. Grasping her by the shoulders, he looked down at her earnestly. "We made a good start this morning, didn't we? We've got to be able to work out our own problems without turning to others for the answers. Let's get off this train at Denver and go back to the ranch, sit down, and calmly finish our conversation."

"It's too late for that, Giff."

"How can you say that, Angie? We haven't really tried."

She smiled despite his seriousness. "I meant that it's too late to get off the train. It isn't stopping at Denver. This is an express freight and it's going straight through."

"Well, you're a part owner in the line; I can't believe they won't stop long enough for us to get off."

"Giff, they weren't even going to stop at the Junction until O'Hara saw that it was me flagging them down. There's two armed guards on board. They're carrying a large shipment of cash to some town near Amarillo."

Astonished, he asked, "You mean Texas?"

"That's right. Like it or not, Giff, this train isn't stopping for about ten more hours."

"Dammit!" he cursed.

Turning away, disgusted, he plopped down on a chair at the small table set in the corner. Angie sat down on the cot, the only other piece of furniture in the tiny caboose.

For several minutes they sat in silence except for the steady drumming of his fingers on the table.

Angie finally spoke up. "Must you do that?"

"Do what?" he asked.

"Drum your fingers on the table. It's quite nerve-racking."

"Oh, sorry," he said, tucking his fingers into the waist band of his pants. He leaned back in the chair and was soon rocking back and forth on the rear legs.

Expecting him to topple over backwards any minute, Angie watched it as long as she could before blurting out, "Giff, for heaven's sake! Will you please stop before that chair tips over?"

"Sorry," he said, relaxing. "Guess I'm a little nervous."

"I guess you are and I bet you wish now that you hadn't been so hasty in jumping on this train. Daddy always warned us that if you act in haste, you repent in leisure. Well, you've got plenty of that now, because you're stuck on this train for the next ten hours without anything to do."

He turned his head and studied her, a speculative gleam in his eyes. "Oh, don't be too sure of that." He rose slowly to a standing position. "Matter of fact, I've thought of something already." The speculative gleam had been replaced by a heated glow of desire.

The staccato beat of her heart pounded in her breast as he lazily approached, his blue-eyed gaze compelling, magnetic—and irresistibly seductive. Her whole being filled with excitement as she waited, her body heated by a flush of expectancy. When his arms closed around her, she shut her eyes, tantalized by his intoxicating male muskiness.

His fingers tipped up her chin. Anticipating his kiss, she felt instead his warm breath ruffling the hair at her ear.

"We have ten hours, Angel."

She opened her eyes to the tenderness of his gaze—an overwhelming assault of wistfulness, longing, and passion that shattered any hope for resistance. Not that she could offer any—not that she would try.

Eagerly she parted her trembling lips, and he hungrily devoured their softness. She burrowed deeper into the bracing excitement of his arms, savoring each spine-tingling kiss he showered on her lips, her nose, her eyes, along the curve of her jaw, her neck, her face. Time and time again, he reclaimed her lips, each kiss becoming more intense, more lingering—more demanding, until their bodies throbbed with a combined urgency, and he eased her gently down onto the cot.

*   *   *

A loud blast woke both of them.

"Did you hear that?" Angie asked.

"Yeah, it sounded like a gunshot. And the train's stopping." Giff shifted her aside and got out of bed. "You said there's two guards on that money, right?" Angie nodded. "Anyone else on the train?"

"Only the engineer and fireman; Pat O'Hara and Dan Harrington have worked for our line for years."

"What about the guards?" Giff asked, pulling on his pants. "Are they with the railroad?"

"I don't think so. Daddy never employed detectives. They're probably with Wells Fargo, or the company who's shipping the money."

"Do they know you're here?"

"They'd have to, Giff. The train stopped to pick me up."

"Did you see what they looked like?"

"No. I never paid any attention to them. I don't even know if they came out of the car and saw me."

By the time Giff finished dressing, the train had come to a full stop. "Wait here." He stepped out cautiously on the platform.

Angie was almost dressed by the time he slipped back inside. "It's a robbery, all right. The money car is about three up from here. There appears to be only one man transferring the money to a horse. There's also a rider down at the engine, holding the train crew at gunpoint. I want you to stay here and keep the door locked. Dammit! What a time not to be wearing my gun belt!"

"What are you planning on doing, Giff?"

"I'm going to try and reach that money car without being seen. They don't know I'm with you, so I've got a pretty good chance."

"Don't try it, Giff. It's too dangerous, especially since you're not armed."

"If I can disarm the man at the car, I can get his gun."

"Please, Giff, stay here. I'm afraid for you."

"Angie, they may intend to kill the rest of you."

"If they did, they would have done it by now. You said they're loading the money. Obviously they'll take off then."

"I won't take that chance with your life at stake. Just do as I say, Angie. Lock the door when I leave and don't open it for anyone."

She put a hand on his chest and glanced up worriedly. "Be careful, Giff."

He pressed a light kiss to her lips. "Lock this door."

Giff moved along the back of the cars until he reached the third car. Pausing to listen, he could make out sounds of the outlaw scurrying in and out of the car.

The body of one of the guards lay facedown on the ground. Giff stared at the dead man. There was something peculiar about the body. It took Giff a moment to realize the man's Colt was still in the holster—he had been shot in the back.

Suddenly the whole picture became clear to him: why there was only one shot fired; why the door had been opened without more of a gun battle; why the guard had been shot in the back. It was an inside job. The other guard was an accomplice to the robbery. And he could tell by the sounds that he was dealing with only one man at this time.

Giff knew he could not get to the dead man's pistol without being seen. Furthermore, any gunshot would alert the robber at the front of the train. Hoisting himself to the top of the car, he crawled on his stomach along the surface until he reached the midpoint. Cautiously peering over the side, he couldn't see any sign of the robber. Glancing quickly down the track, he saw that there were at least a dozen or more flatcars, piled high with rails and ties, between him and the engine, where the other outlaw was keeping an eye on the crew members in the cab.

Raising himself to a painful squatting position, due to his injured thigh, Giff prepared to jump down.

As soon as the robber came out of the car, Giff leaped on him, knocking him to the ground. It was a sorry mismatch. Giff had at least fifty pounds in weight and six inches in height on the man. Before the startled outlaw could utter a sound, Giff delivered a powerful blow to the man's jaw. Then, grabbing the pistol out of the dazed robber's holster, he yanked him to his feet and shoved the man back into the car.

The outlaw rallied enough to throw a punch at Giff, but he blocked it and delivered a muscular blow to the man's midsection. Clutching his stomach, the outlaw doubled over, and Giff followed through with an upper cut to the jaw that flattened the man.

Within seconds, he had the man firmly trussed and gagged, using the outlaw's own belt and bandanna.

Shaking his head in satisfaction, Giff looked down at him. "Tough luck, pal. I've hogtied calves that put up a better fight than a back-shooting son of a bitch like you."

"Hey, hurry up, Walt. We ain't got all day," the other gunman shouted from down the line.

By this time his injured thigh had begun throbbing, but Giff was relieved to see his pants leg was dry, so he knew the wound had not broken open.

"You're a great little seamstress, Angel," he murmured aloud.

"Thank you."

Startled, he spun around. Angie stood behind him. "What the hell are you doing here? I told you to stay in the caboose and lock the door."

Her eyes sparked with anger. "I wasn't about to stay back there locked in a railroad car while you were up here risking your life!"

"Well, can I trust you to stay here and guard this guy while I try to take out that gunman up front?"

"I suppose so."

"Dammit! I should have grabbed that guard's Colt when I had the chance. Here, take this," Giff said, holding out the pistol, "and shoot this bastard if you have to."

"I don't need that. I have one." She held up a Colt. "I took it off the dead man on the ground."

Giff rolled his eyes in frustration. "Dammit, Angie! You've got more guts than brains. You could have been shot!"

"Well, I wasn't," she said smugly. "Where is the other guard? O'Hara told me there were two of them."

"Unless I miss my guess, he's the one trussed up in the corner. I figure he shot the other guard." After checking the chamber of the gun, he handed it back to her. "Listen, honey, you can help me. I need a diversion. Give me two minutes to get down to the front of the train, then fire a shot. That should distract him enough for me to come up behind him."

"Why don't you just shoot him when you have the chance? After all, he has a drawn pistol and could shoot you on sight."

"My, my! You are a bloodthirsty little creature, aren't you, sweetheart? Maybe you aren't cut out for the fine arts, after all."

"My daddy never raised any stupid daughters, Pete Gifford."

"Two minutes," he said, grinning. Then he slid out of the door, crawled under the train, and hurried down the track. Skirting the engine, he peeked around the front of it and saw that the gunman's attention was still focused on the men in the cab.

Okay, Angel, get that shot off, he thought, waiting to make his move.

The sudden shot shattered the twilight calm.

"What the hell!" the outlaw mumbled.

As he jerked his head toward the sound, Giff came up behind him and shoved the gun into the man's back. "Okay, pal, drop it!" The outlaw froze in position, and Giff nudged the point deeper. "I said drop it or I pull this trigger."

As soon as the pistol fell to the ground, Giff said, "Mr. O'Hara, will you and your assistant get down here and give me a hand?"

"Glory be to God!" O'Hara exclaimed. "I thought we wuz goners for sure," he added, as the men climbed out of the cab. "Seems like I've seen you before, lad. Ain't you the foreman of the MacKenzie ranch?"

"That's right. Name's Pete Gifford—I'm Angie's husband. Sorry I can't offer a handshake, but as you can see, I've kind of got my hands full right now."

Dan Harrington picked up the gun. "What can I do to help, Mr. Gifford?"

"Have you got anything we can use to tie up this hombre?"

"Got a skein of rope in the cab," the young man said, climbing back up to fetch it.

In checking the outlaw for any other weapons, they removed a knife from his boot and had him securely bound by the time Angie ran up to them.

"Sure glad to see you weren't harmed none, Miz Angie," O'Hara said.

"I'm fine, Paddy, but unfortunately the guard is dead."

"Apparently the other guard was in on the robbery and shot him in the back," Giff said.

"Where is the bas . . . ah, blackguard?" O'Hara exclaimed, looking sheepishly at Angie.

"We've got him tied up back there, but rope would do a better job."

Giff and Dan tossed the trussed man over the back of his horse and they all returned to the other car. After dumping the outlaw inside the car, they lifted the guard's body in as well. While Giff retied the killer, Angie and Dan toted all the money to the caboose, and O'Hara went back to fire up the engine.

Giff locked up the car, then tied the two outlaws' horses to a rail on one of the flatcars. "I guess we're ready to pull out. We can turn these hombres over to the sheriff in Amarillo," he said.

"It'll be me pleasure to be buyin' ya a drink when we get there, lad," O'Hara said to Giff.

"I'll be looking forward it to, sir," Giff replied.

He slid an arm around Angie's shoulders as they walked back to the caboose.

"The Lord only knows what might have happened if you hadn't come along today, Giff."

"Yeah, I'm kind of glad I made the trip, too," he said as they reached the caboose. Grasping her around the waist, he swung her up on the platform. "And as I calculate, I reckon we still have about three more hours before we get there."

Angie's eyes flashed mischievously. "I'm sure we can think of some way to pass the time."

Hopping up on the platform, he lifted her in his arms. "You've sure got that right, Mrs. Gifford," he murmured, as he carried her through the door.

Chapter 24

Being a man who prided himself on being punctual, if not early, Patrick Michael O'Hara downed his drink and glanced at the clock for the dozenth time in the last five minutes.

He was anxious to depart. The delay had been over an hour already: the banker had gotten his money and left under an armed escort, the town's mortician had picked up the body of the dead guard, and the sheriff had carted off the two outlaws in a Black Maria.

He and Dan had had time to hoist a couple of drinks. And if Gifford and Miz Angie didn't get back soon from the sheriff's office, that frizzy-haired blond whore sidlin' up to Danny Boy would soon have him upstairs between her legs.

Glancing at the clock again, Paddy motioned to the bartender. "Fill her up, and pour one for yerself, Timothy O'Leary."

"That railroad yer workin' for sure has made a difference to this town, Paddy," O'Leary said. "Last week I got in a case of imported Scotch. Got a customer who won't drink anythin' but that."

"God bless the Rocky Mountain Central Railroad," O'Hara said. The two men raised their shot glasses in salute, then downed their drinks.

"Heard tell ya had yerself a bit o' a fray on this trip, Paddy."

"That we did, lad. And I'm thinkin' 'tis takin' a mite long to be fillin' out 'em forms about it, too. At this rate, if I hope to make up any loss, I'd have to be openin' it up to forty miles an hour, and I have to tell ya, lad, that's not to me likin' at night. Ya never know what could be on the track. One of 'em damn steers or the like. After me two wrecks last year, I've not the heart for another."

"And the sad part, Paddy, is that yer not more than fifty miles from the end o' the track."

"Yeah, I know. A damn shame it is that a good punctilious railroader..." He grinned broadly. "Dave Kincaid always calls me that—fine lad that he is."

"What does it mean?" O'Leary asked.

"I've not the knowin' of it, but I'm thinkin' it's good 'cause Davey Kincaid is a fine lad."

O'Leary nodded. "That he is." He poured them each another drink.

"To Davey," O'Hara said, raising his glass in the air.

"To Davey," O'Leary replied.

"And to Pete Gifford. For 'twas him and him alone who captured them thievin' bastards. If it weren't for him, O'Leary, I might not be here to do the tellin' of it."

"That's deservin' of another drink, Paddy," O'Leary said, nodding, and refilled O'Hara's glass.

O'Hara gulped down the shot, and smacking his lips, he put the empty glass down on the bar. "So as I wuz sayin', Timmy me lad, 'tis a sad state of affairs when a good punc...punc...railroader like meself is kept from doin' what he's meant to be doin' 'cause of the need for someone to be fillin' out papers that . . ." His voice faded when he slumped down and his head banged against the bar. Only O'Leary's quick hand prevented the whiskey bottle from suffering the same fate.

"Hey, Dan, O'Hara's got a problem here," O'Leary called out.

Dan Harrington unwound the saloon girl's arms from around his neck and got up from the table. " 'Pears like he ain't gonna be drivin' any train tonight."

"Whatta ya gonna do with him?" O'Leary asked.

"Guess I'll take him back to the train. There's a couple cots we brought along for them fellas that was guardin' that money. He can sleep it off there."

"You coming back, sugar?" the woman asked, when Dan hoisted his grizzled companion over his shoulder.

"Reckon not. I better keep an eye on Paddy."

"He looks old enough to take care of himself, sugar," she said, clearly disappointed at losing the opportunity for a romp with a guy who looked like he changed his britches more often than once a year.

Dan shook his head. "Paddy fools a lot of folks with 'em there whiskers he sports, but Lord knows what would happen to him if I didn't look after him." He flashed a wide smile and tipped his hat. "Night, Miz Delilah. Sure appreciated your company."

Dan had just left when the doors swung open. O'Leary's glance shifted to the tall blond stranger who stood in the doorway. "Whiskey or beer, stranger?" he asked when the stranger walked up to the bar.

"Whiskey. Have you seen anything of Pat O'Hara or Dan Harrington? They work for the Rocky Mountain Central Railroad."

"Friends of yours?" O'Leary asked cautiously.

He'd been a bartender too long to volunteer infor-
mation to strangers.

"Yeah. I was supposed to meet them here."

"Did you try the sheriff's office? Heard tell there
was a holdup."

"I just came from the sheriff's office. I was on the
train at the time of the holdup."

Relieved, O'Leary asked, "Now, would ya be
that Gifford fella what busted up that train holdup
by yerself?"

Giff couldn't help smiling. "That's right. Name's
Pete Gifford."

O'Leary reached out for a handshake. "Pleasure
to meet you, Mr. Gifford. Paddy told me how ya
done in them back-shootin', blackhearted dev'ls."

"So O'Hara was here, then. I wonder where he's
gone."

"He was here, all right. Passed out colder than a
fish. Harrington took him back to the train to sleep
it off. If you're plannin' on goin' any farther tonight
by train, you're plumb out of luck, Mr. Gifford."

Giff downed the shot of whiskey, then shoved
his hat to the top of his forehead. "Looks like I'll
be needing a room."

"You're in luck, good-looking. I just happen to
have one," Delilah said, sidling up to him. She
slipped her arm through his. "And my bed will fit
a big fellow like you just fine."

"That's a mighty generous offer, Miss . . ."

"Delilah," she said.

"Well, you see, Miss Delilah, that bed of yours
would have to fit three."

She arched a brow and smiled lewdly. "The
more the merrier. Especially if they're as good-
looking as you."

"Oh, my wife's much better-looking. In fact,
she's downright beautiful. But she doesn't like a
crowded bed." Grinning, he removed her hand

from his arm. "But let me buy you a drink, Delilah, for your kind offer."

Just then Angie entered the saloon. The first thing she saw was Giff standing at the bar with a blonde hanging on his arm. She felt the same rush of jealousy she had experienced when she saw him with Stella Crawford and Diane Divine. Then her anger cooled when she saw him gently lift the woman's hand off his arm. Composing herself, she walked over to them.

"Howdy, ma'am," O'Leary said.

"Angie!" Giff said, surprised. "Did you get the wire off to Thia?"

"Yes, I did."

"Well, you should have added that we won't be in tonight. Paddy is . . . indisposed."

"Oh, what's wrong with him?" she asked, concerned.

"Drunk as a skunk, honey. Passed out right here on the bar," Delilah said.

Up to that time, Angie had intentionally ignored the woman at Giff's side. Recalling the exhibition with Stella Crawford, Angie was determined to try and avoid a scene. Now she had no other choice but to look at the bar girl.

"Really?"

Giff cleared his throat. "Ah, Angie, this is Delilah . . . ah . . ."

"Divine. Delilah Divine," the woman said pleasantly.

"What a coincidence, Miss Divine. My *husband* has an acquaintance in Denver with the same name. Diane Divine. Are you related, by chance?"

"Naw, honey," Delilah said. "Delilah Divine's not my real name. I just took it 'cause it sounds kinda—"

"Divine," Angie offered.

"You said it, honey," Delilah said, patting the back of her upswept, frizzled hair.

Giff cast a bewildered glance at Angie. "Delilah, this is Angie MacKenzie—"

"Gifford," Angie interjected. His wife," she added distinctly for Delilah's benefit.

"Can I get you something to drink, Miz Gifford?" O'Leary asked. "Maybe a glass of sarsaparilla?"

"No, I think I'll have a beer, Mr. . . . I'm sorry, I didn't catch your name."

"O'Leary, but most folks call me Tim."

"Then Tim it will be."

"How about sitting down at a table," Giff suggested. Angie seemed to be busting for a fight, and he hoped to ward off a confrontation between the two women.

"My goodness, Giff darling," Angie cooed sweetly. "I would have thought you'd want to stand for a while, since you spent practically the last nine hours *lying* on your back." She looked up at him with an innocent smile, and batted her eyelashes outrageously at him.

Giff had had enough innuendo for the evening. "Yeah, but you know I don't cotton to standing, Angie *darling*. Must be because I spend most of my time on horseback." Taking her firmly by the arm, he led her over to a table.

Much to his annoyance, Miss Delilah Divine followed them and sat down uninvited.

Angie appeared unperturbed. "Tell me, Miss Divine—"

"Delilah, honey."

"Of course. Tell me, Delilah, have you done much riding?"

"Done more than I can count . . . but not on horses." Poking Angie with an elbow, Delilah pounded the table and broke into loud, raucous laughter.

Angie couldn't help smiling. She was beginning to like her. After all, the woman had only been doing her job—and furthermore, why should she blame Delilah for being attracted to Giff? It seemed like every woman they met was attracted to him.

Angie took a long look at him. She must have been blind not to have realized through the years what a totally attractive man he was—both physically and sexually. However, at the moment he looked as uncomfortable as she'd ever seen him.

"Funny thing about names, honey. Guess there's more than one coincidence tonight. I remember a gambler with the same name as you. Most gamblers are tinhorns, but not this one. He's one gambler I'll never forget. Handsomest fella I ever met." Delilah sighed deeply. "It's been ten years, and I'm still pining over him, watching the door now and again in the hopes he'll come through it. Name was Cleve MacKenzie."

"That *is* a coincidence, Delilah, because I have a cousin named Cleve MacKenzie."

"Tall fella? Black hair? Blue eyes? A grin that could charm the skin off a snake?"

"I've never seen him, Delilah," Angie said. "But it sounds almost identical to the way my sister described him."

"Let me take a deep look at you, honey." Delilah gazed into Angie's face, then nodded. "Yep, same blue eyes—the color of sapphires. He must be your cousin, all right. What's the good-looking devil up to? Still dealing?"

"No, he's settled down. He's a cattle rancher now. From what I understand, he and his two brothers have a big spread in Texas."

"Oh, yeah, I remember; he did talk about having two brothers."

"Yes, Luke and Flint. According to the letters Cleve writes us, his wife had a baby girl a few months ago. I believe that's his fourth child."

"Well, tell me all you can about him. I sure liked that fella."

"You probably know more about him than I do."

The two women put their heads together and continued chatting as if they'd known each other for years. Giff sat back and just listened. He managed to get a word in long enough to ask Angie if she was hungry, and after a nod, Angie turned back to her conversation with Delilah.

By the time he and Angie left the barroom, the two women had made a pledge to write to one another. The only problem was that Delilah didn't know how to write—but she promised to learn.

Cyrus Fulton, the town banker, was just leaving the hotel's dining room when Giff and Angie arrived. Upon hearing that they were spending the night in Amarillo, in gratitude, Fulton insisted that dinner and the hotel be at his expense.

"My goodness, this was very generous of Mr. Fulton," Angie said, as soon as they were seated at a table.

"Fulton owns this hotel, Angel, so his offer is no big burden to him. I'm curious to know if you're going to insist on separate rooms though. Now, *that* would be prevailing on his generosity. As it is, it's a good thing that these free offers are coming our way, because I'm not carrying any money with me. What about you?"

"Of course I have money with me," Angie said. "You never know when you'll have a need for it."

"Angel, I can't recall a single incident when I needed money in my pocket while riding the range. If you remember, I left rather unexpectedly."

"It seems so long ago. And your leg, Giff. We should change the dressing on it."

"As soon as we finish dinner we can go to the general store and get whatever we need."

"You can get what *you* need: I have everything I need. And while you're gone, I'm going to bathe."

"If you hold off until I get back, we can do that together," he suggested.

"That's a wicked gleam in your eye, Mr. Gifford. I don't think the tub would be big enough for both of us. Besides, a bath is a luxury I dearly love." She closed her eyes. "I can't think of anything more delightful than sinking down into a tub of warm water and just relaxing."

"Well, I sure can," he said. "You mean you and Edward never took a bath together!"

Her eyes popped open in shock. "Of course not! Why . . . why, I never actually saw him naked. He was considerably more modest than you are, Pete Gifford."

He chuckled warmly. "Seems kind of untimely to worry about modesty when you're making love."

"Oh, is that right? Is that another one of those *man things* of yours? There are some people who have inhibitions, you know."

"I sure didn't notice any from you today. Especially when you—"

"Enough!" She put her hands over her ears. "I don't want to hear another word. Only a cad would remind a lady of what she says or does in the . . . in the . . ."

"In the what, honey?" he asked, leaning over with a devilish grin.

She couldn't contain her giggle. "In the heat of battle. Furthermore, I wish you would stop mentioning Edward Emory. He represents a part of my life I am trying desperately to forget."

"In time, I'll have you convinced he never existed."

"And just how do you expect to do that?"

"Like this, Angel," he said, claiming her lips. As the kiss deepened, their passion accelerated. He grabbed her hand, and they hurried from the dining room.

That night, Giff never made it to the general store, and Angie never did get her bath.

Chapter 25

～○○～

The next morning, Cynthia and Dave were waiting to greet them when the train puffed into Tent Town.

Giff had never seen the migrant town before, and he was fascinated by the rows of tents that housed the families of the workers, the makeshift schoolrooms where Cynthia and Lydia Rafferty conducted classes for the children, the infirmary, and general store. There was even a forge to make the heavy iron rails malleable when necessary, as well as to service the extensive livestock so necessary to the railroad's construction. In addition, there was a dormitory car for the single men, a dining car and kitchen that fed the crew, and tents that stored the supplies.

"It's a self-contained city," Giff said.

"Not much different than the ranch you run, Giff," Dave said.

"And you move all of this periodically?"

"Yeah, anywhere from thirty-five to fifty miles of completed track. Depends upon the area. You have to make sure you have fresh water and fairly level terrain. I'll take you to end of track, where you can see the men actually laying the rail. It's a sight you'll never forget."

As soon as the men left, Angie and Cynthia sat down in the luxurious private railroad car.

"All right, the men won't be back for hours," Cynthia said. "So what did you come all the way down here to ask me, Angie?"

"I need some advice, Thia. I don't know what to do."

"Advice about what?"

"About marriage. I don't think I'm ready for marriage."

Cynthia looked stunned. "A little late for that, isn't it? But if you have these kinds of doubts, apparently you aren't. So why did you get married?"

Angie got up and began to pace the floor. "I was desperate."

"Desperate!"

"I'm going to tell you the whole story, Thia. I haven't even told Beth. Nobody knows the whole truth but Giff and myself."

She sat back down and reached for Cynthia's hand. "But first, I have to ask you how you knew you loved Dave enough to marry him. You're glamorous, intelligent, worldly-wise. You always loved beautiful clothes, traveling to all the exciting places of the world, and meeting famous and interesting people. You could have accomplished anything you set your mind to do—married any man you wanted. Yet you've forsaken all that for this life: hard, unsettled, living in a railroad car— certainly nothing glamorous about it. Why?"

"That's pretty obvious, isn't it? I'm in love with Dave."

"I know. But that's too simplistic an answer, Thia. I need to know how *you* knew you loved him enough to choose one way of life over the other. Why you felt you could be content the rest of your life living in this constant state of upheaval."

"Angie, not everything a person wants in life is always attainable at one time. You have to recognize what is most important to you—and Dave is that, to me. Pumpkin, I love you and Beth dearly, but there is no one or nothing in the world more necessary in my life than Dave. Fancy clothes, marble palaces, glamorous capitals, are shallow substitutes—they mean nothing compared to glancing across a room and seeing him, hearing his voice, just knowing he's near."

"That's what I've been struggling to understand. How can you be sure it was worth the sacrifice you made?"

"Sacrifice? Oh dear God, Angie, is that how you see it? Sacrifice is giving up something of value and getting nothing in return. *I got Dave's love, Pumpkin.* Do you think any of those other things you mentioned can compare to that? The Cynthia you once knew no longer exists. Through our love I have become part of Dave and he is part of me—and because of that, I'm richer, wiser, and happier than I've ever been. What has this all got to do with you and Giff?"

"It all began when I quit school and got a job in the chorus on a riverboat. The star of the show was Edward Emory. I fell in love with him and . . . we became intimate." She glanced at Cynthia to see her reaction.

"Pumpkin, if you expect me to cast stones, you're mistaken. Nothing you've told me so far is worse than what I've done in the past."

"Well, that was the simple part of it, Thia. I thought I was carrying his child, and I told Edward. He deserted me and ran off with another woman."

"So you're pregnant, Angie?"

"No. I was mistaken about that."

"Please tell me you aren't still in love with this man. Is that the problem?"

"For a time after Edward left, I thought I *was* still in love with him. I've since seen how mistaken I was. But at the time, I was miserable—and so full of self-pity that I couldn't think properly."

"I don't have to guess what happened next. This is where Giff enters the story." Angie nodded. "I bet you confessed all to him, and he offered to make an honest woman of you."

"That's right. He didn't want any MacKenzie born a bastard. He insisted I marry him to give the baby a name."

"Insisted? Hmmm," Cynthia said, "sounds like you're holding him responsible."

"No, I don't mean to sound like I blame Giff. In fact, I felt guilty for getting him involved in something that affected his own life so much. I was thinking of the baby's welfare—and I suppose, deep down, my own as well—and in desperation I grasped at his offer. I didn't really stop to consider how it would affect Giff's life: whether he was in love with someone else, or that being married to me would keep him from seeking other women's companionship."

"And it didn't occur to you that Giff might be in love with you, when he made the offer?"

"In love with me? Of course not. Giff's always been like a brother to me. As a matter of fact, he even told me just the other night that he's only loved one woman—and he's still in love with her."

"Oh, I see," Cynthia said.

"Thia, I know that smirk. What do you know that I don't? I suppose he's told you who she is!"

"Did *you* ask him her name?" she questioned with the same knowing smile.

"No. It seemed to be a very private thing to him. I didn't want to pry into his personal life."

"Angie, you *are* his personal life. You're his wife. If I were you, Pumpkin, I'd ask him who she is. Well, go on with your story. So you married Giff, and the two of you returned to the Roundhouse to await the birth of the baby."

"We weren't back more than a couple days when I discovered I wasn't actually pregnant. I guess all that moping and crying I had been doing affected my system."

"If I recall correctly, you never were regular as it was, Angie," Cynthia said. "Why didn't you go to a doctor? He could have confirmed your condition immediately."

"That's the same thing Giff said. He had assumed I had seen a doctor."

"Well, Angie, I know it's hindsight, but it would have been the logical thing to do."

"I know that now, but I told you, I wasn't thinking clearly, Thia. Looking back now, I can't believe how stupid I was about everything: Edward, the baby, getting married." She cradled her head in her hand.

Cynthia got up and put an arm around Angie's shoulders. "There is some good that came from it, Pumpkin. As long as you're not having this Edward's child, at least you're rid of that fellow."

"I thought I was until he and Stella showed up at the Roundhouse. Edward said he came to marry me."

"Who is Stella?"

"Stella Crawford worked on the riverboat. She's the woman he ran off with. Pretty bizarre, isn't it? When Edward found out Giff and I were married, I guess he figured out why."

Cynthia shrugged. "So what!" She folded her arms across her chest. "Frankly, Angie, I still can't see where there's a problem, unless . . ." Apparently horrified by the thought that had just entered her mind, Cynthia stopped and looked at Angie. "Are you in love with Giff?"

Anguished, Angie lifted her head and looked up at her sister. "Yes, I am."

"Oh, thank God." Cynthia slumped down in a chair.

"I love everything about Giff. He's a fine, beautiful human being. He deserves more than a wife he married out of loyalty."

"How do you know he didn't marry you out of love?"

"He would have told me. He's never said he loves me."

"Love has a way of sneaking up on people before they realize it. Often one person will recognize it a lot sooner than the other one." She cleared her throat. "A *lot* sooner! So just because he hasn't said it, Pumpkin, you can't be certain he doesn't love you."

Angie jumped up and began to pace the floor again. "Right now, I'm not certain of anything. That's my problem, Thia. I can't explain or understand what's happening to me—my feelings. I don't know how to identify them—put a name on them. I know I get insanely jealous when I see another woman so much as touch Giff. And I'm in ecstasy when he makes love to me. Yet at the same time, I'm afraid to admit to him that I love him because it means I would have to give up dreams I've had for years, and remain on the ranch because that's Giff's life."

"What kind of dreams, Angie?"

"Oh, pursuing my art, or maybe my desire to perform on the stage."

"Which is it? One or the other?"

Angie shook her head helplessly. "That's what I mean. I don't know. I just don't know what to do," she cried, and burst into tears.

Cynthia put her arms around Angie. "Pumpkin, I can't tell you what to do. You have to follow your own instincts. Sometimes in doing so, you end up hurting someone you love dearly. I know I hurt Daddy running off the way I did."

Tears streaking her cheeks, Angie looked up at her. "I don't want to hurt Giff, Thia. That's the last thing in the world I want to do. But I need to prove to myself that even if I'm not talented enough to be a star, I can make it on my own. I just can't continue always wondering if I could do it or not."

"So it's not really about love or dreams. It's really about you trying to prove your independence. The stage or your art isn't as important to you as proving you can be independent."

"They go hand in hand, don't they?"

"You performed on the riverboat, didn't you? What did that prove to you?"

"That was under the worst conditions. The other day Edward suggested we open a repertory in Denver."

"You'd actually consider associating with this man after the way he's acted?"

"No. I've been thinking of doing it on my own. It would give me the opportunity to occasionally perform, under conditions that I control. Not on a riverboat dressed in a sleazy costume. I can't believe it wouldn't be a satisfying experience, as well as a real chance to prove my independence."

"Angie, independence is a sense of self-satisfaction—contentment with being who and what you are."

"And that certainly doesn't describe me," Angie declared in scorn. "Thia, you proved your independence before you fell in love with Dave. I did just the opposite: I proved how dependent I am on Giff before I fell in love with him."

"You're looking for some sign of confidence,

Pumpkin, and you believe it's necessary to leave the Roundhouse to attain that sense of self-assurance. It's *not* necessary. You're very accomplished at ranching skills. On the other hand, if performing on the stage is a driving need within you—a dream of fulfillment—then that is what you must do. But they are two *separate* issues. Don't try to combine them, and believe that one is dependent on the other. I think you must make that distinction in your own mind, Angie, before you can come to a decision about Giff and your marriage. It would be tragic if you and Giff ended up losing something that is very precious. All I ask is that you think it over long and hard, Pumpkin."

The next morning Angie and Giff prepared to return to Denver. As the two women shared a final kiss and hug by the train, Cynthia whispered, "Remember, follow your instincts—and your heart, Pumpkin."

"I will, Thia. I love you," Angie called out with a final wave.

"Well, did you get the answers you came for?" Giff asked, once they settled down in the caboose for the return trip.

"Not exactly. Just some sisterly advice."

"And you don't want to talk about it?" he asked.

"Not yet, Giff. I will sometime, but there's a lot I have to work out before I do."

He lay down on the cot and closed his eyes. She could tell he wasn't satisfied with her answer, but he didn't intend to press the issue.

She felt a twinge of guilt—and gratitude. Giff was a proud man and had always been a private person. Although he knew whatever was bothering her affected him, too, he respected her privacy enough not to force answers from her.

She sat down on the edge of the cot. He opened

his eyes when she gently brushed back the hair on his forehead.

"Tired?" she asked softly.

"Not really."

"Giff, I appreciate your understanding. The last couple of weeks—I guess I should say months— have been pretty bizarre. There've been so many changes in my life, and I know it's been the same for you, too."

She was rewarded with the tantalizing slide of his hands up her arms, his fingers curving around her shoulders.

Lowering her head, she kissed him. The sensation was too sweet, too stimulating, to stop. Tracing his lips with her tongue, she began to lightly tug and nibble at them. His grasp tightened as he parted his lips and sucked in a breath.

Aroused, she covered his mouth and, as the kiss deepened, slid her tongue between his parted lips.

His fingers dug into her shoulders. "Oh, God! Oh, sweet God, Angel!" he murmured, pulling her down to him.

Chapter 26

U pon returning to the Roundhouse, they discovered Middy moving around listlessly with a bad case of the sniffles. When Angie tried to convince the housekeeper to forget her duties for the day and return to bed, Middy immediately balked.

" 'Tain't that serious, gal," she said, pulling out a huge white handkerchief to blow her nose.

"Middy, you're trying to do too much around here. You never should have fired the cook. Tomorrow when Giff and I go to Denver for the concert, I'm going to place an advertisement for another one."

"Do what you want, but it's a waste of time and money, Missy. Now get out of the kitchen and let me be."

"Since Beth still isn't home, you don't have to worry about dinner tonight. I promised to cook Giff a meal at his house."

"Ain't that boy ever gonna move into this here house proper-like?"

"He claims so. He's just taking his time getting around to it."

"So now my cookin' ain't good enough for the two of you," Middy complained.

"I didn't say that; it's just that we want to be alone."

"You sayin' I bother you? You just listen here, Missy: I serve the meal, get back into the kitchen, and mind my own business."

"The trouble is, you old dear, you think we *are* your business."

"Smart talk comin' from you, considerin' it was me swaddlin' the both of yuh when you was babes in arms."

"And it's time you let us take care of you." Angie kissed her on the top of her white head. As Angie hurried out of the kitchen, Middy pulled out her handkerchief again and blew her nose.

Angie found Giff in the barn getting ready to ride out. "How would you like to have a quiet, candlelight dinner at your house tonight?"

He arched a brow. "With whom?"

"With me, of course. I just told Middy that you and I made plans to eat at your house. It looks like she's coming down with a cold, but she's too stubborn to go to bed. I want her to rest."

"Good idea."

"Anything special you'd like?"

He pulled her into his arms. "Just the pleasure of your company, Angel." The slide of his hands up her arms sent a titillating shiver through her. She slipped her arms around his neck and settled into the pleasant warmth of his embrace. "You're no help, Giff. I want to make this dinner very special."

The heady sensation of his kiss carried to the pit of her stomach. "I'll help to make what'll follow that dinner very special. How about that?" He kissed the tip of her nose, then swung up on his gelding. "See you later, Angel."

Still feeling the afterglow of his kiss, Angie leaned back against the fence and watched him ride away. He wasn't making her decision to stay or go any easier.

When Calico trotted over and nuzzled her on the head, Angie turned and patted him. "And you don't make my decision any easier, either."

By the following day, Middy's sniffles had developed into a constant sneezing. She finally bowed to Angie's pleas and took to her bed.

Before leaving for Denver, Angie took her in a cup of tea generously laced with honey and whiskey.

"Here, drink this. It should help you sleep. String and Red said they'd check on you later." She puffed up the pillows behind Middy's head.

"Quit your fussin', gal, or I'll be spillin' this tea. 'Sides, it's just a summer cold. Ain't nothin' that a night in bed won't cure."

"Oh, really! Isn't that what I've been trying to tell you?"

"That don't mean I want those two dumb cowhands stompin' through my kitchen with their dirty boots," Middy grumbled. "Why, the two of 'em could tramp through a pile of manure and pay it no mind."

Angie sat down on the edge of the bed and waited until Middy drank the tea. "We'll be back as soon as the concert is over."

"Just be off and have yerselves a good time, darlin'," Middy said, yawning. Her eyes began to droop.

By the time Angie tiptoed out of the room, Middy was sound asleep.

As they mingled with the theatergoers amassed in the lobby of Denver's opera house, Angie and

Giff made a striking couple: she with her dark hair and wearing a white dimity gown, he with his light hair and dressed in a dark suit. They were stopped repeatedly by well-wishers who had heard of their marriage.

Angie was sipping a lemonade, awaiting the start of the performance, when Michael Carrington approached them.

"What a pleasure to see you again, Angeleen. You look positively radiant," he said, kissing her hand. "And I heard of your marriage. Congratulations, Giff."

As the two men shook hands, Angie couldn't help but notice that the rich Texan, whose family owned a rival railroad, looked exceptionally handsome in a black custom-fitted, tailcoated suit.

For several minutes the two men talked of the declining beef market before Carrington turned back to Angie. "Where are your lovely sisters?"

"Thia and Dave are at end of track, and Beth's been in Washington on business for weeks. We just got a wire today saying she'll be home by the end of the week. I know she feels bad about missing the concert."

"That is regrettable," Carrington agreed.

"Yes, this concert is one of the few diversions Beth allows herself. She works so hard all the time. Are you here alone, Mr. Carrington?" Angie asked.

"Yes, I am." He frowned. "Angeleen, can't we do away with this formality and drop the 'Mister'? Just call me by my first name."

Angie smiled. "Only if you call me Angie, then I'll be delighted to call you Michael. Why don't you join us in our box, Michael? With Beth and Thia both gone, there's two extra chairs."

"I'd like that very much."

"I wonder what's holding up the start of the concert," Giff said, glancing at his pocket watch. "It's almost thirty minutes late already."

"Angeleen!" The exclamation came from a short, gray-haired man who had rushed up to her.

"Mr. Bellemey, how nice to see you again," Angie greeted her former piano teacher.

"My dear Angeleen, you are Heaven-sent," the concert director exclaimed. "May I prevail upon your sweet nature to do me a big favor?"

"Of course, Mr. Bellemey," Angie said. "What is it?"

"Our pianist, Teresa Chambers, has become ill and it appears she will be unable to perform. Would you be kind enough to fill in for her?"

"Oh, good heavens, Mr. Bellemey, I haven't played seriously in months."

"My dear, you could play this particular Mozart piece blindfolded. It's the very one you played at your own recital."

"Yes, but that was years ago, sir."

"There is no piano solo throughout the whole concert," he pleaded. "It will just be a matter of accompanying the orchestra, and one time it will be necessary to accompany the soloist when she does an aria."

Angie looked helplessly at Giff. "I don't think I can."

"Sure you can, Angel," he said.

"I've never played before such a large audience, Mr. Bellemey. What if I make a mistake?"

"Nonsense. You'll do wonderfully. My dear, you were my best student. I would never ask this of you if I thought for a moment you were incapable of doing it."

"Angie, I can't believe you won't be outstanding," Michael Carrington said. "I remember hearing you play last year at your home. You play beautifully."

"Very well," Angie agreed. "But don't say I didn't warn you,"

Bellemey took her arm. "Come, dear, we must begin."

Angie threw a woeful glance at Giff and Michael as the harried man led her away.

"Well, the evening has certainly taken an unexpected but interesting turn," Michael said. He slapped Giff on the shoulder. "Shall we be seated?"

From his seat in the MacKenzie box, Giff had a clear view of Angie at the piano. At first he could see her nervousness, her tentative touch on the keys, but as the concert progressed, so did her self-assurance. Every round of applause gave her added confidence and soon she was enmeshed in the music, caught up in the brilliant flow of the melody.

His heart swelled with pride for her. How could she doubt her musical ability? Her long, slim fingers moved across the keyboard adroitly and assertively. For her to deny her gift was a travesty: she had talent, and more important, she had the understanding of the music—the mood the composer hoped to convey to the listener. He regretted that Beth and Thia weren't there to share this night with her, because he knew they would be as proud of her as he was.

Giff's gaze rested on her face. Angie glowed with enthusiasm as her fingers flew across the keys. With every note, every chord, her increased confidence was reflected not only in the movement of her hands, but in the set of her shoulders, the angle of her head.

And with this bold assurance, she unknowingly sent a signal to every musician in the orchestra to meet this challenge.

When the concert ended, the audience leapt to

their feet with cheers and applause. The maestro took his bow, and then the soloist. Finally the moment came for the much-deserved salute to the orchestra. The applause grew thunderous.

Angie stood up, her eyes searching the box to meet Giff's. He smiled at her as their gazes locked. She was flushed with exuberance. And in that bittersweet moment, as his heart swelled with happiness for her, he felt a tugging pain in his chest, knowing that this was a facet of her life far removed from him and the Roundhouse.

Angie's exhilaration continued on the ride back to the Roundhouse. As they passed MacKenzie Junction and the evening neared an end, she still bubbled over with enthusiasm. "This was the most thrilling night of my life, Giff," Angie said. "Well, maybe the second most," she added, tucking her arm through his.

"What was the first?" he asked, amused.

"The first time you made love to me."

"That's encouraging, anyway."

"Was I really good, Giff?" she asked.

"You were great—fulfilled my every fantasy."

"Oh, you know what I mean, silly!" she said, poking him in the side.

He chuckled. "I couldn't resist."

"Was I really good tonight?"

"Angel, you were great."

"You're not just saying that to be kind, are you?"

"No, I am not. You've got to start believing in yourself, Angel. You're very talented, so stop thinking you aren't. And quit trying to compare yourself to the great musicians or art masters. If everyone had their talent, there'd be nothing unique about them."

"I know what you're trying to say. I tell myself that all the time to avoid getting too depressed.

Giff, what do you think of the idea of my opening a repertory in Denver?"

This was the moment he'd dreaded. From the instant he had seen her on the stage that evening, he knew this moment was inevitable. He pulled the carriage to the side of the road and stopped. "I guess I don't quite know what you mean." His chest felt knotted and he climbed down and walked over to the stream that ran parallel to the road.

Angie followed him. "I have the money Grandfather MacGregor left me. I thought perhaps I'd invest it in a small theater to put on performances every month."

"You mean musical performances?"

"Not always. Sometimes it could be theatrical performances, too. Mr. Bellemey said—"

"Bellemey! You've already discussed this with him?"

She lowered her head guiltily and began to toy with a ruffle on her gown. "Yes, backstage tonight . . . after the performance."

"I see."

"I'm sorry, Giff. I realize I should have discussed it with you before mentioning it to him."

"I suppose that's why you went to see Thia?"

"Partly."

"And what does Bellemey think of the idea?"

"He's in favor of it. He said he has a brother who is a theatrical director who might be persuaded to join in the venture."

Giff said nothing, but began skimming stones into the water.

Finally Angie broke the silence. "It's a very good idea, Giff. Denver only has two concerts a year, and occasionally a famous performer comes to town. This would be a pleasant diversion for the people interested in the performing arts. We would form our own resident company of performers instead of depending on a traveling troupe."

"And you would be part of that resident company."

"Only musically. I have no desire to perform theatrically; I never have. I'd be content just to play the piano once or twice a year. That's what I dreamed of doing."

"Sounds like you'd have to spend a lot of time in Denver."

"Probably at first," she said. "At least until we get organized and operating."

"I see," he said. "So do you intend to live in Denver?"

"This has happened so fast that I haven't thought it all out yet. Certainly I can't travel between there and the Roundhouse every night. But maybe I could come home weekends, or you could come to Denver."

"Is that what you consider a marriage, Angie?"

"No. But we don't have a true marriage anyway."

"We could," he snapped. "If we tried. I want a real marriage."

"Giff, you and I don't even live in the same house now. What difference does it make if I'm in Denver and you're here?"

"Because I'm in love with you." He turned back to skimming stones.

The unexpected statement caught her unprepared. "What do you mean?"

"It means I want you near me. It means I want to come home every night and see your smile, to know you're near. It means I want to smell you— see you—taste you—touch you. To hear the sound of your voice, your laughter. It means I want you to have my children. I want to grow old with you." He turned his head and the pain in his eyes felt like a knife thrust in her heart. "It means all the things I've held within me for three years."

Suddenly Cynthia's words of advice became very clear to her. "Giff, you told me you were in love—that you've only loved one woman your whole life. I'm that woman, aren't I?"

"Yes." His reply was so soft, she had to strain to hear it.

"Oh, I'm so stupid." She shook her head, torn between bewilderment, astonishment—and an overpowering, heartwarming, pulse-pounding joy. Life just didn't get any better than that moment!

"I can't believe how stupid I've been! Every time we made love, I thought it was just that man thing we've joked about. When in truth you were—"

"*Making love to you*. Good God, Angie, I've wanted to make love to you since you were eighteen."

"Why didn't you tell me, Giff? Why did you hold it inside of you all these years?"

"I figured you didn't want to hear it."

She went over and put her hand on his arm. Tears glistened in her eyes when she looked up at him. "Did you ever stop to think that by your remaining silent, I might have married Edward, or someone else?"

"I thought about it every day. I would have had to live with it."

"Oh, Giff, I love you, too." She slipped her arms around his neck. "Hold me, Giff." She gloried in contentment when he drew her tightly into the circle of his arms. "Don't ever let me go again. No matter what I say or do—whatever crazy notion enters my head. Just put your arms around me as a reminder of what I need and want. Because I want all the things you do, too. I want to be with you. To have your babies."

His warm touch moved to her chin, tipping her

face to meet the tenderness and understanding in his clear blue eyes.

"My dream has always been you and the Roundhouse, Angel. I can't think of one without the other. But you must be free to pursue your dream, too. I'd never forgive myself if I were the one preventing you from doing so."

"Giff, I love you so much." She shook her head in mock anger. "Dammit, Peter Gifford, why didn't you tell me sooner? It would have saved me a whole lot of soul searching!"

"I didn't hear any confessions of love coming from you, either," he teased.

"I'm afraid in the future, you're going to get tired of hearing me say it."

Sighing deeply, she buried her head against his chest, a sense of peace filling her as his arms closed around her.

"I must have loved you from the day you were born, Angel, and I'll never let you go. That's why I'm not going to let you give up something you've loved your whole life, either—your music. Tomorrow we'll drive to Denver and you get those plans you talked about in motion. We'll work this out between us somehow. After all, Denver isn't at the other end of the world." His grin tore at her heartstrings. "But don't think I'll ever let you stray farther away than that."

He kissed her long and deeply, sending exciting shivers to every nerve end of her body. Her legs were trembling when he broke the kiss.

"Like it or not, Angel, you're wearing a Roundhouse brand."

She threw her arms around his neck and they sank to the ground. "Then brand me again, Giff. Make it deep and permanent, so nothing and no one can ever threaten it again," she murmured, before recapturing his lips.

Chapter 27

Dawn was just creeping over the horizon when Angie awoke and found Giff already dressed and ready to leave.

"Go back to sleep, Angel," he said, sitting down on the edge of the bed. "String and I are riding out to check the herd. I'm leaving Red behind in case you need him." He leaned over and kissed her. "We'll be back early." He grinned wickedly. "But take care of yourself while I'm gone. No more of that rolling around buck-naked in the moonlight. You could catch a cold."

"Then we're both at risk, aren't we?" she replied with a cocky smile.

As soon as he left, Angie got up and went to the window. String was already mounted, and Red was holding the reins of Giff's gelding. When Giff joined them, the men exchanged several words of greeting and low laughter, then Giff slapped Red on the shoulder and climbed on Brick.

Angie sat down on the window ledge and leaned her head back against the frame. She could almost guess what they had said; she had been a part of that flow of camaraderie so often that she felt a nostalgia when she watched Giff and String ride away. Grumbling about getting up before the sun, Red hobbled, in his bow-legged gait, back to the bunkhouse.

Angie smiled. Life on the Roundhouse was good. There was nothing she didn't love about it. Granted the hours were long, because of the need to make the most of daylight. And physically the work was strenuous: long, back-aching hours in the saddle, roping obstinate steers that didn't want to budge, miserably hot summers, and bone-chilling winters. But these mountains were a temple of worship that stirred her soul; for what compared to the hushed serenity of the dawn of a new day or the breath-robbing beauty of a day's-end sunset?

And what could ever compare to the crackle of a campfire's burning logs, the smell of fresh pines, a hillside carpeted in wildflowers in the springtime or ablaze with golden aspen in the fall? Even Red's incessant carping held a place in her heart.

She thought of her feeling of awe at the birth of a calf, and the heart-tugging sight of a spindly-legged colt taking its first steps. She could see a vivid image of Giff wrestling a steer to the ground, and her heartbeat quickened recalling the countless times he had turned to grin at her during a roundup. Closing her eyes, she lifted her face to the morning breeze, reliving the feel of the wind in her hair as she galloped across the countryside on Calico.

These were but a few of her images of the Roundhouse—sights and sounds she had known all her life that had delighted her, fed her, nurtured her until they had become as intrinsic to her being as the color of her hair.

Last night Giff had told her that she and the Roundhouse were one and the same to him. Now she understood the depth of his words. She could not envision a life without Giff—and Giff was the Roundhouse. And so was she!

She was a rancher—as good as any hand on the ranch! Giff had tried to convince her of this. Thia had tried to tell her. So had Beth. What could she ever prove to herself on any stage or in any art gallery that she hadn't already proven every time she climbed on horseback, swung a lariat, or hazed a steer? And no one, not even Giff, could love the Roundhouse more than she!

"This above all: to thine own self be true."

I will, Mr. Shakespeare. Thank you. And thank you, Giff, my beloved. And thank you, Thia . . . and Beth, String, and Red.

And thank you, God!

Smiling gloriously, she turned away from the window.

Middy was running a fever, and over her protests Angie sent Red to Denver to get a doctor. Then donning an apron, she tucked her hair back under a bandanna and set to dusting the house while she waited for the doctor's arrival.

The heat of the day quickly closed in on her, and perspiration soon dotted her brow as she polished the newels and banister of the stairway. In the hope of drawing in a breeze Angie opened the front door, then returned to the task at hand, singing lightly as she toiled.

The chore was made easier because her thoughts were on the previous night's conversation with Giff. To know he had not been forced into an unwelcome marriage had not only lifted the burden of guilt off her shoulders, but his confession of love had opened her heart and mind to the realization of just how much she loved him. Last night, for the first time since they were married, she truly felt like Giff's wife. Her heart began to flutter as she recalled the thrill of making love uninhibitedly beside the stream under a starlit sky—giving themselves to each other with no restraint, no withheld admissions of love. Those incredible moments in his arms had totally eclipsed the earlier excitement of her concert performance.

"It pains me to see someone so talented reduced to the menial labor of a charwoman."

Startled by the intrusion on her thoughts, she turned to discover that Edward Emory had entered through the open door.

"It is customary to knock, Edward, before entering the privacy of another person's home. What are you doing here? I would have thought you'd left town long ago."

He smiled smugly. "I believe we have some business to transact, Angeleen."

"No, we haven't, Edward. I specifically told you that I did not want to see you on the Roundhouse again."

With an effeminate flick of his hand—the sight of which came near to nauseating her—Edward brushed away her objection. "My dear Angeleen, I recognized your words were said in anger, so I gave them little credence."

Angie put aside the polishing rag and walked down the stairs. "Then I shall repeat them in a calmer vein, Edward, so there will be no misunderstanding. I want you out of here, and if I see you on the Roundhouse again, I shall have you arrested for trespassing on private property."

He threw back his head in laughter. "I suggest that before you whistle for the sheriff, my dear, we sit down and have a calm conversation."

"I would sit down in a bed of snakes before I'd sit down again with you."

"Tsk, tsk, tsk, my dear, such hyperbole! But very well, I shall comply with your wishes and be gone as soon as I get my five thousand dollars."

"What are you talking about, Edward?"

"That is what it will cost you for me to leave Denver without telling my story to the newspaper."

Now it was Angie's turn to laugh. By the time she finished, Edward's arrogant stare had changed to a steely glint of anger. "What do you find so amusing, Angeleen?"

"Extortion! Really, Edward, is there no level to which you are unwilling to stoop?" Her disgusted tone conveyed her loathing for him. "You really are more detestable than I thought possible. I am not intimidated, and since this conversation has become quite boring, please leave at once."

"Since you aren't interested in listening to what I have to say, I am sure your local newspaper will be. After all, when the daughter of a locally renowned citizen has an illicit affair, it does create quite a stir in the community."

"Do you believe I'm so naive that I don't see that you'd continue this blackmail in the years to come? My sister endured a scandal, and if necessary, I'm prepared to do the same before I'd ever consider cowering to your demands."

"I've looked into the gossip about your sister's shameless affair with some foreign count, Angeleen, and it's my understanding the man was a bachelor."

"Of course."

"Then that is considerably less notorious than your . . . ah, dalliance with a married man."

"What are you implying now, Edward? I have never had an affair with a married man. You know I was virginal when you met me."

He patted his mouth to stifle a yawn. "Yes, how well I remember your inexperience and . . . ineptness. It was very arduous on me physically. I am curious, Angeleen, how that cretin you married endures your sexual, ah, shall I say reserve."

Days before, his remark might have fueled the feeling of inadequacy she had suffered about herself, but last night had bolstered a self-confidence she had denied herself for too long. More amused than offended by the caddish remark, Angie folded her arms across her chest.

"Perhaps you should ask him, Edward. I think I would enjoy watching him smash that smirk off your face."

"I doubt that he'd be so quick to deliver blows when he, too, hears of your promiscuity with a married man."

"And just how do you intend to prove such an accusation, Edward?"

"With this." He pulled a document out of his pocket and waved it in her face. "A marriage license, dear Angeleen. Stella and I have been wed for five years."

"I should have guessed that, especially after you showed up here with her. You and Stella are the two most decadent individuals I've ever encountered. How could she not only endure your behavior, but encourage it?"

"Stella is a realist."

"Stella is as much of a degenerate as you are, Edward," she snapped. "You both are beneath contempt, and I am not frightened by your threats." Angie stalked to the door. "Get out of this house. By allowing your presence inside this door, I've defiled the memory of the man who built it."

His eyes glinted with malevolence. "You're not getting off that easy, you little whore. If I can't get the money one way, I'll get it by another—even if I have to beat every dollar out of you." He grabbed her by the arms. "You're coming with me."

"Let me go," she cried out, and began to struggle. Edward doubled his fist and punched her in the jaw. Unconscious, she dropped to the floor.

"What's all the shoutin' goin' on?" Middy asked from the hallway. Upon seeing Angie on the floor, she cried, "What have you done to my baby?" The feverish woman grabbed at his arm.

"Get away from me, you old crone," Edward snarled. With a forceful shove he pushed her aside, knocking her off her feet. She fell to the floor, her frail body slamming against the marble tile, and she lay there groaning.

Dazed, Angie sat up. Edward yanked the drapery tiebacks from one of the windows. Pulling her arms behind her, he tied her wrists together, then did the same to her ankles.

Her head was pounding, her jaw ached, and bound helplessly, Angie tried to clear her blurred vision. She managed to focus on the figure on the floor. "Middy!" Horrified, she groaned, "You've hurt her! You're insane!"

"Shut up." He pulled the bandanna off her head and tied it around her mouth. Hastily scribbling a note, he tossed it down on the floor next to Middy. After struggling unsuccessfully to pick her up, he yanked her bound wrists over her head and dragged her out to the carriage. Grunting, lifting, and shoving, he finally managed to get her onto the floor of the buggy. Pebbles flew in all directions when he whipped the horses to a gallop and raced away in a cloud of dust.

As Giff rode up to the house, he saw the dust cloud in the distance. "Red must be really racing the team to raise that kind of cloud," he said.

String shook his head. "Ole Red oughta have more sense than to whip a horse like that."

"Maybe the doctor has to get back to Denver in

a hurry." Giff dismounted and tied Brick to the hitching post.

"That's the Chief's favorite harness mare. Ain't no call to treat good horseflesh like that. Hope you tell him so, too, when he gits back, Giff. Red don't pay me no never mind when I get on him," String grumbled, dismounting.

"Well, I hope the doctor did Middy some good," Giff said, as they walked up to the open door. "Hate to see her feeling any worse than she did this morning."

As soon as he stepped inside, Giff saw Middy trying to sit up. He was at her side at once. "What happened? Did you fall?"

"My baby—he took my baby," she cried.

"What are you talking about? You mean Angie? Someone took Angie!"

When they tried to help her to her feet, Middy winced with pain. "My arm!"

"Middy, who took Angie?" Giff said anxiously as he and String led her over to the stair and sat her down.

"That Emory fella's got her. Trussed her up like a steer."

String picked up the note lying on the floor. "Looks like he left you a message, Giff."

Giff read the scribbled ransom note damanding five thousand dollars if he wanted to see Angie alive again. "How long ago did he leave, Middy?"

"Just now . . . I think. Head ain't too clear," Middy said, racked with pain and fever.

"Has Red showed up with the doctor yet?"

"No, sure hope he gets here soon. I think my arm's busted."

"Then that dust we saw is Emory's trail. String, Red should be back with the doc any minute. Do what you can for Middy until he gets here," Giff yelled, on his way out the door.

Unhitching his gelding, Giff grabbed the reins and saddle horn. "Get moving, Brick!" Responding to the urgent command, the horse bolted to a gallop. Giff adroitly swung a leg over the saddle and dug his heels into the stirrups, and the well-trained animal stretched out to a speedier gait.

If that bastard has hurt one hair on Angie's head, I'll kill him. I should have kicked the shit out of him the first time I laid eyes on him! The carriage was out of eyesight, but from the dust cloud in the distance it was clear that Emory was following the Denver road. Giff knew he had to overtake it before Emory reached the city, or he'd lose the trail.

He left the road and cut across the countryside to a bluff that overlooked the road. From that vantage point he had a good view of the racing carriage being pulled by a black horse. He recognized it as the same horse and buggy Emory had used before. Wheeling his horse, he turned away and headed for the road.

When he reached the outskirts of Denver, he slowed his pace and started looking for livery stables where Emory might have rented the rig. He had his first bit of luck when he found the carriage itself behind a dingy building.

Giff dismounted to examine it. Lathered and sweating, the poor horse was still attached to the buggy. "Sorry, fella," Giff said, patting the exhausted animal, "that bastard sure has no respect for horseflesh."

Seeing a scruffy-looking lad nearby amusing himself by rolling the rim of a wagon wheel with a stick, Giff motioned him over. "Son, did you see the man who was driving this buggy?"

"Yep."

"Did he have a woman with him?"

"Yep. When I came out, he wuz jest goin' inside the back of that there saloon, so I didn't get a look at her, but she sure musta been drunk 'cuz he looked to be almost carryin' her."

Giff pulled out a gold dollar. "Tell you what, son. If you give this horse a good rubdown and water him, I'll give you this gold dollar."

Wheel and stick hit the ground. "A dollar! Mister, I ain't had a whole dollar in my life."

"Got one now." He tossed the boy the coin.

When he entered the saloon, he saw several closed doors and a battered stairway leading to the floor above. The hallway reeked of beer from the half dozen discarded barrels that were piled up against a wall. Giff climbed the stairs cautiously, trying to avoid making any sound. A stair creaked loudly under his weight and he paused, listening alertly. When it didn't attract any attention, he continued up the stairs.

There were four rooms on the floor above. The walls were stained yellow from tobacco smoke and appeared not to have seen a coat of whitewash from the time they were built. Rubbish was heaped at one end of the hallway.

Giff listened by the first door, but there was no sound coming from the room. At the second door he could hear the low murmur of two women. He moved to the next door.

"You aren't so smart now, are you, you little bitch?" Stella lashed out with a backhand and delivered a stinging slap to Angie's cheek with such force that her head slammed against the chair's back.

The room began to spin. Light-headed, Angie gasped for air, but the gag on her mouth prevented her from drawing a deep breath. *Stay calm, Angie. If Edward intended to kill you, he'd have done so at the ranch. Just keep your head, and figure a way out of this.* She began to work at the rope binding her wrists.

"Why'd you bring her here?" Stella snarled, turning her wrath on Edward.

"Where else could I go with her?"

"It was dumb to snatch her. What if that husband of hers goes for the sheriff? That nosy housekeeper knows it was you."

"Once Gifford comes up with the money, we'll get out of here. By the time they find her, we'll be long gone."

As the two continued to argue, Angie intensified her effort to free herself. She finally succeeded in loosening the knot at her wrists enough to give her more play with her hands. If they'd only continue to argue for a few more minutes, she'd have her hands free! Fortunately, Edward had untied her feet to get her into the hovel, and with Stella hollering at him as soon as they came through the door, the fool had forgotten to rebind her ankles. Once her hands were free, if she could make it to the door ahead of Edward, she could easily outrun him.

She wanted to cry for joy when she finally slipped her hands out of the bonds and flexed them to get the circulation back into her wrists. As much as she'd have liked to loosen the gag, she didn't dare attempt it until she was out of the room. Besides, from what she had seen of the place, a cry for help probably wouldn't raise any response.

Still arguing, Stella and Edward were on the other side of the room pouring themselves drinks. It was evident from Stella's slurred speech that she already had drunk more than her share, but that would work to Angie's advantage too—the drunken woman would be no threat to her.

Angie gauged the distance to the door. Ready to make her move, she was just about to bolt from the chair when the door crashed open and Giff barged into the room.

Edward was too startled to speak, but Stella began cursing at the top of her voice. Picking up the whiskey bottle, she threw it at him. Giff sidestepped it and the bottle smashed against the wall, its contents running down the wall to form a puddle on the floor. The smell of the spilled alcohol became overbearing in the small room. Releasing the gag from her mouth, Angie joined the fracas.

Giff was fighting off both Edward and Stella. The drunken woman had jumped on his back, wrapped her legs around his waist, and was pulling on his hair.

Giff threw a punch at Edward, sending the coward sprawling against the wall. Edward slid to the floor as Giff groped to try to dislodge Stella from his back.

Angie yanked Stella by the hair in an effort to pull her off. "I told you to keep your hands off my husband!"

Screeching like a witch, Stella fell off him and swung a blow at Angie. She ducked beneath it and shoved Stella away, sending her stumbling backwards. Only the wall kept the woman from falling. Snarling, Stella sprang forward and threw her weight at Angie. Both women tumbled to the floor. For a long moment they rolled in close combat, Angie struggling to keep Stella's long nails from clawing her face and eyes. When Giff succeeded in pulling Stella off her, the raging woman began beating him in the face and head with both hands. He had all he could do to keep her at arm's length.

"For heaven's sake, Giff, punch her out," Angie shouted, jumping to her feet.

"I can't hit a woman," Giff said, trying to stay out of range of her swinging arms. Stella began to kick at his groin when she couldn't connect with her blows.

Angie spun the harridan around and delivered a

punch to the chin that not only landed Stella on her backside, but knocked all the fight out of her. Breathless, with clenched fists, Angie stood above the stunned woman who was rubbing her jaw. "That's for that slap in the face, you drunken slut!" she said victoriously.

Giff yanked Edward to his feet. "Let's go, Emory. I'm marching the two of you down to the sheriff's office."

"I wouldn't do that if I were you, Gifford," Edward said smugly, dabbing at his bleeding lip with a handkerchief. "I'll tell the whole story to the newspaper, and that pretty young wife of yours will be shown up for the whore she is."

Giff's blow caught him in the nose.

"My nose! My nose! You've broken my nose," Edward cried frantically. He rushed over to the mirror to observe the damage, trying vainly to study his profile.

"Giff, don't hit him again," Angie yelled when Giff clutched Edward by the shirt and yanked him away from the mirror. "You can call me all the names you want, Edward, but it won't keep you out of jail."

"It's our word against yours," he said. "You broke in here, Gifford, and started a fight. Stella will back me up."

"You're a bigger ass than I thought you were, Emory. Have you forgotten about the ransom note you wrote? Or the old woman you beat up and left lying on the floor? You and your girlfriend are going to spend the next few years in a cell. Kidnapping is a serious offense."

"Well I've got some news for you, Gifford: Stella is my wife. Your precious Angeleen had an affair with a married man. How is that going to look in the Denver newspaper?"

The revelation came as a shock to Giff. He looked at Angie for confirmation.

"I didn't know he was married, Giff. He lied about that, too. He just told me the truth today."

"What do you want to do, Angie?"

"I want him in jail and out of my hair forever. I'd rather suffer the gossip than wonder when he'd show up again with his hand out."

Giff smiled at her. "You're doing the right thing, honey."

" 'You're doing the right thing, honey'!" Stella parroted in a shriek. "Time someone with an ounce of sense got into this conversation. I'll see that Edward won't say anything about your affair with him if you drop the kidnapping charges."

"You aren't telling me what I'm going to do," Edward said.

"Oh, shut up, you damn fool. If you weren't so stupid, we wouldn't be in this mess."

"Well, if you hadn't thrown yourself at Gifford, I'd have gotten the money out of her without any problem."

"You never intended to open a repertory with that money, did you?" Angie said.

Edward snorted. "Of course not, you fool. Once I got my hands on your money, Stella and I were going to Europe."

"I'm afraid you missed the boat, Emory," Giff said. "Let's go, you two. You can read all about Europe in your jail cells."

Sheriff Willie Joe Benteen had been a lawman for the better part of his sixty years, and Denver's sheriff for twenty-five of those years. The former plainsman had fought the Comanche in Texas, the Apache in Arizona, and the Utes in Utah before settling down in Colorado. There wasn't too much good or bad he hadn't seen in his fellow man, and it was said he could sniff out a polecat lurking in a woodpile "a mite better than a yeller-eared hound dog."

While Matthew MacKenzie had been alive, Sheriff Benteen had also been one of Matt's weekly poker-playing pals, his best friend, the best man at his wedding, and the godfather of his firstborn daughter. The confirmed bachelor had once even entertained the notion of asking Betsy MacGregor to marry him before Matt had up and married her.

On this particular morning, Sheriff Benteen bent forward, spit a stream of tobacco juice into a nearby cuspidor, wiped the spittle off his drooping mustache, then leaned back in his chair with his feet on the desk and leveled a leery eye at the man and woman standing in front of him.

"You know, stranger, I don't take kindly to that kind of talk," he said in his slow, distinctive drawl. "I've knowed that little gal all her life, even bounced her on my knee when she was a young'un. Kind of sets my old bones to achin' when I hear you say those unkind things about her."

He glanced at Giff, who was standing at the window with his arm around Angie. "Broke his nose for it, did yuh?"

Giff nodded. "I kind of lost my temper, Will."

"Amazin' you didn't pump some lead into the fella, Giff."

The sheriff lowered his feet and leaned forward. "Did I mention that I've even bounced that young fella on my knee a time or two?"

Edward Emory dabbed at the perspiration that had formed on his forehead.

"Yep," Sheriff Willie Joe said reflectively, "I sure don't take kindly to that kind of bad-mouthin' about that little gal. Got half a mind to put some lead into you myself."

He sat back when a young man entered the office and handed him a telegram. " 'Scuse me, folks."

After reading the telegram, he glanced up at the two people before him.

"I'd say this marriage license of yours ain't worth the paper it's writ on. Don't appear there's any record on file in St. Louis of the two of you gettin' hitched like you said. And this Silas Waters who signed this document ain't ever worked for St. Louis County. You folks ain't hitched, are you?"

"I told you that fake wedding license wouldn't convince anyone," Stella grumbled.

"Shut up. It's your fault we're in this trouble."

"If you weren't so stupid, we wouldn't be," she railed back. "Kidnapping! Anyone has better sense than that! You shouldn't be let out alone."

"Hush up, you two. I ain't interested in hearin' you spat, or them lies you've been spewin'. Any more of it and it's for dang sure you're gonna be eatin' lead." He fixed his steel-gray-eyed stare on Edward.

"Yes, Sheriff," Edward said meekly. He cleared his throat nervously. "I have nothing to say to the press."

"Same goes for you, ma'am," he said to Stella. "Fine-lookin' lady that you are."

Stella patted the back of her hair. "Why, thank you, Sheriff. I hope you realize I had nothing to do with Edward's attempt to kidnap Angeleen."

"Hope not, ma'am, 'cause I'd sure hate to see a fine figure of a woman like you wastin' away behind prison bars." He turned his attention back to Edward. "Oughta warn you, mister, that my deputy told me Doc Fielding just got back in town and said Mattie McNamara's arm is broken. When Slim Collins hears that news, it ain't gonna sit too well with him, either. You sure have worn out your welcome in this town, stranger. I'm gonna have my hands full just keepin' you in one piece 'til the U.S. marshall shows up."

Sheriff Willie Joe Benteen tossed a ring of keys to his deputy. "Lock 'em up."

Chapter 28

Angie had a couple stops to make before leaving Denver. One was the newspaper office, to place an advertisement for a cook.

"Like it or not, Middy is going to have to tolerate one while she's laid up with a broken arm," she said.

"I think it will be the 'or not,'" Giff said, amused.

Her next stop was the doctor's office to check on Middy's condition.

"Middy will be just fine, Angie," the doctor assured her.

James Fielding had been the family physician for almost thirty years, and had delivered the MacKenzie girls. Small in stature, he had a boundless energy that exhausted most men half his age. He also had been one of her father's weekly poker-playing friends, and took great pride in being Angie's godfather.

"I gave her tonic for her cough, an antipyretic for the fever, and put a cast on her arm. I also left some laudanum for the pain. Fortunately it's only a slight fracture, but knowing Mattie McNamara, I thought the cast and laudanum would be the best way to immobilize her."

"You're sure it's just a head cold, Uncle Jim?"

"Yes, her lungs are clear. Summer colds are the worst; they tend to hang on. It would speed her recovery if she'd stay in bed for a couple more days."

"And just how am I going to get her to do that? You know Middy."

He chuckled. "Yes, and you have my sympathy."

He put his arm around her as he walked them to the door. "I was hoping your visit was for a different reason." He gave Giff a reproachful glance. "It's high time there's some young'uns running around the Roundhouse, son. I delivered Matt's gals, and I'd sure like to deliver his grandchildren, too."

"I'm working on it, Doc," Giff said as they shook hands.

"And the next time you pay me a visit, young lady," he said, turning back to Angie, "it better be for that reason."

"So should we rent you a mount or ride back double?" Giff said, once they were outside.

"Definitely double. It's cozier and I get to put my arms around you."

"Just make sure you keep your hands where they belong."

Her eyes gleamed with devilry. "That's exactly what I intend to do."

With the doctor's reassuring words about Middy, and the final end to Edward's interference in her life, Angie felt like a new woman. She told Giff so.

"It has been a busy enough day, Angel," he said as they reached the ranch.

Angie tightened her grasp around his waist and snuggled her face into his back.

"And this has been the best part."

Giff reined in when they reached the swimming hole by the waterfall. "Brick could probably use a rest. He's been carrying a double load for the past five miles."

Angie slid off the back of the horse and sat down on the bank, watching with a contented smile as Giff loosened the cinch on Brick and then led him over to drink. When Brick trotted over to a shady copse and began to chew on some clover, Giff plopped down beside her and lay back, his hands tucked under his head.

"It's a hot one today," he said, expelling a deep breath.

"And that water looks so inviting," she said wistfully.

"So-o-o, what's stopping you from taking a swim?"

"I just happen to have forgotten my suit this morning, when Edward dragged me from the house."

"So-o-o?"

As she guessed his meaning, her eyes rounded. "Do I dare?"

"I don't mind . . . and I'm the only one around."

"Will you keep watch?"

"It's a sure bet; I won't take my eyes off you for a minute."

"I meant the road, silly."

Before she could talk herself out of it, Angie quickly pulled off her boots and hose. Her gown and slip followed, and she put a foot in the water.

"Take it all off, Angel."

She turned her head and looked at him, shoving back the long curtain of dark hair that had fallen across her eyes. His steady gaze was fixed on her.

For a long moment, a sensuous gleam arced between them, then she pulled the camisole over her head and released the tie on her drawers. They dropped to her ankles and she stepped out of them with fluid gracefulness, and stood before him like an alluring wood nymph.

Wading into the water, she reached midpond before looking back. "Are you coming in?" she asked, in a voice unintentionally laden with seductiveness.

He had already cast aside his boots.

The water felt refreshing, made cooler by the heat of the day and the fire her passion had ignited within her. She dove beneath the water, and when she surfaced Giff was there beside her.

She dove under again, and he followed. They emerged beneath the waterfall, their bodies cocooned in the curtain of water.

Giff stood up, the water lapping at his waist, and drew her into his arms. "I love you, Angel," he whispered.

"I love you, too, Giff. I love you, too."

His lips felt firm and warm despite the cool water that coated them. The contrast was tantalizing, splintering her body with erotic shivers. Then the slide of his hands caressed her, bathing her with a sensual warmth. Closing her eyes, she threw back her head, the cascading water showering over her. His mouth feasted at her breasts, fueling a heat within her that even the coolness of the plunging waterfall could not extinguish.

Her moans of ecstasy attracted his attention to her mouth, and he reclaimed her lips. His tongue stroked . . . tasted . . . savored.

Aflame with lust, she clasped her arms tightly around his neck and rained quick, hot kisses on his face and mouth. Cupping her derriere, he lifted her, and she wrapped her legs around his hips, gasping into his mouth when he entered her. Sensation built toward eruption. Her heart hammered in her chest, her pulses pounded, and her head swirled in mindless ecstasy as she matched the tempo of his thrusts, their breaths combining in quick, short gasps. His kiss smothered her cry at the explosive moment of climax—and he filled her with his love.

Middy was sleeping peacefully when they returned to the house, but it tugged at Angie's heartstrings to see Middy's arm lying in a plaster cast on top of her sheet.

The medicine had been effective, because when she awoke, her temperature was normal and her coughing had diminished considerably. After another day in bed, the cough was gone entirely, but Angie would not let her attempt any housework.

"Like it or not, Middy, you are a woman of leisure for a while," Angie declared emphatically.

Being a nursemaid to Middy kept Angie at home, so she used her free time to finish a painting she had begun.

Slim Collins showed up bright and early the next morning to check on Middy's condition, bringing with him a telegram from Beth informing Angie that she'd be home in the late afternoon.

"As long as Slim's here to keep Middy company, this would be a good time to drive you into town to talk to Bellemey," Giff said.

"That's a good idea. Giff, I've decided that I'm going to put up the money to get the repertory started, but I want Mr. Bellemey and his brother to organize and operate it. They don't need my help."

He looked puzzled. "What do you mean? I thought you planned to move to Denver to get it started."

She tried not to laugh, since he was trying so

hard not to show his relief. "Now, how could I ever do that when I've already hired myself out as a hand here on the ranch? Matter of fact, it's very satisfying to know that I'm a darn better rancher than I am a pianist or painter."

"Angel, you're good at anything you do. You've just never recognized that."

"I do now. I've finally convinced myself that I can do something very well—and that's ranching. Now I have the best of both worlds: the Roundhouse and you. We've got a few years to make up for, remember. Furthermore, whenever I have an urge, I have a piano at my fingertips and beautiful landscapes to paint. But most of all, I have you near me—"

"Whenever you feel an urge."

She smiled into his grinning face and brought his palm to her lips.

"And I've thought of another brilliant idea. I know you don't want us to take Daddy's room, so what do you think of remodeling the two guest rooms at the end of the hall into a bedroom suite for us? We could have a sitting room and our own bathroom in it. That would leave my bedroom and Daddy's for guests . . . until we need them for nurseries."

"I like it—especially the nursery part. But if you convert all the rooms to family use, what about overnight guests?"

"I've thought of that, too. Let's remodel your house into a guest cottage."

"You *have* been giving this a lot of thought, haven't you?"

"This is our home, Giff. We're here to stay. It's time we accept that reality—you, especially. I never know which bed I'm going to find you in."

"Whichever one you're in, honey," he teased.

"Someday we could even expand the guest

house into a larger house—maybe a place for Thia
and Dave when they bring their children home for
a visit. Or we might even consider connecting the
two houses."

"I like the idea, Angel."

"Good. I'll get an architect out here—after I talk
it over with Beth when she gets back today." Angie
rubbed her hands with satisfaction. "Now, as soon
as I check the pantry to see what supplies we need,
I'll change my clothes and take you up on your
offer to drive me to town. You can get the supplies
while I talk to Mr. Bellemey. That will give us
plenty of time for me to get back and prepare dinner for Beth's homecoming."

He stood up and pulled her into his arms.
"Sounds like you've got it all worked out, Miz Gifford."

"Are you really pleased with the whole idea,
Giff?"

"I love it, Angel. And I love *you,* Angel," he murmured, before he kissed her.

"I'm still not convinced that this is what you really want in your heart," Giff said, after she left
Bellemey's house.

Angie took his hand and pulled him over to a
park bench. "Giff, since I returned to the ranch, I've
learned a lot about myself. It took a while, I admit.
I had to recognize the difference between childhood dreams and what is really needed in one's
life to feel fulfilled. And the one glaring truth is
that there's nothing more important to me than you
and the Roundhouse."

"That's how I feel about you, Angel. But you can
have both. It's not necessary to give up a dream."

"I did fulfill a dream the night of the concert. My
experience on the riverboat, dressed in those
ghastly red tights, was debasing—a hideous night-

mare that destroyed all my self-confidence. The concert succeeded in obliterating that memory. But more importantly, I proved to myself that I could do it. Thia tried to tell me that how I feel about myself is the real issue, not the music and art." She laughed gaily. "And I feel good about myself, Giff."

"You should, Angel," he said, smiling down into her radiant happiness.

"But as rewarding as it was, what I felt on that stage can't compare to how I felt when you told me that you love me. It caused me to take a long look at how I feel about the Roundhouse, too. Remember when you told me that you consider me and this ranch as one and the same? I realized that I feel the same about you. And now that I've acquired this newfound wisdom and confidence, Mr. Gifford, I'm no longer compelled to make a choice between dreams and the man I love."

She raised his hand to her cheek. "Besides, dreams are to fill the void in the lives of people who are dissatisfied . . . or feel inadequate. That's not me anymore. I have you and the Roundhouse; I'll have the repertory a couple times a year; and I have beautiful landscapes to paint whenever I wish. I'm the luckiest person in the world."

"No, honey, I am: I've got you."

She smiled the serene smile of one who has found inner peace. "The only other thing I need to know complete fulfillment in my life is to have your child."

He offered a crooked smile. "I'm working on that."

"Now, that's a sight to make a man believe that romance is still alive in the world."

Angie and Giff turned their heads toward the unexpected speaker.

"Mr. Carrington. I mean, Michael, how nice to see you," Angie said.

Giff stood up and the two men shook hands.

"I'd think there'd be a city ordinance against making love on a park bench." He grinned at Giff. "You're a lucky fellow, Giff. I wish I had a woman look at me the way Angie does you."

Giff smiled down at her. "I never realized until a few minutes ago just how lucky I really am, Michael."

"You two are embarrassing me," Angie declared, rising to her feet. "Are you free to join us for dinner at the Roundhouse tonight, Michael?"

"I hate to keep imposing on the MacKenzie hospitality, Angie."

"Nonsense, it's no imposition. Beth is finally getting back and we're having a dinner to celebrate. It seems like she's been gone for months."

"If you're sure another guest won't be in the way, I must confess I'd love to join you."

"I'm so glad, Michael. We're just on our way home now. Why not come with us?"

"Unfortunately, I'm on my way to an appointment or I would."

"Well, dinner's at seven. We'll look forward to seeing you then," Angie said, barely able to contain her excitement.

"Until seven." He tipped his hat and hurried away.

"What do you think?" she asked, her sapphire gaze following Michael Carrington as he crossed the street.

Giff shrugged. "I think he's coming to dinner."

"Oh, you know what I mean." She tucked her arm through his as they walked back to the buckboard. "What do you think about Michael Carrington?"

"Angie, I'll be honest with you—I never think about Michael Carrington."

"Will you stop that! I'm serious, Giff. I think he's sweet on Beth, that's what I think. Did you see how he jumped at the dinner invitation as soon as I mentioned Beth would be home tonight? So what do you think about that?"

"Angie, do not try to pull me into any female intrigues. Carrington seems a nice enough fellow. Other than that, I have no opinion one way or another."

"Well, Beth seems to really dislike Michael for some reason."

"In her eyes she has a good reason. He's trying to buy out the Rocky Mountain Central."

"Oh, you men have no instincts for matters of love," she said, as he assisted her into the buckboard. "I wish Thia was home so I could discuss it with her. A complex situation like this calls for some clearheaded female analysis!"

"Well, you two lovestruck romantics sure are the ones to do it." Shaking his head, Giff climbed up on the seat beside her. "Women!" he murmured, flicking the reins.

"What does that mean?"

"Why do women feel they have to hurry the situation along when it comes to matters of the heart? I don't understand why they just can't let nature take its course."

She glanced at him askance. "Maybe because we women think three years is too long to wait to hear a man say he loves you."

He threw up his hands. "I don't believe it! Are you blaming me for the time we lost?"

"Keep your hands on the reins before we have an accident."

"You were the one who was too blind to see how I felt."

"I'm not blind; I just can't read your mind," she snapped in return. Then Angie started to giggle. "If I could, I wouldn't have taken the risk of letting you drive this wagon."

His face broke in a grin. "Okay, you win. I can't think of anything to best that remark, so you got the last word. But how do you feel about one hand on the reins?"

When she shifted over and cuddled next to him, he slipped an arm around her shoulders. "Uh-uh," she warned. "Both hands on the reins, Peter Gifford."

"Always, my love. Always," he said, sliding his hand down to her thigh.

"Are you coming with me to meet Beth?" Giff asked, an hour after they got home.

"I can't," Angie said, placing a fresh rose centerpiece on the table. "I'll just have time to finish setting this table and get dinner started by the time Beth gets home."

"It's too bad you haven't had any response to the advertisement you placed for a cook. Honey, you're as bad as Middy in trying to do everything yourself."

"I just want everything to be special for Beth's return. After eating in hotels and restaurants all this time, I imagine she's looking forward to a home-cooked meal."

"I doubt she's looking forward to sharing that meal with Michael Carrington. When are you telling her about your dinner guest?"

"Not a moment before I have to. I'm hoping she won't even peek in the dining room. If she knew Michael was coming, she'd likely find an excuse to remain in her room for the rest of the evening. And before you give me your 'I Don't Like Doing This to Beth' lecture, remember, I would never do anything to intentionally hurt Beth. I'm doing this for her sake, Giff. It will do her good to spend an enjoyable evening with a superbly handsome—not to mention as rich as Croesus—man for a change, who also happens to be exceptionally charming."

"Angie, you know what I think about this. You're being manipulative."

Her eyes glowed with warmth. "I know, but I promise you—just this once."

As soon as he left, Angie hurried to finish the table. Once satisfied, she rushed to the kitchen to begin the dinner preparations. By the time Giff returned with Beth, Angie had everything under control.

The two women immediately put their heads together, chatting away to make up for the time they had been separated. Beth finally left to unpack and dress for dinner.

After finishing dressing herself, Angie left her room. "By the way, we have a guest for dinner," she told Beth as she passed her room.

"Oh, who is it?" Beth called back.

Angie hurried down the stairs without replying.

Michael Carrington had arrived by the time Beth came downstairs and joined them in the parlor. Her displeasure was evident, but she maintained a reserved graciousness toward him.

"I was just admiring your sister's sketches and paintings, Elizabeth. They're very good."

"Yes, Angie is very talented," Beth said, with a disgruntled glance at Angie. "One never quite knows what she'll surprise you with next."

"Have you ever thought of selling your paintings, Angie?"

"Oh, good heavens, Michael, I paint for the pleasure of it. I'd never expect anyone to want to purchase one."

"I have a friend who operates an art gallery in

New York. Would you object if I show him these two paintings? This one of a horse grazing in the corral, and the other of ranch hands branding cattle, are both quite impressive, Angie."

"I'd be flattered, of course, if you took them with you. But I really don't expect anything to come of it." Trying to hide her pleasure, she hurried to the kitchen to check on the meal.

"I have a big surprise for you," Beth said, when they sat down to eat. "On my return, I had to make a quick trip to end of track, and you know how Thia's been keeping in touch with our cousins in Texas."

Angie nodded. "Oh, yes. She's very impressed with them."

"It seems Thia has convinced them all to come up here to attend the wedding when you and Giff repeat your vows."

"What!" Angie began choking on the wine she had just swallowed.

Giff and Michael both rose to come to her assistance, but she waved them back. "Whoever said Giff and I are going to get remarried?" she managed to sputter after clearing her throat. "We were legally wed in St. Louis. I thought we agreed that there'd be no further ceremony."

"Thia told me she changed her mind after your recent visit."

"Oh, she changed *her* mind."

"Thia feels we have to do this for your own good."

"And you agreed with her?"

"After she told me of your discussion, I certainly did."

"That's Giff's and my decision to make—not yours and Thia's. Neither of you has any right to try and manipulate our . . ." She cut herself off, realizing how hypocritical she must sound to Giff.

Stealing a guilty glance in his direction, she saw the amusement on his face.

"I understand how you feel, Angie. I know how much I resent it when it happens to me," Beth said pointedly.

"Just when is this wedding to take place?" Giff asked.

"A week from Saturday. She and Dave will be coming in with the MacKenzies a few days before."

"Well, that doesn't mean we're going to go along with her plans, does it, Giff?"

"I'd like to meet these MacKenzie cousins of yours. And since Thia's already extended the wedding invitation to them, I suppose we'll have to go through with it."

"Peter Gifford, you're just saying that to teach me a lesson," Angie accused.

"A lesson for what?" Beth asked. She looked at Michael Carrington. "Mr. Carrington, do you have any idea what they're talking about?"

"Not in the least, Elizabeth, but I find this whole undercurrent very intriguing."

"I hope you'll be able to attend, Michael," Angie said.

"Thank you; I'd be honored." Then he chuckled. "Besides, I wouldn't want to miss it for the world."

Angie didn't dare look at Beth.

The evening passed swiftly, and after Michael Carrington departed, with her paintings under his arm, Angie strolled out and sat down on the swing her father had hung when she and her sisters were youngsters.

Suffused with contentment, she was unaware that Giff had joined her until he kissed the back of her bare shoulder.

"Hi," she said tenderly. "I didn't even hear you coming."

"What are you sitting out here daydreaming about?"

"A person can't daydream when it's night. I'm nightdreaming, only with my eyes open," she said lightly.

He lifted her up and sat down, shifting her on his lap so that she faced him. "Seeing you now in the moonlight, Angel, with that ribbon tied around your head and all your hair brushed out hanging past your shoulders, it's hard to believe you're the same woman I made love to last night."

"I'd better be," she teased.

"I meant that you look sixteen again, Angel."

"I never want to be sixteen again, Giff. I was very stupid when I was sixteen."

"So, what were you dreaming about?" He began to push them on the swing.

"Oh, I've been sitting here thinking about how happy I am. How much I love you. Why did we wait so long to find this contentment, Giff?"

"Reckon so we can appreciate it more now," he said. "And that's what I intend to do. But I want you to know, I'll understand if you change your mind about your decision today."

"Peter Gifford, I have a question: you don't have to be a cook to enjoy a meal, do you?"

"No."

"And you don't have to be an artist to appreciate a sunrise?"

"Reckon not."

"Or even a concert pianist to play a melody, isn't that right?"

"Yeah."

She put her face up to his; their noses practically touching. "But you do have to know cattle to be able to raise them."

"And you know cattle."

"You bet I do!" she said, with a firm thrust of

her chin. "And I know them really well, too!"

"You sure do!" he agreed.

Jokingly she made a fist and put it up to his chin. "I even saved the herd, didn't I?"

"You sure did," he said, no longer able to keep a straight face. "I reckon there's a point you're trying to make here."

"My point, Pete Gifford? I'm a damn good rancher! I should have listened to you sooner."

She threw her arms around his neck to kiss him, but the movement unseated them. Laughing, they tumbled off the swing, and Giff ended up stretched out with Angie on top of him.

" 'Pears you're pretty good at steer wrestling, too," he murmured, pulling her head down to capture her lips.

Chapter 29

Despite a hectic week of making the necessary arrangements for a large wedding in so short a time, Angie managed to slip away for a few minutes of relaxation on the morning Cynthia was due to arrive with their cousins. With her sketch pad in hand, she climbed the hill overlooking the house and began to draw some distant peaks.

After a short time, she sensed she wasn't alone and she turned her head, expecting to find Giff or Beth. To her surprise, there was no one there. Shrugging off the thought, she returned to her sketch.

Her hand slowed as once again she had the feeling of being watched. Yet when she turned, she saw no one. Reluctantly she resumed her drawing, but she could no longer concentrate on the work in front of her. The feeling became overpowering, and a chill raced down her spine.

"Angie."

She dropped her pencil when Giff spoke behind her. "Giff, please don't do that again!"

He looked perplexed. "Do what?"

"Sneak up on me like that. It's not funny!"

"I just came up to tell you if we don't hurry, we'll be late getting to the Junction."

"All right, I'm coming," she said. Gathering up her pencil and pad, she stood up.

"I'm sorry if I frightened you," Giff said, slipping an arm around her shoulders. "Angel, you're trembling!" he said in surprise.

"You scared me, that's all. Please, Giff, don't do that again."

With feral eyes fixed on Angie, the figure watched from the concealment of the bushes as they moved down the hill, before slowly backing away without stirring a leaf.

Waiting with anticipation, Angie and Beth stood on the platform of MacKenzie Junction and watched the train grind to a stop. Cynthia waved from the observation deck of the private car, and as soon as it rolled to a stop she stepped off to encompass them both in a hug.

"This is all so exciting!" she exclaimed exuberantly.

Angie's mouth gaped open when she saw the three men who followed David Kincaid off the train. Turning to Beth, she saw the same astonishment on her sister's face.

"*Those* are our cousins!" Beth whispered.

"What are you thinking?" Angie whispered.

"Tall!"

"Incredibly handsome!"

"Formidable! Definitely formidable," Beth muttered. "They look to be an army unto themselves."

The tallest of the men carried an infant in his arms as naturally and confidently as if he were carrying a package. Angie couldn't imagine him ever looking awkward or self-conscious at anything he did.

To her surprise, he wore a gun belt. Quickly checking the other two men, she saw gun belts on their hips also. Then suddenly they were in front of her.

Excitedly Cynthia made the introductions to them. "It's my great pleasure to introduce you to our cousins Luke, Flint, and Cleve MacKenzie," she said. "Gentlemen, I'd like you to meet my sisters, Elizabeth and Angeleen, and my brother-in-law, Peter Gifford—known affectionately as Beth, Angie, and Giff."

The brothers doffed their hats, and as they shook hands with Giff, Angie had a chance to study them closer.

All three men appeared to be in their early forties. Luke, the eldest of the brothers, had a scattering of gray at the temples of his dark head. Although just as dark, Flint's hair was longer and tied back with a strip of rawhide. Cleve wore his dark hair clipped short at the neck. While Luke and Cleve sported mustaches, Flint's face was clean-shaven. The one identical and mesmerizing feature they all possessed was the same color of eyes: a deep sapphire—the same shade that she and her sisters shared.

"So you're the blushing bride," Cleve MacKenzie said to her, flashing a devastating grin.

"Not exactly, Cousin Cleve," Angie replied. "Giff and I were married in St. Louis, but my sisters wanted us to have a big wedding. We're really thrilled that you all were willing to attend."

After they'd each given her a hug and kiss on the cheek, the three men stepped aside and Angie got her first glimpse of their wives.

Though the men were similar in coloring, the women were entirely opposite. Luke's wife, Honey, was an exquisite honey blonde with light blue eyes; Garnet MacKenzie had gorgeous red hair, green eyes, and a smattering of freckles across her nose; and Cleve's wife, Adriana, who appeared to be the youngest of the women, was a stunning beauty with black hair, brown eyes, and the olive complexion of her Spanish ancestry.

"And this young beauty in my arms is our daughter Linda," Cleve said proudly.

Impervious to being the center of attention, the infant yawned and closed her eyes.

"Where are your other children?" Beth asked.

"We didn't bring them," Garnet said in a soft Southern accent.

"And you can thank us for that," Honey added, her blue eyes sparkling vivaciously.

"Cleve and I have two sons and another daughter," Adriana interjected. "Once a year they spend a week on my papa's ranch. It's the only time their grandfather gets to see them."

"Our two children, Josh and Kitty, stayed home," Honey said. "Though Josh really isn't a child anymore—he just turned eighteen last week," she added proudly.

"Yeah, and I think Josh's hankering for the neighbor girl had a lot to do with that decision to remain home," Luke said.

"And naturally," Honey interjected, "when Kitty heard her brother and cousins weren't coming, she chose to stay home, too."

"Flint and I have a son and daughter, also," Garnet said. "Andy's nine and Sarah is seven."

"What are the ages of your children, Adriana?" Angie asked.

"Cole is seven, Jake is five, Lily is three, and Linda here is just three months—too young to leave behind. Besides, I couldn't bear to leave her for a week. It's hard enough doing so with the older children. Why don't you give me the baby, Cleve; you must be tired holding her."

Cleve smiled down at the sleeping infant. "She's doing just fine in her daddy's arms, Raven."

"As you can see," Adriana said, "her daddy is very attached to her."

"And rightfully so. She's adorable," Beth said. "I just wish you'd brought all the children with you. We would have loved to meet them."

"We did you all a big favor, Beth," Honey said, giggling. "And we left the children in good hands. Their aunt Maud has helped raise all of them, and we hired two girls from town to help her. Plus there's eight hands riding for the Triple M."

"Eight riders besides your husbands! You must have a pretty big spread."

"A little over a couple hundred thousand acres," Luke said.

Giff emitted a low whistle. "Well, it's kind of stretched out in the last ten years," Cleve offered, sounding almost apologetic. Then he added with a grin, "But in Texas, there's a lot of room to stretch."

"Do you all live in the same house?" Angie asked.

"No, each family has their own house, Angie," Cynthia said. "You should see it—it's a compound. A much larger version of what we have here on the Roundhouse, because there are four houses besides several barns and other outbuildings. Dave couldn't believe the size of it all. You have to see it to believe it."

A loud neighing disrupted the conversation and drew their attention to the train, where Flint had just unloaded a large black stallion.

Angie recognized the quality lines of the horse at once. "What a gorgeous animal."

"We thought you'd like him as a wedding gift," Cleve said.

"Are you serious?" Giff asked, as awestruck as

Angie. She followed Giff and Luke to where Flint waited with the horse.

"He sure is a fine-looking stallion," Giff said.

Luke nodded. "He's a beauty, all right, and you'll find he's strong and speedy."

"Faster than a gelding," the reticent Flint added.

Grinning, Luke said, "And he's sired some fine colts. Nothing like a Texas-bred horse to strengthen your herd."

"You won't get an argument from me," Giff replied, patting the huge stallion. "I can't wait to get a saddle on him."

Angie grinned at her two cousins. "Just look at him! Giff's like a young boy who's just been given a peppermint stick."

Hugging her to his side, Giff said, "Well, there's no sense in spending the day here, is there? Let's head back to the house; these folks are probably tired from the train trip and would like to sit down and relax." He said to the men, "We brought a rig to hold the ladies, mounts for all you fellows, and a wagon to haul the luggage."

"It'll sure feel good to get some horseflesh under me again," Flint said. "I've had enough of ridin' them rails."

"Hey, my husband helped to build those rails," Cynthia spoke up good-naturedly.

"No offense intended, ma'am," Flint said quickly.

"You have to understand my husband's devotion to horses, Cynthia," Garnet teased. "You have no idea what trouble I had convincing him that his horse can't sleep with us."

"Well then," Angie interjected, "that makes the wedding gift to us even more priceless. Giff and I thank you from the bottom of our hearts, Flint."

String had all the luggage loaded in the wagon,

and as soon as Giff tied the stallion to the tailgate, the ranch hand pulled out.

Chattering and laughing, the women were soon seated in the buckboard. Angie took the reins, and as soon as the men mounted up, they headed for the homestead.

There, Beth and Cynthia headed to the kitchen to help Middy as Angie assigned rooms to their guests.

"I think Adriana and Cleve would be more comfortable with the baby in my father's room. It's roomier and has a connecting bathroom. Giff, why don't you go up and get a crib from the attic," Angie said.

"I'll need a volunteer to help carry it down."

"I'm right with you, pal," Cleve said, following him up the attic stairway.

"You other two couples can take the two guest rooms at the end of the hall. They don't have as nice a view, but both catch a pleasant breeze at night."

"Let the women make the choice, Big Brother," Flint said to Luke. "Let's bring up all those bags they toted with them."

The five men swiftly put the luggage in the proper rooms and cleaned and set up the crib, eager to get out of the house. Giff took them on a short tour of the ranch while the women settled in and unpacked, laughing and calling to one another up and down the hallway.

By the time the men returned at dusk, it seemed as if the MacKenzie sisters and the MacKenzie wives had been close friends all their lives.

"So that's Uncle Matthew," Luke said, looking up at the painting of Matthew MacKenzie as the men enjoyed a brandy and cigar in the study.

Cleve raised his glass in tribute to the portrait. "You did well, Uncle Matthew."

"You would have liked him," Giff said. "The Chief was a hell of a man. He died last year. Too bad you didn't get a chance to meet him."

"I would have liked that," Cleve said. "But I didn't get a chance to meet my own father, either."

"I don't understand," Giff said.

Flint ground out his cigar. "Ma was still carrying Cleve when our pa died at the Alamo."

"I was only two years old," Luke said, "and Flint was one."

Intrigued, Dave asked, "Were you raised in Texas?"

"Yeah, Ma raised the three of us alone," Cleve replied. "Of course, the ranch wasn't anywhere near the size it is today."

"It's a shame the Chief didn't know your whereabouts," Dave said. "He'd have helped to raise you. He always wanted sons."

Luke spoke up at once. "I'd say he did a pretty good job raising those daughters of his."

Giff and Dave exchanged amused looks. "I don't think you'd hear any complaints from either of us," Giff said. "I grew up right here on the Round-house, too. My mother died when I was born. Dad became the foreman here."

"What about you, Dave?" Luke asked. "Were you born in this part of the country, too?"

"No. I'm from Massachusetts. When I was sixteen my folks died in a fire and I came out here and worked on the railroad. That's when I fell in love with this country. After I got my engineering degree, I came back here and started working for the Chief. Then last year when Cynthia came home, she convinced me to marry her."

The men broke into laughter.

"You know, when I was a lawman," Luke said,

"I could usually size up a man pretty good. Often my life depended on it. I'd have figured you for a man who made up his own mind."

"So how did she *convince* you?" Flint asked.

"I think it was the first time she smiled at me."

Flint eyed Dave skeptically. "Is that all it took?"

"Just about," Dave replied. "What did Garnet do to get a dyed-in-the-wool bachelor like you to give up your freedom to roam?"

"Think I was a goner the first time I caught sight of that red hair of hers. Figured it was too damn pretty to end up on some Comanche coup stick. And that's where it would have ended up, too, if she hadn't followed me—the Comanches wiped out the wagon train she was traveling with. There were no survivors," he added grimly.

"And let's hear your story, Luke. How did you and Honey meet?"

"I arrested her—then I married her."

"That's how you get a wife in Texas?" Giff joked.

"Heck, no. That happened in California when I was sheriff of Stockton."

Cleve cleared his throat. "In truth, gentlemen, unlike my brothers, I am the only one who actually married a Texas-born gal; Adriana's father has a ranch near San Antonio. I took one look at her and I was in love." He shook his head. "No second thoughts." He finished his drink and put aside the glass. "And speaking of those lovely ladies we were fortunate enough to marry, shall we join them, gentlemen?"

Returning to the parlor, they found the women grouped around the piano, with Angie playing and Honey strumming a guitar as the other women sang along with them.

"Sounds like there's more giggling going on than there is harmonizing," Cleve teased, seating himself.

"Honey, why don't you and Angie sing a song together? You two are the talented ones," Garnet said.

"What'll it be, Angie?" Honey asked.

"How about 'I'll Take You Home Again, Kathleen'?" Angie suggested, riffling through her sheet music.

"Oh, yes, I love that," Honey agreed.

The others listened in rapt silence as the two women's voices blended together in the haunting ballad. The demand for more echoed through the room when the song ended. Soon they were all gathered around the piano, the men adding their baritones and basses to such favorites as "The Old Gray Mare" and "The Yellow Rose Of Texas." They even got a makeshift square dance going to a rousing rendition of "Blue Tail Fly."

Finally, nearing midnight, they called it a night and retired to their rooms. To help reduce the congestion upstairs, Angie and Giff had elected to spend the night in his former lodgings, so hand in hand they crossed the yard to his house.

Angie couldn't understand how people could just *decide* to go to sleep. To lie down, close your eyes, and automatically fall asleep had always been a mystery to her, because she had to be on the verge of sleep before she even considered going to bed. And with all the excitement of the wedding and meeting her cousins, she was too exhilarated to even think about sleep. Hearing the tinny sound of the clock striking two, she glanced at Giff sleeping soundly beside her and slipped out of bed, deciding to pick out a book to read.

After thirty minutes, she put aside the book and walked over to the door. Hoping to catch a breeze, she opened it and stood in the doorway. This week they were in the clutches of an exceptionally unseasonable hot spell, and even the nights didn't cool down that much.

A light neighing from the barn attracted her attention. Smiling to herself, she pulled her gown on over her nightdress and walked barefoot down to the barn.

Calico's ears perked up as soon as she opened the barn door.

"What's the matter, sweetheart? Can't you sleep either?" she cooed in his ear as she patted him. "Or is that new arrival in the next stall keeping you awake? You're still the important one in this barn, my love." Calico nuzzled his nose into her hand. "I bet you're just as restless as I am. With all the excitement around here this last week, I've been kind of ignoring you." She grabbed a halter from a peg.

Leading Calico out of the barn, she swung up on his back and began to trot him around the corral for some exercise. When she heard a loud disturbance coming from the henhouse, Angie jerked up her head. The sound of frenzied clucking and flapping wings carried as loudly as raucous laughter on the still night air.

Leaving the corral to investigate, Angie passed Giff, who'd been awakened by the noise.

"What's going on with those hens?" he called from the doorway.

"I don't know. I'm just going to see."

"Wait until I get my pants on, Angie."

"It's probably just a fox that will take off as soon as it hears me coming. Let's go, Calico."

"Damn it, Angie, wait!" he yelled, grabbing for his pants.

As the ruckus continued, lights began to appear in the upstairs windows of the main house, and a baby's cry joined the sounds in the once quiet night.

The commotion seemed to have an adverse effect on Calico, as well. He began to whinny and fight the halter strap. Alarmed by the horse's behavior, Angie tried to turn him around to return to the corral.

But Calico reared up on his hind legs and she lost her grip on the halter, slipping off the rear of the horse and falling to the ground just as a cougar leaped onto the frightened animal's back from the roof of the coop.

Angie screamed as the snarling animal dug its claws into Calico, its powerful jaws clamping into the back of his neck and driving him to the ground. Horrified, she watched the whirling, thrashing struggle, chilling feral snarls and the terrified screech of her horse filling the night.

"Help! Somebody help!" she screamed.

Giff was already running toward the noise with a rifle in hand, but his vision was obstructed by the main house. Hearing her screams and Calico's frightened neighing, he fired two shots in the air, hoping to scare off whatever was menacing them. As he rounded the corner of the house, he saw the cougar racing away, and managed to get off a quick shot before the cat disappeared into the trees.

The front door slammed as the MacKenzie brothers, with pistols in hand, rushed out of the house. String and Red raced over from the bunkhouse.

"Sounded like a big cat," Flint yelled.

Giff nodded on his way past them, running to the huddled, weeping figure on the ground. Throwing himself to his knees, he asked frantically, "Angie, are you hurt?"

"Calico—help him. Giff, help him," she cried, staring at the twitching body on the ground. Even in the dim light, he could see the blood pooling around the head of the horse.

Giff gathered Angie in his arms and rocked her

back and forth as she cried uncontrollably. The others examined the unfortunate animal; then Luke MacKenzie came over to them and shook his head.

"No!" Angie screamed. "Not Calico! Please, God, not Calico!"

"Come on, honey. I'll take you back to the house." Giff lifted Angie to her feet.

"No! I won't leave him," she cried out, shoving aside his hands. "I won't leave him like this."

"Angel, he's suffering. We have to put him out of his misery. I know you don't want him to suffer any longer."

She looked up at him, her eyes stricken with anguish. "It's all my fault. If I hadn't taken him out of his stall, he wouldn't—"

"Angel, don't start blaming yourself." He pulled her back into his arms. "You've ridden that horse hundreds of times at night. There was no way you could have forseen this disaster."

Cleve touched Giff's shoulder. "Giff, we can't let that poor animal continue to suffer. If you don't put it out of its misery, I will." He drew his Colt.

Giff nodded. "I'll do it." He motioned to Beth and Thia, who were standing nearby waiting to comfort Angie. "Take her inside, girls."

"No," Angie said, swallowing her tears. "Calico's my horse. I'm the one who should do what has to be done."

She failed dismally to square her shoulders and reached out a hand. "Cleve, may I borrow your pistol?" Without a word, he handed it to her.

The other men stepped aside as Angie walked up to the dying horse. Kneeling beside it, she gently patted Calico, and as if he felt her touch, the horse tried to raise its head.

Angie's finger trembled as she cocked the pistol and put it to Calico's head. His ears perked up at the sound and he looked up at her, his brown liquid eyes glazed with pain. Angie could barely see through the tears that filled her eyes. She faltered, uncertain if she could go through with it.

Suddenly she felt a strong hand close around her own. "We'll do this together, Angel."

For a brief moment she thanked God for Giff— for his strength that she depended upon so greatly, for always being there when she needed him the most.

With his finger pressed to hers, she closed her eyes and pulled the trigger.

Chapter 30

❦❦

"**H**ow is she doing?" Honey asked when Beth and Cynthia joined them in the parlor.

"She's finally sleeping," Beth said.

"She'll be fine in the morning," Cynthia added. "It was the shock of seeing the attack on Calico right before her eyes that caused her reaction."

"The poor dear," Garnet empathized. "And so close to the wedding. It certainly spoils that pleasure for her."

"Middy made coffee. Would you like a cup?" Honey asked.

Cynthia shook her head. "None for me, thanks."

"I'll have some," Beth said. "There's no sense in thinking about any further sleep this morning." She offered a weak smile when Adriana handed her a cup. "Thank you. Did the baby go back to sleep?"

"Yes, she's sleeping like a little lamb."

"You ought to go to bed yourself, Adriana. You didn't get that much rest, and once the baby wakes up again, I doubt that you'll get any more."

"I'll go back to bed as soon as the men come in."

Garnet walked to the doorway and looked at the lit torches flickering from among the nearby trees.

"I wish they'd come back," Cynthia said nervously. "What do they expect to see out there in the dark? That cat could have gone in any direction once it reached the trees."

"You don't know Flint," Garnet said. "He'll find something that will give them a clue."

"That's right," Honey said, nodding. "Luke always said that Flint could trail an ant in a sandstorm."

"Just the same," Cynthia replied, "it makes me nervous that they're out there in the dark. That cougar might still be around."

"It looks like they're on their way back now," Garnet said, returning to her seat.

"Did you find anything?" Cynthia asked as soon as Luke and Dave came through the door.

Dave nodded. "Flint found some fresh blood."

"That means Giff wounded it. Thanks, Jaybird," Luke said when Honey handed him a cup of coffee.

Cleve came in, followed by Giff and Flint.

"How's Angie?" Giff asked immediately.

"She's finally asleep, Giff," Cynthia said.

"That's good. Beth, where's your key to the gun cabinet? I don't have mine with me. We'll need the rifles and shells."

"I'll get it for you," Beth said, hurrying from the room.

Middy came in, wheeling a cart. "I made some sandwiches in case anybody's hungry."

Each of the men grabbed one, then grouped around the table as Giff drew a crude sketch of the layout of the ranch.

"Okay," he said, "we moved the cattle over to the south range a few weeks ago. Other than strays, the herd is here." He wrote the word *cattle* across the area on the map. "We had a recent fire in that same general area. About ten acres of it was blackened."

"How long ago was that?" Flint asked.

"About eight or nine days." Giff looked up at him. "Why?"

"My guess is that the cat won't head in that direction, then. It would still smell the smoke and stay away, which is probably why it's not picking off your herd."

"Aren't there any deer in this area?" Cleve asked. "That's usually their favorite food."

"The deer's on the other side of the basin. We don't get too many over here."

"Deer or not, I didn't think wild cats came this close to a house," Dave said.

Cleve nodded. "You're right. Cats are pretty smart and normally they wouldn't."

"There was a fellow killed by a cougar last year not too far from the Roundhouse," Giff said.

"Is that right?" Luke said. "More than likely by the same cat. It's probably been stalking you out there before it made its move."

"So that's why them hens ain't been layin'," Middy spoke up. "I've been wonderin' what's upsettin' them these past couple days."

Cynthia shuddered. "I get goose bumps just thinking what would have happened if Angie hadn't fallen off Calico's back. She would have been the one—"

"I've thought of nothing else since it happened," Giff said.

"Yeah," Luke said grimly, "Angie was most likely its intended victim."

"So what we've got on our hands is a wounded cat who's not afraid of humans." Cleve gave a low whistle. "That's a pretty dangerous combination if anyone accidently strays in its path."

"Cats like high ground," Flint said. "Where's the closest high ground?"

"That would be over here," Giff said, marking the area *Devil's Peaks*. "It's a treacherous area."

"I bet my best pair of boots," Flint said grimly, "that's where that cat is headed."

Luke nodded. "We'll leave at first light."

"That's not necessary," Giff said. "I'll take String and Red with me. As much as I appreciate your offer, I don't expect you fellows to risk . . . ah, to come along. After all, this isn't your problem."

"Last I heard, this ranch was wearin' a Mac-Kenzie brand," Flint said.

Cleve slapped Giff on the shoulder. "What Brother Flint is trying to say, in his own inimitable way, is that we're family. That makes it our problem, too."

"And mine," Dave added succinctly.

"Well, we've got a couple hours 'til daylight," Luke said. "If anyone wants to grab a snooze, now's the time to do it."

Flint stood up. "Think I'd like to get the feel of the rifle I'll be using."

"Of course." Giff got to his feet. "Come with me and you can pick out what you want. The Chief had a couple of good rifles. Dave, you've got yours, right?" Dave nodded. "Beth, where are yours and Angie's? I remember the Chief gave both of you rifles the Christmas before last."

"They're in the gun cabinet with Daddy's," Beth said, handing him the key.

When the five men left the room, the women remained in their chairs. They all looked from one to another, apprehension in all their eyes.

Quietly and grimly the five men went about the preparations to ride out on the hunt. None of them looked at what lay ahead as sport, but as an unavoidable duty that *must* end in success.

When they kissed their husbands good-bye, Cynthia, Honey, and Adriana stoically disguised their anxieties, but Garnet voiced her fear.

"Flint, remember that wounded cat is dangerous and could spring at you from anywhere. I know how you like to ride ahead when you're following a trail, but promise me you'll stay with the others. There's safety in numbers."

He traced her lips with his finger. "You aren't gonna worry about me, are you, Redhead?"

Her mouth curved in the faint suggestion of a smile. "Of course not."

"Bet you will." He kissed her lightly on the lips and swung up on his horse.

"What makes you think so, Flint MacKenzie?"

"Because you're crazy about me, Redhead."

She folded her arms across her chest and watched him ride toward the trees. Drawing a shuddering breath, she went back inside to see Angie coming down the stairs.

"Where is everybody?" she asked.

"They're outside, honey. The men are just leaving."

"Leaving? Where?"

"To hunt down that wounded cougar."

Angie hurried outside in time to see Giff about to ride away. Upon seeing her, he dismounted quickly, and she ran into his arms. "How are you feeling, Angel?"

"I'm okay now."

He tipped up her chin and stared into her eyes. "You sure?"

She nodded, forcing a smile. "It'll hurt for a while, but my very wise husband once told me that pain is like a wound: eventually it heals, even if a scar remains. I'll be fine, Giff. After all, in two days

I'm getting married. I have to be at my best, don't I?"

"I heard the groom is so crazy about you, he'd take you any way he could get you. I've gotta go, Angel. The others are waiting. I told String and Red not to budge from this yard. And until we get back, my orders are that not one of you women are to go even as far as the privy without an armed escort—just in case that cat doubles back."

"How long do you think you'll be gone?"

"With luck, we'll be back tonight. We took along a few provisions just in case we don't make it. But we'll certainly be back by tomorrow. After all, I'm getting married in two days." Drawing her into his arms, he kissed her long and hard. "I love you, Angel." His arms tightened. "God, baby, when I think of what might have happened to you—" For a long moment he just hugged her, then he stepped away and climbed on his horse. "Take care, love."

When Giff rode up to the others, Flint was squatting down, examining the ground. "There's drops here leading off to the right." He stood up and walked ahead, studying the ground. After several more yards, he remounted. "Okay, there's a pattern here. The cat was running hard, and I figure from the distance between the blood drops that it's got a pretty long stride. The cat's gotta be at least seven feet or longer. At that size, it's most likely a male." He moved on, studying the ground.

Dumbfounded, Dave Kincaid looked at Cleve. "How did he ever figure all that out from a few drops of blood on the ground?"

"Did I mention Brother Flint once was a wagon scout? This is nothing compared to how he used to read Indian signs. But what makes him so good at following a trail is his instinct. It's uncanny."

"I can believe it," Dave replied, awestruck.

Their pace was slow. The blood drops became

fewer and farther between. Frequently it became necessary for Flint to get off his horse in order to pick up the trail of the wily cat. And time after time, the cat veered off the trail, but it ultimately led them to the rocky base of Devil's Peaks.

He found the first sign on a rock about fifteen feet above.

"Not a bad leap for a cat that's been losing blood," Luke said.

Wiping out the inside of his hat with a bandanna, Giff expelled a long breath. "Well, he's in there somewhere. It's a maze of crossed trails, narrow gullies, and ravines. No vegetation. No water."

"And that goddamn cat is probably watching us from behind one of those rocks," Luke said, glancing up at the granite cliffs.

Suddenly a wild, screaming shriek from somewhere above froze them in place, and they jerked their heads upward, seeking the source of the cry.

"Sounds like our friend knows we're here," Cleve said.

"And he ain't pleased about it," Luke added.

Flint pulled his rifle out of the scabbard and nudged his horse forward with his knees. One by one the others did the same, following him up the narrow trail in a single file.

With every passing hour the temperature rose, the hot sun bouncing off the shirred walls adding to the heat of the day. Once or twice Flint's keen eye spotted a telltale spot of blood to indicate the cat was moving, drawing them deeper and deeper into the labyrinth.

With one hand holding the reins of their horses and the other their drawn rifles, they carefully picked their way along the path, avoiding the many fissures that crossed the trail while watching the rocks above for any sign of the cat. Broken pieces of shale ground under the horses' hooves, and each man knew that one false step into one of the narrow cracks could cause a horse to stumble and go down, or worse, break a leg.

Finally, near dusk, when none of them had even caught a glimpse of the elusive animal, Giff called a halt. "There's a dried-up spring near here that's level enough to make a camp tonight. It's the only flat ground in this whole damn maze."

The sun had set by the time they set up their camp. Huge boulders and overhanging precipices ringed the small circle that once had been a mountain spring, long withered by time and erosion. The men quickly lit the lanterns, and the bag of dried cow chips Giff had brought along furnished the fuel for a fire to boil a pot of coffee. Sitting back to back in the small circle of light, they sipped their coffee and ate the sandwiches that Middy had packed.

On the distant horizon, brilliant flashes of heat lightning formed the core of the reds and golds, blues and greens, that flowered out around it.

"What a phenomenon!" Cleve said. "I never can get used to it."

"Kind of reminds me of the aurora borealis," Dave said.

"Except for the lightning streaks in the center," Cleve replied.

"Yeah, the northern lights are soothing to watch," Luke said, "but not heat lightning. Even without the thunder boom, it's kind of scary."

"I didn't think anything scared you, Big Brother," Cleve joked.

Luke looked up when another radiant flash lit the horizon. "Yep, Little Brother, ain't too much that's human that does, but Nature can sure scare the hell out of me now and then."

"I'll tell you what scares the hell out of me," Flint

spoke up cantankerously. "It's you fellas watching that sky instead of those rocks around us. That damn cat's out there right now. I can feel it watching us. Waiting."

"You figure it will go for one of us, or the horses?" Giff asked.

"Most likely one of the horses. They're in the dark."

"Soon we will be, too," Giff said. "This fire's going to burn itself out before daylight. Looks like it's gonna be a long night, so I think we better have a two-man watch. Who wants the first one?"

"I'll take it," Luke said.

"So will I," Cleve offered.

"I ain't tired right now, either," Flint said.

"Then Dave and I will take the next watch. Wake us in two hours."

The fire had burned down to glowing embers as Giff and Dave scanned the darkness. The others were sleeping, or appeared to be while Giff and Dave kept watch, talking in whispered tones.

"You and Angie going away after the wedding?" Dave asked.

"No. Angie's planning on remodeling a couple of bedrooms."

"Yeah, Cyn told me. She told me about Angie's plans for a repertory, too. Sounds like a good idea."

"I was kind of worried she'd get a notion to give up her music just to keep me happy. This'll give her a chance to stay in touch with it; she's too talented to give up music completely."

"It'll all work out, Giff. Damn!" Dave said. "I wish I hadn't drunk all that coffee."

"I'll cover you if you have to pee."

"I'll be okay. I can hold it until we change shifts."

"Well, it sure has been quiet. Maybe that cat will leave us alone."

He no sooner had murmured the words when the horses suddenly began to shift restlessly, emitting frightened neighs as they tugged at the reins that tethered them.

Rifle in hand, Flint jumped to his feet. "This is it!"

"I should have kept my mouth shut," Giff grumbled.

Rising, they strained their eyes, trying to pierce the darkness around them.

"There it is!" Giff shouted. The light was too dim for a clear shot, and his bullet grazed the rock. The cat leaped behind a boulder.

They broke into a run toward the horses as Luke and Cleve scrambled to their feet.

"Watch it!" Dave yelled, as they advanced toward the granite wall. "It's in those rocks to the right."

"Look out, Luke!" Cleve shouted. "It's right above you!" He raised his rifle, but this time Giff's quick shot found its mark, catching the big cat as it prepared to leap. The cougar rolled off the precipice and fell to the ground in a lifeless heap.

They all ran over to it and Flint cautiously leaned down. "It's dead. Clean shot through the head, Giff."

"Thanks," Giff said. "We'd better quiet those horses." He and Dave headed over to calm down the agitated animals.

"Thank God that's over," Luke said, after they all had returned to the fire and laid aside their rifles. "We can still get in some sleep before daylight."

"You're slipping, Brother Flint," Cleve said. "Thought you said that cat would be male—it was a female."

"Yeah, that's sticking in my craw," Flint replied, deep in thought. "I'd have bet my boots that cat was male."

"I don't much care what it is, as long as it's finally dead," Dave said. "I thought I'd have to wet my pants before then."

Reaching for his fly, Dave headed for the darkened periphery of the granite wall just as Flint's instinct kicked in.

"There's two of them!" he yelled, right before they heard the mesmerizing growl.

Petrified, Dave looked up with horror at the snarling mouth and yellowed fangs of the cat perched above his head, its eyes gleaming like green coals in the darkness.

The MacKenzies drew their Colts, and three shots rang out as the huge animal sprang at Dave, knocking him off his feet.

The four men ran over and shoved the dead animal off him.

"Did it get a claw into you?" Giff asked.

Dazed and trembling, Dave sat up, rubbing his head. "I don't know. I don't think so. I've never been so damn scared in my life. Who brought him down?"

"You can thank them," Giff said, pointing to the MacKenzies. "I've never seen anyone draw a Colt as fast as you three did."

"I don't know what to say," Dave said, still stunned by the brush with death. "How can I ever thank you?"

"Reckon you could let us ride free on that railroad you're building," Luke said jokingly.

"You and your family's got a lifetime pass," Dave said, shaking his head. "The same goes for you two," he said, gratefully shaking the hands of Flint and Cleve. "God, I sure married into the right family!" Still slightly unsteady on his feet, Dave walked back to the fire with Giff's assistance and plopped down alongside it.

After examining the animal, Flint stood up grinning at Cleve. "Well, Little Brother, sure hate to remind you, but I was right again—just counted four bullet holes in this here *male* cat."

"How could I have ever doubted you, Brother Flint!" Cleve said, slapping him on the shoulder.

Laughing, the MacKenzie brothers walked back and joined the others.

Chapter 31

❦

Cynthia breezed into the kitchen and found Dave and Giff seated at the table. "What a perfect day for a wedding." Leaning over, she kissed Dave on the cheek, then sat down. "You certainly don't look like a happy groom, Pete Gifford," she remarked with a sideways glance at him. "Speaking of happy grooms, you'll never guess who just got engaged."

"I suppose if I don't ask, you'll tell me anyway," Giff grumbled.

"Jamie Skinner and that former girlfriend of yours, Diane Divine."

"She was not a girlfriend of mine," Giff declared emphatically.

"This is really a victory for poetic justice," Cynthia said. "I can't think of anyone more deserving of her than that weasel Jamie Skinner." She looked at Dave and winked. "The woman's a real man-eater, honey. *P* as in piranha."

"Now that we've heard the morning news, how about telling me something I want to hear? Just where is everybody this morning?" Giff asked.

"I'd have thought you could *hear* it down here.

It's a madhouse upstairs. Honey, Garnet, and Adriana are packing and trying to get themselves dressed for the wedding. You can't move without bumping into someone," she said, laughing.

"That explains why all three MacKenzies are down at the corral," Giff said. "They probably wanted to get out of the house."

Cynthia's eyes flashed with merriment. "I love it; it's so exciting."

"Exciting? It's havoc. The men have the right idea," Dave said. "I think I'll go down and join them."

"It's been wonderful having them all here."

Giff nodded. "Yeah, they're fine people. And those three brothers sure came in handy on that cougar hunt."

Dave shook his head. "I still can't believe it. Have you ever seen anyone who could follow a trail like Flint MacKenzie?"

"Amazing, wasn't it? Almost as amazing as their draws. You wouldn't have believed how fast the three of them drew their Colts."

"I'd probably be a goner right now if it weren't for them."

Until that time, Cynthia had been listening with avid interest. Now all the humor left her face and she turned pale. "What do you mean by that, Dave?"

"Oh, just a close brush out there with one of those cats." He grinned and squeezed her hand. "It's over and done with. You're stuck with me for a few more years yet, Miz Sin." The words were not too reassuring to Cynthia, and she still looked stricken.

"What's Angie doing, Thia?" Giff asked, wisely changing the subject.

"She's staying in her room. Beth is keeping her company. I took a tray upstairs for them. After all, we can't risk her encountering the groom."

"This whole wedding thing is ridiculous," Giff said. "Good Lord, Angie and I are married. This nonsense of keeping us apart—separate beds last night, not being able to see her this morning. It's the dumbest thing I've ever heard."

"Grin and bear it, Giff. It's considered unlucky for the groom to see the bride before the ceremony."

Exasperated, Giff threw up his hands. "Thia, Angie and I are *already* married. Today we're merely repeating our vows to satisfy my wife's *meddling* sisters. Both of whom I love dearly," he quickly added. He looked helplessly at David for support.

Dave shook his head and shrugged. "Women," he replied in sympathy.

Cynthia patted Giff's hand. "All things considered, dear Giff, I wouldn't defy the gods if I were you."

Giff drew back in surprise. "Just what is that supposed to mean?"

"Considering the circumstances and complications that resulted from your earlier marriage, beloved brother-in-law, I'd think you'd welcome an opportunity for a fresh, new beginning."

"All those complications have been resolved," Giff said. "And guess what, beloved sister-in-law. Angie and I are still man and wife."

"Would you deny your bride her girlhood dream of standing before God and company in a white veil and wedding gown when she enters the state of matrimony?"

"A white gown!" Giff scoffed. "Isn't that stretching it a bit? We're married, remember? Angie's not exactly a virgin."

"I agree with Giff," Dave said.

"That is a big misconception and just shows how little the two of you know about weddings," Cynthia declared. "A white gown denotes a first wedding, not necessarily virginity."

"I guess the schoolmarm's right again," Dave said. "I did recently read that at the turn of the century, a third of the brides in New England alone were already pregnant by the time they married. It would be pretty outlandish to infer virginity from their white wedding gowns. However, the article went on to say the incidence of pregnant brides has declined."

Smiling wickedly, Cynthia said, "Undoubtedly due not to abstinence, my love, but the fact that you and Giff are no longer available bachelors. Not to mention Jamie Skinner," she added devilishly.

Dave cast a suffering look at Giff. "You see, pal, how quickly they turn on you."

"So having ruled out Angie's virginity," Giff said, "I'll remind you again, Thia, that this isn't her *first* wedding either."

Grimacing, Cynthia said, "Oh, Giff, that's not true. It is *too* her first wedding. She's repeating her vows, that's all. Furthermore, I didn't say she was wearing a white gown, did I? You just have to wait and see."

Middy entered the room and, in a silence heavy with tension and obvious disgruntlement, put a cup of coffee down on the table in front of Cynthia.

"Good morning, Middy," Cynthia said sweetly.

"Humph!" the housekeeper said, and stomped off.

"What's that all about?" Giff asked.

"Middy's upset with Beth and me because we hired a caterer for the wedding."

"I'd think she'd be happy not to have to work all day," Dave said. "Especially with an arm still in a cast."

"We thought so, too. We wanted her to enjoy the

day with the rest of us and not have to spend her time in the kitchen."

"Middy's happiest when she's working," Giff said.

Middy returned with Cynthia's breakfast. "I'll be obliged if the three of you stop puttin' your heads together and whisperin' about me behind my back."

Cynthia jumped to her feet and hugged the woman around the shoulders. "Now, Middy dear, you know how much we all love you. And this is a big day for you. We can't have you sweating away in the kitchen, banging that cast on your arm around as if it were a baseball club. After all, you're practically the mother of the bride. That's a very important role at a wedding." She kissed her on the cheek. "And you're going to look so lovely in that blue gown we got you."

"Ain't nothin' wrong with my gray dress," Middy said, more subdued, but still unwilling to concede defeat.

"Oh, but the blue gown matches your eyes perfectly."

"That ain't sayin' I'm gonna wear it," she said, and walked away.

"You're slipping, Miz Sin. You used to be able to charm the skin off a snake," Dave teased.

"Well, you all know how territorial she is about this kitchen," Cynthia said, and sat down to eat.

Giff nodded. "Yeah, but it doesn't stop with the kitchen. Still, what would we have done through the years without Middy to fuss over us? She's the only mother I've ever known."

Cynthia squeezed his hand. "That's right. In all the excitement, I forgot she has a dual role: mother of the groom, as well as the bride. Hey, Giff, how about softening her up a little by reminding her?"

"I think she's just putting on a show," Dave said. "I suspect she's pleased as punch."

"Of course she is." Cynthia winked at Giff. "Soften her up anyway, Giff. You know how she loves it." Finishing her light breakfast, she took Dave's hand. "You come with me, Kincaid. I want to hear more about that cougar hunt. What did you mean you'd be a goner now?"

As soon as they left, Giff got up and went over to the sink where Middy was washing dishes. Moving up behind her, he slipped his arms around her waist.

"Saints alive, boy! How many times must I tell you not to do that! You scared the life out of me and I near broke one of these dishes."

"This is my wedding day too, Middy, and you're the only mother I've ever had. I was hoping to see you sitting in the front row."

She raised her hand and brushed aside the tears that began to streak her cheeks. "Course I'll be there. You don't think I'd miss seein' my boy and my baby gettin' themselves hitched, do you?"

"I love you, Middy." He kissed her cheek and stepped away.

"Course you do. Now, get off with you, so's I can get this kitchen in order afore that passel of strangers come trompin' in to take over and mess it all up."

Giff was halfway out the door when she called out to him, "Son, you need your shirt ironed or somethin'?"

"I'm all set, Middy," he said.

The gentle breeze carried a perfumed welcome to the people seated in the rose garden that had been planted by Elizabeth MacGregor MacKenzie as a young bride. The expectant crowd hushed in anticipation as the string quartet struck the first chords of the wedding march.

Side by side, dressed in princess-style pink gowns of crepe de chine and carrying small nosegays with pale pink satin streamers, Cynthia and Elizabeth walked down the aisle between the rows of chairs rented for the occasion.

Standing beside the minister beneath the rose covered bower, Pete Gifford anxiously sought a glimpse of Angie. His gaze filled with love at the sight of his bride, who followed a short distance behind her sisters on the arm of her godfather, Dr. James Fielding.

Her dark hair was tucked back under a fragrant spray of woven apple blossoms. In lieu of the traditional white gown, she wore a pale pink crepe de chine dress covered with white silk gauze, the transparent sleeves of the gown fluttering like angel wings as she moved down the aisle.

Angie's gaze never wavered from that of her husband as he stepped forward and took her hand. The sunlight caressing his light hair turned it into silky gold that she yearned to thread her fingers through.

As the young couple recited their vows, Middy, dressed in the new gown, dabbed at her eyes repeatedly with a handkerchief. Slim Collins, seated beside her, patted her hand in understanding.

Dressed in their Sunday best, String and Red Bean filled the next two seats of the front row. In their nervousness, both fidgeted continually with their uncomfortable and unaccustomed stiff collars.

The MacKenzies filled a row of seats on each side of the aisle. Luke reached for Honey's hand; the less demonstrative Flint stole a lingering look at Garnet, who was listening enthralled to the ceremony; and Cleve brought Adriana's hand to his lips and kissed it, his eyes crinkling with a warm smile as her dark eyes met his.

Even Charles Reardon, the normally impassive family lawyer, pulled out a monogrammed handkerchief and blew his nose.

Cynthia had been determined to get through the ceremony without shedding a tear, but as she listened to Angie and Giff say their vows, she couldn't help reliving her own wedding day. Tears slid down her cheeks as she glanced at her husband, seated next to the aisle where she stood. Smiling tenderly, Dave looked up at her, then clasped the hand she reached out to him.

Elizabeth MacKenzie's eyes were misted with tears as she followed the words the young couple recited. She had prayed often for this moment, and her heart overflowed with joy that these two people she loved so dearly had found their happiness, like Cynthia and Dave. She couldn't think of two finer men to have as brothers-in-law. She thought of how proud her parents would be of these men whom her sisters had married. If and when she married, she could only hope her choice of a husband would be as outstanding as her sisters' had been.

The ceremony ended with a shared kiss between the bride and groom, then Angie turned to face the beaming smiles and glistening eyes of her sisters. Forsaking any attempt at restraint, she flung herself into their arms. And as they had always done on joyous occasions and reunions, the three women embraced together, laughter and tears flowing uninhibitedly.

As the couple accepted congratulations, Angie spent as much time answering questions about her cousins and their wives as she did about her future plans as Giff's wife. The striking presence of the handsome MacKenzie brothers from Texas gener-

ated a great deal of interest among the guests—
especially the women.

Michael Carrington approached and congratu-
lated Angie and Giff, then said to Beth, "And you
look very lovely, Miss MacKenzie."

"Thank you," she replied. "You appear to spend
as much time in Denver as you do in Texas, Mr.
Carrington."

"I thought so, too. That's why I recently pur-
chased a home here. I believe it once belonged to
the White family."

"The Sanford White mansion!" Giff let out a
long, low whistle. "Must be twenty rooms in that
house."

"Did I overhear you say you bought the White
mansion?" Cynthia asked, joining them. "You told
me you were a bachelor, Michael. I imagine it
would get very lonely in a twenty room mansion."

"I know. Maybe someday I can fill it with children." He looked pointedly at Beth, and she spun
on her heel and walked away.

"I've brought you some good tidings on your
wedding day, Angie," Michael continued. "En-
rique Gallo bought your paintings."

Angie gaped in astonishment. "Are you serious?"

"As a matter of fact, he wants to buy more. He
said there's a big demand for Western art on the
East Coast."

Angie clasped Giff's hand. "Oh, darling, did you
hear that? I can't believe it."

Grinning, Giff said, "I'm happy for you, Angel.
Looks like you're going to have to get back to that
paintbrush and easel as fast as you can."

"But not today," Michael said, laughing. "At
least not until after I've had a chance to dance with
the bride." He offered his arm to her. "Do you
mind, Giff?"

"Go ahead," Giff said, amused. "I'd say you've earned the right."

When she returned from the waltz, Giff pulled her aside. "Angel, can you come with me for a minute? I have something to show you." He took her hand and they slipped away from the crowd.

"What is it, Giff?" she asked, as they headed toward the barn.

"You'll see. Close your eyes and no peeking until I tell you to open them."

"This is exciting," she laughed, complying with his wishes.

He steered her by the shoulders to one of the stalls. "Okay, you can open up now."

Angie opened her eyes and gasped. Blinking several times, she gaped in disbelief at the dun colt in the stall. "It's . . . it's Calico!"

"Calico sired him," Giff said. "Sheba was the dam."

Angie opened the stall for a closer inspection. "He has the same blaze as Calico did," she said in awe, rubbing the white patch between the colt's forehead and nose. Her glance quickly shifted to the horse's mane, then its tail, and finally its feet. "And the same black points, too!" Tears glistened in her eyes when she turned and looked at Giff. "Oh, Giff, he's identical."

"We sold the colt to Ben Danforth at the beginning of the year. I bought him back as a wedding gift for you."

"I couldn't have hoped for a better gift." She walked into his arms. "I love you so much, Giff—I think that I've loved you my whole life. I know that I will for the rest of it."

She kissed him: a gentle one, not one with the fervor of passion—but a kiss with the promise of everlasting love.

*   *   *

The day passed into an evening of bright stars and a pleasant breeze, and as the night lengthened, the guests slipped away in twos and threes.

Then came the only flaw in what had been a perfect day: the time to say good-bye to the Mac-Kenzies. After the hugs, kisses, tears, and hand-shakes were exchanged, they all loaded into two wagons.

"Just follow Slim's wagon into Denver and he'll lead you to your hotel," Giff said. "You can leave the wagons at the livery and we'll pick them up tomorrow."

"I still don't see why you couldn't have stayed and gone back with Dave and me," Cynthia protested.

"We've been away too long as it is," Cleve said. "Besides, Adriana won't last another day away from our other kids."

"And now it's your turn to come to the Triple M," Honey reminded them.

"You'll be seeing us sooner than you think," Dave said. "The railroad should reach Dallas by next spring."

"We'll be there for the celebration," Flint said. " 'Bye, folks."

"Have a safe trip home," Beth called out as Flint flicked the reins of the wagon. "And let us know how the service was on your train trip back home—we aim to please on the Rocky Mountain Central."

"Thanks again for coming to our wedding," Angie yelled. "Giff and I really appreciated it."

The wagons rolled away with another exchange of waves and good-byes from the women.

Then wearily, the family entered the house.

"I'm not even going to look at this mess," Elizabeth declared. "Good night, all; I'm going to bed."

"That's a good idea," Dave said, grabbing Cynthia's hand. "Let's go, hon."

Left alone, Angie and Giff strolled hand in hand down to the barn so she could look at the colt again.

"Do I dare call him Calico, Giff?" she asked, stroking the horse.

"Why not, if that's what you want to do?"

"Do you think it would be fair to Calico?"

"I think naming his son after him would be the greatest compliment you could give him."

Sighing, she leaned her head against Giff's chest. "Oh, Giff, this is the most exceptional gift I could ever hope for. I'm so grateful, my darling."

He kissed her, and when they separated, he took her hand. "We'd better think about getting to bed. Tomorrow will come sooner than we want."

"But I can't wait until tomorrow to ride him."

"Angie! I've seen that look in your eye before. It's too late now."

"Oh, Giff, just a little canter around the corral. Please, please, please," she beseeched irresistibly.

He shook his head indulgently. "This is not how I planned to spend my wedding night," he grumbled, opening the stall. When he finished putting a halter on the horse, Angie pulled up the skirt of her wedding gown and he lifted her up on the horse's bare back.

"Remember, just a couple times around the corral, Mrs. Gifford."

She lightly nudged the colt with her knees and the horse jogged out of the barn.

Giff leaned on the gate and smiled as she trotted the horse around the corral. Laughing with joy, Angie threw him a kiss in passing, her dark hair bouncing on her shoulders with every step of the horse.

He had never known such a moment of unequivocal contentment.

When she trotted the horse back into its stall, Giff

lifted her off and carried her back to the house. They made love and spoke of their love and happiness until, exhausted, they both drifted into sleep.

Sometime later, Angie awoke. For a long moment she gazed at the sleeping moonlit figure beside her, then she slipped out of bed.

Donning a robe, she opened the dresser drawer, took out a worn envelope, and then reached for the small music box set on the dresser.

Barefoot, she padded down the stairway and went into the den. After lighting the desk lamp, she went over to the fireplace and gazed up at the portrait of her father.

"Did you enjoy the wedding, Daddy?" she asked. "I felt you near me all day. And I think this is the time to open your letter—to share more of today's happiness with you."

Her fingers shook as she wound up the music box, and as the little equestrienne circled the box to the music, Angie broke the seal on the envelope she had handled so often and began to read the letter written in her father's familiar script.

My Dearest Angie,

Not knowing how long you will wait to open this letter, I found it the hardest of the three to write; for you are my youngest daughter—my baby— and at the time of this writing there is still so much that must occur in your young life before you will know true contentment. There are rites in life we all must experience before we reach a stage where we recognize what we are seeking. Perhaps as you read this, you have passed through many of these rituals and know of what I speak.

Hoping not to stumble, we leap from one stepping-stone to another, challenged by a swirling river of doubts, confusion, a multitude of difficulties to overcome, hurdles to leap, and errors to right, before we step safely on the opposite shore.

I fear that if you open this letter before you have attempted that crossing, the journey will be made more difficult by something I might say within these few scattered lines that will divert you onto the wrong course.

In my letters to your sisters, I made no attempt to influence the path they choose to follow in their search for ultimate happiness. But I find myself unable to ignore that temptation with you—not because I do not trust your judgement to make that choice for yourself, but rather because I knew from the moment the doctor placed you in my arms, and those little fingers—even then long and delicately formed—curled around mine, that they were meant to one day grace the keys of a piano or ply an artist's brush.

Thus the message of the music box is simple, my dearest Angie, yet so expressive. The notes of a favorite song are symbolic of the draw that the creative side of your nature will always hold on you. But lest you forget, I seek here to remind you that like a coin, your nature has two sides.

So look, too, for the message in the words of the song taught to you and your sisters by your precious mother. Words that express this very significant other side of your nature—for therein lies your struggle, sweet child.

Heed those words of the song carefully, my dear. Weigh them with your heart, as well as your mind—for I believe them to be the real measure of your future happiness.

Angie glanced down at the cherished keepsake she held. As the haunting melody neared its end,

she softly half sang and half murmured the closing
words to the song.

"And in that place, I thank the Lord content to be.
For it is home; the home God gave to me."

Angie softly rubbed the letter against her cheek,
then brought it to her lips and kissed his signature.
Tears misted her eyes as she smiled up at the beloved face in the portrait.

"You were right, Daddy—you and the words of
the song. This is where I belong, where my contentment lies. Right here at the Roundhouse, at the
side of the man I love. I may have struggled with
the notion along the way, because it took me a
while to see that I don't need a stage to sing the
song in my heart, or a gallery in which to hang my
paintings. What matters is that I have a song to
sing, a landscape to paint. And I do. It's always
been here all the time . . . right before my eyes. And
what's more, it's been in my heart—because this is
where Giff is. That's your real message, isn't it,
Daddy? It's not only about the Roundhouse—it's
about Giff, too."

Brushing the moisture from her eyes, she
grinned up at him. "And I'm proud to say, I came
to that conclusion myself. I finally made a decision
and stood by it. No reservations, no doubts, and
no regrets. I may have stumbled a time or two
along the way, but I made it, Daddy. I made it
across that river."

"Angie, honey, what are you doing down here
at this hour?" Giff asked worriedly, entering the
room. He looked all tousled and sleepy-eyed. He
looked beautiful.

She gently put aside the letter and music box,
then reached out a hand to him. He clasped it,
holding it in the warmth and strength of his own.

Smiling serenely, she turned back to her father's portrait.

"Are you okay, Angel?" Giff asked tenderly.

"I'm fine, my love."

Enfolding her in his embrace, he pulled her back against the firm wall of his chest and body. For a long moment they stood in a love-filled silence gazing up at the portrait.

"Do you suppose he guessed this would happen? That one day we'd marry?"

"I don't doubt it, Angel. He was so wise about everything."

She turned in his arms. "While his daughter still has a great deal to learn."

"Oh, I don't know about that," he said, kissing the tip of her nose. "She seems pretty smart to me. Look who she picked out for a husband fifteen years ago."

Angie frowned in reflection. "You know, that's right—I *am* pretty smart, aren't I?" Then her eyes flashed with mischief as she smiled up at him. "But I actually wasn't referring to that. What I was thinking is that I really need to learn more about what that *man thing* is all about. Maybe an additional demonstration would help."

Grinning, he swooped her up in his arms. "Angel, you've come to the right person."

And their laughter blended in love as he carried her up the stairs.

Dear Reader,

With a new year coming, don't miss a new year of exciting romances from Avon! We've got some of the writers you already know and love, along with some fresh voices you're sure to fall for.

A writer you know and love is January's Treasure author, Tanya Anne Crosby. *On Bended Knee*, Tanya Anne's latest, is an unforgettable love story of passion and promise, and she returns to the Scottish setting that her readers love so well. Don't miss this sinfully sensuous historical love story.

Rachel Gibson's first contemporary, *Simply Irresistible*, made readers sit up and take notice. Now, she returns with another witty and wonderful contemporary called *Truly Madly Yours*. When a young woman returns to her hometown of Truly, Idaho, she never dreams the handsome man she left behind would still be there...laying in wait for her!

If you're looking for a spectacular new writer, don't miss Gayle Callen, author of next month's *The Darkest Knight*. A young woman is on the run from a forced marriage, and is rescued by the one man she can never have in this sensuous, exciting medieval historical romance.

And with a title like *Once a Mistress* how can you resist buying the latest from Debra Mullins? A dark handsome rogue sweeps our heroine off her feet and rescues her from an evil abductor in this wonderfully swashbuckling romp.

Until next month, enjoy!

Lucia Macro

Lucia Macro
Senior Editor

AEL 1298

Avon Romances—
the best in exceptional authors and unforgettable novels!

KISS ME GOODNIGHT
by Marlene Suson
79560-4/ $5.99 US/ $7.99 Can

WHITE EAGLE'S TOUCH
by Karen Kay
78999-X/ $5.99 US/ $7.99 Can

ONLY IN MY DREAMS
by Eve Byron
79311-3/ $5.99 US/ $7.99 Can

ARIZONA RENEGADE
by Kit Dee
79206-0/ $5.99 US/ $7.99 Can

BY LOVE UNDONE
by Suzanne Enoch
79885-9/ $5.99 US/ $7.99 Can

THE MEN OF PRIDE COUNTY:
THE OUTSIDER
by Rosalyn West
79580-9/ $5.99 US/ $7.99 Can

WILD CAT CAIT
by Rachelle Morgan
80039-X/ $5.99 US/ $7.99 Can

HIGHLAND BRIDES:
HIGHLAND SCOUNDREL
by Margaret Evans Porter
79435-7/ $5.99 US/ $7.99 Can

HER NORMAN CONQUEROR
by Malia Martin
79896-4/ $5.99 US/ $7.99 Can

THROUGH THE STORM
by Beverly Jenkins
79864-6/ $5.99 US/ $7.99 Can

We've got love on our minds at